RANDOM
HOUSE
LARGE
PRINT

ALSO BY CURTIS SITTENFELD
AVAILABLE FROM RANDOM HOUSE LARGE PRINT

Eligible
You Think It, I'll Say It

RODHAM

RODHAM

A Novel

CURTIS SITTENFELD

Rodham is a work of fiction. While some characters have real-life counterparts, their characterizations and the incidents in which they are depicted are products of the author's imagination and are used fictitiously. **Rodham** should be read as a work of fiction, not biography or history. The characters who are not recognizable are drawn from the author's imagination, as are the incidents and dialogue that concern them.

Published in the United States of America by Random House Large Print in association with Random House, an imprint and division of Penguin Random House LLC, New York.

A few paragraphs of this novel were previously published in **Esquire** in the story "The Nominee."

Cover design: based on a design by Jo Thomson/TW
Cover photograph: Boston Globe/Contributor/Getty Images

The Library of Congress has established a Cataloging-in-Publication record for this title.

ISBN: 978-0-593-29499-4

www.penguinrandomhouse.com/large-print-format-books

FIRST LARGE PRINT EDITION

Printed in the United States of America

10 9 8 7 6 5 4 3 2 1

This Large Print edition published in accord with the standards of the N.A.V.H.

For L,
with love and gratitude

My marriage to Bill Clinton was the most consequential decision of my life. I said no the first two times he asked me. But the third time, I said yes. And I'd do it again.

—Hillary Rodham Clinton,
What Happened

The world has no right to my heart.

—Lin-Manuel Miranda, **Hamilton**

RODHAM

PROLOGUE

May 31, 1969

There was a feeling I got before I spoke in front of an audience and sometimes also before an event that was less public but still important, an event that could have consequences in my life—taking the LSATs, for example, which I'd done in a classroom on the campus of Harvard. The feeling was a focused kind of anticipation, it was like a weight inside my chest, but it never exactly came from being nervous. I always had prepared, and I always knew I could do it. Thus the feeling was a sense of my own competence blended with the knowledge that I was about to pull off a feat most people thought, correctly or not, they couldn't. And this knowledge contributed to the final aspect of the feeling, which was loneliness—the loneliness of being good at something.

My Wellesley graduation occurred on the green near the library, and I was scheduled to speak after Senator Edward Brooke, who was from Massachusetts. As I listened to him, I sat on the temporarily erected stage in my black gown and mortarboard. My father had traveled from Park Ridge, Illinois, without my mother or brothers, and was seated many rows back. I would be the first-ever student speaker at a Wellesley graduation.

I'd slept little the night before, between finishing my speech and being gripped by nostalgia. Even though Wellesley had, during the upheavals of the last four years, come to seem an almost embarrassingly cloistered place, I'd loved being a student there, loved the green lawns and the lake; loved the wood-paneled classrooms where I'd listened to lectures on Spinoza and quantum mechanics and argued about what it meant to live in a just society; and, of course, loved my friends, who were now headed in many directions.

Senator Brooke's speech was winding down, and he still hadn't explicitly mentioned recent protests or assassinations, civil rights or Vietnam. I understood then that addressing them fell to me. In a way, I'd understood this before the ceremony even started, and it had been the reason that my classmates and I had pushed for a student speaker. But the speech I'd written suddenly seemed inadequate, and I knew I needed to start with a rebuttal, a generational rebuttal, to the senator's evasiveness. Because I was the one who'd be standing at the podium, doing so was my obligation.

Wellesley's president, Ruth Adams, introduced me by saying that I was a political science major, president of the college government, and—perhaps this was a warning or form of wishful thinking on her part—"good humored, good company, and a good friend to all of us."

Walking to the podium seemed endless and then was already finished, forever finished. So many people sat in front of me, most of them strangers and some my confidantes. I began by saying, "I am very glad that Miss Adams made it clear that what I am speaking for today is all of us, the four hundred of us. And I find myself in a familiar position, that of reacting, something that our generation has been doing for quite a while now. We're not in the positions yet of leadership and power, but we do have that indispensable element of criticizing and constructive protest and I find myself reacting just briefly to some of the things that Senator Brooke said. This has to be quick because I do have a little speech to give.

"Part of the problem with just empathy with professed goals is that empathy doesn't do us anything. We've had lots of empathy; we've had lots of sympathy, but we feel that for too long our leaders have viewed politics as the art of the possible.

And the challenge now is to practice politics as the art of making what appears to be impossible possible."

I could feel a shifting in the audience, a taking of sides: those who considered it disrespectful for a college student to chide a senator and those who, given the stakes, considered it admirable. There were also, and this may have been the majority of people, those not paying attention; there are always those people. But the division I'd created—it would be a lie to say I didn't find it bracing.

I knew I'd do at least a good job delivering the rest of my speech and maybe a great job; good I could control, while great was more nebulous and chancy, arising from the feedback loop of energy between me and the audience. But I didn't know yet that my speech, probably due to the extemporaneous part, would cause my classmates to give me a standing ovation; I didn't know that the standing ovation would offend or anger many of my classmates' parents, remaining in some cases a point of intrafamily contention for decades to come (my father said afterward, with derision, "You sounded like a hippie up there"); and I didn't know that my speech would attract national media attention, including from **Life** magazine. Yet I clearly remember that I felt the feeling: the focused anticipation, my competence, my loneliness. I understood how I appeared to other graduates and their families, a confident and idealistic young woman standing behind a podium, even as I inhabited my own body, as I **was** me and could hear my voice magnified across the green. The feeling was in the collapse, the simultaneity, of how I seemed to others and who I really was. In retrospect, I think what I felt in that moment—I'd felt it before, but never quite so brightly—was my own singular future.

PART I

The Catch

CHAPTER 1
1970

THE FIRST TIME I SAW him, I thought he looked like a lion. He was six foot two, though I knew then only that he was tall. And in fact, his height seemed even greater because he was big-tall, not skinny-tall. He had broad shoulders and a large head and his hair was several inches longer than it would be later, which drew attention to its coppery color; his beard was the same shade. I suppose I thought he looked like a handsome lion, but even from a distance, he seemed full of himself in a way that canceled out his handsomeness. He seemed like a person who took up more than his share of oxygen.

This sighting took place in Yale Law School's student lounge, in the fall of 1970—my second year of law school and his first. I was with my friend Nick, and Bill was speaking in his loud, husky, Southern-accented voice to a group of five or six other students. With great enthusiasm, he declared, "And not only that, we grow the biggest watermelons in the world!"

Nick and I looked at each other and began laughing. "Who **is** that?" I whispered.

"Bill Clinton," Nick whispered back. "He's from Arkansas, and that's all he ever talks about." The next thing Nick told me was actually, at Yale Law School, less notable than being from Arkansas. "He was a Rhodes scholar."

After I'd been accepted at both Harvard and Yale, I'd decided where to go using a rule I'd established for myself at such an early age—probably in third or fourth grade—that I had trouble remembering a time when I hadn't abided by it. Though I'd never discussed it with anyone, I thought of it as the Rule of Two: If I was unsure of a course of action but could think of two reasons for it, I'd do it. If I could think of two reasons against it, I wouldn't. Situations arose, of course, where there were two or more reasons both for and against something, but they didn't arise that frequently.

Should I, as a high school freshman, take Latin? Because I'd heard the teacher was outstanding and because it would help me with the SATs—yes.

Should I attend my church youth group's retreat

at Gebhard Woods State Park if it meant missing my friend Betty's sweet sixteen party? Because the date of the retreat had been announced first and because a church event was inherently more moral than a party—yes.

Should I style my hair in a beehive? (Yes.) Should I major in history? (No.) Should I major in political science? (Yes.) Should I start taking the pill? (Yes.) After Dr. King's assassination, should I wear a black armband? (Yes.) That my "reasons" were often simply articulations of my own preferences wasn't lost on me. But in the privacy of my own head, who cared?

The reasons I'd ultimately chosen Yale were: (1) its commitment to public service, and (2) when I'd attended a party at Harvard Law after my acceptance there, a professor had declared that Harvard didn't need more women. As with Yale, the number of female law students at Harvard was then at about 10 percent, and I was slightly tempted to enroll just to spite this professor. But only slightly.

One evening in March 1971, shortly after spring break, I was studying in the law library, which was in a striking Gothic building. The library occupied a long room filled with carrels. Above the bookshelves were large, arched stained-glass windows, and bronze chandeliers hung from the wood ceiling.

I'd been sitting at a carrel for ninety minutes, and every time I looked up, I made eye contact with Bill Clinton—the lion. He was about twenty feet away, perched on a desk and talking to a man I didn't know. I wondered if Bill was confusing me with someone else. Then again, since only twenty-seven students my year were women, it shouldn't have been that difficult to keep us straight.

I stood, approached him, and said, "I noticed you looking at me. Is there something you need?" I extended my hand. "I'm Hillary Rodham."

He smiled slowly and broadly, and in his warm, husky, Southern voice, he said, "I know who you are." (Oh, Bill Clinton's smile! More than forty-five years have passed since that night in the library, and at times it's crossed my mind that his smile may have ruined my life.) He added, "You're the one who told off Professor Geaney on Ladies' Day."

This—Ladies' Day—was a ritual observed by some professors who called on female students to speak just once a semester, on a designated day. But Professor Geaney, who taught Corporate Taxation, which was an upper level class Bill wasn't in, took the tradition further than most: Every Valentine's Day, the professor started class by announcing that it was Ladies' Day and asking all the virgins to assemble in the front of the room. When he'd done it a few weeks before, I along with the other two women in the section stood but remained at our seats, as we'd planned to do in advance, and

I spoke on our behalf. I said, "This is an offensive custom that has no place in an academic setting. The female students present should be treated as full members of the law school community, with the same rights to participation in this class as the male students."

When I'd finished, I'd felt some of the defiant satisfaction I had at my Wellesley graduation, and the feeling hadn't been diminished when Professor Geaney said, "Fine then, Miss Rodham. You ladies may stay where you are, but since you seem particularly keen to share your viewpoints today, I'll let you begin our discussion by summarizing **Gregory v. Helvering.**"

"I'd be happy to," I said.

In the law library, to Bill Clinton, I said, "Yes, that was me."

Bill rose then from the desk, all six feet two of him, with his coppery hair and beard, and took my still-extended hand (I was five-five). He said, "It's a pleasure to officially meet you. I'm Bill."

"Are you interested in working at the legal aid clinic?" I asked. For the last eighteen months, I'd volunteered at the New Haven Legal Services office.

He seemed amused, though I didn't see why. Our hands were no longer moving but still clasped—his hand was enormous—as he said, "I might be. Would you like to get a cup of coffee sometime and we could discuss it?"

As I extracted my hand, I said, "If you're considering the clinic for this summer, you should apply as soon as possible. The slots will definitely fill up."

"No, I'll be organizing for McGovern down in Florida. But what about coffee?"

Was he asking me out? In a matter of seconds, I considered then dismissed the possibility. There were, as it happened, two reasons why. The first was that Bill Clinton had a palpably impatient and acquisitive energy, and while, at Yale Law School, this energy wasn't unique, his was more extreme than most. He did, obviously, want something from me, but it seemed unfathomable that the something was romantic. And the reason it seemed unfathomable wasn't that men weren't interested in me; they sometimes were, but the men who were interested in me were never outrageously charismatic and handsome.

Therefore I wasn't playing hard to get, I wasn't being coy, as I said, "I'm busy until the weekend, but I have time to meet you on Saturday afternoon."

The room at the legal aid clinic where we did intake contained four desks and one massive file cabinet, and when I arrived on Friday morning, another law student, named Fred, was already there and on the phone. He raised his eyebrows twice in my direction in a friendly way, even as he said into the receiver, "Unfortunately, we don't handle criminal matters, but I can give you the name of a volunteer lawyers' organization." I set my tan leather satchel under a desk. About thirty of us worked at the clinic per semester—you received course credit the first semester, and after that it was both uncredited and unpaid, which we joked was good practice for a career in public-interest law—so no particular desk in this room belonged to anyone. I hadn't yet sat when the phone on my desk rang, and I fielded intake calls for the rest of the morning, as did Fred and another student, named Mike, who arrived after I did. We couldn't help the vast majority of callers—their incomes weren't low enough, or they lived outside the geographic boundaries where we were authorized to work—but we weren't supposed to hang up on them without providing the names and phone numbers of other resources.

It was a little after one o'clock when my supervisor, whose name was Harold Meyerson, said, "Hillary, at your earliest convenience, please come to my office."

"I can come now," I said and followed him back to his desk. Harold was in his midforties, a staff attorney and also a lecturer at Yale.

He rifled through a few manila files and passed two to me. "It's a noise-complaint eviction in Section 236 housing, but I suspect the landlord just wants to raise the rent. See if there are any warranty-of-habitability violations."

I held up the files. "There's a copy of the lease in one of these?"

"There should be."

"When is the defendant supposed to vacate the premises?"

"March thirty-first."

This was less than two weeks away, and I said, "Oh, man. Should I try to negotiate with the landlord first or just file for a stay of execution?"

"Do some investigating, then tell me." Harold smiled. "I know you enjoy a challenge."

At noon on Saturday, I and the four other leaders of the Yale chapter of Law Students United for Change met at the student union to read and sign the final draft of an open letter—collaboratively written earlier in the week and typed that morning by me—to U.S. House Speaker Carl Albert. After much lobbying by antiwar activists, Albert was rumored to be on the brink of endorsing an amendment to lower the national voting age to eighteen. Meanwhile, that evening, I was planning to attend a potluck dinner hosted by Richard and Gwen Greenberger. Richard taught Constitutional Law as well as Political and Civil Rights, a seminar that had been my favorite class so far—perhaps not coincidentally, Richard was the only professor I called by his first name—and Gwen, who herself had graduated from Yale

Law in '63, ran the university-affiliated National Children's Initiative, where I'd worked the previous summer. For the potluck, I'd offered to bring chocolate chip cookies, which was one of the few foods I could confidently make.

Between the letter signing and the potluck, I was meeting Bill at three. When I arrived at the café, he was waiting outside. He cocked his head to the right and said, "I have a better idea. I passed the art gallery on the way here. You interested in the Rothko exhibit?"

"The gallery isn't open," I said. Because of a labor dispute, several university buildings were currently closed.

"Exactly," he said. "Want to see me work some Arkansas magic?"

I couldn't help myself. I said, "Does it involve watermelons?"

He laughed. "I **thought** you might have been eavesdropping in the lounge." This had been six months prior, and although I remembered the day, I was a little surprised he did. He added, "If you want to get specific, it's the town of Hope, in the southwest part of the state, that grows the very best watermelons of all. I grew up mostly in Hot Springs, but Hope is where I was born. The soil there is nice and sandy because of the river, and we once sent a melon that was almost two hundred pounds to President Truman."

" 'We' as in your family?"

" 'We' as in the town, though my uncle Carl, who was married to my grandmother's sister Otie, was a watermelon-growing champ. To be honest, it's not the really big watermelons that taste the best. The small ones are the sweetest."

"I promise not to tell Truman that you short-changed him," I said. "And yes, I'm interested in the Rothko exhibit. As for Arkansas magic, I'm willing to temporarily suspend disbelief."

"If that's the best I can do, I'll take it." He then gave me a kind of once-over and I had the strange thought that he might be about to take my hand, but instead we were soon walking side by side, and I wondered if I'd imagined the strangeness. As we walked, I was conscious of his height and heft next to me; I had to crane my neck to meet his eye.

I said, "How are your classes?" In the days since we'd spoken in the library, I'd concluded that if the purpose of this meeting wasn't to pick my brain about working at the clinic, it might be that he wanted advice about which courses to select in his second year.

"I can't lie," he said. "I'm a terrible procrastinator. I have a bad habit of taking on more projects than I ought to off campus, and I usually finish the reading about three minutes before class starts." He winced before adding, "That's assuming I come to class at all."

"What are you doing the rest of the time?"

"I'm teaching criminal law at the University

of New Haven, for one. It's to make money, but it's not a bad gig. The students are studying to be policemen, so I get an interesting window into their lives. I also do errands for a lawyer in town, delivering papers and whatnot. But the best job, until all of a sudden it wasn't, was campaigning for Joe Duffey last fall."

"Ah," I said. "I'm sorry." Duffey, a seminary professor who'd run for U.S. senator from Connecticut on an antiwar platform, had lost to a Republican named Lowell Weicker.

Bill shook his head. "Classic example of the right guy having the wrong message. Joe grew up blue-collar, but he couldn't convince factory workers he understood them. Have you worked on any campaigns?"

I said, "I actually walked precincts for Duffey the Saturday before Election Day. And in college, I'd go to New Hampshire on the weekends to volunteer for McCarthy. But this might make you want to end our conversation right now. My first campaign experience was going door-to-door for Goldwater."

"Oh, Hillary." Bill's expression was a mix of appalled and amused. "Say it ain't so."

"I started to see the light gradually. In '68, I attended both the Republican and Democratic conventions."

Bill squinted. "Is that legal? Or even possible, metaphysically speaking?"

"I'm a staunch Democrat now, and it's because

I carefully considered the alternatives. But honestly, I'd already switched sides and wouldn't have attended the Republican convention except that the Wellesley intern program assigned me to work for the House Republican Conference that summer. I did meet Frank Sinatra at the convention, though."

"Well, that's something." Bill hummed a few bars of "Strangers in the Night." "What are your plans for after Yale?"

"It depends on the day." I laughed a little. "I definitely want to work in Washington at some point. This summer, I'm clerking at a firm in California, and I can see how litigation would be exciting. But I've also been doing research for Gwen Greenberger at the National Children's Initiative. Do you know the Greenbergers?" In addition to admiring Gwen and Richard professionally, I was fascinated by them personally. He was white and Jewish and from Georgia, and she was black and Baptist and from New York, and they were the parents of three-year-old twin boys. The Greenbergers' life and home charmed me—their many bookshelves, the fact that he sometimes cooked the meals, the way they joked around **and** fought for justice **and** were both dazzlingly yet casually brilliant. It was all so different from the way my parents interacted.

"I'm in Richard's Constitutional Law class right now," Bill said. "He's fantastic."

"I'm having dinner at their house tonight," I said. "What are **your** plans for after Yale?"

"I'll go back to Arkansas and run for either Congress or attorney general." Bill wasn't the first person at Yale I'd heard express this kind of goal, but he expressed it with the greatest certainty.

I said, "I was president of the student government at Wellesley, but I think that may have been it for me—that my involvement with campaigns from here on out won't be as the candidate."

"Why?"

"Well, there's being female, for one thing. Also, I take it you don't mind asking people for money."

"No doubt about it, money-grubbing is part of the game. But I'm pretty shameless."

I laughed.

"I did student government in high school and the first couple years of college," he said. "But I went to Georgetown, and the longer I was in Washington, the more time I spent on Capitol Hill instead of campus. It was hard to resist the lure of the real thing. I was a staffer for Fulbright, and if the choice was attending a Foreign Relations Committee meeting versus listening to twenty-year-olds complain about the food in the dining hall, it wasn't much of a contest."

"Being a member of Congress and being attorney general of Arkansas seem really different," I said. "Don't they? Geographically and also, you know, metaphysically speaking?"

This time, he laughed. "I'll see what makes the most sense once I'm home," he said. "Frankly, I'm prepared to serve in just about any capacity that improves the lives of the people of Arkansas."

"You certainly **sound** like a politician."

We were turning onto Chapel Street, and he seemed unbothered as he said, "You mean I sound like a phony?"

"Maybe rehearsed more than phony."

"Is there a difference?"

"Sure," I said.

"There's a real piece-of-shit GOP congressman, a Nixon crony, up in the third district, which is mostly rural besides Fayetteville. This man is nice enough if you're talking to him, but when he's in Washington, he forgets all about his constituents. Unseating him would be a long shot, but you've got to start somewhere."

We had reached the front of the gallery, which was in another Gothic building, this one particularly castle-like. I stopped walking, causing Bill to stop, too. I looked up at his face and said, "Why are we here? I don't mean at the gallery. I mean, why are we spending time together? What do you want?"

He smiled. "What do you think I want?"

"No," I said. "Give me a real answer. There's been enough of this"—I searched for the correct words, then landed on a phrase I'd never used before—"this chitty chat."

His expression grew concerned, and when he

spoke, his tone was serious. He said, "We're on a date. I wanted to go on a date with you."

For a few seconds, I stared at him. "Why?"

He still seemed worried, fearful of misstepping, and matter-of-fact rather than fawning, as he said, "Because you're the smartest person at Yale."

I didn't know how to reply, so I laughed. It came out as more of a cackle than I'd intended.

"You must know that's what people say," Bill said. "I knew who you were more than a year ago. My mom clipped the article about you out of **Life** magazine and sent it to me at Oxford."

"And that's your thing? Smart women?"

"Why wouldn't it be?"

"If you're planning on a career in politics, I'd assume you want more of a doting housewife."

"Well, I'm not proposing marriage," he said, and I felt a surge of embarrassment. Then he smiled again and added, "Yet." I suppose this was my first experience of Bill's overlapping flirtatiousness and kindness. He said, "Listen. I'm just happy to be spending time with you right now. I had a hunch you were really cool, and you are." He paused for a half second and, not entirely unselfconsciously, added, "And also really attractive." He tilted his head toward the entrance to the gallery. "Wasn't I about to show you some Arkansas magic?"

• • •

In 1957, my friend Maureen Gurski's tenth birthday party took place at her house in Park Ridge, a block away from where my family lived. Six girls sat at the Gurskis' dining room table eating cake, along with Maureen's younger brother and parents. The subject of baseball came up—I was an ardent Cubs fan, despite their terrible record that year—and I said, "Even if the White Sox are having a better season, Ernie Banks is clearly the best player on either team. If the Cubs build around him, they'll be good in time."

Maureen's father smiled unpleasantly from across the table. He said, "You're awfully opinionated for a girl."

It was not the first time someone had said such a thing. Starting when I was in third grade, my teacher, Mrs. Jauss, had routinely asked me to be in charge when she left the room, a task that sometimes necessitated my telling John Rasch to sit down or stop poking Donna Zinser and resulted in John reminding me that I wasn't a teacher. In fourth grade, I'd been elected co-captain of the safety patrol, which occasionally elicited similar resistance from my peers. But Mr. Gurski's remark was the sentiment's clearest and most succinct expression in my life thus far and gave me, henceforth, a kind of shorthand understanding of the irritation and resentment I provoked in others. Not all others, of course—plenty of people admired that I was eager and responsible—but among those provoked were both men and women, adults and children.

Is it odd that I feel a certain gratitude to Bud Gurski? It's for (yes) two reasons. First: He said what he said at just the right moment. I was still in possession of the brazen confidence of a nine-year-old girl and didn't take him seriously, the way I might have if I were twelve or thirteen. Second: He used less ugly terms than he could have, far less ugly than I've encountered in the years since. Opinionated for a girl? Of course I was opinionated! And indeed I was a girl. He was stating facts more than offering insult.

Mr. Gurski was about thirty-five at the time of Maureen's tenth birthday, which seemed to me rather old for putting a grade school girl in her place. I hadn't yet learned this is an impulse some men never outgrow. But he was easy to dismiss, even though I was aware that to convey my dismissal wouldn't have been respectful. **You're awfully dumb for a grown-up,** I thought. Aloud, I said, "Well, Ernie Banks is a great ballplayer."

On his way to meet me at the café, Bill had noticed that trash had accumulated in the gallery courtyard, presumably because the janitors who usually picked it up were part of the strike. He'd started talking to a security guard and asked the man if he'd let us into the museum if we cleaned up beforehand. The guard was a black man who looked to be sixty or so, whose hand Bill shook warmly. Extending an arm toward me, Bill said, "And this is Hillary, the girl I'm hoping to impress."

The guard's name was Gerard; he and I also shook hands. The next thing I knew, Bill and I were striding around the courtyard picking up discarded soda cans, cigarette stubs, and bits of paper, and throwing them away. We were calling to each other as we passed in front of and behind an oversized bronze sculpture of a reclining human figure, and it was some of the strangest fun I'd ever had. Was I enjoying myself because it was a cool but sunny spring day and I was outside and moving around? Because everything about this afternoon was surprising? Because Bill was tall and silly and handsome and flirtatious?

It was ten to four when Gerard let us in a side door, into the cavernous and shadowy museum proper; the lights were not on. We wandered past an ancient Greek vase and a ceiling tile from Syria and a bust of the Roman emperor Commodus. We paused at a nineteenth-century American oil painting of pink jungle orchids, and Bill pointed at one of the leaves and said, "Look at that level of detail."

I pointed, saying, "I like the hummingbird."

Bill's index finger fleetingly brushed against mine as he said, "There are two hummingbirds."

I hesitated—it was plausible he was a person who did such things without deciding to, but I wasn't—then I fleetingly brushed my finger against his. "They look like they're telling secrets."

He laughed. "How do you know they're not debating important jungle policy?"

He turned from the painting then, and I turned, too, and he set his hand on my back just below my left shoulder. Inside me, there was a ripple, a kind of swooning. He wanted to be on a date with **me**? I was the person he wanted to be alone with? Being courted, being found "really attractive" by a man like Bill was not a type of good fortune I'd expected or even actively wanted; to want it would have seemed ridiculous and indulgent and possibly greedy. I'd had crushes, of course. In fact, I'd had many crushes. But I tended to feel excitement for the other person in inverse proportion to his excitement for me. And I didn't even aspire to men like Bill, to anyone magnetic or exceptional—I pinned my hopes on guys who were smart but ordinary, and still it worked only when they were the ones who liked me first.

In front of an Edward Hopper painting of a woman in a hotel room, Bill said, "This is my favorite piece in the museum. Sometimes I stop by just to check up on her."

The woman wore a sleeveless red dress with a low-cut neckline and high-heeled brown shoes and sat on the edge of a made bed, some kind of dunes or mountains in the picture window behind her, beneath a blue sky. The painting wasn't overtly sexual, but it wasn't entirely unsexual, either.

"Why do you like it?" I asked.

"The intensity of her expression—what's she thinking? Is she heartbroken? Is she angry? Is someone else in the room with her?"

Now that he mentioned it, it did seem another presence, perhaps that of the painter, was implied.

"How do you have time to come here?" I asked. "Between working on Senate campaigns and procrastinating?"

He grinned. "Coming here **is** procrastinating." He pointed at sunlight against the wall in the painting and said, "Aren't the shadows and light remarkable?"

"I wouldn't have guessed that you were such an art aficionado."

"You mean because I'm from Arkansas?"

"Because you're so busy." Sheepishly, I added, "And maybe partly because you're from Arkansas, although I promise I'm not an East Coast snob. I grew up outside Chicago, so I can't be."

Bill appeared enthused rather than offended as he said, "I have a hard time getting people to believe this, but Hot Springs is incredibly sophisticated. The sulfur springs have always attracted people from all over the country and, really, the world—everyone from Hernando de Soto to Al Capone to Teddy Roosevelt. De Soto literally thought he'd found the fountain of youth. Now there's different religions, there's beautiful houses and hotels, there's arts and culture, and it's even where a lot of baseball teams come for spring training. Admittedly, there are seedy parts, and some avid fans of the seediness include people near and dear to me, but I think it's a mix of activity that makes life interesting. Don't you?"

There really was something ridiculously endearing about the man beside me. "Yes," I said. "I do."

"And there's an alligator farm **and** an ostrich farm. Oh, and a zoo with a mermaid skeleton."

I smiled. "Did anyone ever mention that to Darwin?"

"You do realize," he said, and he was smiling, too, "that it's entirely possible to be from Chicago and still be an East Coast snob?"

In the spring of seventh grade, I ran for student council president, as did four other rising eighth graders. When the list of candidates was posted on the bulletin board outside the principal's office, it didn't surprise me that all my opponents were boys, and if anything, it pleased me: I immediately understood the advantages conferred if students voted along gender lines.

On a warm May afternoon, following lunch in the cafeteria, the four boys and I gave our speeches to the entire junior high. We'd been told by Mr.

Heape, the student council adviser, to speak for a maximum of five minutes.

My father, who was sarcastic, exacting, and often mean, helped with my speech. Starting in grade school, I'd write papers in their entirety then give them to him, and he'd mark them up with a ballpoint pen: crossing out entire paragraphs, flagging repetition or soft arguments, writing **puerile** or **vacuous** in the margins. I'd make changes based on his suggestions but not show him second drafts. There was a joke my father told about a piano tuner whose surname was Opporknockety, which allowed for the punchline "Opporknockety tunes but once," and early on, when I'd asked him to read a revision, he'd replied, "Hugh Rodham tunes but once." By profession a supplier of drapery fabric and window shades, my father was also a Republican, a political junkie who disdained most politicians, a cheapskate, and a man not only easily bored but disinclined to conceal his boredom. It was he who provided me with the introduction to my student council campaign speech.

"Hello, fellow Ralph Waldo Emerson Junior High students," I said into the microphone. "In the words of Winston Churchill, a good speech should be like a woman's skirt—long enough to cover the subject but short enough to create interest."

Most students looked at me blankly. A few teachers tittered, and a few more exchanged perturbed glances. I won the election with eighty-two votes.

The next fall, student council meetings occurred every Monday, in Mr. Heape's classroom, during lunch period. I and a boy named Bruce, who was the student council treasurer, were always the first to arrive because we packed our lunches rather than buying them. In the ten minutes that we waited for everyone else, Bruce and I discussed upcoming math tests or his family's springer spaniel, Buster, or who had been on **The Ed Sullivan Show** the night before. During these conversations, I sat in a chair desk I'd moved to the front of the classroom, with the chalkboard behind me, and Bruce sat in the front row of chair desks, facing me. In October, we made a bet about whether "Save the Last Dance for Me" would remain a Billboard number-one single for more than a week. He thought it wouldn't, and I thought it would, and in a way we both were right, because it was bumped the next week from the top slot then returned for two weeks. When I got a haircut, he said as soon as he entered the classroom, "You look different with bangs." Bruce himself had a blond crew cut, hazel eyes, and a collection of authentic Indian arrowheads he once brought in to show me, acquired on a trip to Ohio with his family.

When Mr. Heape and the other students arrived, bearing cafeteria trays of meatloaf and cottage cheese and peach slices in syrup, I would open the manila folder where I kept student council notes and call the meeting to order; I had used my mother's typewriter to make a label for the folder that read, STUDENT COUNCIL PRESIDENCY 1960–61.

On Thanksgiving morning of 1960, I woke up from a dream of kissing Bruce. The dream shocked me and then, as I lay beneath the covers, made an abrupt sense; after all, wasn't the ten minutes Bruce and I spent alone together in the classroom my favorite part of each week? But realizing this, admitting it to myself, was both troubling and exciting. I had never in real life kissed anyone. As I helped my mother squeeze lemons for the cranberry relish and roll the pie dough, I wondered if she'd sense that now I wished to. For all of Thanksgiving break, as I skated with my brothers at Hinkley Park, as we trimmed our Christmas tree, as I watched a movie at the Pickwick Theater with my friend Maureen, the idea of Bruce accompanied me, my jittery and valuable secret. Certain weather and certain times of day—the sun setting early, or snow—filled me with a new yearning, a wish to share the sadness or loveliness of the world with this other person.

The following Monday, Mr. Heape's classroom was empty when I entered it, which threw me off. In my imagination, Bruce had already been there when I arrived for our post-Thanksgiving reunion. As I moved a chair desk around to face out, my own body felt unwieldy, and when I sat, I couldn't remember how I usually positioned my legs or what expression my face ought to settle into. I was probably in the classroom for all of a minute by myself, when Bruce entered and casually said, as if in my mind we had not spent the last five days kissing each other, "It smells like spoiled milk in the hall."

He was so cute! His blond crew cut and his hazel eyes and the maroon sweater vest he was wearing. At first, I had to pretend to act normal, but soon enough the rhythm of the conversation absorbed me and I was wondering with only a part of my brain, rather than with all of it, if he thought I was cute, too. At the student council meeting that day, a boy named Gregory said, "It's dumb to sell Valentine's Day dance tickets before Christmas," and I said, "Some people like to plan ahead," and Bruce said, "I agree with Hillary." Before the meeting the next week, when we were discussing Bruce's neighbor's dachshund, who'd died of old age over the weekend, I said, "I love dachshunds," and he said, "I thought cocker spaniels were your favorite." Which I'd told him back in September, and he'd **remembered.**

A few weeks passed thusly: I still raised my hand in social studies class and math, read propped up on two pillows in my bed at home, helped my mother set the table and wash the dishes, played pinochle with my brothers, and all the while, my body thrummed, my heart clutched, with thoughts of Bruce.

On the last day of school before Christmas break, I gave him a note I had written in pencil on a piece of lined paper and folded twice:

Dear Bruce,

If you ask me to be your girlfriend, I will say yes.

Sincerely,
Hillary

I'd thought giving him two weeks to formulate a response was wise; the erroneousness of this logic was apparent by the time I arrived home after school and was too keyed up to eat my usual snack of peanut butter and saltines. Had he read the note yet? Had he shown the note to anyone else? What was his answer? These questions were the drumbeat of Christmas 1960, and what was usually my favorite holiday was contaminated by doubt and anxiety. And what if I ran into him **during** the winter break? Would that be better or worse? I considered calling him and telling him the letter was null and void—I located his number in the white pages that we kept on its own white-pages-sized shelf under the telephone nook in the front hall, at the bottom of the staircase (his father's name was William D. Stappenbeck, and their address was 4633 Weleba

Avenue)—but what if one of my family members overheard?

By New Year's Day, my agitation had started to wane; it flooded back as soon as I awakened on the morning school resumed, and the very halls of Ralph Waldo Emerson Junior High seemed to pulsate with the shame of my forwardness. When I'd written the letter, I hadn't expected that Bruce would respond over break, but if he did like me, wouldn't he have wished to convey it as quickly as possible?

Finally it was lunchtime. When I entered Mr. Heape's classroom, Bruce was the only one there, seated in a chair desk in the front row. He said, "Hi, Hillary."

"Hi," I said.

There was a pause, then he said, "For Christmas, I got a pogo stick and a new Monopoly set because my brother left our other one out in the rain."

"Oh," I said. "I got a cowgirl vest."

Soon enough, the rest of the student council members were arriving, and neither Bruce nor I had mentioned my note. By the following Monday, a part of me was convinced I ought to pretend I'd never written it, as Bruce seemed to be doing. (Or could he have dropped it before reading it? And if so, where? **Please, please,** I thought, **not at school.**) But I also wanted clarity and resolution; there was something about pretending that seemed silly.

What if, before he'd read it, the note had fallen out of his pocket in his bedroom, then his mother had thrown it away, also without reading it? And what if he'd have been thrilled to be my boyfriend but had no idea I wanted it? (In the years since, on the occasions when I've been accused of being a pessimist, I've yearned to hold up this counterexample.)

On the third Monday in January, which was a few days before John F. Kennedy's inauguration, Bruce said as he removed his sack lunch from his book bag, "My cousin told me that the mafia got Kennedy elected."

From my desk, facing Bruce, I asked, "Did you read the note I gave you before Christmas?"

Bruce didn't seem nervous as he said, "Janet Umpke is the girl I like."

A tidal wave of disappointment crashed inside me, while calmly (this was my first experience of needing to act like I wasn't devastated when I was) I said, "Okay."

Bruce pulled an apple from the brown bag and set it on his desk, then pulled out his baloney sandwich. He didn't say anything else. Many seconds passed.

"Have you ever talked to Janet?" I asked.

"Once," he said.

"Do you have any classes with her?"

"Social studies." The room was quiet again, then he added, "She has pierced ears." I knew this about Janet; I had mentioned it to my own parents at dinner one night, and my father had said, "Pierced ears are for Gypsies."

Bruce's revelation about Janet would have made more sense if she were unusually pretty, but weren't we about the same? I considered myself medium-pretty: not beautiful like Emily Geisinger, who had the blond ringlets of a fairy-tale princess, but certainly in the same general category as Janet.

Bruce took a bite of his sandwich. He said, "You're more like a boy than a girl."

This was another tidal wave, which is to say another opportunity to practice composure. I said, "How?"

He was silent, seeming to consider the question. When he spoke at last, he spoke decisively. He said, "The way you act and the way you talk."

Around dusk, Bill and I ended up back outside, in the courtyard. As the door to the museum shut behind us, he said, "Where do you live?"

"On Orange Street. I have a roommate named Katherine who's getting a doctorate in history."

"Is she the lousy kind of roommate or the good kind?"

"She's the cousin of someone I went to Wellesley with, and we're not close friends, but we get along well enough. I'm really only home at night, and she has a fiancé in New York so she's there at least half the week."

"Do you know Keith Darrow or Jimmy Malinowski or Kirby Hadey?" Bill asked. "I live with those guys out on Long Island Sound, in Milford. It's an authentic beach house, which is more romantic in theory than in practice. Or at least warmer in the winter in theory than in practice. But I'd love to have you down for a sandy picnic."

"Is Kirby the nephew of Senator Hadey or is that just a rumor?" Already, I regretted not responding flirtatiously to the mention of a picnic—regretted responding to the concrete question he'd asked rather than to the open-ended statement—but it seemed too late to fix my mistake.

"No, it's true," Bill was saying. "Kirby never brings it up, but it is true. The funny thing is that his family is so rich, it seems like being related to a senator is the least of it. I went home with him over Thanksgiving, to his parents' penthouse on Park Avenue in New York. It was about the size of the Taj Mahal, with their own private elevator from the lobby. We arrived on Wednesday night, and his parents invited us to join them for drinks in the living room with some guests, but Kirby wanted to go meet his prep school friends at a bar. Before we leave, we stop by the living room to say goodbye, and it turns out one of his parents' guests is William Styron, another is an editor from **The New York Times**, and yet another is undersecretary of the treasury. Their wives were there, too, all of them just chatting like mere mortals. I was practically salivating."

I laughed. "Was the prep school bar fun?"

"It was all right." Bill grinned. "But I hope you don't think I missed the opportunity to get Styron's phone number for next time I'm in New York."

"Did you really?"

"I told him what a fan I am of **Nat Turner** and **Lie Down in Darkness**. I got the editor's number, too."

"How long were you in the living room? Two minutes?"

"More like ten. I have a notebook where I write down the name and, if I get it, the number or address of everyone I meet. I started in high school. If it's someone influential like Styron, I send a follow-up note saying I enjoyed meeting them and when I'm next in their neck of the woods, how about if I say hello? The worst they can say is no."

"This is all in preparation for when you run for office?"

"Yes, but if I got to have lunch with William Styron in New York City, that in itself would be an experience."

"And you think someone like him will take an interest in a congressional race in Arkansas?"

Bill looked impish. "Maybe I have bigger goals."

"Like what? Senator?"

He held up a thumb and jabbed it skyward.

A little incredulously, I said, "President?"

"Apparently I'm not supposed to say that I'm prepared to serve in just about any capacity because that would sound phony. But you know how you can tell if someone is truly thinking of running for president? He'll never admit it until he publicly announces. Anyone who goes around noodling over the idea is a lot less likely to do it than the fellow who holds his cards close to the vest."

"Does that mean you will or won't?"

In a faux-ingenuous tone, Bill said, "Running for president—what an interesting thought, Hillary! That's never occurred to me." More seriously, he added, "There's something about you that makes me want to tell you everything. Do you think that's a good or bad idea?" He was looking at me again with an expression that no one had ever looked at me with; it was intensely attentive, and it also was as if his words were simultaneously a joke and not a joke at all.

"I think it's worth trying to find out," I said. And really, in spite of the many crushes I'd had, there was a feeling Bill Clinton gave me that I'd never previously experienced: There was so much—an infinite amount—for us to discuss, there were so many topics I'd like to talk about with him, so many questions I had and things I wanted to tell him about myself. Telling personal anecdotes sometimes seemed tedious to me, or pointless, but

I felt a powerful desire for us to know each other extremely well.

He said, "I'm planning to run for president as soon as 1984 and I hope no later than 1992. I really have been laying the groundwork since I was in high school. You ever heard of Boys Nation? I was big into that, and I went to Washington the summer I was sixteen and met Kennedy. I know this probably sounds crazy, but I realized then, it has to be someone, so why not me? I love people, I'm passionate about improving the world, and I'm willing to work like hell."

"Wow. I think of myself as a planner, but—"

When I didn't say anything else, he said, "Am I scaring you?"

"No," I said. "You're impressing me. A lot of people underestimate their ability to change the status quo or they're too lazy to try." We had wandered over to the large bronze sculpture, and we stood next to it, facing each other. "You know what I was just thinking?"

Bill cocked his head to one side expectantly.

I said, "I was thinking that a sandy picnic with you sounds really, really nice."

Unlike Mr. Gurski's observation that I was opinionated for a girl, Bruce's statement that I was boy-like had not been easy for me to dismiss; if anything, that it had been delivered without apparent animus made it more distressing. Even so, the lesson he offered proved to be one I needed to learn more than once. The lesson was this: You will encounter boys and men with whom you think you enjoy chemistry. A boy or man will find you funny and interesting and smart, just as you find him funny and interesting and smart. The pleasure you take in each other's company will be obvious, but, crucially, while this pleasure will make you feel as if you're in love with him, it will not make him feel as if he's in love with you. He might remark on how much he likes talking to you, but there will be girls he wants to kiss, and you will not be one of them.

In high school and again in college, there were more Bruces, Bruce stand-ins. After hours or weeks or months of robust conversation, when I finally said or did something I considered overtly flirtatious—declared how handsome they were or how lucky a girl would be to date them, or when I stood or sat close enough to kiss, tilting up my face—these boys seemed surprised and uncomfortable. This happened in high school with a boy named Norman, and it happened my sophomore year at Wellesley with an MIT senior named Phil, and it happened again my senior year at Wellesley with a Harvard graduate student named Daniel.

In the meantime, in eleventh grade, I had my first kiss; I attended prom with a date; I seriously dated a different MIT student named Roy, to whom I lost my virginity. (Premarital sex held no stigma for me, though getting pregnant would have, and I'd started taking the pill in advance of our first time.) I had discovered that the key to opening the door of dating was to agree to go out with boys and men to whom I was not physically attracted. This trick, if such a defeatist stance could be considered a trick, involved a passivity I brought to no other area of my life. But choosing the guy, liking the other person first, **never** worked for me; dating worked only when I let them choose me. Was it because, around boys and men I wasn't attracted to, I was freed of some heaviness of expectations I couldn't otherwise conceal? Was it because, in the hierarchy of appearance, I liked guys who were more good-looking than I was entitled to like? (But really, they didn't need to be extraordinarily handsome—there were so many kinds of men I could fall for, such different physical types and mannerisms and personalities, just as long as they weren't boring or meek.) Or was I pretty enough but, per Mr. Gurski, spoke with an off-putting sharpness or surety of tone?

Roy, to whom I lost my virginity, was boring, meek, **and** arrogant. On our first date after we'd met at a Wellesley-MIT mixer, I steered the entire conversation, which was tiring—I inquired about his upbringing, his Judaism, and his academic studies—but before we parted, he asked if next time I'd like to go out for dinner. In the seven months we were a couple, he rarely made conversation and rarely complimented me yet seemed to take for granted my wish to be involved with him. Did he, in a way he was unable to articulate, actually like my strong will? Or did he mistake me for a typical woman, was he game to be my boyfriend not because I was Hillary and distinctly myself but because I possessed the standard feminine qualities that a college-educated man in the late 1960s might wish for? Did he not understand that I was special?

Just before I returned to Chicago at the end of my sophomore year, when Roy raised my conversion to Judaism as a precondition of our eventual marriage, I broke up with him. I had, all along, seen him as a kind of experiment, a test to determine whether ongoing involvement with a man I wasn't initially infatuated with might create infatuation; and while a sample size of one wasn't wholly revealing, the answer in Roy's case was no. For a time, the novelty of sex had offset our boring conversations and lackluster physical compatibility, and then, eventually, it hadn't.

I was soon spending time with Daniel the Harvard Divinity graduate student, whom I'd met at a Vietnam protest in Harvard Yard. Though our campuses were just sixteen miles apart, we began corresponding by letter, which progressed after a month to meeting for tea on Saturday afternoons. During these get-togethers, which occurred in either the town of Wellesley or Harvard Square, we'd discuss Martin Luther and Dietrich Bonhoeffer and Reinhold Niebuhr; we once spent three hours debating all the ways the word **good** could be interpreted in John Wesley's dictum "Do all the good you can, by all the means you can, in all the ways you can, in all the places you can, at all the times you can, to all the people you can, as long as ever you can." Daniel was from Indianapolis, had attended Indiana University as an undergraduate, and was wiry and dark-haired, with black horn-rimmed glasses.

One cold day in early March, we were walking along the Charles River, and I said, "I'm not sure how you feel about undergraduate activities, but there's a mixer coming up at Wellesley a week from Saturday, and I'm wondering if you'd like to join me for it." I had rehearsed this language. I also had decided to pat his upper arm as I issued the invitation, but my execution of the gesture was more halting and less carefree than I'd imagined.

Daniel stopped walking and turned toward me, the river behind him. It was 4:00 P.M. and about twenty degrees, and parts of the Charles, especially near the shore, were still frozen. Really, it was a bit cold to be walking for pleasure, except that my crush on Daniel had ballooned to the point where I didn't care about the temperature. And might not the banks of the Charles be a perfect place for our first kiss?

"Hillary, I really enjoy discussing theology with you," Daniel said, and I knew, after those eight words, that if we ever again spent time together, it would be only to prove to one or both of us that I wasn't ending our friendship because he didn't reciprocate my romantic interest. There were additional words he said then, with the river behind him, the cold air, the wintry afternoon light, but they didn't matter. How many times, I wondered, would this pattern repeat itself and still surprise me? I was twenty-one, meaning absurdly young yet old enough to consider myself newly worldly and to see my limited experiences as conclusive.

Back on the Wellesley campus, I cried while describing the conversation to my friends Nancy and Phyllis, though already it felt like the tears were for a general sense of romantic discouragement rather than a Daniel-specific lamentation. Nancy was a tall, extremely rich English major from Greenwich, Connecticut, and Phyllis was a short, working-class biology major from Baltimore, and they'd been roommates since our freshman year and were my closest friends.

"I'm sorry, Hillary," Nancy said. "But all that time you were talking about God and man, you should have been wearing a dress with a low neckline." Nancy was sitting with her desk chair turned out toward the room, Phyllis was cross-legged on her bed, and I was on the floor with my back against Nancy's bed frame.

"It was fun talking about God and man," I said, and they looked at each other and laughed.

"Once a guy doesn't think of you as someone to date, it's hard to change that," Phyllis said.

"You need to flirt more," Nancy said. "From the beginning, you need to make it unmistakable. Don't be subtle."

"I gave him a biography of Reinhold Niebuhr," I said.

"Yes," Nancy said. "That's the problem."

"I realize that's not the same as batting my eyelashes, but it showed that I was thinking about him when we weren't together. And it was hardcover. It cost twelve dollars."

"I don't think it matters what **you** do," Phyllis said. "He's paying more attention to how you react to what **he** does."

As it happened, Nancy had applied to the Peace Corps, and Phyllis had applied to medical school. That all of us believed in equal rights went without saying.

"I don't know if this sounds pathetic or conceited," I said. "But I always hoped a man would fall in love with me for my brain."

Again, Phyllis and Nancy exchanged a glance. Phyllis's voice was kind as she said, "Hillary, no man falls in love with a woman's brain."

In the gallery courtyard, I was perched against the bronze sculpture—because the sculpture was an oversized human figure, I was essentially sitting in her lap—and Bill stood facing me, intermittently lifting his right leg and setting the sole of his shoe against the sculpture's base, a few inches from my left thigh. Describing where I'd grown up, I said, "When I started at Wellesley, I'd have said that I was from a middle-class background. Meaning, compared to girls who rode horses and went to boarding school. Park Ridge is nice but not fancy. But the people I work with at the clinic and through the National Children's Initiative—I'm sure my family would seem rich to them. My dad owns a drapery business that's done well. My mom had a really hard childhood, though. She mostly wasn't raised by her own parents, and she had to support herself from a young age. Ironically, it's my dad who has more of a chip on his shoulder, even though he grew up in a regular family."

"You think your mom's childhood is what drew you to the clinic?"

"I'm sure. My mom doesn't talk that much about her past, but she always thinks of other people, whether it's my brothers and me or a child she hears about through our church who needs a winter coat."

"When my mother was pregnant with me, my father was killed in a car accident."

"Oh my goodness," I said. "I'm so sorry."

"Her next husband died on her, too, though I can't say I was entirely sorry to see him go. Daddy was a mean old drunk, and we had some ugly times with him, me and Mother and my brother, Roger.

In fact, Mother divorced him once, but it didn't stick."

"When did your stepfather pass away?"

"In '67, of cancer. Now Mother's married to a fellow named Jeff, and we all love him. Admittedly, he's colorful in his own right. Not a drinker like Daddy, but Jeff did do time."

"You mean in prison?" Rapidly, the chip on my father's shoulder, and even the challenges of my mother's childhood, were seeming like minor inconveniences.

"Stock fraud, and he was in for less than a year," Bill said. "This was long before he and Mother became an item. The real problem when they got together was that he was still married to someone else."

"Yes," I said. "I can see how that would be a problem."

"Jeff and his wife were separated," Bill said. "They just weren't legally divorced. Personally, I've always had a soft spot for the guy. He adores Mother, which matters the most. Plus, Mother's beauty regimen is very important to her, and he's a hairdresser. Talk about mixing business and pleasure, huh?"

Our conversation had for me taken on a careening quality—one rather shocking detail was following another and another, without leaving time to absorb them, even as we swerved between seriousness and levity. Then Bill said, "Does this all sound crazy to you? Does it sound like I have a terribly disreputable background?"

Carefully, I said, "It sounds different from what I'm used to. But it makes me respect the fact that you've overcome challenges and made something of yourself."

"Remember how I told you that in high school, I spent a week in Washington through Boys Nation?"

I nodded.

"There were two delegates from every state. We all stayed in a dorm at the University of Maryland, and it was the first time I'd been outside Arkansas. From the minute I started meeting the other boys, I could tell that some of them, especially the ones from bigger Northern cities, thought I was a hick. I had an accent, I was kind of fat, I talked a lot." Bill smiled wryly. "I'm sure you haven't noticed any of those things."

"You're not fat," I said.

"I was then. In any case, I realized I could observe these other boys and emulate them, even if that meant concealing parts of who I was, or I could say fuck it and be myself. Let the chips fall where they may. Mother loves betting at the racetrack. She wears gobs of makeup. She's been married four times to three men, one of whom was violent, and I've never even asked her about this, but a cousin of mine told me there was a rumor my real father, the one who died in the car crash, was already married when he married her. But Mother has a heart of gold, and so do so many people in my extended family and so many of our neighbors. I've met lots of wonderful people at Georgetown, at Oxford, here, but the people in Arkansas are something special. And I'm not just saying that because I plan to run for office there." He paused. "I said fuck it and decided to be myself."

"I think you made the right choice." I hesitated then added, "My father was never violent, but he's a real asshole." This wasn't a way I'd ever previously described him, even to Phyllis and Nancy at Wellesley. "I assume he's unhappy," I continued, "but I never understood why he had to take out his unhappiness on us and especially on my mom. If we left the cap off the toothpaste, he'd throw it out the bathroom window and make us go get it, even if we were already in bed. He once made me go out in the snow in my bare feet. He also—" I took a deep breath. "He didn't let my mom come to my college graduation. He's very cheap, and he got angry at her because she bought the more expensive brand of chicken at the grocery store so he said he wasn't paying for her to come to my graduation. Obviously, the chicken was just the excuse. But for him to do that—I guess you know from that **Life** article that I spoke at my graduation. And the fact that I even went to Wellesley, my mother would have loved to have that chance. She'd been sent to live in California when she was eight, and after she finished high school, her mother said she would pay for my mom to go to Northwestern if she came back to Chicago. But it was just a trick to make my mom come work as a housecleaner. Anyway, I think my father had to poison my graduation **because** it meant so much to her and me."

Bill's brow was furrowed. "None of your family heard you make that speech?"

"My dad flew in the night before, stayed at a hotel near the airport, took the T to Wellesley for the ceremony, then went back to the airport. I told people my mom couldn't travel because she was on blood-thinning medication." I glanced down, and then he was next to me—he had joined me in the sculpture's lap. The sides of our torsos and legs touched, and when he set his arm around my back, I leaned into him. The odd part was that none of this seemed odd. We both were quiet.

At last, after a minute or so, Bill said, "It's beyond me how anyone could have you as a daughter and not be bursting with pride."

"My mother is proud," I said. "So maybe it's not a bad thing if my dad is critical. Midwesterners aren't supposed to get swelled heads."

"You're very forgiving."

"It depends on the situation."

"Well, I'm sure that speech was just the beginning. There are a lot more amazing things you'll do, and your dad won't be able to keep your mom from seeing them all."

"Thank you," I said. True dark still hadn't

descended, but if I'd had a book, there would no longer have been enough light to read. Through my jeans, I could feel the cold of the sculpture contrasting with the pleasant warmth of Bill next to me, his bulk and closeness. Certainly there was nowhere else I wanted to be in this moment; there was no one whose company I'd have preferred. My heart spasmed a little, because of how significant the moment felt—it felt like a threshold between my youth and adulthood, or the exact instant of love coming into existence.

It seemed he felt it, too, because he removed his arm from my shoulder and took my hand, my left with his right. In addition to being enormous, his hands were beautiful, his fingers long and slender. I could sense him turn his head toward me, and I knew that if I turned my head toward him, we'd kiss, and I wanted this to happen and also was overwhelmed and immobilized. A few more seconds passed, seconds that were silent and massive and terrifying and thrilling, and then his lips were against my neck. Softly but firmly, he kissed my neck over and over. It felt very good, and I was very happy. And eventually I could turn to him, our mouths could find each other, our lips and tongues, and then we were kissing fully.

At some point in the courtyard, perhaps in our third hour together, it had fleetingly occurred to me that there was no longer enough time left to make chocolate chip cookies for the Greenbergers' potluck, and I'd decided to instead pick up a bottle of wine. But then Bill and I had started kissing, and when we left the grounds of the gallery, I was already an hour late for dinner and still empty-handed. Bill wanted to walk me to the Greenbergers' house, and in his company, my various breaches of etiquette seemed insignificant—how could a baked good or a bottle of wine compare to the sensation of Bill Clinton's mouth on mine?—but the breaches seemed less so once I was standing in the dining room, facing eight people who were in the middle of dinner. Two of these people were law professors, one was my boss and mentor, one was a law professor's wife, and the others were law students. John Coltrane was playing on the record player, and the Greenbergers' twins, Otto and Marcus, were shouting and jumping in the living room. I had let myself in the front door, and I blurted out, "I'm so sorry. I fell asleep and completely lost track of time."

"I was worried," Gwen said. "I'm glad you're here." She stood, and walked around the table to embrace me as Richard said cheerfully, "Better late than never." The other professor, a man named Jeffrey Larson who taught criminal procedure, said, "The spicy goulash should wake you up."

Gwen led me into the kitchen, and as she scooped the meat and macaroni from the pan, I said, "I really am sorry."

She looked at me intently. "Are you sick?"

"No. I just—" I didn't like lying and especially not to Gwen. But to need to lie or else reveal my rudeness—these were not my usual choices. "I'm fine," I said. "How are you?"

"I called your apartment a few minutes ago, but you must have just left." She set the large wooden spoon back in the pan. "I have great news. My friend Ida's nephew will be in Los Angeles this summer, and you can sublet his apartment in Berkeley. It's furnished."

"Oh, that's fantastic. Thank you." It was Richard who had helped me secure the clerkship with a small firm, one of whose partners had been his Harvard Law classmate.

Gwen said, "I can't vouch for how nice the apartment is, but it's near the campus, which should be convenient."

"Gwen, I didn't bring any cookies," I said.

"Well, we have some ice cream," she said, and then, breathlessly, I said, "I think I'm in love. Do you think it's possible to fall in love with someone in four hours?"

Her expression turned to one of amusement. "Who?"

"Do you know who Bill Clinton is?"

She shook her head.

"He's a first-year from Arkansas." I lowered my voice to a whisper. "He's very, very good-looking."

"Well," she said, "that never hurts."

"Did anyone ever kiss you on the neck the first time they kissed you? Instead of on the lips?" She looked confused, and I added, "I'm just wondering if that's unusual or not unusual."

"Did you like it?"

I nodded rapidly.

A thud and the sound of crying came from the living room and Gwen called, "Boys, what did I say about jumping off the couch?" To me, she said, "I have about fifty questions, and I can't ask any of them now. Don't forget what you were going to say. But if both people like something, I'm not sure it matters whether or not it's unusual."

As she went to attend to her children, I carried my plate into the dining room and took the open seat, which was between my classmates Herb Buchsbaum and Elman Deeks. A conversation was under way about whether the recent tenure denial of a law professor was due to his role in the protests the previous year in support of a Black Panther on trial for murder. Though both Elman and I had attended the trial as ACLU volunteers monitoring for possible government abuses, I was far too wound up to contribute. And I was certainly too wound up to eat more than a few bites of goulash.

As Bill and I had stood on the sidewalk outside the Greenbergers' house just a few minutes before, it had crossed my mind to invite him in, though I was relieved I hadn't. It also had crossed my mind to skip the potluck and take him back to my apartment, but wouldn't we end up in bed, and wouldn't that be rash, even if it **was** 1971? Thus I'd said, "Thank you for the Arkansas magic today. I had a great time." I'd stepped in and reached up to hug him, a gesture simultaneously bolder than what I'd normally initiate after such a brief time and less than what the situation seemed to call for. Very fleetingly, I was being embraced by Bill, and it really was like being embraced by a lion, or at least a fairy-tale version of a lion; he was enormous and tender and he subsumed me. Then the hug was finished, and I was taking a step backward.

"I had a great time, too," he said.

We eyed each other, and I hoped he would try to arrange another date. When he didn't, I hoped I hadn't squelched the impulse with anything I had or hadn't said. Bill's interest in me seemed incontrovertible, but I had such a bad track record; what if, even though he'd been the initiator, I reciprocated too enthusiastically and drove him away? My voice was misleadingly steady as I said, "See you soon?"

"Absolutely." In his voice, there was real warmth. "Enjoy the dinner."

Sitting at the Greenbergers' table, I wondered, was he about to become my boyfriend? It seemed impossible. But, already, his not becoming my boyfriend seemed impossible, too. The way it had felt when he'd kissed my neck, and the way it had felt when we kissed on the lips—

"Hillary," Elman said, and when I glanced at him, he pointed to my other side and said, "The butter?"

I could tell by his puzzled expression that it was not the first time he'd made the request.

In my satchel, I always carried both a fold-up map of New Haven and a bus schedule, and I'd used them to determine that the apartment in the eviction case was about two miles north of the law school. The bus I boarded on Monday morning went straight up Dixwell Avenue, and although the area around campus wasn't particularly quaint—it featured grad student apartments and cheap restaurants—the streets became dingier as I rode north: laundromats and beauty salons where it didn't look like business was booming, multistory brick buildings with boarded-up windows, empty lots behind torn chain-link fences. The ages and skin colors of the people I observed through the bus window also changed, the young whites like me being replaced with Mexicans or blacks.

The Suarez family lived a few blocks off Dixwell, in a clapboard triple-decker. The front door of the building opened onto a small vestibule in which three vertical mailboxes hung from the wall; a filthy mustard-colored carpet led up two steps to the first-floor unit, and I kept climbing the staircase to the second floor. I paused before knocking on the door, listening, and heard nothing. I rapped my knuckles against the wood.

The man who opened the door was just a couple inches taller than I was, with olive skin, dark hair, and a neat mustache. He wore royal-blue cotton coveralls with an oval Neely & Cooke badge—Neely & Cooke was a commercial aircraft engine manufacturer located nearby—and he was smoking a cigarette.

"I'm Hillary Rodham from the New Haven Legal Services office, and I'm here for the tour of your apartment," I said. "To confirm, you're Robert Suarez?"

"Yes, ma'am," he said. "That's fine."

On the phone the previous week, he had uttered the phrase **Yes, ma'am** no fewer than twenty times, and I had wondered if he'd be surprised when he realized how young I was.

Inside the apartment, the curtains were drawn in all the rooms, and no lights were on; in the living room, an older woman, a toddler, and a baby were watching a soap opera on a black-and-white television. Given that I was there in part due to a noise complaint, I noted that the volume of the TV was average. Robert Suarez didn't introduce me to the woman, who also was smoking, and, following his lead, I didn't introduce myself; I assumed she was his mother-in-law. Over the phone, he'd told me the names, ages, and estimated sleeping schedules of everyone who lived in the apartment, which included his wife, who was on the cleaning staff at a high school, and their oldest child, a seven-year-old girl.

The apartment had two bedrooms, and the tour did not take long. I spent several minutes in the sole bathroom, leaving the door ajar as I opened the cabinet below the sink and found a mess of toiletries. I debated whether I ought to explain to Robert Suarez that I was looking for plumbing problems or whether it was self-evident and to explain would be condescending; in my clinic work, I routinely felt unsure if I was being overbearingly friendly or standoffish. When I ran the sink, the pipes appeared to be in working order. The toilet also flushed normally. Leaving the bathroom, I returned to the kitchen and looked beneath the sink there, too. I walked again through the various rooms, opening and closing windows—none stuck—and turning on lights to examine the walls. There was a two-foot-long crack in a bedroom wall, but the paint wasn't peeling.

I asked to see the basement, and Robert Suarez led me out of the apartment and down two flights of stairs. When I inquired about rodent or insect problems, he said sometimes there were mice in the winter, which wasn't enough for a warranty of habitability violation.

In the basement, a bare lightbulb illuminated a bulky boiler and heater, stacked wood planks, and a rusty push lawnmower. This was when I saw it, just below the ceiling's exposed beams: Where a major pipe connected to the stucco wall, a lopsided circle of gray mold billowed around the pipe's foundation. "See the mold?" I said to Robert Suarez. "That's definitely a violation." He looked alarmed and I added, "No, that's a good thing for our defense. We can use it to file an objection to the eviction notice." I pulled the clinic camera, a Kodak Instamatic, from my satchel and took photos of the mold close up and from a few feet away.

As we returned to the ground floor, I said, "Do you know your neighbors?"

He shook his head. "Not much."

"I have letters to put under their doors. I'm hoping that at least one of them will give a written statement saying that the noise levels in your unit don't bother them, and we'll be able to use those in court." I took the folder containing the letters out of my satchel.

For a few seconds, Robert Suarez looked at me with searching eyes. He said, "The landlord—will he make us leave?"

"I'm working as hard as I can to prevent it."

Robert Suarez did not appear to be reassured. His expression was grim as he said, "We don't have nowhere else to go."

On arriving home at night—often this was at nine or so, after a lecture or meeting—I'd eat something quick if I hadn't had dinner: peanut butter on toast or soup from a can, followed by a pot of chamomile tea. Then I'd change into blue pajamas and a white quilted nylon robe that my mother had given me before my freshman year at Wellesley. I'd pull my hair into a ponytail, set a cup of tea on my nightstand next to the lamp, sit on my bed with two pillows propped between my back and the headboard, and make a list of what I needed to do the next day. In addition to using a spiral notebook, I kept a daily planner, which was eight by four inches and which I reordered by mail every October. I thought of this arrangement of tea, pillows, notebook, calendar, and textbooks as my nest.

When the to-do list was complete, I'd read or write for three or four hours. Routinely, I'd become immersed in my work, look up, and realize two things: that it was well after midnight—sometimes several hours after—and that, due to all the tea I'd consumed, I desperately needed to urinate.

In college and law school, these had been the hours when I felt most like myself. I liked being around other people during the day, and I was relieved to be alone late at night; it was the latter that made the former possible. In fact, setting up my nest often made me think of a Wordsworth phrase I'd learned in English class as a high school junior: **emotion recollected in tranquillity.**

On that Monday night, it was not yet ten and I'd

been in my nest less than an hour when my phone rang. When I answered, a male voice said, "This is Chitty Chat Clinton. I'm wondering if you'd like to have dinner."

"Now?"

"Are you busy?"

"Well, I've already had dinner." I certainly wasn't trying to rebuff Bill; I just was surprised by the call.

"Then meet me at Elm Street Diner and I'll buy you an ice-cream sundae for dessert."

I glanced down at the notebook in my lap, my pajama-encased thighs below it. "What about tomorrow?"

"Alternatively," he said, "what about five minutes from now?"

When I entered the Elm Street Diner, he was sitting at the counter, his back to the door, and I hesitated—he was wearing a brown wool sweater that was unfamiliar to me, and I was reminded of just how much about him was unfamiliar—but then he turned, held up his hand, smiled, and said in a joyful tone, "Hillary!"

Bill stood as I approached, hugged me, then ate the french fry he'd been holding in his left hand. "I'm so happy to see you!" he said. What was the catch? Wasn't there a catch?

As I sat on the vinyl-covered stool next to Bill, a middle-aged waitress on the other side of the counter said to me, "I hear you'd like a sundae. Whipped cream and nuts?"

I'd had a sense of the sundae being more metaphorical than literal, but when I glanced at Bill, he nodded. "Sure," I said.

Bill gestured toward the waitress, whose uniform was a white apron over a pale-pink collared dress. "Edith voted for Nixon but thinks McGovern might have what it takes in '72." Edith smiled indulgently. "And two spoons, Edith," Bill added as she turned away from us. There was on the counter in front of Bill a large oval plate, half-full, which was the source of the french fries he hadn't stopped eating even as he'd greeted me. He nudged the plate toward me. "Help yourself."

"Are you a regular here?"

"How could I not be? Tell me you've ever in your life tasted better fries." He held one out, in the vicinity of my mouth, and although I didn't think of myself as a prude, it felt practically obscene to bite it—to do it there in the brightly lit diner, when I'd been in Bill's company for about a minute. Instead, I plucked the french fry from his fingers. As I chewed—it tasted both ordinary and delicious—he was grinning. "Yeah?" he said.

I laughed. "It's good."

"What were you doing when I called?"

"I was drafting an affidavit for a clinic case. What have you been doing?"

"As I just told Edith, I drove to Boston today to

meet with a fellow from the McGovern campaign. I'll be opening an office for McGovern here in a month or two. Oh, and I got a great letter from a woman in Hope who I'm crazy about." For a split second, I felt a sense of displeasure, then he said, "Her name is Lou, and she's eighty-eight. She's rereading all of Shakespeare's plays, and every time she finishes one, she writes and tells me what she thinks and I reread it and write back telling her what I think. She just finished **Troilus and Cressida,** which, truth be told, I've always considered a lesser work, but Lou had some great observations about whether it should be classified as a tragedy or a comedy. Lou is the widow of a real character. His name was Walter, and she was his tenth wife. Talk about a leap of faith, huh? I asked Walter once if he remembered the names of all his wives, and he said, 'All except two.' But he and Lou were married thirty years and from everything I saw, they seemed pretty damn happy."

In the fifty-one hours since I'd parted ways with Bill, I'd thought of him frequently and felt both eager to see him again and anxious that it would be awkward when I did. It also had occurred to me that our time at the gallery might have been a one-time thing, that he might be a person whose enthusiasm was intense but ephemeral. But the energy between us in the diner—it was as if we were picking up exactly where we'd left off outside the Greenbergers' house.

I said, "Do you think people in Arkansas are born more interesting than people in other places, or is it Southern storytelling that makes them more interesting?"

"Oh, Hillary." Bill seemed delighted. "We're just getting started."

Edith set a stainless steel ice-cream bowl, really more of a goblet, in front of me, and Bill pointed to his plate and said to Edith, "And how about some more fries?"

"Wow," I said. "When did you last eat?"

"I know," Bill said. "This is why I'm so fat."

I'd been joking—flirting, or so I thought—and it wasn't the response I'd expected. Though many women I knew watched their weight, it seemed strange to me that this was the second time he'd mentioned his own. "Oh—" I said. "No. Not at all."

"It's the salty-sweet thing that does me in." Even as he spoke, he was dipping one of the two spoons into the sundae. "Do you know why sundaes are called sundaes? It's because soda shops would make them using the leftover ice cream from the weekend, but they'd put toppings on in case the ice cream had turned."

"How appetizing."

"That was before refrigerators. I'm sure it doesn't apply to this fine establishment." He took another spoonful of ice cream and said, "How was the Greenbergers' potluck?"

"Good," I said. "I may have been a little bit distracted."

"Oh, yeah?" He smiled, reached out, and rubbed his fingers against the back of my hand. Just this skin contact gave me some of the same swoony feeling as in the gallery.

Then Edith set a fresh plate of french fries in front of Bill, and he glanced over with a sheepish look.

"Please," I said. "Don't hold back on my account."

"I'm calculating how disgusted you'll be when I dip a fry in the ice cream."

"One of my brothers does that. I'll feel right at home."

He did it, and as he was chewing, he said, "What's the affidavit you were working on when I interrupted you?"

"A landlord is trying to evict a family for excessive noise, but I think it's pretextual. I'm very glad you called."

"You are?" He was looking at me intently.

"Yes," I said. "I am."

We were still making eye contact and smiling, and Bill said, "How would you feel about being kissed inside a diner?"

I didn't hesitate; I leaned in, under those bright lights, and I kissed his mouth. I said, "Does that answer your question?"

He looked very happy. "Your fearlessness," he said, "did your parents instill that in you, or did you come out of the womb that way?"

"I wish I were fearless."

"You weren't afraid to take on Professor Geaney for his Ladies' Day nonsense."

"He was clearly in the wrong," I said.

"Exactly."

"Didn't Mark Twain say something about courage being the mastery of fear rather than the absence of fear? Although this might answer your question. My family moved into the house where my parents still live when I was three, and another little girl in the neighborhood immediately started trying to fight with me. Physically, I mean. When my mother realized I was running away and hiding inside our house, she very calmly told me that the next time Kathy hit me, she wanted me to hit her back. Not even 'You **can** hit her back' but 'I **want** you to.' I did, and it solved the problem."

"Kathy started hiding from you?"

"Actually, we became friends and still are."

"Of course she wanted to become your friend. I'm sure everyone does." He ate the last spoonful of ice cream. "Is your roommate here tonight or in New York with her fiancé?"

"She's in New York." I paused. "Would you like to see where I live?"

"I'd love to see where you live. But before we get out of here, should we order one more round of fries and a sundae?"

For the first time, I was genuinely taken aback

by Bill. More than I was put off, I was confused by his simultaneity of appetites. Wasn't this moment about sexual tension rather than eating? But Bill, apparently, could be hungry for multiple things at once. Though it wasn't a word anyone used at the time, he could multitask. I'd have far preferred to leave immediately and continue kissing, to kiss for real, but because of his earlier reference to being fat, I didn't want to make him self-conscious.

"Sure," I said, and he flagged Edith, and when the next order came, I took one bite of the sundae. When he'd polished off the food, he grinned and said, "Does the offer of the apartment tour still stand?"

We were lying in my bed, him on top of me, both of us on top of the covers, the only light on in the entire apartment the small one on my nightstand. I was wearing jeans, socks, underwear, and a bra, and he was wearing jeans, socks, underwear (or so I assumed), and a white T-shirt. His sweater was on the floor, and we'd been kissing for a long time and it had been wonderful. I loved how his neck smelled and I loved his chest pressed to mine and I loved how his back felt when I ran my hands up inside his T-shirt and I loved how sometimes we were talking and joking around and sometimes we were just making out.

He propped himself up, as if doing a push-up, and looked down at me, our faces perhaps six inches apart. He said, "You're not a virgin, are you?"

I smiled. "You sound like Professor Geaney."

"You know that's not how I meant it."

"No, I'm not a virgin," I said. I was joking as I added, "Are you?"

"Yes, so please be very, very gentle."

"I'm on the pill, if that was your next question."

"At the risk of scandalizing you even more than I already have," he said, "I lost my virginity when I was fourteen."

"Wow," I said. "I was nineteen."

"Who was the lucky fellow?"

"My college boyfriend."

"Were you in love with him?"

"Not really."

To my surprise, he laughed.

"Were **you** in love?" I asked. "At fourteen?"

"I was in lust. She was sixteen and I thought she looked like Anita Ekberg. You know who that is?"

I shook my head.

"A very voluptuous actress."

"Half of me is tempted to ask how many women you've slept with, and half of me doesn't want to know."

"Maybe we ought to defer to the second half of you."

With our faces close together, I scrutinized him, and he added, "For as long as I can remember, even when I was just a kid, I've had a weakness for a nice figure. A girl in a skirt walks by, and I'm like a dog drooling over a bone. But it's—" He paused. "It's infatuation. Not love." His face remained a few inches above mine as he watched me absorb his words. "You and me," he said. "This isn't infatuation."

"At the risk of making an argument I don't want to win, you wouldn't really know, would you? Presumably, infatuation never feels like infatuation until it's over."

"No." He shook his head. "I haven't told you this yet, but soon after that day in the lounge when you heard me talking about watermelons, I saw you at a lecture. It was when Judge Motley came to campus. Do you remember that? I was sitting in the row behind you, and when it was over, I thought, I'll introduce myself to her. I reached out my hand to touch your shoulder, and I felt—I realize this will sound strange, but it was like an electric shock. I knew I'd be starting something I couldn't stop."

It was difficult to know what to make of this story. I was flattered, yes, but also confused.

Then he said, "Can't you feel it, too, how this is different from everything else? I want this—us—to last forever."

Prior to two days earlier, we had hardly spent time in each other's company. But with Bill's face so close to mine, waiting for my response, with our bodies pressed together, it seemed that either of us might blurt out "I love you"—that I was just as likely to do it as he was. And, almost impossibly, that it would be true. However, **I love you** wasn't what I said. Soberly, I said, "Yes. I feel it, too."

Soon after that, we weren't talking much. We were kissing a lot, and removing the rest of each other's clothes, and his fingers were stroking me in different places and I was overwhelmed with wanting to be as close as I could to him—him, Bill, a specific person. With Roy, and with another law classmate named Eddie whom I'd dated my first year at Yale, the sex had been enjoyable enough but not personal. It had felt like we were doing pleasurable things that human beings did, in a fairly consistent sequence, but it hadn't felt relevant that I was specifically me and the other person was specifically the other person.

And then I could feel the nudging of Bill's erection, it was probably going to happen, then it was definitely going to happen, he was entering me, and I gasped—I gasped both because it felt so incredibly good and because I couldn't believe I was naked with this man. And then he really was inside me, it **was** happening, and we would eternally from this moment on be two people who'd had sex with each other. Even as he thrust into me, as I arched up against him and gripped his buttocks, there were a few seconds in which our eyes met and we looked at each other, both of us unblinking. Neither of us was smiling; smiling would have been trivial, or beside the point. To be with him in this way was an almost intolerable ecstasy. It was the most precious thing I had ever experienced.

The girl was named Kimberly, and she was seven years old, though as I watched her through the mirrored window of the room at Yale New Haven Hospital where her clinical session was occurring, she looked so small I'd have guessed her to be four; she also had dark hair and pronounced circles under her eyes.

The room was furnished with a regular-sized couch, a child-sized table and chairs, and an assortment of wooden blocks, toy trains, dolls, and books. Kimberly sat on the floor, her back against the couch, holding but not interacting with a doll, a blank expression on her face. A psychologist was crouched in front of her, saying things to Kimberly that didn't elicit a response. On the other side of the window, I stood beside Dr. Hormley, who was one of the physicians, a gentle, white-haired grandfather of eleven.

"Has she spoken at all since she was admitted?" I asked, and Dr. Hormley shook his head.

He said, "We're trying to determine if there was a previous mutism diagnosis."

Early Sunday morning, a neighbor had called the police, apparently not for the first time, after hearing a dispute between Kimberly's parents. Police officers had found Kimberly tied to the radiator, sitting in her own urine and feces. Thirty-six hours later, the father remained in jail, while the mother had been released. The question, and the reason I'd been summoned, was whether Kimberly ought to be returned to the custody of her mother or placed temporarily in foster care—whether the mother was also a victim of the father's abuse, an accomplice, or somewhere in between. As in similar cases, Gwen had tasked me with gathering information in order to make a custodial recommendation.

I said to Dr. Hormley, "How underweight is she?"

"She's height/weight proportional, but her height is in the fifth percentile for her age."

Though Dr. Hormley had a kind presence, I had learned to keep my questions to him factual rather than subjective—he was not the person to ask about, say, the nature of a patient's family relationships. Also, no matter how horrifying the situation that had brought a child under his care, he and I did not editorialize about the horrors. I wondered if he discussed such matters with his wife or colleagues or if not discussing them was part of what allowed him to maintain equanimity.

Dr. Hormley passed me Kimberly's chart and said, "I need to check on an appendectomy. Leave this at the nurse's station when you're done."

In retrospect, the only thing more staggering than the seriousness of the outcomes I shaped as a twenty-three-year-old graduate student was the carte blanche with which I conducted my research, but patient privacy laws were lax to nonexistent then. I followed Dr. Hormley and other physicians as they met patients, I evaluated children by observing them in clinical settings like the one Kimberly was presently in, and I led case meetings. I spoke directly to police officers, social workers, and family members.

I took a few more notes on Kimberly's interactions with the psychologist, dropped off her chart, and rode the elevator to the fourth floor. The National Children's Initiative—Gwen's fledgling organization—was a tiny office inside the hospital devoted to reforming federal policies around children's health and education. Gwen truly was a pioneer, responsible for introducing the concept of child abuse to the general public.

When I stepped off the elevator, I was next to a large picture window facing southeast, providing a view of the medical school campus and the modest neighborhood known as the Hill. I stood by the window for a minute—it was a gray, overcast day—organizing my thoughts before walking down the hall to speak with Gwen. I'd never had an inordinately rosy view of human nature, but the circumstances that caused children to end up in the hospital still shocked me. What could cause an adult to unleash such savagery? Drug addiction, insanity, sometimes in combination with crippling poverty—these were all factors, but at some point, it seemed that cruelty or even sadism were the only explanations for a three-year-old who had been drowned in the bathtub by his uncle or a nine-year-old whose back was covered with burn marks from a mother's iron. Sometimes when I returned to the law school after observing or even just discussing such children, it was like emerging from a grim trance I'd been unaware of having slipped into. The privileged bustle of Yale, all of us with our sparkly eyes and theoretical notions about justice, our clever conversations, our impending diplomas—they seemed a kind of illusion or pretense. Soon after starting law school, I'd decided to eschew makeup and opt for pants instead of skirts or dresses, which made me consider myself down-to-earth, but I recognized in such moments that this was a negligible distinction. I was as obscenely lucky and fancy as everyone else.

Early on, I'd occasionally wept in private after seeing an abused child. But quickly my tears had come to seem not just unprofessional but self-indulgent. And the truth was that, looking out the window that day, I didn't need to suppress tears. An image came into my mind of Kimberly—her big dark eyes, her unresponsiveness, her tight grip on the doll—and then, unexpectedly, another image followed, of what Bill looked like when he smiled. The contrast between Kimberly's tragic neglect and my new connection with Bill, how sustaining and generous his presence was, made me feel something that may have been elation or terror or certainty or lust. I often secretly experienced my own good fortune as slightly shameful and my impulses toward activism as a form of contrition, but what if I could lead a life that made me worthy of luck? What if getting what I wanted most could be a fuel for my own morality, and additive rather than unfairly advantageous?

Out the window, four floors below me, a man rode a bicycle on a street lined with shabby houses. I didn't want to go talk to Gwen about Kimberly's awful parents; I wanted to find Bill and wrap my arms around him, to hold him and be held, even if we were clothed, even if we weren't talking. I just wanted to lie there with him.

None of this was what I did. Instead, I took a deep breath, tucked my hair behind both ears, turned away from the window, and walked to Gwen's office.

The second and third times with Bill had been the same night as the first time, and the fourth and fifth times had been the following night, also at my apartment, and the sixth, seventh, and eighth times were at my apartment between 3:00 and 5:00 P.M. on a Wednesday, instead of my Corporate Tax class, and that was when I stopped counting.

There were other milestones, too, including the

public presentation of ourselves as a couple, which happened that Friday at the twenty-fifth birthday party of Nick Chess, who was the editor of the **Yale Law Journal** and the friend I'd been with when I'd first heard Bill talking about watermelons. Bill and I entered the party holding hands and I felt a few people notice, but no one said anything until a bunch of us were standing in the kitchen, and he and I were leaning against the counter, both of us drinking beer, his arm around my shoulders. His classmate Charlie Kulik's wife, Prudence, nudged me from the other side and whispered, "You and **Bill**?"

I smiled and said, "I guess so."

"Nice job," she said.

As we left the party around one in the morning, Nick himself, who was clearly drunk, yelled after us, "Try not to actually fall in love, because I don't think it's legal for the president of the United States to be married to the Supreme Court chief justice."

Over his shoulder, Bill called back, "Then how about if I don't aim any higher than the U.S. Court of Appeals?"

It was also that weekend that I first visited Bill's house, riding in the passenger seat of his rather improbable orange Opel station wagon. When we arrived, around nine o'clock at night, Kirby and Keith were playing cards in the living room, and Jimmy was in the kitchen washing dishes and listening to a Jackson 5 record at a high volume.

When Jimmy saw us, he said to me, "I'd say that you're the reason Bill's never around, but Bill's never around anyway."

Because it was dark, I could sense and hear the Atlantic Ocean behind the house more than I could really see it. Bill and I took off our shoes and walked over the cold sand and, for a few seconds, into the even colder water. Then we went back inside and washed our feet off in a grimy tub, and after we were in his room, he shut the door behind us and I was gripped by that particular happiness that I truly had only ever felt with him. What could be better than being alone in a room with Bill Clinton? He had a double bed without a headboard, a red armchair, an overstuffed shelf, a desk, and a desk chair. Almost right away, we'd taken off our clothes and were in bed and under the covers, and again there was the closeness of our bodies, the warmth of his skin, the way he touched me, the way he smelled and felt, how alert he seemed to me and how alert I was to him. Afterward, he lay on his back, his head on a pillow, and I lay on my side, my head on his chest, and he enfolded me with one arm. He said, "Is there anything you need so you're comfortable spending the night? A glass of water or another blanket? Do you want to borrow my toothbrush?"

In addition to the map and bus route in my satchel, I always kept a yellow grosgrain cosmetics bag that contained a toothbrush, toothpaste, a hair brush, a small tube of hand lotion, and no makeup. I kissed Bill's bare shoulder. "There's nothing I need besides you. But what's that?" Next to the armchair, a black rectangular case about two feet in length had caught my eye. Like a suitcase, it had a handle and two metal clasps.

"It's my saxophone."

"You play the saxophone?"

"No, I just left the case there to impress you. It's empty." Lightly, he flicked my clavicle with his thumb and middle finger. "Of course I play."

"You'll have to show me sometime," I said, and the next thing I knew, he'd bounded out of bed, and I was offered an unobscured view of his pale buttocks as he bent, opened the case, and pulled out the golden instrument. Still naked, he turned around, inserted the mouthpiece between his lips, and began playing "When the Saints Go Marching In." Our eyes met, and I started to laugh, even as I worried what his roommates might think or whether any of them would open the door to tell us to quiet down. But he continued playing, and I continued laughing. He was laughing, too, while he blew on the mouthpiece and held his fingers over the buttons. Finally, he had no choice but to stop and give in to his laughter. I was by then on my back, propped up on both elbows, and he put the instrument away and returned to bed.

"I can tell you're **very** impressed," he said.

"Your musical skills are dazzling." I leaned in and

kissed him on the lips. "I've never been serenaded by a naked man before."

As he settled back in beside me, we kissed again and kept kissing—now my mouth knew his mouth, this was becoming familiar and was also still wondrously new—then he pulled his head back an inch or two. He was regarding me with such warmth and affection, with such **focus**. "I love you, Hillary," he said. "I'm in love with you, and I love you. I can't believe that you exist."

"That **I** exist? You're the Arkansas Renaissance man and future president." I looked at him more seriously. "I'm in love with you, Bill, and I love you, too."

I had dropped off the film containing the photos of the mold in Robert Suarez's basement at a camera store a few blocks from my apartment, and I wanted to pick up the prints before I tried to get statements from the Suarezes' neighbors; if the photos had turned out horribly, I could take them again without making yet another trip.

I opened the stiff envelope before I left the photo store, and the photos inside were fine. While I wouldn't be mistaken for, say, Ansel Adams, they captured clear images of the moldy wall.

By design, I stepped off the bus on Dixwell Avenue a little after six; I figured that the dinner hour was the likeliest time to catch people, none of whom had responded to the letters I'd slid under their doors on my earlier visit. There were just three units in the Suarezes' building, and when the man on the first floor opened his door, I said, "My name is Hillary Rodham, and I work at the New Haven Legal Services office. There's a noise dispute between your landlord and the Suarez family, who live above you, and I wonder if you have a few minutes to discuss it with me."

The man squinted at me as I spoke. When I finished, in an emphatic tone, he said, "Your name is **bitch** from the New Haven Legal Services office." Then he slammed the door.

The second floor was where the Suarezes lived. The television was in fact audible from the hall, but it also was just on the other side of the wall, close to where I passed without knocking.

On the third floor, a very old, very small woman answered the door, and the scent of what seemed to be steaming vegetables billowed out. When I repeated what I'd said to the man on the first floor, she said, "Which family?"

"The Suarez family. The people who live right beneath you. Can I ask you a few questions and write down your answers?"

"Robert and Maria don't do anything wrong," she said.

"I'm glad to hear that. The landlord said they're loud, and he's trying to evict them, but if you're telling me they don't make too much noise, that will help them stay in the apartment."

"There's a dog around the corner who barks and barks." She was pointing north. "That's who's loud. He barks day and night."

"Does the dog belong to someone in this building?"

"It's not right to leave an animal out in the yard till all hours."

I had pulled a notebook and pen from my satchel, and I said, "Just to confirm, the Suarezes don't make excessive noise?"

"No."

"How long have you lived here?"

"I've been here for years, dear. Since the Johnsons were in that apartment and the family before the Johnsons, too. Do you know Gladys?"

"I don't know Gladys," I said. "You've never experienced any noise disturbance with the Suarez family?"

The woman looked at me intently. "The problem is the dog that barks all the time. It's not a big dog, but the fur is matted something terrible."

"I'm sorry its owners don't take care of it." I closed my notebook. "Thank you for your help."

At nine, I joined Bill at the Elm Street Diner, where he'd been finishing dinner with two of his

Constitutional Law classmates. As we walked back to my apartment, we held hands and I was, for some reason—not because it felt urgent or even cathartic but more because there was nothing it wasn't fun to discuss with him—describing Daniel the Harvard Divinity student and our final conversation on the banks of the Charles River, the one in which I'd invited Daniel to the Wellesley mixer and he'd replied "Hillary, I really enjoy discussing theology with you."

Bill snorted. "What a pretentious fool."

As I pulled out my keys, Daniel seemed so distant, and also so inferior to Bill, that I was inclined toward generosity. "He was fine," I said. "His best quality was that he was very intelligent, and his worst quality was that he didn't have a sense of humor."

"Not having a sense of humor isn't a 'bad quality,' " Bill said. We were standing outside the door of my apartment, and I inserted the key. "It's a crime."

"True," I said, "although— Oh, hello." My roommate, Katherine, and a friend of hers named Sandra were both in the living room. They sat on opposite ends of the couch, each of them holding a glass of red wine. Before I could make introductions, Sandra said, "Hi, Bill." In her voice, there was a degree of amusement, or even mockery, that made me understand immediately there had been some kind of flirtation between them.

"Hi, Sandra," Bill responded warmly, and his

tone gave away nothing. But it didn't need to. "Hi, Katherine. How have both of you been?"

"It's such a small world, isn't it?" Sandra looked between us. She was pretty and red-haired.

"Hillary, I should warn you that I roasted a chicken," Katherine said. "I promise to clean everything up before I go to bed. Would either of you like a glass of wine?"

"I won't be using the kitchen tonight." I made eye contact with Bill, then said, "And no thanks on the wine. Nice to see you both."

"Sandra, I have to thank you for recommending that book by E. H. Carr," Bill said. "Very thought-provoking."

"I thought you'd find it interesting," Sandra said.

"I'm not convinced he's as secular as he claims," Bill said, and I tugged his hand. As I pulled him away, he added, "I'd love to talk more sometime."

In my bedroom, I dropped my satchel by the door and kicked off my shoes, and Bill did the same. He flopped backward on my bed. I was still standing as I said, "Did you date her?"

"It was nothing serious."

"Did you sleep with her?"

His brow furrowed. "This was months before you and I ever spoke."

The implication that I was being too sensitive—he wasn't wrong. If I found Bill attractive, was it any surprise that other women did? And he'd never pretended he hadn't had girlfriends before me.

I said, "Maybe I just feel pathetic that I was describing someone from my past who rejected me at the exact moment we ran into someone from your past that you successfully dated."

He shook his head. "It wasn't successful. I'm sorry to tell you that you hardly have a monopoly on failed relationships."

"But the men I've dated besides you—it was like I was dating them so I could check off a box and prove I'd had a boyfriend. No one like you has ever been interested in me. You're so much handsomer and more appealing. And I realize I'm not beautiful, and I realize you could easily find someone who is. It doesn't make sense that someone like you wants to be the boyfriend of someone like me." I was on the verge of tears as I said, "See how fearless I am?"

"Hillary," he said in a crooning voice. "My sweet baby. First of all, I'm the lucky one. I can't believe **you** think I'm worth your time. You're amazing. Whether you know it or not, you are beautiful. And not beautiful like your insides are so impressive they make your outsides attractive. Your outsides are attractive all by themselves. I don't know if I'm supposed to say this during the women's movement, but you have great tits. And your little waist, and your nice soft bum, and your delicious honey pot—" I laughed, and he said, "I mean it. Your whole body is perfect, and you have such a pretty face, your eyes and lips and your skin.

I love playing with your hair, and I love how you smell and how you move when we're in bed. Isn't it obvious I can't keep my hands off you? I love your whole body. I love all of you. You're brave and funny and hardworking and you're so goddamn smart, but you know what? You're beautiful, too. And there's nothing about you that's pathetic. Nothing."

A lesson I learned from Bill, a lesson that perhaps should be obvious, though there's evidence that most other people don't know it, either, is that direct and sincere compliments are shockingly effective—that they feel wonderful. What in theory should sound saccharine or manipulative rarely does in practice, so long as you believe the other person really means it. And we crave praise not, I think, because most of us are egomaniacal. It's because we're human.

I joined Bill in bed, and when I was lying on my back naked and he was lying on top of me naked, he looked at me and smiled. He said, "Hillary, I really enjoy discussing theology with you. I also enjoy doing lots of other things with you," and then he plunged inside me.

The exterior of the courthouse was a classical Greek structure that resembled a smaller version of the Supreme Court, including similarly tall white marble columns and a pediment. The courthouse's interior was also architecturally impressive but so crowded that Robert Suarez and I needed to wait for an hour in the hall before we could enter the courtroom itself. We then waited another hour and a half in the gallery, listening to the adjudication of other housing cases. The judge, a man who looked at least seventy, had a brisk and focused air. Intermittently, a baby on the other side of the gallery bawled and someone very close to Robert Suarez and me broke wind. The first time, I pretended not to notice the smell while fearing Robert Suarez would think it was me. The second time, I wondered uncomfortably if it was **him**. The third time, we glanced at each other, simultaneously made expressions of dismay, then simultaneously started laughing.

When finally our turn arrived, we took seats at the defendant's table and were sworn in, as was the landlord, whom I still knew by name only. He was balding and kept his raincoat on.

"Your Honor, this isn't a nonpayment case," I said to the judge. "My client is a family man, a churchgoer, and a responsible tenant. He's also a Section 236 tenant, and while this might not be desirable from the standpoint of some housing owners, I sincerely believe that the claims of noise violations are pretextual. I have a statement from a neighbor of the defendant who says she's never been disturbed by noise. I also have documentation of mold in the basement of the building, but when I raised this issue in a response, the plaintiff never filed a reply."

The judge asked the landlord what the disruptive noise was (the landlord said "very loud conversations, often in Spanish") and who had complained. ("Lots of people," the landlord said, and when the judge asked for specific individuals, the landlord said he didn't know their names because it included tenants in the next building, which he didn't own.) The judge asked what floor the unit was on and how much of its interior was covered in carpet. After answering, the landlord added, "There's six Mexicans in a two-bedroom. Six of them, and three are adults."

"There are no grounds to evict these tenants," the judge said. "This eviction proceeding is dismissed with prejudice. So ordered." The entire proceeding had lasted a few minutes.

I turned to Robert Suarez, who looked confused. "We won," I said. "The case has been dismissed permanently. He can't try to evict you again for any reason having to do with noise."

An expression of relief overtook Robert Suarez's features, and he crossed himself.

The bailiff had already called the next case, and I didn't take the time to insert my manila folder in my satchel before leaving the courtroom; I did this in the hall, which remained crowded. Outside the courthouse, I shook Robert Suarez's hand and said, "I wish you and your family the best of luck."

"Thank you for the help," he replied.

The following week, I received a package at the

clinic addressed to **Hilarie Rodman.** Inside was a piece of paper with small handwritten print that read in its entirety, **Thank you, Suarez Family,** along with a white crocheted tablecloth that looked to be handmade—I assumed by Robert Suarez's mother-in-law, though I never knew. I own this tablecloth still.

In April and May, Bill and I rarely spent a night apart. As the end of the semester approached, we had papers to write, exams to study for, year-end meetings to attend, and a few farewell gatherings for our friends who were graduating. Plus, of course, for me there was the clinic and the National Children's Initiative, and for Bill, there were already obligations with the McGovern campaign. Though Bill would be based in Florida for the summer, he'd started organizing in Connecticut and was looking for a spot near campus to open a headquarters in the fall. I accompanied him one afternoon to see a storefront on a particularly questionable street; outside, on the sidewalk, were not one but two smashed glass syringes with intact needles. Even before we stepped inside, I said, "No. I'm sorry, but no, and I have a feeling you're showing it to me so I'll tell you no."

I felt the busiest I ever had, and happily so; with Bill underpinning my days, there was such a fullness to them. I'd have imagined spending so much time together to be depleting, but it was the opposite. The nights alone in my nest had ceased to exist, or maybe it was that Bill himself had become my nest. We often lay side by side and read, and there was a series of conversations we were having, or possibly one long conversation, that gave me precisely what my nest once had. This fact was miraculous.

I knew plenty of smart people, but I'd never before encountered a person whose intelligence sharpened mine the way his did. His perspective both overlapped with and differed from mine so as to be challenging, reassuring, and never boring. I also, though I knew it would have sounded arrogant to express this to anyone other than Bill, enjoyed the rare experience of being the less impressive person—I was less articulate than he was, less charismatic, less knowledgeable about obscure congressional districts and Southern authors. How marvelous! It wasn't that I was without an ego, immune to the gratification of seeming impressive, but impressing others wasn't for me a goal unto itself, a kind of sport; for Bill, it was definitely a sport, which perhaps, I thought, was one of the reasons a person eventually ran for office.

And certainly he was practicing running for office, practicing winning people over. Yet his was such a nimble and omnivorous mind that he could exert himself publicly and still have an abundance of private energy, of complex opinions and ideas to exchange with me; he didn't need to ration his energy or thoughts. What was unfolding between us felt continuously replenishable, regenerative. Sometimes in the past when I'd worked on various projects—fighting at Wellesley to be allowed to have interdisciplinary majors, for example, or to wear pants to class—I grew close to others who were involved, then the project concluded, and though I could still feel affection for the people I'd been working with, there simply wasn't as much to say to one another. We'd been linked by something larger than ourselves, but we'd been linked temporarily.

In contrast, the conversations I had with Bill never felt provisional; as long as we went about our daily lives, we had more to talk about than time to talk. We discussed the Supreme Court's ruling on **Swann v. Charlotte-Mecklenburg Board of Education** and if the Gulf of Tonkin resolution was constitutional; we discussed whether food tasted the same to everyone and people liked or disliked the taste, or whether it actually tasted different to different people; and we discussed our childhoods and our plans for the future and all the people either of us had ever known, including Bud Gurski and Bruce Stappenbeck and Bill's grandparents Mammaw and Papaw and the nun who was his teacher in both second and third grades and the so-called scout—I teased him that it sounded like a butler—who had made his bed at Oxford. At Wellesley, I'd once babysat for a professor's nine-year-old daughter, and she'd said as I was putting her to bed, “Tell me a story that’s long, interesting, and hilarious.” Having Bill as my boyfriend, loving Bill, felt like living inside such a story.

And then there was the sex. I recognized only in retrospect that it wouldn’t have been difficult, with my two former boyfriends, for me to transgress and not in a manner they found arousing. That I could have made a sound that alarmed them, that I could have shown my body from an unflattering angle, that I could have seemed assertive or greedy when they’d planned to be the assertive, greedy ones. Once, with Roy, when the way he was using his fingers on me wasn’t working, I had finished with my own fingers, while also kissing him, and it was afterward, due to a certain sulkiness on his part, that I realized he’d been put off. I had never again touched myself in his presence.

In contrast, Bill was not only unfazed but actively delighted by any sound I made, any way I moved. Sex with him was fun and tender and barely embarrassing or awkward, or amusing in its embarrassment and awkwardness. (At one point, he said, “I want you on top of me,” and I started to shift and had to say, “Okay, but my arm is stuck under you.”) The general impression Bill gave was that he found me irresistible, at least as irresistible as french fries and an ice-cream sundae; that nothing I did could repel him; that there was nothing in the world he’d rather be doing than stroking my body or kissing me all over. As impatient as he naturally was, he never rushed when we were in bed. He was leisurely, and I was the one who became increasingly, gloriously frantic.

And the truth was that when he was thrusting into me, I had such a strong sense of wanting him to come inside me, wanting no barriers between us, wanting the things we did with each other to be different from the things we did in the rest of our lives, with other people. None of this was remotely like what I'd felt with Roy or Eddie. I'd regarded their semen as, if not disgusting, then as messy and mildly regrettable, like a spilled glass of water.

When Bill was inside me, sometimes I was mindless with how good it felt, and sometimes I was aware, with a kind of granular precision, of the unlikely sequence of events that had made our lives intersect: his Arkansas upbringing, his stepfathers, his ambition and intelligence and hard work, and the more ordinary circumstances of my childhood that had nevertheless set me on a path, primarily because of the fierceness of my mother's belief in me, to travel east and enter law school and meet this very particular person, this distinct and exceptional man. I'd think of my earlier belief that the things that made me most myself were a romantic turn-off, that no one would simultaneously value my intellect and find me attractive; I had wanted so badly to be wrong, and I'd struggled to find evidence that I was.

Yet here we were, with all of his skin touching all of my skin; he was kissing my neck, next to my ear, or we were kissing with our mouths open and our tongues mashing together. His body in my arms, pressed against me, was shocking. Looking into his eyes was shocking. That we were literally fused, that his erection was inside me and my legs were wrapped around him, hooked through the backs of his knees—all of this was shocking. It was shocking that we'd found each other and it was shocking how natural yet thrilling having conversations with him was and it was shocking that we were naked, even though we'd never spoken until a few weeks earlier. Falling in love was shocking, shocking, utterly shocking.

Richard Greenberger invited some of his Constitutional Law students, including Bill, over for an end-of-semester dinner. I was reading when Bill rang the doorbell of my apartment afterward, and when I let him in, I said, "How was it? Isn't Gwen great?" The fact that my boyfriend and my mentor had just met without my being present made me intensely curious what they'd thought of each other. As it happened, the next morning, Gwen and I were attending a conference for elementary school teachers and principals in Hartford, and I couldn't wait to learn her impression of Bill.

"She's terrific," Bill said as we settled onto the

living room couch. "I understand why you're crazy about both of them."

"Doesn't their life seem like the ideal?" We'd sat close together, my legs angled over his, and he was rubbing my thighs. "It's such a brave, optimistic experiment. I assume not everyone in his family was thrilled that she's black and maybe not everyone in her family was thrilled that he's white or Jewish, but they got married anyway. They didn't make a choice out of fear. They also didn't do that thing of getting married and forgetting about the greater good, the collective good. They still care. And their kids are adorable."

In a not-exactly-casual tone, Bill said, "You definitely want to get married and have children?"

"Yes," I said. "Definitely." When our eyes met, I said, "Did you think I didn't?"

"I hoped you did," he said. "Because I want to." There was a kind of atmospheric thickening, the lack of necessity of acknowledging the conversation's significance. After a few seconds, he said, "I can't see getting my political career started anywhere other than Arkansas. That's always been the plan, and I always thought, Maybe I'll meet someone from home or maybe I'll meet someone from somewhere else and I'll bring her back. But it's different to ask **you** to move to Arkansas. Truthfully, I think you could be happy there, whether it's Little Rock or a different city. There's much more going on all over the state than people realize, and it's such a beautiful place to live. I'd love for you to visit so I can show it to you. But I know you have other choices."

"I'd love to visit," I said. "I can't promise that I'll move there, but I'm not necessarily opposed to it."

"Really?" There was such unconcealed relief on his face that I laughed.

"Sweetheart," I said, "of course. It's not what I ever imagined, but I've thought about this, too."

"The things you care about, children's rights and women's rights—you could do a world of good as first lady of Arkansas and practice law at the same time. You could be a whole new kind of first lady."

I laughed again. "You're already governor now? I thought Congress or attorney general was first."

But Bill was serious as he said, "I wouldn't be showing you respect if I didn't think about this in the long term."

"If you were governor, do you really think people there would accept a first lady who worked?"

"It wouldn't be their choice. And you'd be such a role model."

"The thing about if you ran for Congress is that, couldn't we both live in Washington and you'd go back and forth?"

"It's absolutely a possibility, but that race in the Third District—I'd be the underdog. I don't want to pretend otherwise."

How surreal this was, that we'd been a couple for

only two months, and talking about where we'd live next felt responsible rather than rash; it felt headily grown-up.

"I want to be a good man," Bill said. "It probably sounds corny, but I want to be honorable. I want to be an honorable elected official, an honorable father, and an honorable husband."

"I'm sure you will be."

"I know I'm far from perfect. Sometimes I really can hear the angel and the devil arguing on my shoulders."

I reached up and tapped my fingers against his left shoulder. "Which one is on this side?"

He gripped my hand in his. He said, "I don't want to lose you."

I realized only when it didn't happen that I'd imagined Gwen and I would discuss Bill right away, as soon as I got in her car, and then I realized only when it also didn't happen that I'd imagined she'd be as effusive about him as he'd been about her. Instead, Gwen and I talked in detail about the conference in Hartford, the focus of which was children who weren't attending school because of disabilities or, as we called them then, handicaps. One of Gwen's goals in the next year was to collect statistics on how many such children there were in the state of Connecticut.

We were past Wallingford by the time I said, "Bill really enjoyed meeting you last night."

Warmly, she said, "Isn't he something?" But I knew her well enough that I immediately wondered if—it seemed almost impossible—she hadn't liked him.

"He thought your family was great," I said.

"I certainly learned a lot about Arkansas," she replied, and her odd tone—I couldn't ignore it.

I said, "Did you not like him?" The only time I could remember disagreeing with Gwen about anything was when I'd said my favorite Supremes song was "Stop! In the Name of Love," and she'd said their best song was "Someday We'll Be Together."

In the car, she said, "Richard thinks he's brilliant. He just **talked** so much. This is what he did on Joe Duffey's campaign and this is what he's doing for McGovern and he'll serve in Arkansas where he's most needed and at some point I thought, You could let someone else get a word in edgewise."

"He does like to talk," I said. "That's true. But I've also found him to be a great listener."

"What I think of him matters a lot less than what you think."

"Maybe he was trying to impress you because he knows how much I look up to you."

She was quiet before saying, "Some people who run for office want to create change, and some want everyone to fall in love with them."

"Bill wants to create change," I said, and I didn't like the thin, defensive sound of my own voice. "I'm certain of it."

The following afternoon, Bill met me outside the clinic and as we cut across campus, I said, "Katherine told me Pan Am is having a sale on flights to San Francisco, and I'd love for you to come visit me this summer. I'll split the price of the ticket with you."

"How am I supposed to survive being apart from you for a whole goddamn summer?" Bill sounded genuinely unhappy.

"That's very flattering, but you did a respectable job of making it through the first twenty-four years of your life without me."

"It might have been less respectable than I've led you to believe." But he grinned. "Fuck McGovern. I'm coming with you."

I glanced at him. "To Oakland? Don't be ridiculous."

"There'll be other campaigns," he said. "But there's only one Hillary Rodham."

"I'll be back in three months."

"What if your feelings about me change? What if a hippie in Haight-Ashbury with a daisy in his hair sweeps you off your feet?"

"That doesn't seem very likely."

"Then what if it's a needle-nose law clerk?"

We were passing a dorm outside of which two

undergrads were tossing a football as I said, "I wonder if there's a campaign you could work on out there."

"Or I can take a sabbatical. I have some money saved. I could read and explore."

"But you'll make a lot of valuable connections working for McGovern."

"You think I'm teasing," he said. "But there really is only one Hillary Rodham."

"I can't imagine anything more fun than spending the summer together, but I don't think it's fair to ask that of you."

"You're not asking."

"I mean that I don't think it's in your long-term best interest."

A silence arose between us, filled with the hum of the campus, which was, like that of Wellesley, absurdly beautiful: A nearby dogwood tree filled the air with a sweet spring scent. Bill's voice was serious when he spoke again. He said, "I really don't think you understand. All this time, I needed you. I needed you, and I was looking for you, and now I never want to let you go."

The day of my Corporate Tax exam, I took my seat in the auditorium, set my satchel down at my feet, then reached into it to remove a pencil. I saw the scrap of paper then, torn from a lined notebook. Just three words were written on it, in blue ink: I

cherish you. It was nine-twenty in the morning, and the exam would last for three hours and consist of three essay questions.

The part of this that I'm struck by now, decades later, is that I felt so flush with Bill's love, so ensconced in our relationship, so confident of its durability, that the note didn't seem significant. Earlier that very semester, I had been uncertain I'd ever meet a man I could truly love and be loved by, and already Bill was such a fixture of my days that being showered with his affection was sweet but unremarkable. Did I imagine that my life would be full of such emotional extravagance? I must have, because to save the note did not occur to me.

CHAPTER 2

1971

BILL WAS DOING IT—INSTEAD OF working for the McGovern campaign for the summer, he was going with me to California, and we were driving there in his orange Opel station wagon. On our final night in New Haven, he slept at my apartment and rose at six in the morning to go back to Milford and pick up his duffel bag and books, with the plan of returning to me by 8:00 A.M. so we could get on the road. In fact, he returned to my apartment closer to noon. Though he didn't come out and say it, it became clear he hadn't begun packing until that morning, but how could I be irritated with him? He was giving up so much for me.

It would be a fifteen-hour drive from New Haven to Park Ridge, Illinois, where we were stopping to visit my family: through the southern parts of Connecticut and New York then across the entirety of Pennsylvania, northern Ohio and Indiana, and around the tip of Lake Michigan. Because of our late start, we decided to spend the first night in a Howard Johnson's outside Akron; it occurred to us that the clerk at the front desk might not rent a room to an unmarried man and woman, so I waited in the car while Bill entered the lobby to pay the twenty dollars. The May sky darkened as I sat in the passenger seat.

After Bill had the key, which was attached to an orange-and-blue plastic tag, we drove forty feet to park facing the room's exterior door. The room itself was Spartan, with a sink outside the bathroom proper. We both used the toilet, after which I washed my face as well as my hands, and I thought we'd get dinner right away, but as I was drying my hands, Bill approached me from behind, placed his palms on my shoulders and began kissing the side of my neck. It still was astonishing to see our reflection in the mirror, to see what we looked like together—his bent head, his taller body behind mine, his beard against the skin on my neck. Would it always be astonishing or would I become accustomed to it? I turned around so we could kiss on the lips, and he tugged me toward the bed and very quickly we were lying down, entangled and unclothed. We ate dinner afterward in the adjacent diner—meatloaf for Bill and a tuna sandwich for me—and by the time we finished, it was nearly eleven.

In the morning, we drove for six hours, and suddenly we were just minutes from my childhood home, at the intersection where my friend Maureen's brother had once thrown a rock at a car, then passing the house where I had taken piano lessons from a woman named Mrs. Cacchione. I was the one driving, turning onto Wisner Street, approaching the yellow-hued brick house where we'd moved in 1950, and my heart was beating quickly. The self I was with Bill felt both true and aspirational, the self I most wished to be: worldly and beloved. Whereas the self I was with my family was less mature and more contradictory, pulled between the tensions of my mother believing me capable of anything and my father expressing little support or interest. When **Life** magazine had excerpted my Wellesley commencement address and sent a photographer to my family's house to take my picture, his sole comment was "If they're printing your words, they should pay you." And when I'd called to tell my parents I'd chosen Yale, he said with confidence, "Yale is the Ivy League school where the homosexuals go." In my youth, I had respected my father's intelligence, not recognizing how much sharper my mother's was because hers was concealed by being pleasant and female. In the last six years, I'd undergone a slow but nearly complete shift from taking his opinions seriously to disregarding them, which had had the strange effect of making me more deferential. I no longer saw arguing with him as worth the effort.

I parked on the street in front of the house, and as I turned off the ignition, I looked over at Bill and forced a smile. "Ready?"

"What a beautiful neighborhood," Bill said. On this sunny afternoon in mid-May, I agreed—Wisner was an avenue of large houses, tall trees, and well-tended lawns. He set his fingers on my right knee and said, "Don't be nervous, baby. I'll love them because they're your family, and I love you." I said nothing, and he added, "Do you love me?"

"Oh, God," I said. "So much."

We walked up the flagstone path to the arched front door, and though I owned a key, I had no idea where it was. After I'd rung the bell, I could hear my brother Tony yelling, and then my mother opened the door and was in front of us in a pale-blue sleeveless blouse and a pleated black skirt and she was hugging me then hugging Bill and my father was behind her in khaki pants and a brown button-down, saying, "Nice of you to stop by while you were in the neighborhood." When we'd stepped inside, I hugged my father, and Bill shook his hand, and Tony, who was sixteen, materialized in the front hall and also shook Bill's hand and embraced me. My other brother, Hughie, was twenty then and still finishing his junior year at Penn State, which was where our father had gone.

Bill's tallness in my childhood home, Bill's Southern accent, Bill's warmth and charisma—it was profoundly strange. In the kitchen, my mother gave us each a glass of water, and Tony said to me, "Did you hear the Cubs had a walk-off win last night?" Bill was complimenting my mother on our home. My mother seemed to regard him with a hopeful and slightly amused curiosity, and my father seemed to regard him with a slightly amused suspicion.

"We're going to Vandy's tonight," Tony said and wiggled his eyebrows in a way I understood to be a reference to how expensive Vandy's was; it was a steakhouse where we'd been just a handful of times in my life.

"Because heaven forbid a Rhodes scholar eat Hamburger Helper," my father said.

Cheerfully, Bill said, "As I'm sure you can tell by looking at me, I'm happy as a clam eating absolutely anything, including Hamburger Helper. For that matter, including clams."

"Our reservation is at six," my mother said. "Is that all right? Bill, do you like steak?"

"I love steak!" Bill said. "That sounds terrific."

"Your beard," my father said to him. "Do you find that it makes people wonder if you're a communist?"

Bill grinned. "Not usually."

• • •

We spent the afternoon walking around the neighborhood, then I took Bill on a driving tour of Park Ridge, including my elementary, middle, and high schools. At five, we met my friend Maureen for ice-cream cones at Benzer's, and Bill got two scoops. Maureen was a nurse at Baptist Hospital and lived with her parents, which she said was making her crazy. The three of us sat on Benzer's rickety chairs at a tiny white marble table.

Bill said to Maureen, "Do I get to hear what Hillary was like before she was the amazing woman she is now?"

"Hillary was always amazing," Maureen said. "In grade school, she was already raising money for United Way."

"That wasn't until junior high," I said, and both Maureen and Bill laughed. Maureen leaned forward and squeezed my hand. "Also, she's always been opinionated for a girl."

"That's what I love about her," Bill said.

My eyes met Maureen's, and she set one hand over her heart.

When Bill stood to get a napkin, Maureen mouthed to me, **He's so good-looking**. Then, either for emphasis or for our amusement, she fanned herself.

• • •

Opening the menu at Vandy's and seeing that the osso buco cost six dollars and the filet mignon eight dollars made me nervous; surely my stingy father wouldn't let us enjoy such a meal without some form of punishment.

After a waitress whose name tag read ANGELA had taken our drink orders—bourbon for my father, scotch for my mother, beer for Bill and me, Coke for Tony—Bill cheerfully said, "Mr. Rodham, please tell me everything I don't know about the drapery business."

"I assume you know nothing about it," my father said.

"Bill, what led you to Yale?" my mother asked.

"It wasn't an easy decision. At one point I joined the ROTC and signed up to attend law school at the University of Arkansas, but I reconsidered and entered the draft again. I still have mixed feelings about getting a high draft number. On the other hand, in college, I was a clerk for the Foreign Relations Committee, and I was privy to papers that a lot of Americans don't even know exist, with information that muddies the water even more about our involvement."

My father made a snorting noise. After the bombing of Pearl Harbor, he'd joined the navy and served in Illinois, at Naval Station Great Lakes. When he and I had argued about the Vietnam War in the past—I thought it was imperialist, he thought it would stanch communism—I'd never had the nerve to say that I thought not having seen action undermined his credibility.

Quickly, before the conversation could get derailed, my mother said to Bill, "Did you grow up in Little Rock?"

"In Hot Springs," Bill said. "I've been telling Hillary what a fantastic place it is."

As the waitress set down our drinks, he detailed its charms—Hernando de Soto, the Ouachita Mountains, watermelons—and I thought about how it wasn't that Bill wouldn't let someone else dominate the conversation, more that he **couldn't**. Yes, he retained a boyishness that made him deferential around, say, a particularly august professor. But you could always feel Bill's impending, increasing charisma, how if he wasn't the smartest and most charming man in a room, he would be soon. I was looking at the menu when I heard my father summon the waitress back and say, "Angela, there's a problem."

I glanced up and saw a peculiar sight: My father had inserted a thermometer into his glass of ice water. The bulb was pointed down, the mercury rising to less than midway up the capillary. He then removed the thermometer, peered at it in a theatrical way, and said, "This says that my water is forty-eight degrees, but the ideal temperature for hydration is between fifty-five and seventy degrees."

With evident confusion, the waitress said, "Would you—would you like me to replace it?"

"Yes, with water between fifty-five and seventy degrees."

"I'll replace it right away, sir."

As the waitress carried away his glass and the thermometer dripped on the tablecloth, Tony was snickering; my mother looked irritated in a way that mirrored my own irritation; and Bill observed the proceedings with an open smile, as if my father was making an intelligent observation about a worthy subject. Oh, how I wished Bill and I were back on the road, on the highway at dusk, just us and a staticky radio.

The most striking parts of my father's performance were how apparently premeditated it was and how not funny it was. Taking the temperature of water in a restaurant wasn't some sort of shtick with him, and I'd never seen him do it. But the general impulse to destabilize a group, to reclaim attention and make life mildly unpleasant for everyone—these were tendencies I knew well.

I thought of how I'd told Bill on our first date, in the gallery courtyard, that my father was an asshole. I hadn't realized at the time that I was issuing a warning.

My father had gone up to bed, Tony had also disappeared to his room, and Bill was getting settled in the basement, where he'd be sleeping on a pull-out couch. In the downstairs den, my mother and I half watched a TV show about a private investigator. I was curled up against her, and she was running her hand over my hair, just as she had on countless nights in my girlhood when she'd tucked me in.

"I'm sorry Dad decided to be so silly at dinner," she said, and I said, "It's certainly not your fault."

"Bill is nice," she said. "I think you'll have a good time in California."

Because of the tilted angle of my head, I couldn't see her as, a little sheepishly, I said, "Us renting an apartment together—does it bother you?" The fact that in an hour or so I'd be sleeping on the second floor while Bill slept in the basement, an arrangement I hadn't protested, indicated as much.

"Oh, honey," she said. "You're a grown-up now. And society is so different than it used to be." We both were quiet—rather incongruously, the private investigator onscreen was being punched in the face by a gangster—then my mother said, "A new community college opened in Morton Grove, and I've signed up to take some classes in the fall."

"In what?"

"One in ancient Roman history and one in philosophy. Just for fun. Rosemary Munroe did it, and she said it was very stimulating."

"How's the soup kitchen?" This was affiliated with my family's church, and for as long as I could remember, my mother had volunteered there on Tuesdays and Thursdays.

She said, "Busy." We were quiet again, for longer

this time. The reality was that I didn't often pour out my heart to my mother and that I experienced her support more in deed than in word—in the form of her spending hours playing cards with me when I was young, teaching me to type, buying a fake ponytail for me at the Ben Franklin five-and-dime after, as a high school freshman, I was distraught about a drastic and unflattering haircut. But then, softly, she said, "I'm glad you've found someone who appreciates you."

After midnight, I went down to the basement, where Bill lay under a sheet on the pull-out couch, reading **Newsweek**. Immediately, he set the magazine down and whispered, "Baby, I was hoping you'd come visit." He scooted toward the center of the mattress and patted the space next to him. When I lay beside him, he turned onto his side and wrapped his arms around me. "I was reading the obituary of a woman who survived the sinking of both the **Titanic** and the **Britannic**. Can you imagine? She just died of heart failure at the age of eighty-three. She also was aboard an ocean liner that collided with a British warship even before she was on the **Titanic**."

"Does all that make her lucky or unlucky?"

He pondered the question. "Both?" Our faces were at the same level, and he kissed my forehead then said, "I'm not surprised your dad gave me a hard time. I'm his daughter's boyfriend, so it's almost a requirement. But I couldn't believe the way he treated you."

"How so?"

"The relentlessness of his nasty comments. I don't think I've ever heard a father talk to his daughter that way."

I was genuinely perplexed. "Like what?"

He adjusted his voice to what I understood was an approximation of my father's, though the mimicry wasn't particularly adept. " 'That's an impressive insight for someone of your limited intellect.' 'You look good since you've put on all that weight.' 'Maybe you're not as awful as everyone says.' "

"Oh." I laughed. "He's said those exact same things hundreds of times. They're like his personal proverbs."

We still were making eye contact, and Bill said, "Hillary, that stuff is **awful**. He's your **father**."

"He's joking," I said.

"It's not funny."

"Well, I agree with that. But it's how he's always been. I assume you noticed he did it to Tony, too, and he does it to Hughie. The thing he always says to Hughie is, 'Does your face hurt? Because it's killing me.' It's not personal, though."

"How on earth is it not personal? Does he say things like that to people other than his children?"

"Presumably, he realizes he can't get away with it."

"That illustrates my point. Daddy—my stepfather—was no prize. Once when I was four, he and Mother were arguing, and he pulled a gun on her and shot it into a wall. I was in the room. She and I ran over to the neighbors, and they called the police. He had to spend the night in jail. Another time, when I was a lot older, Daddy was beating up on Mother so much that I went after him with a golf club to get him to stop. Now, is your father like that? No. He's not. But there's something very ugly in the way he is with you."

I found Bill's stories of his family and his observations of mine both interesting and disturbing. I said, "Why did your mother stay with your stepfather?"

"Well, she didn't always. She got all the way through a divorce once, before they reconciled. When he wasn't drinking, she loved him. They had a life together."

"Remember when you asked about my fearlessness?" I said. "Maybe it **is** my dad who made me—not fearless, but less fearful than a lot of women. When a man is a jerk, or tries to insult me, whether it's a professor or another student who doesn't think women should speak at a protest, it doesn't seem like a big deal. I hardly pay attention."

"I think you're giving your father too much credit."

"I'm not being a Pollyanna," I said. "I agree with almost everything you're saying." We both were quiet, and then I said, "I'm sorry your stepfather shot a gun while you were in the room, and I'm sorry you had to use a golf club to get him to stop hitting your mom."

Bill didn't say anything, but his eyes filled. I had never seen him cry.

"I love you very much," I said.

He blinked, and no tears slid out. He still didn't speak.

I said, "Seeing you with my family makes me feel so lucky."

The landscape in California was different—the green and tan mountains, the glittering water, the Bay Bridge—and the sky was different and the light was different and the way the air smelled was different. I felt right away how having arrived with Bill made this an adventure, and how if I'd come by myself, I'd have been fine—earnestly fine, responsibly fine, the way I always was—but probably lonely, at least at first.

The apartment Gwen had helped find—her friend's nephew's—consisted of a bedroom, a bathroom, a galley kitchen, and a space off the kitchen with a round table and two chairs. If it wasn't technically a studio, it was close. The unit was on the first floor of a four-story white stucco building with yew trees on either side of the front entrance and bars over the windows, and the building was located on a hill, with the east side of the foundation built to accommodate the hill's slope.

We arrived on a Wednesday evening, and the next morning, when we went grocery shopping together for the first time, we bought bananas and yogurt and hot dogs. Then we went for a hike in Muir Woods. In the shade of the massive, spectacular redwoods, I asked Bill, "Are you **sure** you won't be bored not working?"

"Bored?" He laughed. "I'll be in heaven."

That weekend, we'd been invited for dinner at the home of Phil Howard, the friend of Gwen and Richard's who'd hired me for the summer. This dinner was when I'd meet the firm's partners and my fellow summer associates, and I decided that Bill and I should take a peach pie, using a recipe I'd found in an issue of **Reader's Digest** in the Berkeley apartment. The pie was fresh out of the oven as we drove through the hills of Berkeley to the Elmwood neighborhood, the dish still so warm that I had to sit with a tea towel covering my lap. I had never before baked a pie, never before been a summer associate at a law firm, and never shown up to an adult dinner party with a boyfriend.

The Howards' house was modern—rectangular, big windowed, minimalist—and set high enough up that it resembled a tree house. The person who answered the door was their daughter, Margaret, who said she was a sophomore at Stanford. Bill and I followed her into the living room, where we met all three partners, their wives, Margaret's younger brother Bob, and their dog, Apollo. I followed Irene Howard, Phil's wife, into the kitchen and set the pie on a burner of the stove, and she peeled back the foil and said, "Oh, it looks fabulous."

I drank a gin and tonic and made a point, during the cocktail hour, of speaking to each of the three partners. Phil Howard asked me about Gwen and Richard, and Mark Guion and I discussed new special education laws pending in Massachusetts, and Dan Schau and I discussed the Giants and the Oakland A's. Place cards around the dining room table told us where to sit, and at dinner I was between Mark and an associate named Rick who'd just finished his second year at Berkeley's law school and who informed me that, locally, people referred to Berkeley as Cal.

As I cut into my piece of chicken Kiev, Mark said, "If your boyfriend is also at Yale, you won't need to practice law for long."

I was taken aback and said, "Well, Bill is very interested in public service, and it's no secret that that doesn't pay a lot." It felt strange—to say the least—to imply to a man I'd met a half hour earlier not only that I'd marry Bill but that I'd be the breadwinner when I did. Other than circling the topic of marriage with Bill himself, I'd discussed it with no one.

Mark laughed. "Just don't become a litigator, because then there won't be anyone to iron the clothes or go to the market."

Was he kidding or not kidding? I tried to sound upbeat, to accommodate either possibility, by saying, "Isn't that what weekends are for?"

"Trust me, trial lawyers don't have a free minute to themselves. They need wives. Even when you're home, even on the weekend, you're poring over files."

I was almost certain he wasn't kidding. And I didn't want to appear defiant to a superior before I'd started, but I also felt uneasy pretending that I agreed. Noncommittally, I said, "That's an interesting point of view."

He snorted. "It's not interesting at all," he said. "It's a statement of fact."

In the mornings, I'd leave the apartment at ten after eight, board a bus on College Avenue, and ride south on Highway 24 to downtown Oakland. Howard, Schau and Guion specialized in civil liberties cases, and Phil Howard assigned me to work on a case defending a woman in her thirties named Mary Buck, who was raising the seven-year-old son of former neighbors killed in a car accident four years prior. Initially, it had seemed the arrangement would be temporary, but the child, whose name was Teddy, had lived with Mary ever since his parents' death. Then, six months earlier, Teddy's maternal grandparents, who lived in Reno, had petitioned for guardianship. Mary, with our support, was filing her own petition for guardianship. In order to write briefs and legal motions, I often went to the Berkeley Law Library to research similar cases.

Sometimes during the day, I'd think about Bill reading at the apartment or in a park, or exploring the Bay Area, and I'd again feel disbelief that I got both—I got to work in a way that mattered, and I got to go home, talk to the most interesting person I knew, and kiss the most attractive person I knew. Did I deserve such abundance? Did anyone? I'd leave the office at five-forty, take the bus back up 24, and when it turned onto College Avenue, I'd feel myself smiling with anticipation.

Once, on a weekend, Bill and I climbed up and down the steps on Lombard Street then walked along the Golden Gate Promenade. On another weekend, we ate afternoon ice cream in Ghirardelli Square and dinner in Chinatown, and in between we stopped by City Lights bookstore, where I bought **North Toward Home**, which was a book about the South that Bill loved but hadn't brought with him for the summer, and Bill bought a biography of Robert Frost. On yet another weekend we went for a hike in Joaquin Miller Park, which was a fifteen-minute drive from the apartment, and on a trail thirty yards in from the parking lot, Bill kissed me and we kept kissing and soon both were sufficiently far gone that we decided to skip the hike, go back to the apartment, and get in bed.

Once, on a weekday, when I got home, he was listening to a George Harrison record and making chicken curry, and instead of saying hello to me, he sang, "I really wanna know you / Hallelujah / I really wanna go with you / Hallelujah / I really wanna show you, Lord / That it won't take long, my Lord."

I laughed and said, "I didn't know you knew how to make chicken curry," and he said, "It's not clear that I do."

It was around this time that I sent a postcard to Phyllis, my Wellesley friend. The card featured the Golden Gate Bridge, and I sent it to her in Baltimore, where she'd just finished her second year of medical school at Johns Hopkins.

Dear P,

I have found a man who loves my brain. Stop the presses!

Love, H

P.S. His name is Bill.

• • •

On our drive to the West Coast, Bill had said we should live together in the fall, back in New Haven, and I'd said we might as well test the idea for a few weeks in California before deciding. On the first day of July, when I returned to the bedroom to get dressed after a morning shower, still wrapped in a towel, he said from the bed, "Has it been a few weeks? Have I earned the right to be your permanent roommate?"

I said, "No offense to Katherine, but you're much more fun to snuggle with."

He raised the sheet, and his erection was visible inside his white underwear. "Come back to bed," he said.

"That's not something she was ever able to offer me. Unfortunately, I need to catch the bus." I opened the top drawer of the bureau and pulled out a bra.

"Eddie Shinske is moving out of a place on Edgewood Avenue that I always liked. It has a fireplace in the living room. I'll call and see if he knows if anyone has rented it."

"Can you wait until the weekend to call? Or at least until after seven tonight?" This was when the rates were cheaper.

"Is that a confirmation that we get to live in sin?"

I fastened the bra then walked over to him, leaned down, and kissed his lips. "I guess it is."

He slipped his hand underneath the bra's left cup and squeezed my nipple. He said, "It's such a shame to cover these up."

On a morning in late July, Mark Guion appeared in front of my desk and said, "You can't really be planning to move to Arkansas."

He said this as though we'd been discussing the pros and cons of such a decision, but in fact I'd spoken to him little in the eight weeks since he'd warned me against becoming a trial lawyer.

I said, "Pardon me?"

"Phil told me it's where your boyfriend wants to run for office. Do you know what a backwater that state is?"

Did Mark intend for this unsolicited advice to dovetail with his previous unsolicited advice—I ought not to live in Arkansas while not going into trial law—or was it entirely separate?

I said, "Oh, I didn't—I haven't—" I paused and said, "I didn't realize you'd spent time in Arkansas."

Mark's expression was disdainful. "I wouldn't set foot there if you paid me. What happened in Little Rock is a blight on our nation's history."

"Well, it was a very dark moment," I said. "But racial injustice isn't unique to Arkansas."

He was practically sneering. "They'd still lynch people down there if they thought they could get away with it."

• • •

Bill and I had decided to meet at six-thirty at a noodle restaurant on Fourth Street in Berkeley, a place where Bill previously had eaten lunch on his own and had thought I'd like. I ended up spending the afternoon at the library, which was closer to our apartment than to the restaurant, so at quarter to six I began to walk home. It was about seventy degrees out, a breezy summer evening, and I thought that over dinner we ought to make a list of the things we wanted to do and see before we left the Bay Area. Impossibly, our time there was almost finished—it was mid-August, just over a week before we were to drive back east.

Half Moon Bay, I thought as I walked north on Piedmont Avenue, my satchel hooked over my right shoulder. And what about Sausalito? And we still hadn't even made it to the Botanical Garden on the Cal campus. On our final remaining weekend, we were planning to see friends of Bill's, another Rhodes scholar and his wife who were driving up from Los Angeles.

A few seconds after I'd turned from Hearst Avenue onto Leroy Avenue, I saw a man and woman outside the stucco apartment building, kissing in an open-mouthed, passionate way. The man was tall and sandy-haired and leaning down, and the woman was dark-haired and leaning up. The sight of them would have been notable on the street I'd grown up on, but in Berkeley, in 1971, it was less so. It was less so, except that, as I realized with a start, the man wore Bill's white T-shirt and jeans; the man's wavy hair was cut just like Bill's. I was ten feet away when I knew for certain that the man **was** Bill.

Later, when I described the moment in a letter to Maureen, she wrote back that she'd have turned around and bolted in the other direction. This didn't occur to me. I blurted out, "What are you **doing**?" and when Bill raised his head and saw me, his expression turned from one of casual pleasure to one of horror.

He said, "Oh, Jesus. Oh, shit." He stepped back from the woman, who was now looking at me, too—she was young and pretty—and she said, "Oh!" and I realized she was the daughter of my boss. She was Margaret Howard, the Stanford student.

She said, "But I thought—" then didn't finish the sentiment. She seemed to be in a daze, which made me consider what induced such a daze. What was it that had already happened?

In a quiet but firm voice, Bill said to her, "You need to go."

Even given the circumstances—my own shock and distraughtness, her confusion—I sensed her wish for some more ceremonial farewell from him.

She said, "But—" and he said, "Now."

Bill had turned toward me, and neither of us

spoke. "Bye?" the girl said then repeated, "Bye." I was conscious of her walking away, but I didn't watch her leave.

Bill closed the space between us and set his mammoth palm on my shoulder and upper arm. His voice was thick with emotion as he said, "Hillary."

I shrugged off his hand and glared up at him. Without speaking, I turned and walked inside and down the hall to our unit, which wasn't locked. Bill followed me to the bedroom. Although whichever of us got up second, usually Bill, made the bed each morning, the sheets on the mattress were in disarray, and one of the four pillows was on the floor. I felt nauseated and shaky. I dropped my satchel, walked into the galley kitchen, leaned my back against the sink, folded my arms, and said, "You just had sex with her in our bed." It wasn't a question.

He was standing at the kitchen's threshold, and he stepped toward me. "Sweet baby," he said and brought his face close to mine. I pushed him away.

"You were kissing her thirty seconds ago, and now you're trying to kiss **me**?" I shook my head. "What's wrong with you?"

"It wasn't—I didn't—" He paused.

"You didn't what?"

"Even while it was going on, I regretted it. She flirted with me, and I had a moment of weakness and gave in to temptation. I regret it with all my heart."

I was so upset that it was difficult to speak. Several seconds passed, and I said, "I saw the two of you kissing, and it didn't look like you were regretting anything."

"No." He seemed to be on the brink of tears. "It was just physical gratification. It was nothing compared to what we have."

"Did you run into her or did you make a plan to see her? Did you call her at Phil's house?"

He didn't respond.

Dumbfoundedly, I said, "You called the house of my boss to ask his daughter on a date?"

Still he didn't speak.

"Have you seen her before today?" I asked.

He sighed deeply and finally said, "A few times."

"How many?"

"Four?"

Again, a silence descended on us. At last, I said, "This is such a betrayal." I waved a hand at myself then at him. "I don't know what the point of this is."

"You'd throw away our love just like that?"

"**I'd** throw away our love?"

"I'll swear on my Mammaw's Bible that I'm passionately in love with you," he said. "I'm a horny bastard, and sometimes I can't help myself. But there's no question that you're the love of my life. I want to be around you forever and ever."

"Then why the hell did you just have sex with that girl?"

He looked pained.

"For God's sake," I said, "we did it last night. Am I not enough for you?"

He looked down as he said, "There's definitely something wrong with me. Because yeah, you and I made love last night, and it was wonderful. And I could have done it again right when we woke up in the morning and again before you left for work and again at lunch and again now. It's the way I imagine it is for people who drink too much. It's a rarer moment that I'm **not** overwhelmed with how much I want to have sex than when I am. I'm thinking about doing it right now, with you."

"Don't get your hopes up."

"That's not what I meant. I just meant it's constant, and I hate this about myself. My male urges—they make a fool of me. That's been true since long before I met you. But if I wreck what you and I have, I'd rather die."

I did still feel furious, and stunned with hurt, but I also felt some slackening; he was telling me something that didn't exactly surprise me but also wasn't something I'd known.

I said, "How long have you been like this?"

"Since I was ten or eleven. I—" He hesitated. "As soon as I figured out it was a thing I could do, I touched myself a lot. And I mean **a lot**. Later, with girls, at first I was shocked any of them were willing to have anything to do with me, but I discovered they were."

"How many women have you slept with in your life?"

He bit his lower lip.

"Just to be clear," I said, "if you tell me the truth right now, I might forgive you, and if you lie to me, I never will."

"I don't know the exact number," he said. "It could be over fifty."

"Did you cheat on your earlier girlfriends?"

"Sometimes."

"If you're going to be evasive, you might as well pack your suitcase and start driving to New Haven tonight. I can fly back next week. It's not as if I need you here while I finish my job."

"I've never been faithful to any girl," he said.

It felt like I'd been kicked in the stomach.

He said, "But from now on, I want to be faithful to you. I want to be worthy of your love."

"If you're saying that it's like a compulsion, how can you change that?"

"With willpower," he said. "And prayer. And with your help, if you'll give it to me."

"Does that mean us having sex three times a day?"

"Maybe—what if—if I wanted it and you didn't, would you think it was disgusting if I lay next to you and touched myself?"

I considered it, then said, "No. I wouldn't think it was disgusting."

"Would it bother you if I looked at magazines?"

"I need to think about that. It doesn't seem like

it's my right to try to stop you, but I don't know if I want to see them."

"That's fair."

Mapping out the future, coming up with strategies and plans—these were things we were good at, things we'd practiced. In a way, strategizing made me feel as close to him as sex.

Again, he took a few steps toward me and when we were less than a foot apart, he dropped to his knees. He looked up at me, took both my hands, and said, "The flesh is weak. Lord knows how weak my flesh has been. But, Hillary, my spirit is yours. My soul and my spirit and my heart—they'll always be yours, no matter what." And then he began to cry, and I don't mean he got choked up like he had in my parents' basement. This time, his face crumpled and tears streamed down his cheeks in a way I'd seen in my brothers in their youth but never in a grown man. Pulling his head toward my navel—it was instinctive, not a decision, as so much about Bill was for me instinctive. Still on his knees, he wrapped his arms around my waist and pressed his torso and face against me, and I petted his hair. I didn't reassure him that my spirit and soul and heart were his, because wasn't it obvious? Instead, softly, I said, "Bill. Oh, Bill, what am I going to do with you?"

• • •

At the office the next day, I finished a brief and ate lunch with the other associates, but my mind wandered. If Bill had met up with Margaret Howard four times, when had the other three been, and where? Did the admission of four really mean eight, or twelve? Had sex occurred the earlier times? If so, had they used birth control? On the days they'd seen each other, what conversations had he and I had that night over dinner, and had he felt uncomfortable with his lies of omission? I tried to recall evenings when he'd seemed preoccupied, and I couldn't.

His apparent talent for deceit—it was so disturbing, so insulting. How could I stay with a man like that? How had I been such a poor judge of character? And yet I believed what he'd said about his spirit and soul, I believed he wanted us to be together forever. I believed that he adored me and—remarkably—that he adored me while understanding not only who I was but who I wished to be. But if that was true, how could he so easily take off his clothes with someone else? Sex was a physical act for me, yes, but what made it precious was that he was the other person; my bond with him felt singular.

There was an odd familiarity to this affront, a variation on the men who'd admired my mind without taking any interest in my body. Was it that all along Bill had taken an interest in my body only because he wasn't picky, because he took an interest in almost all women's bodies? This was crushing to consider; it was devastating. I thought of the stupid, smug postcard I'd sent to Phyllis; I thought of when I'd asked Bill if he'd be bored not working and believed him when he'd said he'd be satisfied reading and wandering the streets of Berkeley. I'd believed this of Bill, the most gregarious person I knew.

As the day wore on, I developed a headache, and I was tempted to leave the office early. But what if I went home and walked in on him with Margaret? Or with someone else? Then I thought if I did, the situation was hopeless, and if it was hopeless, at least I'd know.

He was sitting in the living room reading the Robert Frost biography. He stood when I entered and said in a warm voice, "Hi, baby. I'm so happy to see you." When he embraced me, it was comforting in a way I hadn't anticipated; I wouldn't have thought the same person could cause and assuage my pain. I just wanted to relax with him, to sit close together on the couch and read or talk, but not to talk about the subject that had gripped me for almost twenty-four hours. The questions that had been spinning in my mind—I asked him none of them. I'd told Bill that I wouldn't tolerate evasion, but it wasn't true.

• • •

We had planned to drive back along the southern route, stopping in Hot Springs, but there was a tenderness with which he treated me during those weeks in August, an extra deference, and I think he understood that visiting his home, meeting his mother and brother and stepfather, wasn't something I could do at that point. After he'd called his mother to say that we needed to get back to New Haven sooner than expected because of his obligations to the McGovern campaign, Bill said to me, "Just promise me this. Promise you'll come to Arkansas another time."

Perhaps he realized that if his long-term goal was to persuade me to move there, it was smarter to postpone our first visit so that it wouldn't be tainted.

Sometimes in the night I awakened with a sense of dread, a nebulous apprehension, and it took a few seconds to pinpoint its source. And yet there was a less predictable emotion that at times accompanied my hurt and disappointment. It took until after we'd left Oakland, until our second day on the road, as we were turning in to a motel parking lot in Omaha, Nebraska, for me to admit to myself that it was relief—a strange, perverse, sincere relief. The reality was that I was a hardworking and not beautiful middle-class Midwestern girl with a mean father. I had never believed the world existed for my enjoyment. I'd believed instead that every situation was a trade-off, that there was always a catch. I didn't yearn to be envied by others, and wasn't a great love affair with Bill Clinton enviable? Hadn't it been thrilling and also made me slightly uneasy? Now the catch had made itself known. Bill could be genuinely devoted and at the same time struggle to remain faithful. We had been a couple for five months, and he'd already cheated. Surely this meant that at best, I'd live with the fear that he'd cheat again, and at worst, that he **would** cheat. He wasn't too good to be true. But discerning his flaw meant that if I could live with it, I could keep him.

There also was this: Our relationship was still new enough that the idea that I'd have to exert myself in order to sexually satisfy him, that we'd need, together, to be imaginative and thorough—this was not a wholly unpleasant challenge. It didn't seem like the worst burden. There was an extra intensity to our couplings in those weeks after I'd found him kissing Margaret. And both in and out of bed, I'd think of what he'd told me about himself; his secret had become something else we shared.

On August 23, 1971, we pulled up in front of the apartment on Edgewood Avenue in New Haven, and, as the landlord had agreed to, a key waited beneath a brick in the small backyard. We entered an apartment that did indeed feature a charming living room fireplace and, less charmingly, uneven flooring and such an absurdly small bathroom that the toilet seat touched the bathtub.

Walking through the empty rooms for the first time, I felt older than I'd been when Bill and I had departed from New Haven in May. A certain giddiness between us had been punctured, in part, of course, by his infidelity, but that wasn't the only reason. Having lived under the same roof for three months, shared a bed, driven across the country and back, we knew each other in a far deeper way. We weren't bound only by conversation and chemistry, which can be at once seductive and misleading or at least incomplete. We now knew each other's extended habits and moods, knew each other awake and asleep, not as a novelty but as a daily norm; the way he smelled when he woke up in the morning wasn't a bad smell—I liked it—but it also wasn't the public version of him. We knew each other's animal selves. Berkeley had been practice, a probation from which our survival as a couple hadn't been guaranteed. The return to New Haven felt like the true beginning of our lives together.

Later, I thought about the fact that both Bill's infidelity and my discovery of it had occurred in California—how geography had seemed to contain the sorrow and conflict, allowing us to leave them behind. The only person I confided in about the infidelity was Maureen, with whom I exchanged long letters that I took care never to read or write when Bill was in the apartment. Did I tell Maureen because we'd recently seen her in Park Ridge or because there'd have been too much shame involved in telling anyone at Yale? My reasons, I suppose, were not mutually exclusive.

The episode with Margaret took on the quality of a bad dream—vivid and unsettling but also ephemeral and discrete.

CHAPTER 3

1974

THE GREENBERGERS LIVED CLOSE TO the Yale campus, in a brick house with a front porch. When I arrived there at seven-thirty on a hot Sunday morning in August, all four members of the family were outside: Gwen and Richard sat on the porch steps, both of them holding coffee mugs, while the twins, who had recently turned six, stood in the yard in matching Spiderman pajamas. Otto was eating a piece of toast, and Marcus was running a toy car over a red vinyl suitcase set upright on the path that led from the porch to the sidewalk.

As I emerged from my car, I said, "Hi, everyone," and Marcus said, "I am a flying Camaro and I go seventy thousand trillion miles an hour."

"Hillary, it's a shame you can't drive Marcus's Camaro to Arkansas," Richard said.

I laughed, and Gwen said, "But then Hillary and I would miss out on the pleasure of each other's company."

Richard rose to wedge Gwen's suitcase in the back of my car—it was a new used Buick—among my clothes, books, records, and favorite frying pan. I'd left Washington, D.C., a week before and been driving around the Northeast on a kind of farewell tour, including attending the Boston wedding of my Wellesley friend Nancy, who was out of the Peace Corps and had become a social worker. One morning in Jamaica Plain, I'd pulled clothes from the trunk and discerned that during the night, a back-door lock had been jimmied open, my belongings had been rifled through, and nothing had been taken; I'd been both relieved and a little insulted.

I went inside to use the Greenbergers' downstairs bathroom, and when I came back out to the yard, Gwen hugged the boys.

"Thank you," I said to Richard. I meant, for giving Gwen his blessing to drive with me while he was left alone with their kids.

"Just so long as you know she's acting as a double agent," Richard said.

"I guess now I can't claim I wasn't warned," I said.

Gwen shook her head at Richard, but then

she hugged him and kissed him on the lips, and he looked at me and said, "Drive safely with my favorite passenger."

When Gwen and I were both in the car, she rolled down her window and called, "Boys, be good for Daddy. I love you all. Richard, we're almost out of milk."

"Mommy, will you bring us a present?" Otto said.

"That depends on the reports I get from Daddy about how helpful you are."

"Where are you stopping tonight?" Richard asked.

Gwen glanced at me, and I said, "Indianapolis."

To Richard, Gwen said, "I'll call you from the motel."

We hadn't yet reached Pennsylvania when Gwen said, "I understand why you love him. I promise that I do. I just think he's asking so much of you. You sacrifice your professional future, and what does he sacrifice?"

"But I'm the one who made this decision," I said. "And it's not like I won't have a job."

"Being a professor in Fayetteville, Arkansas—" She was speaking slowly, seeming to choose her words carefully. "You can do anything you want and live anywhere. You—**you,** Hillary Rodham—if you're not the beneficiary of the women's movement, who is? More than any other young woman I know, you have the freedom to choose your own path."

"Do you think important work only gets done on the East Coast?"

"Absolutely not. But you aren't moving to Arkansas for the job. You took the job because you're moving to Arkansas."

"Don't you live in New Haven because of Richard's job?"

She sighed. "Maybe that's part of why I'm saying all this."

Around Dayton, Ohio, Gwen said, "If the talk about him being president is true, can you imagine being first lady?"

I'm sure it wasn't her intent, but whenever people invoked Bill's future this way, I felt pride. I said, "I'm more focused on finishing my syllabi before the semester starts than I am on a Clinton presidency."

"Don't bullshit me, Hillary. Have you really considered it? Hosting teas and talking about the dress you're wearing?"

I thought of Betty Ford, who had moved into the White House days earlier, following Nixon's resignation. She seemed pleasant enough but was a woman of my mother's generation, as was Pat Nixon, who came across as poised, traditional, and now tainted by association. Then again, I'd just finished seven months as a lawyer on the House Judiciary Committee's impeachment inquiry, and there wasn't anyone in Richard Nixon's orbit whom I considered to be unscathed.

"At least imagine being the first lady of Arkansas," Gwen said. "Southerners like women to have their hair, nails, and clothes just so."

I said, "But what if Bill and I are a team and after he's elected, whether it's to Congress or something else, I influence policy? There's more than one way to have an impact."

"Why would you want to work behind the scenes when you don't have to?"

On our second day of driving, an hour outside Fayetteville, Gwen said, "Do you remember when Richard had Bill and some of his classmates over to our house for dinner?"

This had been three years prior, and I hadn't attended but definitely remembered; it had been the night Gwen and Bill met, when he'd liked her and she hadn't liked him. I said, "Of course."

"There was a woman in that class, and I can't remember her name."

"Audrey Belzer," I said.

"I don't have proof of anything. But he was **very** attentive to her that night. Early on, he made an effort with me. He turned on the charm. But after dinner and a few drinks, he was very close to her on the couch, touching her arm. He didn't act like a man who had a girlfriend."

The seizing in my stomach—this was a highly inconvenient moment for it. I said, "Bill is warm and friendly with everyone, sometimes to a fault. I know that about him, and he knows it about himself."

"You don't worry that it could get him into trouble?"

"He isn't perfect, but show me who is. And his talents far, far outweigh his shortcomings." Sitting in the front seat next to Gwen as she drove my Buick, I felt a flicker of resentment. Why hadn't she mentioned this at the time, before my life was so thoroughly entangled with Bill's? Years later, I read that patients in therapy routinely brought up the subjects they were most worried about in the last few minutes of a session, when there was limited time left to delve into them, and I thought of Gwen. She'd waited so long that we were in Arkansas; we were in the lushly green Ozark Mountains, the road rising and falling gently, curving through valleys and around rocky overlooks and shimmering lakes. The scenery was lovely—could Gwen not see how lovely it was? I wished to be out of her company, and the wish made me sad.

"I hope I'm wrong," she said. "Barring that, I hope you know what you're getting into."

And really, my resentment of her was unfounded. Because even by the time Bill had eaten dinner at the Greenbergers' house, by the time I'd known him for two months, it had already been too late.

After graduating from Yale, I'd worked for the National Children's Initiative full-time, while Bill finished his third year of law school. I'd interviewed the families of children in Connecticut who couldn't attend school because of physical and cognitive disabilities, then I'd had the deeply rewarding experience of watching Gwen present my findings at Senate hearings that occurred in the spring of 1973. Among the other projects I'd worked on for Gwen was researching private schools that had been created to avoid complying with **Brown v. Board of Education** yet managed to maintain tax-exempt status. When I'd driven alone to rural Tennessee and pretended that I was moving to town and wanted to find a segregated school for my child, I had felt like a private investigator. Other times under Gwen's tutelage, I felt like a journalist, and still other times, I felt like a social worker.

Meanwhile, Bill had been away from campus as much as he was there, working for McGovern in Connecticut and also in Texas. I joined Bill in late October 1972, canvassing door-to-door, and I was in Austin with him, his young staffers, and his volunteers for McGovern's disastrous loss on election night. By the time Bill graduated from Yale, the dean of the law school at the University of Arkansas had offered him a teaching position, an ideal arrangement given that the university was located in the district of the Republican congressman Bill hoped to challenge. On my first visit to Fayetteville, in the fall of 1973, the law school dean and his wife had us over for ribs and he told me if I'd like to teach there, too, he was sure they could find classes for me. On the ride back to Bill's rental house that night, I said, "Did you put him up to that?"

Bill grinned. "Of course not."

In January 1974, both Bill and I had been contacted by John Doar, a friend of one of our Yale professors and the lawyer leading the Nixon impeachment inquiry for the House Judiciary Committee. When John invited us to join his staff, Bill declined—he had just started telling people he was running for Congress—and I accepted based on my Rule of Two: The job was interesting, prestigious, and an opportunity to make important contacts, **and** it could serve as a transition from working for Gwen to joining Bill. That is, I wouldn't have to tell Gwen I was quitting the National Children's Initiative to move to Arkansas, though I would be quitting the National Children's Initiative and I would be moving to Arkansas.

I was mostly correct about the impeachment inquiry: It was often fascinating, though also sometimes boring as we pored over every word in a document or on the tapes Nixon had made of himself in the Oval Office. I and forty-three other lawyers—two besides me were women—worked up to twenty hours a day, seven days a week, in a federal office building where we kept the blinds closed and security guards stood watch. Based on our findings, Doar presented the proposed articles of impeachment on July 19, and on August 9, Nixon resigned. His televised farewell speech that day felt both surreal and belated.

When Gwen had offered to accompany me on the drive to Fayetteville, I'd suspected she still had reservations about Bill but I hadn't realized the extent of them; I'd hoped she was trying to understand why I was moving to Arkansas rather than trying to prevent it. Bill also had offered to fly east and drive with me, though clearly he was relieved when I declined. In June, he'd won the Democratic primary, and in the last few weeks, it had started to seem as if he might actually win the seat. Accordingly, his schedule was packed with visits to hardware stores and rodeos and fish fries, and the poll numbers between him and his opponent, whose name was John Paul Hammerschmidt, were so close that every encounter with even one voter mattered.

And underlying all our plans and conversations as a couple was something that had happened a year before. Just after his law school graduation, Bill and I had flown together to England; it had been my first trip overseas. We wandered around London, visiting the Tate Gallery and Westminster Abbey and Trafalgar Square. We took the train to Oxford and ate fish and chips for lunch at a pub, and steak and kidney pie for dinner at the home of the man who'd been head porter at University College when Bill was there. Then we took the train up to the Lake District and checked in to a rustic inn near Ennerdale Water, where the proprietor owned a slow-moving, heavy-breathing bulldog whom we decided resembled the Yale mascot.

In the previous two years, Bill and I hadn't done much purely recreational travel separate from campaigns or seeing family. I'd wondered ahead of time if either of us would feel annoyed or suffocated. In fact, spending twenty-four hours a day together was effortless.

At twilight on our first night at the inn, we walked down a path that led to the shore of Ennerdale Water and found ourselves overlooking a placid lake with grassy, craggy mountains beyond it.

"Hillary," Bill said, and I turned. He reached out and took both my hands in both of his, and this gesture maneuvered us so we were standing face-to-face, albeit at different heights. As he looked down and I looked up, he said, "I love you more than anything, and I always will. Hillary Diane Rodham, will you marry me?"

"Oh, God," I said. "I want to. But not now. I can't now."

He seemed surprised more than wounded, though he seemed wounded, too. "We don't have to have a wedding right away," he said. "We can wait as long as you want."

"I love you more than anything, too," I said. "I promise."

"Is it because you don't want to live in Arkansas? Because I thought we said if I beat Hammerschmidt, you wouldn't have to."

I had to look away as I said, "I can imagine moving to Arkansas, and I can imagine marrying you. But I can't do both at the same time, and I don't think I should do either one yet. It's too—it would be—the combination just seems irrevocable."

"You mean you'd feel trapped?"

"I need to be realistic about what I can live with. Once I get married, I want to stay married." When I glanced at him, he was looking out at the water, biting his lip.

Then he said, "How am I supposed to prove myself? How long will I be in the doghouse for what happened in Berkeley?"

"There's no doghouse," I said. "But don't you think you are who you are?"

Even though we were alluding to the topic, not landing on it directly, this was closer than we usually got. The thing I'd failed to anticipate after I'd seen Bill kissing Margaret Howard was that henceforth I'd need to make a decision about my own level of vigilance. Bill and I had sex almost every night that we were in the same bed, but on a night that we didn't, did it mean something? If we attended a campaign event or party together, was it necessary to monitor him and intervene if he talked to any particular woman for too long? If he traveled, was it appropriate to ask for an account of his time away? One night shortly after we'd moved in together, we went to Philadelphia for a youth conference sponsored by the DNC. Based on my role with Yale's chapter of Law Students United for Change, I was one of three speakers at the dinner banquet. I was focused as I stood onstage and spoke into the microphone about the importance of registering young people now that the voting age had dropped to eighteen. But earlier that afternoon, I'd noticed Bill chatting cozily with a curly-haired girl in a halter dress, and after the speeches, when the crowd was mingling again, I tried to track his movements around the ballroom as various people approached me to introduce themselves or praise my speech. Even when a Wellesley classmate I hadn't seen for a few years greeted me, I could hardly concentrate. And it was this experience that provided the answer to my question about monitoring him. I couldn't do it. Even though I'd given the DNC organizers what they'd asked for that night, I'd been preoccupied, and my preoccupation left me exhausted and ashamed. I felt pathetic. It was clear that I couldn't live like this and certainly not for decades. I had to either break up with Bill or trust him.

Had he been faithful in the last three years? I didn't doubt that he'd flirted—paying compliments, touching a woman's elbow or the small of her back. But had he kissed another woman? Had he had sex with another woman? Had his erection been inside another woman's body and then had he pulled out and come on her stomach, or had he taken the risk of coming inside her? Were there women who'd found themselves pregnant following a tryst with Bill, and, either before or after **Roe** was decided in January 1973, had they had abortions? I didn't know. I didn't like to think about it, and I usually didn't and then every few months, at moments I hadn't planned to, I did.

And even if I'd decided to trust him, there were indications that others didn't. Shortly before my graduation, when I told my former roommate Katherine that I was staying in New Haven to work at the National Children's Initiative, she said, "If Bill Clinton was my boyfriend, I'd keep an eye on him, too."

It was for all these reasons that I said what I said next on the shore of Ennerdale Water: "Let's see what it feels like to live in different states and discuss this again in a few months." Then, surprising us both, I added, "And why don't we date other people during that time? Just to be sure."

His expression was displeased. "Sure of what?"

Sure that we can't live apart, I thought. **Sure that you really have ruined me for everyone else.** Aloud, I said, "I don't know what the rush is."

"Fine," he said. "I'll agree to your terms, and you know why? Because I'm sure already."

On the day of my arrival with Gwen, Bill had late-afternoon and evening events in Bentonville, which was on the way to Fayetteville. If we got to Bentonville before five, Bill had said we should go to Don's Cafeteria, where he'd be prior to giving a speech in the town square. At four-fifty, we parked a block off the quaint downtown and walked into a bustling restaurant, where, at a table covered in a red-checked oilcloth, Bill sat with eight men, all of them about the age of my father. Bill was facing the door, and as soon as we made eye contact, he called, "Hillary!" He added, "And Gwen!" He stood and embraced me, kissing me on the lips, then he wrapped Gwen in a similar bear hug. "I am **thrilled** to see both of you," he said.

When he introduced us to the men, I experienced a sensation I'd experienced before around Bill, which was their surprise. I was the girlfriend of Bill Clinton? They did not, probably, think I was ugly; it was more that they'd expected their talented native son to have a girlfriend who was notably beautiful. As it happened, before Gwen and I had left the Best Western in Indianapolis that morning, I'd set my alarm clock twenty minutes early to shave my legs in the motel room tub, and I was wearing the first dress I'd bought in several years, a wrap dress with a brown-and-white geometric pattern. I looked back at them, holding each of their gazes, one after the other. Yes. I was the girlfriend of Bill Clinton.

Bill was talking to the men about coal miners in the Arkansas River Valley suffering from black lung disease. Before we all left, he got up to shake hands with other diners, and a chicken farmer told me he'd never met a lady lawyer before. I hoped the man talking to Gwen wasn't saying anything racist.

Maybe because it was a Saturday, or just because it was a sunny summer evening, there was a larger than expected crowd waiting in the town square to hear Bill—at least a hundred people. After being introduced by the mayor of Bentonville, who was one of the men from the cafeteria, Bill gave his stump speech, adjusted to acknowledge Nixon's recent resignation. He promised that if elected, he'd fight for fairer taxes, better health insurance, additional funding for education, and price controls on gas.

He spoke clearly and intelligently, his Southern accent stronger than when we'd lived in New Haven in a way that I found endearing, though it's possible that after I'd been apart from him since

May, anything Bill did would have struck me as endearing. But there was some particular magic in the air on that hot and beautiful night, the magic of Bill in his native habitat. He'd shaved off his beard just after finishing law school, and he was a little sunburned, which only made him handsomer, his white button-down shirt rolled up to the elbows. The audience clapped and cheered at every opportunity. Afterward, dozens of people shook hands with Bill, and a sizable number took out checkbooks and made donations for ten or twenty dollars on the spot.

Several people approached to introduce themselves to me, including an older woman who was volunteering on the campaign and said with a wink, "Sweet pea, he's been counting down the days till you got here."

After almost everyone had cleared out, I rejoined Gwen, who sat on a folding chair with one leg crossed over the other. She was scratching at a bug bite on her forearm, not smiling.

"I think he was great," I said.

Without enthusiasm, she said, "He likes when people listen to him."

Gwen rode to Fayetteville with Bill's campaign manager, a man named Lyle Metcalf, and Bill drove my car. Even though it was over ninety degrees, the harsh afternoon sun had mellowed into a rich evening light that dappled the crop fields and forests beside the highway. As soon as we were out of town, Bill set his palm above my left knee, ran it up my thigh, and said, "You look beautiful in this dress. When you walked into Don's, I couldn't believe how beautiful you looked."

"Oh, baby," I said. "You were amazing tonight. And you looked so handsome."

He still was rubbing my thigh as he said, "I can't even tell you how much I've missed you."

"I've missed you, too," I said, and it was becoming hard to speak—I was weak with how much I loved him, how miraculous it felt that he loved me back. And the proximity of his hand was making me molten.

Which perhaps he sensed, because he said, "Will you take off your panties and let me touch you while I drive?"

I laughed.

"I'm serious," he said.

With effort—I was almost immobilized, almost mute—I said, "I want you to, but is it safe?" I gestured toward the windshield.

He looked over and smiled. "I'll be very careful."

We were on the highway, not close to other cars or trucks, and I reached up to my hips, hooked my thumbs into the waistband of my underwear, and pulled them to my ankles, above my sandals, without taking them off.

"Please don't get pulled over," I said, and after

that I really couldn't speak. I was writhing against his fingers. I lasted about two minutes, and then I was saying as quietly as I could, "Oh, baby. Bill. Bill. Baby, I love you so much." He stopped moving his fingers and just cupped me, and I whimpered incoherently.

He was alternating between watching the road and turning his head to watch me, smiling, and he said, "I love **you** so much. I really do. And also—" He lifted his hand off me and gestured toward his own lap, where he clearly had an erection.

"I don't think I should do anything while you're driving," I said. "But when we're home, I really, really want to make you feel as good as you make me feel. Is that okay?"

"That's fantastic," he said.

Maybe the reason Gwen didn't understand my move to Fayetteville, I thought, was that I couldn't tell her about this.

Before my arrival, Bill had found a one-bedroom apartment for me near campus. His rental house was eight miles out of town, a tiny place on a large plot of land on the White River, with beautiful views and lots of bugs and rodents. He had matter-of-factly told me that we couldn't live together without being married while he ran for Congress, and I didn't balk, wary of ending up in an argument about marriage. Besides, he said, we could still spend every night together and this way we'd get the best of both worlds—convenience in town when we felt like it, privacy and quiet when we preferred.

I did not explain the situation to Gwen, and even though she could have spent the night in my apartment for free—Bill had already borrowed a bed from a supporter—I made a reservation for her at a hotel in downtown Fayetteville. I stayed at Bill's house, and early the next morning, he and I both picked up Gwen and drove her to the tiny Drake Field airport. We sat with her at the gate while she waited, a thirty-five-minute interval during which four people stopped to greet Bill, including a baggage handler who said he hoped Bill beat Hammerschmidt.

When Gwen's flight started boarding, the three of us stood and I said, "I can't thank you enough."

Gwen said, "I hope your life here is wonderful," and then her chin trembled and she began to cry, which I had never seen her do, even when discussing children in the bleakest circumstances.

"I promise to take care of Hillary," Bill said, and he stepped in to hug Gwen. Like me, Gwen was much shorter than Bill, and our eyes were at the same level when she turned her head while it was still pressed to his chest. Her expression of sincere anguish made me deeply uncomfortable, and I could feel that I might catch her tears. "And we're all just a plane flight apart," Bill said, which wasn't true—we were a minimum of two flights apart.

I, too, hugged Gwen and when she walked outside to the tarmac, I was relieved. It felt like she was the embodiment of everyone who questioned or disapproved of my decision.

After Bill and I left the airport, we were going to a pancake breakfast in Fort Smith, then he was speaking to a local NAACP chapter, then we were distributing yard signs. As we got in his car, I said, "I just think it's hard for Gwen because she pictured me having a different professional path."

Bill looked puzzled, almost amused. He said, "Do you think I don't realize that?"

When Bill and I had eaten ribs at the law school dean's house a year earlier, the other guests present that night had been Ned and Barbara Overholt, both of whom were also law professors; Barbara was the first and, until my arrival, the only woman on the law school faculty. She was in her early fifties, with two children and three stepchildren all in their twenties. She had grown up in Virginia, attended UVA for law school, and moved to Arkansas because her ex-husband was from there, as was Ned.

On my third day in town, Barbara had invited me for lunch at her house, a big tan Victorian with scalloped shingles and Ionic columns, in the historic Washington-Willow district. Before I could ring the bell, she pushed open the screen door—she wore jeans, sandals, and a sleeveless shirt—and said, "Hillary, welcome to Fayetteville! Can I hug you?" As we embraced, she said, "Bill has been beside himself with excitement about your arrival, and I think it's contagious."

"I'm delighted to be here," I said.

"I have something to show you that I hope won't make you regret your move. This happened a few minutes ago, and I haven't decided if it's awful or funny, so maybe you can help me figure it out. I got an anonymous letter in my mailbox, but first I have to show you what inspired it. Follow me." She walked into the yard, which featured a border of ferns set in mulch. Among the ferns, near the sidewalk, stood a plump female figurine that was about eight by three inches. Barbara pointed to it. "Is this woman recognizable to you?"

"It's the **Venus of Willendorf** ? Well, a replica."

"Very good." Barbara reached into the back right pocket of her jeans and pulled out an envelope that was folded in half. She removed a piece of onionskin paper and passed the paper to me, and she was shaking with laughter. The paper had two typewritten lines on it: **For the love of God and all things holy and good, Please remove the fat lady statue from your yard. Each and everyone of your neighbors thinks it is digsusting.**

I began laughing, too.

"My sister just went to Austria and bought this for me," she said. "Do I try to explain to my neighbors that it's a major work of art celebrating female strength or do I cave and hide it? She's only been out here a couple days. I didn't even think anyone would notice!"

"Do you have any idea who wrote the note?"

"I have my suspicions. The first question is, is the person borderline illiterate or trying to disguise his identity by pretending to be borderline illiterate? Did you read Nancy Drew?"

"Of course," I said. "I longed to have titian hair and a roadster."

"Should we say to hell with the university and open a girl detective agency?"

"I think that's a wonderful idea."

"In the meantime, I've made some gazpacho. Do you eat gazpacho?"

"I love gazpacho," I said.

As we ate, I said, "How have you found that the students react to having a woman law professor? Do you have advice?"

"The students are usually all right. It's the other professors you've got to watch out for."

"Really?"

"I'd put them into three categories. Category one is they can't stomach the idea of a female colleague, they're dyed-in-the-wool chauvinist pigs, and nothing you do will change their mind.

Category three, and Bill goes here, obviously, is they're supportive. Category two is the odd one. They tolerate you, but it's because they've decided you're an honorary man."

"What does that mean?"

"You'll know it when you see it. A lot of these men are very well mannered, so some of it is the absence of their manners. They do everything short of scratching their nuts in front of you. Oh my Lord, I forgot the bread!" She stood and retrieved a rectangular steel pan from the stovetop; when she cut pieces for both of us from the whole-wheat loaf, they were still warm.

I said, "I think maybe I've been an honorary man since I was in grade school, but I just didn't know what to call it. The first boy I ever had a crush on told me I was more like a boy than a girl."

Barbara laughed. "Well, thank goodness, because if he'd nabbed you, you'd never have ended up with Bill."

I had taken a bite of the bread, and when I swallowed it, I said, "This is delicious."

Barbara reached across the table, set her hand on top of mine, and said, "From the minute I met you at Dick and Ginny's house last year, I decided we'd be great friends. I'm so glad you're here."

Then, unexpectedly, in the middle of the night and at the age of forty-eight, Bill's stepfather, Jeff, died.

The phone rang at six-thirty in the morning, and when Bill answered, I heard him say, "Oh, Lord. Oh, Mother, I'm sorry." He began to cry. Jeff's cause of death turned out to be heart failure, related to his diabetes. His death made Virginia a widow for the third time.

Bill was scheduled to record three radio ads that day and to attend a chicken fry; he postponed the session at the studio and asked Lyle Metcalf to cancel his other meetings with the influential and not-so-influential men and women, but mostly men, of northwest Arkansas. By 8:00 A.M., Bill and I were on the road to Hot Springs, and by noon we were parking outside the house where Jeff had lived with Virginia and Roger, Bill's eighteen-year-old half brother; Roger was supposed to leave in just a few days for nearby Hendrix College. Inside the house, I hugged Roger then Virginia, and it was the first time Virginia and I had ever hugged. The kitchen was filled with Bill's extended family and friends, and the kitchen table was laden with food, plates of sliced ham and biscuits, and a pink Jell-O mold and an apple pie.

Immediately, Bill took charge of the logistics of Jeff's death, the cremation and funeral. Not for the first time, I was struck by how Bill's protective and solicitous manner toward his mother was, some might say, husband-like. After meeting her a few years earlier, I'd said to Bill that it wasn't that

I didn't like Virginia Dwire, or, more specifically, Virginia Cassidy Dell Blythe Clinton Dwire; it was that we had nothing in common except him. But the truth was that I also didn't like her. I found her manipulative and petty, theatrical and needy. Conveniently, given that it behooved all of us to conceal the natural animosity between Virginia and me, it **also** was true we had nothing in common except Bill.

When Virginia had visited New Haven in the spring of 1972, Bill and I had held a dinner in her honor at our apartment. We made stew, and I was setting out cheese and crackers before our friends arrived while Bill took a shower. Virginia looked me over from the sofa, where she was doing a crossword puzzle. "You're not wearing that when the guests come, are you?" she asked in a cheerful tone. I had on jeans and a paisley smock.

"I am," I said.

"Hillary, honey," she said in the same upbeat tone, "you aren't pretty enough not to make an effort."

As it happened, Virginia spent an inordinate amount of time beautifying herself, and her efforts led her in a direction I found actively unattractive. She dyed her hair black but kept a white skunk stripe going back from her forehead, and she wore heavy foundation, a great deal of mascara, false eyelashes, and bright lipstick. She loved jewelry and gaudy clothing, and she gave off an air of mischief. She knew how to enjoy herself, she wordlessly implied, while I was an uptight stiff. By contrast, the first time I'd met Jeff, which was when Bill and I traveled to Hot Springs together, he'd taken my cheeks in both his hands and said, as if directly rebutting Virginia's observation a few months prior, "Why, I think you have a real pretty face." I adored him immediately. I also felt a natural fondness for Roger, who was sweet and a little dopey.

Now Jeff had passed away and I lived in the same state as Virginia, and I understood, as she wept—both theatrically and, it seemed, sincerely—that there was nothing to be gained from acrimony with her. And seeing Bill's interactions with his mother, his solicitousness and patience, made me love him more. Plus, the way he was of Virginia but not **like** Virginia was proof of his specialness, his exceptionality. When he delivered Jeff's eulogy a few days later, I was struck, even there, by Bill's eloquence and handsomeness. Dozens of people had driven down from Fayetteville, though Bill had lived there only a year—law school students and professors, including Barbara and Ned Overholt; campaign staff and volunteers; the waitress at Bill's favorite diner. Bill could take care of his mother, I thought as he stood in the pulpit of the church, and I could take care of him. The timing of Jeff's death was a cosmic confirmation that I was where I should be.

• • •

In order to campaign full-time, Bill had taken a leave from the university. I, meanwhile, would be teaching Criminal Law and Trial Advocacy, and running the legal aid clinic. Classes started the Tuesday after Labor Day, and Trial Advocacy, in which forty students were enrolled, met first. That morning, I was surprised by how nervous I was—though I usually ate cereal for breakfast, I put down my spoon after two bites, my stomach balking—and, ten minutes before class, I hurried from my law school office on the fourth floor to the women's bathroom on the first floor and had diarrhea. As I washed my hands afterward, I looked at my reflection in the mirror; I had bought the same skirt suit in navy, gray, and black, and I wore the black one, with my hair pulled into a tight bun. I thought, but did not say aloud, **You're more than capable of teaching this class. Just be focused and respectful. It's fine if they don't like you right away. You have a full semester to earn their trust.**

The classroom had three rows of horseshoe-shaped tables, and I stood at the top center of the U, at a desk on which sat a tabletop lectern; a chalkboard hung on the wall behind me. In addition to writing my syllabus, I had typed the words I'd say to introduce myself and greet the students, and I'd estimated how long this and other segments of the class would take:

10:38–10:41 welcome & my background

10:42–11:07 discuss Trial Advocacy & go over syllabus etc., etc.

About half of the students were present when I entered the classroom, and as the rest filtered in, I saw that most looked about my age or a little older; three of the forty were black, and the rest were white. At least 80 percent of them were male, which I had inferred from the class list.

"Hello," I said. "I'm your professor, Hillary Rodham, and this is Trial Advocacy. I'm very much looking forward to this semester. Before joining the law faculty of the University of Arkansas, I worked as an attorney for the U.S. House Judiciary Committee's impeachment inquiry of Richard Nixon. Prior to that, I was the assistant director of public policy for the National Children's Initiative, which is a child advocacy nonprofit affiliated with Yale University. I'm a graduate of Yale Law School. My areas of specialization are civil rights, family law, and juvenile justice. As I'm sure you all realize, trials are at the heart of our judicial system, which is just one of the reasons this course will be relevant to any kind of law you ultimately pursue. I want to start today by distributing my syllabus and going over my expectations then I'll have all of you introduce yourselves."

I walked from the lectern to the three aisle seats on the right side of the horseshoe-shaped tables and handed a stack of syllabi to the students sitting there. As I returned to the lectern, I heard a murmuring that stopped when I began speaking again.

"Let's start on the first page," I said. "Attendance is mandatory." This was egregiously hypocritical—if I hadn't skipped law school classes as often as Bill, I'd still missed plenty—but I planned to compensate for my youth and gender by being strict.

The syllabus was ten pages, and when we'd reached the end, I said, "I'd like you all to take out a sheet of paper and write the following, which you'll read out loud before I collect them."

I picked up a piece of chalk and wrote on the board:

- **Name**
- **Hometown**
- **Undergraduate major**
- **Work experience**
- **Reason for attending law school**

Again, a murmuring arose. When I turned around, I made eye contact with a young woman in the first row, who was looking at me intently and unsmilingly. She patted her left hip three times, which struck me as a peculiar gesture. I gave the students three minutes, then they went one by one reading their responses. All but one of them were from Arkansas, and that person was from Tulsa, Oklahoma.

I proceeded to memorize all their names using a method Bill had recommended: I started on one side of the last row, said the person's name aloud three times—"Charles Shaheen, Charles Shaheen, Charles Shaheen"—then I went on to the next person and did the same—"Howard Bisgard, Howard Bisgard, Howard Bisgard"—then I said, "Charles Shaheen. Howard Bisgard." I repeated the pattern until I'd reached the young woman in the first row—Harriet Early—and had recited the first and last names of all forty of them. "Now just promise you'll all wear exactly the same thing every day from now until December," I said. No one laughed, and I said, "I'm joking. We're finished for today."

As they passed the pieces of paper to me, a high proportion of the students hardly made eye contact, which was unsettling. I thought the class had gone well, and I wondered if, simply due to being a woman and a Northerner, I seemed to them as strange as a Martian. The final person to pass over her paper was Harriet Early, the woman in the front row. By this point, the classroom was nearly empty.

"Professor Rodham," she said, "I'm sorry, but I wanted to tell you your skirt—" Again, she patted her hip three times, and while the gesture was imprecise—she meant buttocks, not hip—I understood this time. Horrifyingly, I understood.

I reached around and, though I couldn't see it, I could feel it. After I'd used the bathroom before class, I had tucked the back of my skirt into my pantyhose. I had just taught my first class, in its entirety, with my underwear and upper thighs exposed. "Oh, God," I said.

Harriet winced, but sympathetically. She said, "I didn't know how to say it before."

I went immediately to Barbara's office. I said, "Something so embarrassing happened that I might need to leave the state of Arkansas and never return."

"This sounds good."

After I'd told her, I added, "The **Venus of Willendorf** has nothing on me in showing off her womanly figure."

Already, I was half as distressed as I'd been before arriving in her office, and wasn't this the alchemy of friendship, to mutually transform the humiliation of life into private jokes? Barbara said, "Once when I was teaching Civil Procedure, I went to sit down during a student presentation and missed the seat. Apart from the mortification, it hurt so badly, I thought I'd broken my tailbone. I nearly burst into tears."

"That sounds awful."

"Welcome to the club."

"Should I say something in the next class?"

"It meets again Thursday?"

I nodded. "The irony is that I've been so concerned about them taking me seriously and showing me respect as a woman." I closed my eyes and pressed my hands over them. "Do you ever wish you could just excise a chunk of your brain?"

"Once a day," Barbara said. "At least. I don't think I'd say anything on Thursday. They may have forgotten by then."

When I told Bill that night, he said, "And here I like to think I'm the only one who gets to see your beautiful bottom."

"I still can't believe that I couldn't feel that my skirt was bunched up."

"Remember when you told me Mark Twain said bravery isn't the absence of fear, it's the mastery of fear?" We were eating potato chips at 10:00 P.M. on the secondhand sofa in my apartment. Bill took my hand and squeezed it. "Maybe life isn't about the absence of embarrassment, it's about the mastery of embarrassment."

On Thursday, I entered the classroom for Trial Advocacy after having stood in my office and run my palms over the back of my skirt no less than eight times. I said, "Hello, everyone. We'll be talking about chapter one in your casebook today, but first I understand there was a little awkwardness on the first day of class. I trust that's now **behind** us." I paused and smiled, pretending I was as charming as Bill, and the odd part was that I could feel it working. Or at least several of them smiled back at me. I said, "Now onward."

I had steeled myself for culture shock, and certainly there was some. The tradition of calling the hogs at the Razorbacks football games made me feel like a visiting anthropologist, and I was constantly reminded of the smallness of the town—the cashier at Chouteau's Market announced as I was paying for cereal and frozen vegetables that her nephew was one of my students, and when I went to open a bank account, the teller told me that his ex-wife lived in my apartment building. Quickly, I developed the habit of looking over one shoulder before discussing anything sensitive in public.

But I liked the quirkiness of Fayetteville—it was an artistic and progressive mecca within the state, and far less influenced then than it would eventually be by the nearby presences of Tyson Foods and Walmart—and the natural beauty of the rural areas was remarkable, especially in late summer and early fall. Highway 23, which Bill and I routinely rode along as he campaigned, was known as the Pig Trail. This less-than-beautiful name notwithstanding, the road curved among dense trees whose leaves turned, during my first weeks and months in the state, from bright green to vivid yellow, orange, and red, the foliage opening at intervals to reveal dazzling vistas of the Ozarks. I also was charmed by the small towns, their awnings over shops and restaurants, their fountains and elegant banks and churches.

Even with preparing for classes, holding office hours, and running the legal aid clinic, I had plenty of time to campaign for Bill. Though I'd been a believer on past campaigns, it was different to work to earn votes for him. When I knocked on doors, I never identified myself as his girlfriend, but I'd beam when people already knew who he was and praised him. And I loved hearing his stories after he'd spent a day traveling around the district and meeting voters: Once while he was going door-to-door in the town of Harrison, a woman noticed his shirt was missing a button and sewed one of hers on right there in her living room. Another time, he entered a barbershop to shake hands and emerged with a haircut.

One evening, as I drove to Barbara Overholt's house to have a glass of wine, I thought to myself that when Bill and I bought a home, we ought to live in the same historic neighborhood where she did. I then realized the implications of this thought, but I wasn't bothered; I felt a stirring of excitement. How curious it was that most people who knew me assumed my move to Arkansas was a narrowing of my world when I was experiencing it as an expansion. But I also understood this assumption because I once had shared it.

Sometimes on weekends, Bill's mother drove up from Hot Springs, often with a friend or two, to volunteer at his campaign headquarters, which was in a one-story house he'd rented near campus; Bill and a friend had painted CLINTON FOR CONGRESS in red and blue paint on the outside of the house. Virginia and the other women would put together yard signs or would phone bank, usually while playing a radio station that featured Elvis Presley songs in heavy rotation. Whenever Bill stopped by, he'd heap praise and affection on his mother, and though she still was clearly grieving Jeff, Virginia would beam.

On a Saturday morning in early October, I entered the headquarters with him to find Virginia, her friend Judy, and a dozen other volunteers stuffing envelopes at the folding tables and chairs set up in the house's living room, dining room, and sole bedroom. A spontaneous cheer arose, and the volunteers clustered in the living room, where Bill greeted everyone individually, hugging and thanking them. I kept looking at my watch—it was after nine, and we were due at eleven at a harvest parade in Boone County.

We finally extricated ourselves and were standing

in the driveway, along with a sophomore named George who'd be driving us that day, when Judy reappeared and said to Bill, "I almost forgot." She passed him a brown paper lunch bag, then puckered her lips. He obediently bent for her to kiss his cheek, and she said, "Drive safely, darlin'."

George drove a Chevy pickup, and I sat in the truck's second row. We were still on College Avenue when I said, "What's in the bag?"

"Just a little present from an ardent fan in Hot Springs." Bill chuckled strangely.

I'd imagined he'd say that it was biscuits or cinnamon rolls. I said, "It's not money, is it?"

From the front passenger seat, Bill turned around and smiled. "Is that a question you do or don't want to know the answer to?"

I leaned forward and grabbed the bag off his lap. When I unfolded the top, I saw many—probably hundreds of—twenty-dollar bills. "What the hell is this?" I said.

"Do you remember meeting Dickie Kinnaman? He's a close friend of Judy's who's made a killing at the racetrack, and he hates Hammerschmidt. He told her to tell me to use it as I see fit in Sebastian County." Bill glanced at George, who was impassive.

I was genuinely stunned. "You can't mean you're planning to buy votes."

"I'm shocked—**shocked**—to find that gambling is going on in here!" Bill said in his best Claude Rains accent. In his normal voice, he added, "I'm not planning to do anything with it besides hand it off to my guy in Forth Smith. What he does with it is up to him." Bill glanced once more at George before saying to me, "You do know that Sebastian County is the biggest, most conservative, and most corrupt county in the district?"

"My God, Bill!" I said. "This is a terrible, terrible idea."

"Then we won't do it. Calm down, baby."

"What are you thinking?"

"What am I thinking?" Bill repeated. "I'm thinking that I'm an Arkansas good ol' boy who wants to win."

For the first time, George reacted, but not by saying anything. He reacted by laughing.

The parade was just a few blocks long, and instead of walking in it with Bill, waving at spectators and handing out flyers, I spent the entirety, as floats passed and a marching band vigorously played John Philip Sousa, standing on a street corner talking to Lyle Metcalf. Lyle was in his late thirties, a bald, slender, married lawyer, and a man of few words who clearly had Bill's respect. He ran his own law practice, and Bill had told me that Lyle went to the office at 6:00 A.M., worked ceaselessly for three hours on his client business, then spent the rest of the day on campaign duties.

"Did you know about this?" I asked.

"No," Lyle said.

"Does Jim?" Jim was the campaign treasurer.

"I can't speak for him."

"This could destroy Bill's campaign," I said.

"Unlikely," Lyle said.

How were intelligent men blind to the damage they could sow? "It's unacceptable," I said. "It can't happen, and it's not going to. Do you hear me?"

Lyle smiled, and his smile was reptilian. "Have you told Bill that?"

We were headed next to a sale barn—a farmer's market, flea market, and livestock auction rolled into one—and I said, "I'll tell him in the car."

When I did, Bill acted as if he were a little boy, and I was scolding him for sneaking extra cookies from the cookie jar.

"Fine," he kept saying as we arrived at the sale barn and climbed from George's truck. "Fine. Can we stop talking about it?" And then Bill had walked away and was shaking hands with a farmer who'd grown a seventy-five-pound watermelon.

One Friday in October, when Bill had gone overnight to an AFL-CIO event down in Hot Springs, Barbara and I went together to hear jazz in Walker Park. That afternoon, I'd received a letter from my friend Maureen in Park Ridge saying she and her husband Steve—he worked at LaSalle Bank, and they had married in the spring of '73—were expecting their first baby.

Barbara had brought a blanket, cheese, and crackers, and I'd brought a chilled bottle of wine, a bottle opener, and two paper cups. As I poured, and the ensemble down the hill played a Dizzy Gillespie song, I said, "Can I ask you a question?"

"Of course."

My voice was far more tentative than usual—with Barbara or in general—as I said, "I suspect you know that Bill can be flirtatious with women."

"Ah," Barbara said, "I was wondering when we'd discuss this."

"When he and I are together, I feel very confident in our relationship, that what we have is real. But when we're apart—well, I'm not even sure what he does when we're apart." After our agreement on the shore of Ennerdale Water to date other people, the only follow-up had been a year later, during a midnight phone conversation when I confirmed I'd join him in Arkansas as soon as the impeachment inquiry wrapped up. I'd said, "If there are other women—" then I'd started over. "If I'm moving there, there can't be other women."

"You have my word," he'd said.

During the previous year, there had not, for me, been other men. One of my colleagues on the impeachment inquiry was a recent graduate of

Columbia Law School named Roland Osborne, a quick-witted guy on whom I might have had a crush if Bill weren't my boyfriend. Would that crush have been reciprocated or, as with the others, unrequited? The question was irrelevant because Roland was pleasant, and Bill was a meteor. Roland was a version of other people I knew, and Bill was unique.

But I did not pretend to myself that Bill had been similarly impervious. During those early weeks in Fayetteville, the women he'd probably touched, kissed, and then some in my absence were often spectral—I knew they walked these streets, perhaps this campus, even if I couldn't pinpoint who they were—and sometimes vividly corporeal. Any young, attractive woman who attended one of his events and seemed to already know him caught my attention.

I said to Barbara, "Do people think I'm a fool?"

She made a dismissive sound. "Who are **people**? There's no monolithic opinion. Though don't forget I got divorced when my kids were in grade school, so I'm used to ignoring gossip. But I think people understand perfectly why you're dating him."

"He proposed to me about a year ago, and I said I needed more time."

We both were quiet—the song ended, and the audience clapped—and as a new composition started, she said, "If I'd known the things that I know now about marriage when I was your age, my head would have popped off. I had such a conventional idea of how it all worked—that you said 'I do' to a man and loved each other forevermore. Back then, you had to get married in order to have sex so I guess it's no surprise lots of marriages of my generation have failed."

"Do you think infidelity doesn't matter?"

"If he's your husband, you decide what matters. Besides, men aren't the only ones who can be unfaithful." I absorbed this, wondering if she was referring to herself, and she said, "Ned and I—and keep in mind this is the marriage I've stayed in, not the one I left—we've had good weeks and bad weeks, but we've also had good years and bad years. At some point, your spouse will absolutely make you angry and absolutely drive you crazy. Those are givens. I would never be so bold as to tell you what to do, but it seems to me you and Bill have something special, in addition to facing the universal ups and downs—that you find each other interesting, that you're intellectual equals. Those qualities would be hard for both of you to find in someone else. The excitement of sex comes and goes, no pun intended, but great conversations make life worth living. Don't they?"

Her advice mattered because Barbara filled a similar role to the one Gwen had occupied for me; her open-mindedness balanced out Gwen's opprobrium.

"There are two kinds of marriages," Barbara said.

"The ones where you're privy to how messy they are, and the ones where you're not."

The **Arkansas Gazette,** which had by this point endorsed Bill, hosted a debate between him and Hammerschmidt just a week before the election. I caught a ride home with the Overholts and Ginny Richards, who was the wife of the law school dean; Bill was driving to Clarksville for a prayer breakfast the next morning. When I'd hugged him goodbye in the parking lot, I'd said, "Please get some sleep." He was averaging three or four hours a night, fueled by caffeine and euphoria.

He had done an excellent job in the debate, focusing on real problems and legislative solutions yet still seeming upbeat while Hammerschmidt chose to disparage him personally. At various moments, Hammerschmidt had implied that Bill's fancy education and years away meant he no longer understood the state; that he was too young to lead; and, most preposterously, that in a 1969 newspaper photo of a man protesting Nixon's visit to an Arkansas football game by sitting in a tree, the man was Bill. Bill had laughed at this accusation, explaining that he'd been at Oxford at the time the photo was taken, which may have been the trap Hammerschmidt was laying. Still, I thought Bill had performed superbly.

Afterward, as I sat with Ginny in the back of

Ned Overholt's Cadillac, Ginny said, "When people say Bill will be president someday, I really and truly believe it."

"I'm worried about this race," Barbara said, "but there's no question that the sky's the limit for him in the long run."

Ginny was smoking a Pall Mall as she said, "Hillary, you must think he'll be president."

Surely it was a sign of Bill's influence that, though I was among the people I was closest to in Fayetteville, I still said, "Oh, I'm sure he'll serve in whatever capacity he's needed most."

The cupboards in both Bill's house and my apartment had been empty for weeks when I decided on the Sunday evening prior to the election to make a quick stop at Chouteau's Market. The store would close at six, and I arrived at five-fifty and hurried through the aisles. Near the cereal shelf, I became aware of a woman watching me. I made eye contact with her and smiled, but the woman quickly turned her head and pushed her grocery cart away. A few minutes later, when I was back in the parking lot and setting my two paper bags in the trunk of my car, I heard a high, hesitant female voice say, "Miss Hillary."

When I turned, I saw the same woman. Though I'd purposely parked by a light pole, it was a dark night and the parking lot was mostly empty. I felt a wariness, a wish to already be in my car with all the doors closed. Still, I was not prepared for what came next. The woman said, "I need to tell you something about Bill Clinton."

She was probably a little older than I was—in her early thirties, I'd have guessed—and pretty. Definitely, for Bill, pretty enough. I felt a familiar exhaustion. This again. But it wasn't this.

In her Arkansas accent, which struck me as thick even though I'd become accustomed to Arkansas accents, she said, "He forced himself on me. I was volunteering for him, and we were alone one night at the headquarters, back in April. When he started kissing my neck, I told him no, no, no, but he forced himself on me."

Some instinct kicked in, a shift from girlfriend to lawyer, and I said, "What's your name?"

She shook her head. "I'm a married woman with two babies. I don't want my private business out there."

I said, "I think you're confusing Bill with someone else."

Her expression became indignant. She lowered her voice but repeated with even greater urgency, "He **forced** himself on me." Then she made a gesture I had not seen for many years, and certainly never from an adult woman; I associated the gesture with junior high. The woman bent her right thumb and pointer finger into a circle and jabbed her left pointer finger three times through the circle's hole.

"I didn't go to the police." She pronounced it, as I'd heard other Arkansans do, **po-leece**. "I didn't think anything would happen except embarrassment." She looked intensely at me and said, "But I thought **you'd** want to know."

Bill and I spent that night in town, at my apartment, but he got in so late, well after midnight, that in spite of my distress, I'd fallen asleep. When I woke around five, he was lying on his back, breathing deeply in the still-dark dawn, and I felt almost certain that I wouldn't say anything before the election. How could I, in the final forty hours, when he was barely sleeping, jubilant and dejected by turns depending on the minute?

He woke at six, showered, and left for headquarters, and a few minutes later, I called Lyle Metcalf. Even though my understanding was that he arrived at his office this early, I still was surprised when he picked up. I said, "I need your advice about something extremely sensitive." When he didn't respond, I said, "It's confidential."

"Okay," he said.

I had learned in my work for the National Children's Initiative that painful topics were not improved upon by preemptive handwringing or by sugarcoating. I said, "A woman approached me in the parking lot of Chouteau's Market last night and said Bill—these were her words—forced himself on her in April at the campaign headquarters. She wouldn't tell me her name, and she said she didn't go to the police, that she just thought I'd want to know."

Lyle was silent.

I added, "I don't think we should say anything to Bill before the election, but I just—"

"Of course you shouldn't say anything to Bill," he said.

"Obviously, she could have all kinds of motives, whether she's acting on Hammerschmidt's behalf or it's extortion or she had a crush on Bill. She said she was a volunteer. My fear is that something could end up in the paper tomorrow, or after the election."

"It's bullshit," Lyle said. My relationship with him had never been warm, but for once, Lyle's lack of emotion was reassuring.

I said, "You don't think there's anything to do?"

"It costs a person nothing to make an accusation, refuse to tell you who they are, and walk away."

The following night, Bill lost to Hammerschmidt by 6,000 votes out of 170,000. We watched the returns at campaign headquarters, and the torturous part was that for most of the night, Bill was in the lead and victory seemed possible. Even though we knew that Sebastian County would be the last to report, it was impossible not to hope. As the night wore on, two thirds of the original seventy or so people who'd crowded into the headquarters departed, and when the Sebastian County results came in around midnight, officially reelecting Hammerschmidt, Bill gave a speech about his appreciation for the energy and devotion of his supporters. He said this was just the beginning and his passion for helping people in Arkansas was undiminished. Like other supporters, Virginia and Roger both wept openly, though it was only from Virginia's eyes that a profusion of mascara ran.

I could feel how Bill's graciousness was a limited resource, how I needed to get him out of there so he could vent and moan. I also could feel how eventually—probably not on this night, but at some point—he would need to point out that if not for my high-mindedness about the bag of money, he'd have won.

Between November 6 and Thanksgiving, Bill hardly got out of bed. I had seen his moods fluctuate before, including when McGovern had lost, but this was an entirely different level of discouragement, a ruminating anger. He barely bathed, and, unprecedentedly, he didn't initiate sex. Sometimes he made lists of things to do, sometimes he read, sometimes he listened to the radio. When I entered the bedroom, he'd speak forcefully, as if we'd been midconversation. He'd say, "People can say what they want about the hubris of running for Congress at the age of twenty-eight, but I'll tell you what—unlike Hammerschmidt, I actually give a damn about the future of Arkansas." He'd say, "It's hard to believe so many voters are stupid enough to really think it was me sitting in that fucking tree." Later, a large stash of Bill's campaign postcards was found mildewing behind a post office, a development that might have set him back emotionally if he'd made any progress. About that, he said, "See, that's the problem with playing clean when the other guy plays dirty." This was as close as he'd yet come to censuring me, but still, I braced myself.

Sometimes his dissatisfaction widened from his electoral results, showing a more generalized bitterness I hadn't observed in him in almost four years together. He'd say, "It's like my family just can't catch a break. What woman besides Mother can you think of who's lost three husbands by the age of fifty?" He wasn't wrong that he and his family members had experienced inordinate loss, and I'd say, "I know, baby. I'm sorry."

To his complaints about the election, I tried to respond with logic. "You came so close. You got so many more votes than anyone could have expected. People here love you."

"The fact that I lost means you're stuck here." Was this a test on his part or an apology?

"Well, I don't feel stuck," I said.

It wasn't exactly a decision, that first I hadn't told Bill about the woman in Chouteau's parking lot because I didn't want to destabilize him before the election; then I hadn't because he was devastated by losing; and after that I hadn't because he was improving, but his improvement remained so tenuous.

It also was the case that I hadn't mentioned it because it was awful to consider. And because frankly her accusation seemed to matter far less than it would have if he'd won.

We spent Christmas in Hot Springs, and after dinner on the twenty-sixth, a bunch of Bill's elementary and high school friends came over and sat in Virginia's living room, chatting boisterously. Bill told a long, high-spirited story about a voter he'd met in Springdale who he guessed was seventy years old and weighed four hundred pounds and who proudly told Bill that once a month, he ordered eleven roses from the florist in town and had them delivered to himself along with a card that read, **You're the twelfth.** When the room exploded with laughter, including from Bill, I understood that he was mostly back to normal.

That night, Virginia was in and out of the room, refilling glasses and the dishes of nuts and trays of cookies on the table. It was clear that she adored Bill's friends and that the affection was mutual. In that moment of group laughter, she and I made eye contact, and we smiled at each other.

Another sign of Bill's improvement was that he wanted to have sex again, which I first welcomed and soon found burdensome. He'd consistently had a higher sex drive than I did, but in the past it hadn't been difficult for him to get me interested. Maybe it was because I now feared he'd pout or revert to self-pity if I refused—maybe the feeling of obligation was an anti-aphrodisiac—but more than once in that late winter and spring, I found myself lying underneath him, his erection inside me and his scrotum bumping against the lowest part of my bottom, waiting for the episode to be finished; of course this either made it take longer or just feel like it was taking longer.

On Valentine's Day, his alarm went off, waking us both, and he turned toward me and said, "I don't suppose you'd like to get married today?"

I laughed. "I do want to but not today." For a few seconds, I was afraid he'd get angry, that the joke wasn't a joke. I set one hand against his cheek. "I want my mother to be there," I said.

"Fair enough," he said. He kissed my fingers. "When you change your mind, be sure to tell me."

Harriet Early, the brave student who'd told me my skirt was stuffed into my pantyhose, had ended up working for course credit at the legal aid clinic that I ran. Harriet was a bright and industrious twenty-two-year-old from Conway, Arkansas, and one afternoon at the clinic, which was in a room next door to the new student radio station, she and I were discussing a case involving a nineteen-year-old mother of two who'd filed for divorce from her violent forty-year-old husband.

Harriet said, "When I meet with Brenda, I always wonder if there'd be a way to hold classes for young mothers who dropped out of high school. Not degree-granting but to give them practical skills, and at the same time, when they testify, they can refer to that."

I said, "I take it you're envisioning classes that aren't specifically prenatal."

"No, more like home ec—cooking, health, budgeting."

"And it'd be a one-time thing or ongoing?"

"Ongoing. Maybe weekly?"

"If it was on a Saturday, that would certainly increase the chances someone else could look after the women's children." I reached for a pen. "There's a professor named Jacqueline Walsh in the College of Education, and I want to run this by her. I'd be curious if any education students would consider teaching it."

"A girl at my high school got pregnant when we were seniors, and they made her leave even though the baby didn't come until the summer," Harriet said. "It seemed like such a waste."

"Can you get numbers about how many girls under eighteen give birth every year in this county? I'll check how many have been referred to us at the clinic."

"I just want to say—" Harriet smiled sheepishly. "It's good you came to the law school, because I would have been embarrassed to bring this up with a man."

During spring break, Bill and I house-sat for Dick and Ginny, the law school dean and his wife, who lived in an immaculate Craftsman that had a hot tub on the deck. The weather was warming, but the nights were still cool, in the fifties, and it was a new pleasure to me to walk outside from the kitchen into the dark backyard in nothing but a towel, set it aside, and sink into the warm bubbling water. The first time we did this, Bill grinned and said, "It's like we're ingredients in a soup." He kissed me on the lips and added, "Haven't I always said how delicious you are?"

When it quickly became apparent that we were about to have sex, I said, "Is this hygienic? And is it okay with the Richardses?"

Bill laughed. "I'm sure they'd be disappointed if we didn't."

We repeated the pattern every night for a week, except for Saturday, when we were joined by a few other young professors. On that night, we all drank a lot of beer, played charades, and wore swimsuits in the hot tub, though I'm sure Bill and several guests would have been just fine skinny-dipping. In the presence of our friends, I kept noticing, as I hadn't for a while, how handsome Bill was; I kept thinking that it was fun to have guests but that I also wanted him to myself.

It was well after midnight when they left, and we decided to clean up in the morning. We were sleeping in a guest room rather than in our boss's bed, but the guest bed was still queen-sized and nicer than what either Bill or I owned. Under the covers, I snuggled against him, and I thought that, although I'd had my doubts, my life in Arkansas was rich and full and, because of Bill, adventurous. I liked that I was on a path I hadn't predicted.

"Baby," I said, and Bill stirred. "You should run for attorney general."

There were two things about the AG race that differentiated it from Bill's congressional race. The first thing was that the job meant being in the state of Arkansas full-time; indeed, it likely meant moving to Little Rock, which was three hours away. The second thing was that if he ran, Bill would probably win.

In mid-April, my mother called to tell me that Maureen had given birth to a healthy baby boy and that they were naming him Stephen Andrew Rymarcsuk, Jr. I immediately purchased a Razorbacks plush toy from the university bookstore and mailed it off, along with a note of congratulations. When Maureen called a few days later and asked if I'd be the godmother, I was touched.

"What's motherhood like?" I asked.

"More undignified than you can possibly imagine in your wildest dreams. For Stevie and for me."

"Are you exhausted?"

"Yes."

"Can I do anything for you?"

"Flatten my stomach, make my nipples stop dripping, and make this weird little creature stop crying."

"Oh, Maureen," I said. "I don't think this part lasts long."

The christening at which my godmother status would be made official would happen in late May, and a few days later, as I was dialing the number for Delta to make my reservation, it occurred to me that as long as I was getting on a plane, I ought to go to the East Coast, too. I'd received a postcard from an impeachment inquiry colleague mentioning that a group of attorneys were having a reunion dinner in Georgetown in early June. I hung up the phone without talking to a reservation agent and looked at the calendar that hung above my desk. First Chicago, I thought, then Washington, D.C., for the dinner, then maybe Boston to see Phyllis and her husband and New Haven to see Gwen and Richard. As I looked at the calendar grid for May 1975, I understood with a jolt that I was retracing my past in order to arrive at my future and that when I returned to Fayetteville, I would tell Bill I was ready to marry him. And once I told him, I thought, we wouldn't wait long. What would the point be? We didn't want a fancy ceremony; we were ready to get on with the rest of our lives. I thought of how happy he'd look—I knew just the expression he'd make, the slight smile broadening into a huge smile, that light and intelligence that was always in his eyes trained on me—and sitting there in my office, I teared up. Finally, enough time had passed, enough testing of the waters. Finally, I was sure.

In Chicago, my father told me I looked good since I'd put on all that weight, my mother and I discussed Lucretius's **On the Nature of Things**—she was taking another philosophy course—and my brother Hughie teased me that I'd developed a Southern accent. At the christening, Maureen's son, Stevie, wore a white lace gown with a three-foot train and howled through the entire ceremony. Afterward, Maureen said, "Now that you seem so happy, I can tell you that I thought you were crazy moving to Fayetteville."

I laughed. "You weren't the only one."

In Washington, the reunion dinner was loud and festive, and an attorney's wife had made so-called Watergate salad, which featured pistachio pudding mix, crushed pineapple, and marshmallows. A lawyer I'd never known well said with obvious surprise, "You're teaching at the University of **Arkansas**?"

"I am," I said. "And I've had a terrific first year."

"My sister just graduated from Harvard Law, and she told me most of the top law schools have a mandate to hire women professors," he said. "She's been recruited by a few places, including Northwestern. Aren't you from Chicago?"

I had wondered if I'd feel jealous of my former colleagues, almost all of whom were working on Capitol Hill or for big firms, and I didn't. "I'm not looking for another job," I said.

In Boston, my Wellesley friend Nancy revealed that she was pregnant and due in October. She said, "Is it too much to ask you to get pregnant, too, so our kids can be friends?"

"Nothing's official yet," I said, "but I don't think it'll be long for Bill and me."

In New Haven, Richard Greenberger requested that I demonstrate calling the hogs—I complied, and Otto and Marcus immediately began imitating me—and I had the feeling that Gwen had decided that if she didn't have anything nice to say about Bill, she wouldn't say anything. In their kitchen, we ate breakfast for dinner, pancakes and bacon and stewed apples. Otto took several bites of his pancake then pushed his plate toward me and said, "What state does it look like?"

I scrutinized the remaining pancake before saying, "Idaho."

Gwen took off work on a Friday morning to drive me to the airport in Hartford. We were just a few minutes from the airport exit when she said with forced brightness, "How is the neck kisser?" She glanced at me, and I suspect I looked confused, because she quickly added, "Do you remember after your first date, when you asked me if it was unusual for a man to kiss you on the neck instead of the mouth? I always thought it was cute how worked up you were that night."

I made myself smile, and I said Bill was doing well, that he was popular with his students. I didn't mention his AG run. But the uneasiness spreading inside me—I could barely conceal it for those last few minutes in Gwen's car, or as I hugged her and entered the airport. I checked my suitcase and walked to my gate, and I was trembling and nauseated. In the last seven months, I hadn't admitted it to myself; I had buried it, though, it turned out, not permanently. But I believed that something had happened between Bill and the woman in Chouteau's parking lot. And the reason I believed it was that she'd said he'd kissed her neck.

On the way to pick me up, Bill had passed a house on California Boulevard that he knew with such certainty we should buy that he used a pay phone inside the airport to call the real estate agent listed on the yard sign. After he'd hung up, he said, "She can show it to us in half an hour."

We drove directly there, and he parked on the street. The house was very small but pretty, a brick Tudor near campus. Before we climbed from the car, I said, "There's something I need to talk to you about."

He must have recognized my unusual tone, because he looked at me with apprehension.

"Last November, right before the election, a woman approached me in the parking lot of Chouteau's Market and said she'd been a volunteer for your campaign and that you'd"—I hesitated but only for a split second—"forced yourself on her."

Immediately, he said, "That didn't happen."

"She said it was in April—April of '74, obviously."

"Did you hear me? I just said it never happened." He seemed irritated, which was mildly reassuring.

"Do you know who I'm talking about?"

"How the hell would I know who made a false accusation against me? Once you run for office, you're a public figure. Anyone can say anything. I just can't believe that you think I'm capable of this."

"I didn't say that."

"But you've been mulling it over for the last six months. Jesus Christ, Hillary."

A part of me felt the impulse to soothe him. But we needed to get to the other side of this by walking through it. I said, "Did you ever have sex with anyone at the headquarters?"

He bit his lip, and I could tell he was moving from irritation to anger. I understood the question I should have asked instead. I said, "How many women did you have sex with at the headquarters?"

"I wasn't the one who wanted to spend a year apart," he said.

"Do you know why I suggested dating other people?" I realized as I spoke that this was true. "Because I knew you'd screw around, and this way we could both pretend I was all right with it."

He glared at me. "What's the point of all this? If you can't trust me, what are we doing?"

"If I can't trust you," I repeated, and I could hear my voice rising, "it's because you've done everything short of taking out a billboard telling me not to. You have no right to act like I'm paranoid when you're the one who betrayed me. I move to fucking

Fayetteville for you, and you can't even keep your pants zipped."

There was something horrifying and refreshing in this bluntness. Since Berkeley, we had only talked around the subject of infidelity.

He said, "It's interesting that you're so sure you're not the problem when plenty of people would think it's your expectations of me that are absurd. Kennedy had liaisons. LBJ had liaisons. Everyone knew it and just turned a blind eye. Maybe I'm a normal man, and it's your self-righteousness that's the problem."

"You're not normal," I said. "You're also not the president."

"And if you keep sabotaging me, I probably never will be." There it was, at long last—the allusion to the bribe money I'd prevented him from using.

"I sometimes question whether you have any ethical standards," I said. "I'm not sure you do."

"You know what you are?" he said. "You're a smug bitch who drives people away because you think you're smarter than everyone else. Of course you don't find it hard to be faithful when you don't have other options."

There was just enough truth in these accusations, or at least enough of our deepest and most private fears about ourselves, to truly sting. Neither of us spoke for close to a minute, then I looked over and said, "And you wonder why I don't want to marry you." I got out of the car and slammed the passenger-side door, and he drove away with my suitcase still in the trunk.

He knocked on the door of my apartment three hours later, and when I opened it, he said, "Hillary," and then his face contorted grotesquely and he was sobbing. He stepped into my apartment, took me in his arms, and held me tightly. I began sobbing, too. "I'm so sorry," he said.

"No," I said, "I'm so sorry."

He said, "If I don't have you, I have nothing."

We hugged and hugged and cried and cried and then we had glorious sex and when I was on top of him, sitting up, and both of us were close but not finished, I said, "I'll marry you. I want to marry you so badly. I love you so much."

He smiled in exactly the way I'd anticipated. He said, "Do you really mean it?"

I nodded.

"Oh, Hillary," he said. "Oh, baby." He pulled me toward him so that we were even closer, without space between us, as close as we could be.

In the middle of the night, he woke me by tapping my shoulder. It sometimes happened that while I was asleep, he'd rub my breasts or below my navel and at the slightest shifting toward him on my part, or when my breathing became ragged, he'd slide into me. But in those circumstances, we didn't speak, and on this night, he was saying my name, asking if I was listening. Finally, I said, "Yes. I'm listening."

"I've never, ever forced myself on a woman. Never."

"Okay."

"And I never would. But you shouldn't marry me. You should leave. I'll drag you down. The thing that's wrong with me is incurable. Do you hear me?"

My eyes had already filled with tears. "Yes," I said.

"In the morning, I'll try to talk you out of it, but what I'm telling you now is the truth. You know your rule about two reasons? One reason is you won't have the career you deserve here and the other is that the problems I have will never go away. When I try to convince you to stay, it's me being selfish. Us staying together is good for me and bad for you."

"Bill," I said. "Baby." But I couldn't say more, and it wasn't because I was too sleepy. It was because I was too sad.

What he'd said during the night was wrong in two ways. The first was that he didn't try talking me out of it in the morning. In the daylight, we treated each other soberly and gingerly. There was between us a careful energy that had never previously existed, an awkwardness, and this energy made me understand that an eventuality I had never truly considered could come to pass. I had never truly planned to break up with Bill because I wasn't capable of it; I just hadn't yet figured out how I'd justify his contradictions.

We drank coffee together and were reading **The Northwest Arkansas Times,** and he said, "I'm going to go home and shower because I have a meeting at ten with Norm Pulaski."

"You don't want to shower here?"

He shook his head. Before he left, he patted my shoulder, which was strangely heartbreaking.

In his absence, I looked around the apartment, which I'd furnished with a few other secondhand items besides the bed and sofa—a coffee table, a rocking chair. If I was going to leave, I needed to do so quickly. Almost immediately. **Now?** I thought. Then I thought, **Not now. Tomorrow morning.**

There was, of course, an alternative. I could call Barbara and ask if she was free to have a glass of wine that evening—it was a Saturday—and I could tell her about the woman in the parking lot and about Bill's warning, and she could help me find a way forward, a way to stay. Or I could pretend that I'd leave in several weeks, by the end of the summer, then not do it. I could escape very quickly, it seemed, or never, and I wanted to do both.

In a state of disbelief, I began packing. I was finished by noon, and because I hadn't eaten breakfast or lunch, I had a bowl of cereal. Was I supposed to call Bill? Was he supposed to call me? If he called, would he act like everything was normal? If he did, I doubted I'd have the strength to contradict him.

Another few hours passed, and I called his house, not expecting him to pick up, but he did. I said, "I'm leaving in the morning."

"Where will you go?" He sounded subdued, perhaps shakily so.

"I guess Washington or New Haven." There was a silence, and I said, "Do you want to get dinner?"

"Sure," he said.

When he came back to my apartment, he looked at the two suitcases by the door and the cardboard boxes I'd brought up from storage in the basement, and he bowed his head and exhaled deeply.

"Would you want to take over my lease?" I asked.

"Oh, God, no," he said. "Living here would be too painful."

As we walked to a barbecue restaurant, I wondered if I should hold his hand. I didn't reach for it. A half block from the restaurant, which appeared even from that distance to be crowded, he stopped and said, "I can't do this. I can't be around other people."

Back in my apartment, he lay on his side in the bed, his shoulders shaking. I spooned him, and we stayed like that through the night. Around four in the morning, we had sex. Was this the last time? How could it be the last time?

The second way he was wrong was that there were more than two reasons. The first reason was indeed Arkansas, and the second reason was indeed his compulsive infidelity. But he didn't seem to recognize that the infidelity gave rise to multiple other reasons. One was that cheating and political ambition were a risky, if apparently common, combination. Another was that already he'd been accused of assault. And the last reason was that he'd warned me. By my calculations, this added up to five, when all I'd ever required was two.

Yet even so, the margin between staying and leaving was so thin. Really, it could have gone either way. Sometimes I think that my years of diligent schoolwork and political idealism had given me the erroneous notion that if one choice, one plan, was hard and the other was easy, doing the hard thing was inherently better—worthier, more upstanding.

Until the moment on Sunday morning when my car was loaded, it all seemed like it might go the other way. It didn't seem possible we'd had sex for the last time, eaten a meal together for the last time, slept in the same bed for the last time. His voice was almost dispassionate as he said, "I can't believe I ruined this. You really are the best thing that ever happened to me."

"You're the best thing that ever happened to me," I said.

We both just stood there, facing each other, holding hands, by the driver's-side door of my Buick. In order to stay, I needed him to ask me to, to tell me to. And he had made the decision that, for my sake, he wouldn't.

"Oh, Hillary," he said, and his eyes welled.

It was unfathomable that we were hugging a final time, that I was climbing into the car, starting the engine. I was so stunned that I actually wasn't crying then, and when I got on the road, I experienced the profoundly strange wish to talk to Bill about having just broken up with Bill. Or maybe it wasn't surprising; Bill was the person I always wanted to talk to about everything.

Fayetteville was far enough north that I hit the Missouri border less than an hour later, and for some reason, this was when I began to cry. I cried in a way I haven't cried since and perhaps hadn't cried before except as a baby, heaving and wailing. I could hardly see out the windshield, but I was afraid to pull over because what if that led to turning around?

What was I doing? How, metaphysically speaking, was this possible? For twenty-three years, I had been myself, alone, and then I had become his and he'd become mine. And I did believe that for all his dalliances, he really had only ever been mine; he had never truly belonged to anyone else. Now that

I knew what it was to be adored by him, to blend my life with his, how could I live in the world not being the person Bill Clinton loved the most?

The margin between staying and leaving was so thin; really, it could have gone either way.

PART II

The Woman

CHAPTER 4

1991

I SOMETIMES KEPT PUBLIC RADIO on in the background while I worked, and, during a morning in late June 1991, as I was revising the fourth chapter of the casebook I was writing with a professor at another law school, I heard that Thurgood Marshall was about to hold a press conference; the news of Marshall's retirement from the Supreme Court had broken the previous day. I hurried into the hall and, because its door was open, knocked on the doorframe of the office next to mine. When my colleague James looked up from behind his desk, I said, "Do you get C-SPAN? Thurgood Marshall is going to speak."

Unlike me, James maintained a meticulously neat office, and also unlike me, he kept a small TV in it, on a table by the door. The only other object on the table was a gold-framed photograph.

As James stood, I said, "I hope I'm not interrupting." I didn't know him well. He'd joined the faculty of Northwestern's law school just a year before, and during that time, we'd interacted amiably but fleetingly.

"Come in," he said. "And yes, I do have C-SPAN."

But as he turned on the television, it occurred to me that I was unaware of his political leanings—James might not view Marshall's retirement as heartbreaking because of what an inspirational figure he was and also alarming because of who President Bush was likely to appoint in Marshall's stead. And, frankly, James dressed like a Republican. I had never, including on this day, seen him in anything other than a suit and tie. Such formality wasn't unusual during the school year but was rare among faculty who came to the office during the summer; in fact, coming to the office during the summer period was rare. On this ninety-degree Friday, I wore a short-sleeved blouse, a denim skirt, and sandals.

Onscreen, Marshall was entering a room in the Supreme Court Building, where he was greeted by sustained applause. As he crossed a maroon carpet, Marshall used a cane but walked steadily. "Just in time," James said to me. He moved two chairs that faced his desk—they were cheaply upholstered, with metal legs—so that they were facing the television, and gestured in a way that made me suspect he was a man who wouldn't sit first if a woman was present. Maybe he wasn't Republican but just very polite? Though, as anticipated by Barbara Overholt back in my University of Arkansas days, some of my colleagues who were probably chivalrous to women in social settings weren't particularly so around me due to my being an honorary man.

Marshall had taken a chair facing dozens or maybe hundreds of reporters. He wore tan plastic glasses, and his gray mustache was neat.

"How do you feel, Justice?" one of the reporters called out, and, deadpan, Marshall said, "With my hands." Raucous laughter and more clapping followed.

As other reporters shouted to him and cameras clicked audibly, Marshall was good-naturedly uncooperative. Among the topics he declined to comment on were pending legislation, the current state of civil rights, and the definition of patriotism. He blithely scowled and squinted, in the way of a man who either knows the audience is on his side, is past caring, or both.

"I can't imagine the court without him," I said.

"Have you seen the picture of him with Autherine Lucy after he won the case for her to go to the University of Alabama?" James asked.

"I don't think I have."

"It's from '55 or '56, when Marshall was with the NAACP. It's just one of those classic images where they all look very purposeful and brave. Not that my life has been like that, but it might have been the reason I became a lawyer."

James! I thought. **You're most certainly not a Republican!** I said, "It's always the pictures of Ruby Bridges that get to me—how young she was in her little dress, with her bookbag."

Onscreen, Marshall's chest rose and fell with what appeared to be labored breathing, and, alluding perhaps to this as well as to the health problems Marshall himself had mentioned at the opening of the press conference, a reporter asked, "What's wrong with you, sir?"

"I'm old," Marshall said. "I'm gettin' old and coming apart."

"Supposedly, he loves afternoon soap operas," I said. "One of my students clerked for him and said he watches them in his chambers."

James laughed. "I wouldn't have guessed that."

Marshall evaded a question about the future of school desegregation—"It's obvious I'm not going to have anything to do with it so why should I be commenting on it?"—and said he didn't know if he'd become involved in the civil rights movement again after retiring. Then a male who couldn't be seen onscreen said, "Thank you very much, Justice Marshall."

"Thank you, thank you," Marshall said—apparently, the press conference was finished—and he scooted to the edge of his chair. Two aides, or perhaps security agents, approached to remove his mic and help him stand, and when the camera pulled back, I said, "Oh, gosh. Look at his socks." They appeared to be white athletic socks, several inches of them visible below the cuffs of his pants.

James said, "I guess he's human after all?"

As Marshall left the room, I glanced at the framed photo next to James's TV, which I'd been glancing at intermittently during the press conference. The photo was probably six by eight inches and featured James; his wife, Susie, whom I'd met a few times in the last year, most recently at the law school dean's end-of-the-year potluck in May; and their son, David, who looked to be about ten. The three of them sat close together on a log with autumn foliage in the background, the adults flanking the boy. They all wore rugbies that were striped, though not matching, and they all smiled broadly.

I pointed to the photo. "So you **have** worn something other than a suit at least once?"

He laughed again. "Only under duress. That picture was a Christmas card, but it was taken so long ago that David is now in driver's ed. I know you don't have children, but do you—are you—" I could tell what he was trying to ask. Many people thought that my single status was akin to a sensitive medical condition. Finally, he said, "Is there a special someone?"

"There are lots of special people in my life," I said. "But I don't have a boyfriend." I stood. "Thanks for sharing your TV."

"I suppose the next thing we'll be watching is the announcement of his successor."

"I know Bush can't be trusted, but—" I held up a hand and crossed my fingers. "Hope springs eternal. I'm going to D.C. next week to see my friend Gwen, who's very well connected. If he's considering anyone in the black legal community, she'll know."

"Keep me posted," James said, and even though the selection of the next Supreme Court nominee was a highly rarefied form of gossip, I thought then how endearing a gossipy man was.

I didn't realize at the time that we'd already learned the name of Bush's pick. Midway through the press conference, as Marshall kept emphasizing that the decision was up to the president, one of the reporters had asked, "What do you think about the discussions of having Clarence Thomas as the person to succeed you?"

Impatiently, Marshall had said, "I think the president knows what he's doing and he's going to do it."

As another reporter had asked another question, I'd said, "Who's Clarence Thomas?"

• • •

That weekend, at my parents' condominium, my father drew a G from the bag of Scrabble tiles, and I drew a Y. This meant he got to go first; he set down the word BARK. Playing off his B, I made the word GLOBE.

"How does it feel to be consistently mediocre?" he asked, and I said, "You tell me."

We each played several more words in companionable silence, and he said, "You should tell your mother not to run the church's coat drive this year. It's a drain on her."

It was actually my father, who'd turned eighty the previous spring, who seemed worn out and saw several doctors at appointments my mother took him to; at seventy-two, my mother remained energetic.

As I pulled three tiles from the bag and set them on the wooden rack, I said, "Mom likes the coat drive."

"She lets people take advantage of her," my father said.

In 1987, my parents had moved from their house in Park Ridge to a condo just a mile away, where my brothers and I, along with Hughie's wife, Bonnie, joined them on Sunday evenings for dinner. Hughie had attended law school at the University of Illinois and worked as an assistant public defender in the Chicago drug court, as did Bonnie; they didn't have children. Tony, meanwhile, had attended Iowa Wesleyan and the University of Illinois without graduating from either, currently lived in Wrigleyville, was a private investigator, and was still single.

The typical Sunday routine was that my brothers would toss a football in the yard or, in the winter, watch the Bears on television, while Bonnie helped my mother cook and I played Scrabble with my father; after the meal, I and one of my brothers would do the dishes.

A few minutes later, as I played the word QUITE, my father said, "I wish Sandra Day O'Connor was my daughter."

I said, "I do, too." Both of us had said exactly these words before. It wasn't that my father was hoping to engage in a real conversation about the Supreme Court. He regularly invoked not only O'Connor but also Oprah Winfrey, whose Chicago-based talk show had become a nationally syndicated ratings juggernaut. Another of my father's tics, ever since my fortieth birthday almost four years before, was bringing up **Newsweek**'s famous article warning that women over forty were likelier to be killed by a terrorist than to find a husband.

Tony appeared then, sweaty from throwing the football outside, and paused by my chair. He touched a fingertip to the edge of my letter rack. "I see something you can do," he said.

Simultaneously and emphatically, my father and I both said, "No help!"

• • •

I decided to work from home on Monday before flying to Washington in the evening, and it was as I was packing my suitcase and listening to public radio that I learned President Bush's Supreme Court nominee was Clarence Thomas. Apparently, both men were at Bush's vacation compound in Kennebunkport, Maine, as Bush declared to the country that Thomas was "the best qualified person." Formerly the head of the EEOC, Thomas was at present a federal judge, though I was surprised to learn he'd held the position for less than eighteen months. He was black, had graduated from Yale Law School just a year after I had, and was, it seemed, quite conservative.

I wondered if my colleague James had heard the news, thought of calling his office, decided that doing so might seem strange, and instead called my friend Greg Rheinfrank. Greg was a Democratic strategist I'd known for years, ever since I'd started volunteering as a state party legal responder, which meant I monitored voting irregularities on election days. I met Greg for a standing monthly dinner at Szechuan Wok in Old Town; that he was gay allowed a certain uncomplicated closeness between us.

"Bush is such a fucking weasel," Greg said when I reached him at his office. "Nominating not just a black guy, but a black guy who grew up dirt poor in the South. Do you know what an Oreo is?"

"The cookie?"

"The person—it's when someone is brown on the outside but white on the inside. No exaggeration, Clarence Thomas is more conservative than Strom Thurmond."

"Has he spoken on the record about **Roe**?"

"I'm sure a million reporters are trying to find out at this very moment."

"What a slap in the face to Marshall," I said.

"Plus revenge for Bork."

"The Oreo thing," I said. "Did you make it up?"

"No, but thank you for thinking I'm that clever," Greg said, and both of us laughed. That we ought not to have laughed, that this conversation between two white people was inherently cringe-worthy, were facts not apparent to me until later. They were far from the only such facts.

Even though I'd told Gwen I could take a cab from National to their house in Takoma Park, she'd insisted on meeting my flight, and we were already discussing Clarence Thomas before we left the parking garage of the airport. She said, "Oh, he's terrible. He's a complete opportunist. Everyone I know at the NAACP and the Urban League is very concerned."

"I don't remember him at all from Yale," I said.

"He used to wear blue jean overalls. That doesn't ring a bell?"

I shook my head.

"When he came to our house for dinner, he was so awkward that I felt sorry for him. But I've seen him over the years at events here, and he's become very abrasive and dogmatic." In 1978, Gwen and Richard had moved from New Haven to Washington for Richard to work for the Carter administration. The National Children's Initiative had broken off then from Yale, and Gwen now had sixty employees and an office a block from Dupont Circle. Richard, meanwhile, led a liberal think tank.

I said, "So Thomas was on your radar long before the nomination?"

"Well, there just aren't that many conservative African Americans. Thank goodness." As we pulled onto the George Washington Memorial Parkway, Gwen said, "Is there anything private and wonderful going on in your life that we need to talk about before we get home?"

"I wish. How are you and how's Richard?"

"We're doing well. And you'll get to see Otto, who's here for the weekend licking his wounds after his girlfriend dumped him."

"Oh, dear," I said, and Gwen shrugged, seeming almost amused. "It's character building."

Richard and Gwen's sons had graduated from college the previous summer, Otto from Dartmouth and Marcus from Harvard. Marcus worked on

Capitol Hill for a Democratic congressman from Massachusetts, and Otto worked in New York for a sports magazine, and, to my delight, both boys joined us on the Fourth for hamburgers and potato salad and coleslaw, for which I chopped the purple cabbage while Gwen shaped the ground beef into patties. As we ate in the backyard, the topic of Clarence Thomas came up once again, and Richard, who was sitting across from me at the picnic table, said, "Gwennie, did you tell Hillary about Clarence and his law school overalls?"

"It sounds like he dressed almost as badly as I did," I said.

Richard raised his eyebrows. "Although I suspect you carried less incendiary material on your person."

Gwen was shaking her head. "I spared Hillary that part, but since you brought it up—" The expression on her face was one of great distaste. "Supposedly, he'd carry pornographic magazines in his back pocket and pull them out to show people."

"Mom," Otto said at the same time that Marcus covered his ears.

Gwen and Richard laughed, and Gwen said, "My apologies for offending your delicate sensibilities, boys." Looking at me, she said, "Clearly, Clarence is just bad news all around. Politically, personally—"

"Sartorially," Richard interjected.

"How a man known for talking wild is going to fit in on the Supreme Court is anyone's guess,"

Gwen said. "Let alone what the right-wing ideologues would think if they really knew."

"Talking **wild**?" I repeated. I wasn't sure I'd heard her correctly.

"It means talking about sex in a graphic way," she said. "Do white people not say that?"

This time, it was Marcus who said, "Mom, seriously. Is this necessary?"

"Sweetheart, if just the word **sex** makes you uncomfortable, you're going to have a very embarrassing adulthood."

I said, "I feel like I should remember an African American law student in overalls at Yale, even without the magazine in his pocket."

Gwen shrugged. "He was an odd bird."

After dinner, Otto and Marcus went to meet up with friends, and Richard, Gwen, and I drove to see fireworks over a field at a middle school, which we all preferred to braving the Mall. Though our location was still crowded, we were able to spread a blanket on the grass, and the three of us passed around a thermos of white wine. Richard lay with his hands behind his head, elbows out, then Gwen was in the middle, propped up on her arms, and I was in the same posture as Gwen. "The thing that would turn this up a notch is some good weed," Richard said, and Gwen looked at me and smiled indulgently. Richard added, "Though it's nice as is."

As darkness fell and I was an individual in the thrumming crowd, I felt what I'd felt since my girlhood, that yearning for someone with whom to share the loveliness and also the sadness of the world. On the middle school field, I simultaneously wished I had found someone else, someone permanent, and I felt grateful for Gwen and Richard's friendship.

The crowd oohed and aahed when the fireworks started—exploding dots and bolts of white and green and purple—and the finale was dozens and dozens of them, rapidly following and overlapping with one another, and I felt the yearning the most intensely then, which I suppose was the point of fireworks or any visually dramatic moment experienced collectively. I was forty-three years old, turning forty-four in a few months, and I wondered if I knew the contours of my own life. Would it continue to unfold more or less as it had in the sixteen years I'd lived in Chicago or would it change in ways I couldn't foresee? Did I want it to continue as it was or did I want it to change?

After we'd all applauded, Gwen and Richard and I stood as the families and couples around us did, too, gathering our belongings. Richard and I made eye contact. He grinned and said, "In spite of our shit-for-brains president, it's almost enough to make you feel patriotic, huh?"

I got back to my apartment in Chicago after ten o'clock on Sunday night, left my suitcase just inside the front door, and walked to the kitchen to wash my hands and drink a glass of water. The red light on the answering machine in the corner of the kitchen counter was blinking, and after I pressed the Play button, the automated voice said, "You have—**nine**—new messages. First message." A loud voice filled the room. "Hillary, it's Bill." After a split second, the voice added, "Clinton. There's something I'd like to discuss with you, sooner rather than later, if possible. At your earliest convenience call this number"—he recited nine digits—"and ask for Arlene Dunagan. Many, many thanks, Hillary, and I hope you're well."

It was shockingly strange to hear Bill's voice. I'd neither seen him in person nor spoken to him for sixteen years. In the days and weeks after I'd left Fayetteville in June 1975, we'd talked on the phone a few times, tortured conversations that ended with no more clarity than they'd started with, and we'd exchanged several letters that were similar in their pain and earnestness. But within a few months, the contact had stopped; I'd begun a reply to his most recent letter, realized I wasn't conveying anything I hadn't already conveyed, and never finished it. The only time I'd laid eyes on him was on television, when he'd delivered the keynote speech at the 1988 Democratic Convention in Atlanta, a role he'd been invited to fill because he was then in his fourth term as governor of Arkansas. I'd thought he'd spoken well, though for too long, and apparently I hadn't been alone because near the end of the speech, when he'd said "In closing . . ." applause had broken out in the convention center. Three years later, Bill was still governor, meaning that in his phone message, he presumably was instructing me on how to reach him at the governor's mansion in Little Rock.

The second message on my answering machine was from my friend Maureen: "Are you leaving town Wednesday or are you already gone? Now I'm thinking you're already gone." Prior to hearing Bill's voice, I'd been tired, relieved to be home and ready to get in bed. Now my mind whirred with speculation about the possible reasons he'd called, though, really, weren't there only two? I erased Maureen's message.

The third message, which I also erased, was from a seamstress saying that a pair of pants were ready for pickup.

The fourth message was, once more, from Bill: "Hillary, it's Bill Clinton again. I realize you might be traveling for the Fourth. It's nothing bad, but can you call as soon as you have a chance?" This time, I wondered if Barbara Overholt had given him my unlisted number; though I hadn't returned to Arkansas, she and I saw each other once a year, in various cities, at a conference for female law professors. Then again, I imagined she'd have asked for my blessing before telling Bill how to contact me. And surely a governor had all kinds of extra access.

After playing the remaining five messages, I went to bed and slept terribly. Like Chicago, Little Rock was in the central time zone, and, at exactly eight-thirty the next morning, I dialed the number he'd provided. I reached Arlene Dunagan's answering machine and left a brief message. Under normal circumstances, I'd have departed for the office at eight, but I'd decided not to give my work number to Arlene Dunagan and to instead wait at home until nine-thirty. Whatever the reason for Bill's call, I didn't want to take it with me to another location; I preferred to keep it contained. Less than fifteen minutes later, I was starting a load of laundry when the phone rang. It wasn't Arlene Dunagan; it was Bill.

"How have you been?" he asked. "Do those law students at Northwestern know they're damn lucky to have you as a professor?"

I wonder what you want, I thought. I said, "I've been well."

"It's great you get to be at a world-class university and at the same time be so close to your family." The faintly patronizing way he said this made me suspect he knew that, unlike him, I wasn't married.

I said, "It's funny because, living in downtown Chicago, I sometimes forget that I'm less than twenty miles from the house where I grew up. I see my parents once a week, but the only other person from my childhood that I socialize with is Maureen, and she lives in Skokie."

"Well, give my best to Dorothy and Hugh. And of course Tony and Hughie. I always had a soft spot for those guys." There were methods Bill Clinton had had of charming me, ways that hadn't even seemed to require much effort on his part, but this pleasantly perfunctory way of feigning interest in my life—it was actually a little repugnant, and mildly insulting.

Mostly to change the subject, I said, "Is being governor of Arkansas everything you dreamed it would be? Congratulations, by the way."

"Funny you should ask," he said. "Because that's tied to the reason I'm calling. It's been a fabulous run here. I've had an amazing team so God knows I can't take credit for doing any of this single-handedly, but I'm damn proud of how we've improved schools in the state and bolstered the economy, to name just two of my major initiatives. Lately I've been thinking, wouldn't it be extraordinary if, with a little luck and a whole lot of elbow grease, I could do for our country what I've done for Arkansas?"

I wondered how many times so far he'd used that "elbow grease" phrasing, and how many more times he would in the future. A hundred? Ten thousand?

"I know you're a busy woman, and I'll cut to the chase," he continued. "I'm going to run for president."

"Wow," I said, though the surprising part was

not his ambition but the passage of time. The future he'd long planned for had arrived. Of the two reasons I'd imagined he could be calling, this had been the likelier one.

"I won't announce for a couple months, but I'm getting my ducks in a row. Quack, quack. Now, I'm not the youngster I was when you and I first discussed this possibility, but my motivations are the same. I want to turn this recession around and make life better for ordinary Americans."

I was tempted to say, **Bill, it's me. You can save the bromides.**

"The more attention my campaign gets, the greater chance there is that you'll hear from the media. You know, portrait of the candidate as a young law student and professor. I know I wasn't a perfect boyfriend, but we always had real respect for each other, and if you're game to talk about me fondly, and about just how long I've been committed to making the American dream a reality for everyone, someone as articulate and successful as you is someone voters will listen to."

"I'd need to think about it," I said. "That sounds kind of—well, personal. I've heard from journalists before about you. This is going back awhile, but there was a reporter from the **Gazette** and a few years later from the **Democrat**. I told them no comment."

"I'll bet it was Danny Griffith from the **Gazette**," he said. "Journalists can be real sons of bitches. Some of them are smart, but Jesus God do they like to roll around in the dirt."

I didn't remember the name of either reporter—one had reached out in 1980, a few months after Bill had been sworn in as governor, and another a few years later—but the first had explained that he was working on a piece about Bill, his family, and his personal relationships. When I'd said Bill and I hadn't been in touch for five years, the reporter had said fair enough, but it was his understanding that I was for Bill the one who got away. The reporter had said this in an upbeat way, without regard for how it might crack apart my heart. In any case, I'd wondered if an article about Bill's "family and personal relationships" was an investigation into infidelity. The topic wasn't written about as frankly in 1980 as it would be later—the implosion of Gary Hart's 1988 campaign seemed to mark the real sea change—but the press didn't entirely look the other way, even then.

"I know what you mean about discussing personal subjects," Bill was saying. "But don't underestimate the impact you could have, especially with other working women. And I'd be remiss if I didn't say how impressed I was by your involvement in Harold Washington's election."

How many people did Bill interact with every day, speaking by phone or shaking their hands or making eye contact as they sat in an audience? Did he feel happy with his life? Did he miss me at all?

Was there enough time or space in the days of a governor planning a presidential run, enough repose, to miss a girlfriend from sixteen years earlier?

He added, "If you ever find yourself in my neck of the woods, it'd be an honor to give you a tour of the governor's mansion."

What if I had known when we were a couple that someday, when we were both in our forties, Bill would say over the phone that it'd be an honor to give me a tour of the governor's mansion? Would it have devastated me or made me laugh?

"Thanks," I said. "And good luck in your quest to become leader of the free world."

He chuckled. "Some people might say you've got to be either stupid or crazy. You don't have to weigh in on which. I'm off now to deliver a speech to a hog farmers association, but if you have thoughts or questions, don't hesitate to be in touch. If you want to bounce ideas off someone before talking to a reporter, I'm sure you remember Nick Chess from Yale, right? He's my media guy now." I hadn't seen Nick for longer than I hadn't seen Bill, but I'd heard through the grapevine that he'd gone to work for Bill.

I said, "I have a pretty clear idea of what to say and not say to reporters."

"No, of course. You've always had great horse sense. Hey, speaking of Yale, did you know Clarence Thomas? I think I met him a time or two."

"I have no memory of him, but Gwen thinks he's awful."

"There's no doubt he could do some serious damage. You're still in touch with the Greenbergers?"

"I just stayed with them in Washington."

"Gwen never liked me, did she?" If this was possible, Bill sounded both amused and sad. But the truth was that he did not seem haunted by me, by us. And that of course had been the other reason he might have been calling, the first one that had occurred to me upon hearing his voice on my answering machine: that he'd realized I was the love of his life. That even though we were now middle-aged and he'd married someone else and had children with her, I was the person he'd never stopped thinking about. To be told instead that I had great horse sense—I can't pretend that it was any consolation.

I lived in the Streeterville neighborhood, on East Lake Shore Drive, and I could see Lake Michigan from my living room and bedroom. I'd bought the apartment the year after getting tenure, and when I'd shown it to my parents, my father had said, "Someone certainly thinks she deserves the finer things." When my call with Bill ended, I walked from the kitchen to the living room, looked out at the vastness of the lake, and felt resentful.

With the Fourth of July behind me and eight

weeks before the school year began, I had planned to renew my focus this morning on the casebook I was writing with a friend at Cornell; I wanted to finish a draft by the end of the summer. Now I felt distracted and injured. From the moment I'd stepped into my apartment and heard his message the night before, Bill Clinton had defined my mood, and I had let him. And good God, what if he **was** elected president? I'd see him in the news every day, watching as he was sworn in on a Bible, as Air Force One touched down on runways in Tokyo and Brussels, as he spoke from behind a podium in the Rose Garden. As **he,** Bill Clinton, the man who'd broken my heart and endlessly delighted me and once given me an orgasm on an Arkansas highway, was addressed as "Mr. President."

Surely, if he was elected, some form of exposure therapy would occur in which I began to perceive him as the national leader rather than my ex-boyfriend. But I no longer felt what I had at Yale or in Arkansas, which had been not just a belief in his talents but an investment in that belief. It was far from clear to me that I hoped he'd succeed. Back when we'd been a couple, I'd thought he was wonderful and brilliant, and I'd loved thinking so. Yet, **was** he wonderful and brilliant? Was he now, had he ever been? Had he changed in the last decade and a half, and if so, how? I was confident, based on our conversation, that he'd still be good company to sit next to at a dinner party, especially if he was trying to extract a favor. But as president, would he be ethically casual, irresponsibly magnanimous, vulnerable to his enemies due to weaknesses that he erroneously believed he could conceal or at least be forgiven for? Besides that, did he have any shot at unseating George Bush, whose approval ratings were around 70 percent? I had heard that other Democrats who might run included Bill Bradley, Al Gore, and Mario Cuomo, but the only person who'd declared so far was the former Massachusetts senator Paul Tsongas.

No more than a minute or two had passed since I'd hung up the phone. I returned to the kitchen, lifted the receiver, and called Maureen. When she answered, I said, "Is this a bad time?"

"I'm standing in my mudroom watching my kids fight over an inflatable raft in the pool."

"Do you need to go outside?"

"Maybe. What are you doing?"

"Bill Clinton just called to say he's running for president and he wants me to tell reporters how great he is."

"Wait, really?" Maureen said. "Oh, geez. Are you okay?"

"Those weren't the words he used."

"I know everyone thought it was his destiny, but it's wild that he's actually running. Can he win?"

"It's not impossible."

"Do you wish you were married to him?"

I hesitated. "No?" I added, "Although sometimes I wish I were married to someone."

"Well, there are plenty of someones who wish they were married to you. I'm sure if you wanted a mediocre marriage like the rest of us, you could have it." After eighteen years together, Maureen often complained that Steve didn't appreciate her or everything she did to take care of their children and make their household function. At the same time, she was candid, at least with me, about how she liked being able to send the kids to private school and to ski in Colorado over spring break—though she hadn't worked as a nurse since becoming a mother, Steve had risen through the ranks at LaSalle Bank. Now her youngest, Meredith, was seven, Johnny was fourteen, and Stevie was sixteen.

I said, "I'm really grateful for everything I have." I thought of my students, my positions on the boards of the League of Women Voters and a Chicago organization that provided services to young adults in foster care, my Election Day work. "Things are good almost all of the time," I continued. "But every so often this gaping hole of loneliness opens up."

"Sometimes a gaping hole of loneliness opens up while I'm in the same room with my husband and children," Maureen said. "Sometimes it opens up while Meredith is literally sitting on me." Then she yelled, "Johnny, I can see you! Do you know that I can see you? Leave your sister alone." Talking to me again, she said, "Sorry, where were we? Oh, right, gaping loneliness. So should I vote for Bill or not?"

"He has the primary to get through before we need to worry about that. If you were me, would you say nice things about him to reporters?"

"No."

"Really?" I was surprised by her certainty.

"Why would you?"

"I think if he could have controlled his behavior, he would have."

"Do people ever say that when a woman does the things he did?"

I sighed. "If I make myself work for a few hours, can I come over around five with a bottle of wine?"

I could hear Maureen smiling through the phone. She said, "I thought you'd never ask."

In February 1976, eight months after I'd left Fayetteville, a letter from Barbara Overholt had arrived at my apartment in Chicago. **Bill has been dating a woman named Sarah Grace Hebert, and I think he'll propose to her soon,** Barbara had written. **I wanted you to hear this from someone who cares about both of you.**

I was living then in an apartment in Lincoln Park, with a roommate who was a friend of Maureen's. That night, as soon as I'd made my nest, I began a reply to Barbara, but in the act of writing, I realized that I couldn't commit to paper any of the questions I wanted to ask; whether this reluctance stemmed from my training as a lawyer or from the questions' patheticness was hard to say. The first was **What's she like?** The second was **Does it seem like he loves her as much as he loved me?** and the third was **Is he faithful to her?**

After leaving Arkansas, I had, of course, been heartbroken. As I'd driven north, I had wondered what to tell people when they asked why Bill and I had broken up—surely I couldn't say it was because he'd cheated, let alone because he may have sexually assaulted someone—and it was in western Ohio that I'd realized **I** was wondering why we'd broken up. Had it been the woman's accusation, or Bill's warning? If I believed that the woman and Bill had had some kind of physical encounter, did I believe that it had been against her will? On the Pennsylvania Turnpike, I understood suddenly that I was freed from deciding what I believed. If I was no longer his girlfriend, and never his wife, I was not responsible for his behavior, not even by extension. This absolution was my reward for losing him; in the years to come, it sometimes seemed like the only reward. As it happened, nobody ever asked me why Bill and I had broken up, even the people who expressed sympathy.

Thirty-six hours after I'd departed from Fayetteville, I arrived at Gwen and Richard's house in New Haven. I stayed for a week on their third floor, sleeping in a single bed and walking down steep steps to the second floor to use the twins' bathroom, where both the toilet and the tiles were splattered with their little-boy urine. I spent several days in bed, weeping and shocked, and when she got home from the hospital in the late afternoon, Gwen would rub my back and say, "This is the best decision you've ever made. Now your life belongs to you again."

I'd had the idea that I'd either resume working for Gwen or get a job in Washington. But I quickly understood that New Haven was haunted, filled with places and people who reminded me of Bill. Though Washington would be less so, I'd still constantly see people who knew both of us, and, as Bill continued to run for elections, he'd visit often and possibly move there. When I reached out to the impeachment inquiry colleague who'd mentioned that law schools were recruiting female professors, he'd referred me to his sister, who'd referred me to her contact at the Association of American Law Schools. I quickly interviewed at Harvard, Penn, and Northwestern. When I accepted the job at Northwestern, it wasn't because it was close to my family, although there was a certain poignance to its being the place my mother hadn't been allowed to attend; but really, it was because I hadn't been offered the positions at Harvard or Penn.

I'd settled in Chicago by late August, started

teaching in September, and soon developed a pattern of seeing my parents and Maureen's family on the weekends. I took up jogging and joined both the local League of Women Voters chapter and a Bible study group at the Methodist church in my neighborhood. I was conscious that fall of forcing myself, going through the motions; routinely, something that was only moderately sad would bring me to tears, and I'd have to hide in an empty hallway or a bathroom stall.

Sometimes I thought of Bill with sincere distaste, believing I'd dodged a bullet. Other times, I felt sympathy for both of us, for our almost-compatibility. Surely we had both done our best and tried our hardest. And at yet other times, and this emotion felt the truest and the rawest, I just missed him desperately. If he had shown up in my office or knocked on the door of my apartment, I'd have tossed aside all principle and logic for his smile and his voice, his hands, his smell, his complicated, unpredictable intelligence, and the way his body felt against mine. If I was damned if I did and damned if I didn't, why not keep having sex with him, even if I was sharing him with other women? I was certain that Tennyson was wrong about it being better to have loved and lost, because now I knew what I was missing. Perhaps, after all, I should have attended Harvard Law.

Because we had talked about everything, everything reminded me of him: Linda Ronstadt's new album and my roommate's recipe for savory crêpes and the colleague who told me family law was a second-rate area of study and President Ford's decision to posthumously restore Robert E. Lee's citizenship. Even in his absence, Bill remained the most interesting person with whom to discuss any book or breaking news or small moment of absurd behavior on the part of a friend, acquaintance, family member, or stranger.

And then, on Christmas Eve, as I drove my Buick from Lincoln Park to my parents' house to attend church with them, I became aware that I hadn't thought of Bill in a few days. This had to be a double achievement in light of the fact that I'd once believed I'd spend all my future Christmases with him.

On that February night when I received Barbara's letter, by the time it occurred to me to call her, it was 9:35, which seemed on the cusp of but not actually too late. I kept my address book in the drawer of a desk in my bedroom, and I rose from my nest to retrieve it.

It was oddly heartening to hear her voice; it reminded me how much I liked her. We chatted a little—she said she was traveling over spring break to see her sister—before she said, "I take it you got my letter."

"I did. Can I ask you a few questions?"

"Of course."

"I don't mean to put you in an awkward position."

"I'll answer any questions you have. I didn't know how much you'd want to know."

I took a deep breath. "What's she like?"

"She's soft-spoken. Sweet. She grew up in Texarkana, and she's a second-grade teacher. I wouldn't say she's the most worldly person."

"How old is she?"

"I think twenty-three or twenty-four."

At the time we were having this conversation, I was twenty-eight.

"I'd say she looks up to Bill," Barbara continued. "I suspect he's the first person she's met with political ambition."

No doubt it would have been more upsetting if he'd found another woman with a law degree, or a woman who'd graduated from Vassar or Mount Holyoke.

"What does she look like?" I laughed self-consciously and said, "Just to be really shallow."

"She has light-red hair and I'd say she's not gorgeous but attractive. She's petite."

"Meaning short or thin or both? Is this too stupid for you to answer?"

"It's not too stupid. And both—short and thin. She's small, and he's so tall that she looks tiny next to him."

"How did they meet?"

"They were at a new pizzeria by campus one night last fall. My impression is that she was there with her parents."

On the one hand, didn't this mean that Bill had thought she was very pretty, as opposed to just ordinarily pretty? On the other hand, did a woman need to be very pretty to catch Bill's eye? And, though some men might have been reluctant to hit on a woman whose parents were present, Bill probably wasn't one of them.

I said, "And you think he's going to propose, which must mean—they must be serious."

Barbara's tone was infinitely sympathetic as she said, "Hillary, they're engaged already. It happened the same day I mailed the letter."

How could I have been surprised, how could I receive this news as a fresh blow, when it was the very reason we were speaking? But I was, I did—right away, I felt worse. Quietly, I said, "Wow."

"I do think he's fond of her," Barbara said. "I imagine he also wants to get things squared away before he announces he's running for AG. And there's more." Barbara paused. "She's pregnant. I'll bet he would have proposed anyway, but this gave him extra incentive."

The ample evidence of his ability to continue without me—oh, how it stung.

"When is she due?"

"I believe late September. She's not quite to the end of the first trimester."

For a few seconds, I said nothing and neither did Barbara. I understood for the first time that when I'd driven away from Fayetteville, I hadn't believed Bill and I were permanently ending our relationship. I had hoped we'd reconcile, once we were sufficiently transformed by time and distance. Our phone conversations and letters after my Arkansas departure—in some, he'd offered to come to Chicago and I'd declined—had seemed like a continuation of who we were; they had seemed too soon. But I'd thought, without clearly articulating it even to myself, that we'd wait, say, two years and then find each other again.

At last, Barbara said, "Sarah Grace is a nice young woman, and I hope Bill can rise to the occasion. But I wouldn't read too much into the timing, the quickness. I think when he understood that he'd never find another you, he decided to get on with it."

I was determined not to cry until I got off the phone, and my voice shook only a little as I asked, "The things he and I struggled with—do you think he still struggles with them?"

"Oh, Bill will always struggle with that," Barbara said.

After Bill's call about running for president and then my conversation with Maureen, I walked to my office. Though the main campus of Northwestern was in Evanston, the law school was downtown, just ten minutes from my apartment, and I arrived most days by eight-fifteen. On this summer morning, when I finally got to Levy Mayer Hall, I noted that the door to James's office was closed even though it was after 10:00 A.M. Usually, he was there before I was, his door open except when he was on the phone, which there were no sounds of. Did his absence mean he was out of town, or perhaps he just had a dentist's appointment? I wanted to discuss Clarence Thomas's nomination with him, to tell him what Gwen had said.

In spite of the distractions of Bill and keeping my eyes peeled for James, I managed to make progress on my casebook. That afternoon, before I left, I stopped in the department office to check my mailbox. I found a letter inviting me to speak at a conference on family law and the Fourteenth Amendment in January at the University of Texas; the latest issue of the Yale Law alumni magazine; a notice that the water in the building would be turned off on Friday; and a manila folder. Inside the folder was a microfiche printout of a black-and-white newspaper photo: a black woman in black heels and a stylish coat, and a tall mustachioed black man in a suit and coat, both of them striding forward with serious expressions. A cluster of other people walked to the man's left, and in the background was a large and imposing-looking building with a row of columns. A Post-it note stuck to the top of the copied image read, **Hillary, This is the picture I mentioned of Thurgood Marshall**

and Autherine Lucy that's always stayed with me. Best, James.

As I stood next to the cubby-style mailboxes, a few feet away from the desk of our department secretary, Sheila, a jolt of electricity passed through me; in examining the piece of paper, I felt almost as if I was doing something I ought to conceal. Today, of course, one could summon this photo by typing a few words into Google, but didn't the photocopy imply that James had tracked it down in a library, that he'd gone to some effort? Which was exactly the sort of thing I would do for a person I had a crush on, though I'd long ago been convinced that this was not, for anyone else, a method of flirting. And, of course, he was a married man. Still, it was nice to know that a person I'd been thinking of had also been thinking of me.

So frequently did I visit Maureen and Steve's house in Skokie that, in the summer, I kept a bathing suit there, a navy-blue tank, as well as a striped linen coverup. When I changed in their downstairs bathroom, I was chagrined to realize that, as was often the case, I'd forgotten to shave my legs, and blond stubble dotted my calves. **Oh, well,** I thought. It wasn't as if any member of the Rymarcsuk family hadn't seen it before.

When I joined Maureen on the patio, Meredith was in the pool; their dog, Alf, was sniffing frantically at the base of the fence that ran between their backyard and their neighbors'; and Maureen had poured a glass of wine for each of us from the bottle I'd brought. I stretched out on the lounge chair next to hers. The sky above us was cerulean, and the leaves on the trees were thick and green, rustling in the hot breeze. Yes, it was over ninety degrees, but still—it was heavenly.

"This is really nice," I said.

"Except for my uncooperative children, my flatulent dog, and the squalid mess in my house."

"No," I said. "Even with that."

"How are you feeling about Bill and the reporter stuff?"

"I'm trying not to think about it."

"In that case, never mind. I have someone to set you up with, but here's the wild part. I haven't met the man, and it's Steve's idea. He's a recently divorced colleague of Steve's named Chuck."

"Does he have kids?"

"I think two between the ages of Meredith and Johnny—middle school age?"

I took a sip of wine. "Does Steve think we have something in common, or is this one of those situations where Chuck is single and I'm single and he's part of the human species and I'm part of the human species?"

Maureen laughed. "What if we invite him over for our Labor Day cookout? Isn't that less pressure than a candlelit dinner?"

At times, I was enthusiastic about being set up—particularly in January, if I'd made a New Year's resolution—but I had come to see marriage as a possible rather than probable scenario. To my own surprise, I had between the ages of thirty and forty dated a fair number of men, at least a dozen, but usually for just a few months and only once for more than a year. My relationship with Bill had left me with both more and less confidence, as well as with a new recklessness or indifference. I didn't care as much about these other men because they weren't him; my not caring seemed to make me more attractive. Some of the men I dated were intelligent, some were interesting (usually less so as time passed), and some were handsome. But none were all three, and none were as intelligent, interesting, or handsome as Bill had been. None ever played the saxophone naked for me. I thought about marrying them only insofar as I wondered if it would be worth it to marry someone I wasn't excited about in order to be a mother.

The person I dated the longest, for fourteen months, was a futures trader named Larry whom I'd met through my brother Hughie. Larry's build was the most like Bill's of any man I went out with, and sometimes in the dark, if I'd had two glasses of wine, I could pretend. Although Larry and I didn't stay together, I also found it endearing that he invested five thousand dollars of my money in natural gas and crude oil, and four years later, when the contracts expired, I received twenty-nine thousand dollars in return.

Ultimately, I had experienced so much ambivalence about marriage and children that turning forty had come as a relief. Two weeks after my birthday, I ended a six-month relationship with Pranath, a partner at a large downtown law firm, because it simply seemed to have run its course. In the almost four years since then, I hadn't gone on more than a few dates, nor had I felt much distress about it.

"I'd be delighted to meet Chuck on Labor Day," I said to Maureen. "Thank you."

"Mom and Hillary," Meredith called. "Watch me!" She was on the diving board, wearing a bathing suit with an image of C-3PO, from **Star Wars**, on the front, and she raised her legs and grabbed them, cannonballing into the water. When she surfaced, she said, "Aren't I great?"

Even though her older brother was my godson, Meredith was my secret favorite; regularly during the summer, we had imaginary tea parties in the pool in which we both spoke in English accents.

"You're fantastic," I said.

Greg Rheinfrank, my political strategist friend, called me at the office and said, "I want to plant an idea in your head, and don't answer yet. Just give it some thought."

"Are we still on for dinner next week?" I asked.

"Yes, but I'm telling you this now to give you a chance to mull it over. If Dixon votes for Clarence Thomas, you should run against him in the primary."

"I should run for U.S. Senate?"

"I'm hearing rumors that the RNC is telling Dixon if he votes for Clarence Thomas, they'll run a soft opponent against him in the general."

Alan Dixon was Illinois's senior senator, a centrist Democrat I'd met at a few fundraisers over the years and didn't find objectionable. In fact, he made himself so available to constituents that he was known as "Al the Pal."

"Who told you that?" I asked.

"Hillary, you know I'm a man of discretion."

"Right," I said. "And I'm a supermodel."

"I heard it from my friend Wallace in George Mitchell's office."

"Obviously, I've given thought to running for office," I said. "But aiming for the Senate in my first go-round—"

"Can I lay out the reasons you should do it? One, you know everyone around here, and everyone respects you. Two, it's fucking ridiculous that in the year 1991, there are a total of two women senators. Three, Dixon is about to pull a Benedict Arnold on the Democratic party."

"If Dixon really does vote to confirm Thomas, that's one thing, but if he doesn't, I can't imagine a better way to make enemies."

"Agreed," Greg said. "For now, just think about it."

James wasn't in the office that day, either, and he didn't appear for the rest of the week, which probably meant he was on vacation with his family. It was likely that Sheila knew his schedule, but asking her about it would have felt strange. What was the point?

When I returned to my apartment after work that Wednesday, there was a message from Nick Chess, my Yale classmate who now did media work for Bill, saying he hoped I was great, he knew Bill and I had spoken recently, and he wanted to know if he could offer any assistance vis-à-vis what Bill and I had discussed or just be a sounding board. I liked Nick, but I didn't want to be strong-armed. Though I copied down his number on the pad of paper I kept by my answering machine, I didn't return his call.

In my nest and on jogs that week, I thought about Greg's suggestion. For starters, it was outrageous that Dixon might vote to confirm Clarence Thomas. Thomas would need the votes of every Republican and seven Democrats, but I could see no justification for Dixon being one of those Democrats.

In general, I'd never had difficulty understanding

why someone would run for office, but I felt less certain that I personally should. Changing legislation, improving people's lives—both were hugely, indisputably important. But I wasn't sure the public hustle of campaigning was for me, the gladhanding, the suffering of fools. Already, by the time Greg floated it, the possibility of my running had arisen twice, and both times, I'd decided against it.

In February 1983, Harold Washington won Chicago's Democratic mayoral primary, which under normal circumstances would have made him a shoo-in to win the general election less than two months later. But Washington was black, the city had never had a black mayor, and the backlash to his primary victory was swift and ugly not only among Republicans but among many white Democrats. Supporters of his Republican opponent, Bernie Epton, wore T-shirts that read VOTE WHITE, VOTE RIGHT and buttons that either featured a watermelon with a slash through it or were just plain white; leaflets were distributed that called Washington "Mr. Baboon"; and in neighborhoods on the West Side and the South Side, which had overwhelmingly black populations, anonymously funded billboards appeared with the words VOTER FRAUD IS A FELONY in huge letters. Along with some of my Northwestern students, I reached out to a billboard company who, for free, posted signs in the same neighborhoods with a different message: HEY CHICAGO, VOTING IS A RIGHT, NOT A CRIME. Our counter-messaging garnered national media coverage, and I ended up giving dozens of interviews; the attention was reminiscent of the time after my Wellesley graduation speech, except amplified. That mayoral Election Day, April 12, was the first on which I worked as a legal responder—I was one of the in-the-field roving lawyers monitoring at-risk polling places and communicating what I saw back to the Washington campaign's boiler room—and when Washington beat Epton by 3.7 percent of the votes, I was overjoyed.

After this, a few people in both the state and national party suggested that I run for the Illinois General Assembly, but I wasn't that tempted. I'd received tenure, and I was thirty-six years old and single. While once I'd moved to Fayetteville for Bill, believing we were starting our life together, I didn't at this point want to spend half my time in a crummy apartment in Springfield, nor did I yearn to constantly make the four-hour drive between Springfield and Chicago.

But one conversation did stay with me. A woman named Bitsy Sedgeman Corker, whom I'd previously met in passing, invited me to lunch. The Sedgemans were a large, multigenerational Chicago family who'd made a fortune in transportation equipment and railroads and had given millions of dollars to various progressive causes. Bitsy, who happened to have graduated from Wellesley six years before I had, was a major donor to Planned Parenthood. At lunch, she, too, encouraged me to run for the Illinois House or Senate—she said, "Down the line, you'd make a terrific governor"—and when I demurred, she said, "I'm curious if you know this. The vast majority of men run for election because they decide they want to, and the vast majority of women run only when someone else suggests it."

I said, "I didn't know that, but I'm not surprised."

"Let's keep in touch," Bitsy said. She had dark hair and a pixie cut, and on this day in 1984, she wore a matching black-and-white polka dot blouse and pants. She said, "And please know that when I decide I'm supporting a candidate, the rest of the Sedgeman clan falls into line behind me, with the exception of crazy Republican Aunt Henrietta."

The second time I thought about running was six years later. The foster care organization I was on the board of worked with young adults who were about to or already had aged out of the system, trying to help them find stability because the population disproportionately ended up homeless, without a GED or a job. I worked with the offices of three state senators to draft proposed legislation to expunge the records of juveniles with criminal records in foster care, in order to increase the likelihood of their finding steady employment. My close contact with the senators and their aides, which culminated in testifying after the bill was introduced in Springfield, made me wonder if my earlier decision against running had been shortsighted. But even by the time I'd driven back to Chicago, the feeling had passed. It was an embarrassingly petty reason, but I really liked where I lived, both my apartment and my neighborhood.

A part of me wanted to call Bill and get his advice about running for Senate, but surely this impulse arose only from our recent contact; I had almost completely outgrown the wish to discuss everything with him. The person I called instead was Gwen.

"If you have even a chance at winning, then yes," she said. "Do you?"

"I'm sure I have a chance. Maybe not much more."

"Well," she said, "why not try?"

And then on Monday, as soon as I stepped off the elevator, I could see that James's office door was open, and my heart began to beat more quickly. Which was ridiculous—he was my married colleague whom I hardly knew. I entered my office, and as I did all the things I normally did, I felt as if I were performing these gestures in a play no one was watching: setting my leather briefcase on the floor by my desk, turning on my computer, radio, and single-serving coffee maker. I expected him to materialize in my doorway, an expectation that intensified as time passed without it happening.

I tried to hear any small sounds coming from his office, but I couldn't above the public radio. I worked on my casebook for about ninety minutes, then all at once I could take it no more, and I stood and walked the twelve feet from my desk to the doorway of his office. He looked up from his desk then immediately stood.

"Hillary, how are you?"

"Were you out of town?"

"We were at Susie's parents' house up in Michigan. We always go the week after the Fourth."

"Oh, fun," I said.

There was a silence, then we both started to speak, then we both paused. "Please," he said. "Go ahead."

"I was just going to say, where in Michigan?"

"Petoskey. Are you familiar with the area?"

"I'm not, though I've always heard it's beautiful." It wasn't that any of the words either of us said were irregular, but somehow the energy in the air was unbearably awkward. Was this my fault or his?

"You were in Washington, D.C.?" he said.

"Yes, and my friend Gwen said she doesn't think the NAACP will support Clarence Thomas."

James looked down at his desk as he said, "I apologize for putting that picture in your mailbox. You must have wondered what I was thinking."

Was this the source of the awkwardness, that he was embarrassed?

"No, not at all," I said. "It was interesting."

"I just thought since obviously you admire Justice Marshall—"

"No, I liked it."

"It was silly," he said.

"Well, no matter what happens, it's abundantly clear Clarence Thomas is no Thurgood Marshall." Another silence descended, and I said, "I'll let you get back to work."

What had just happened? But a part of me understood in a way I wouldn't have when I was younger, when I'd have perceived such an encounter as insulting. What had happened, I was almost certain, was that on the day when James and I had watched Thurgood Marshall's press conference, spending time together had been too enjoyable—not egregiously enjoyable, but still excessively so. Something that wasn't precisely flirting but was a kind of recognition of each other, and that also wasn't the total absence of flirting, had occurred, and now we both were backing away from it.

This shouldn't, I thought, be a great loss—the compressed flare-up and extinguishment of a surprising compatibility with formal, soft-spoken James. I needed to keep working.

At Szechuan Wok, Greg and I ordered mai tais and, to share, shrimp dumplings, moo shu pork, and beef and broccoli. As soon as the waitress walked away, I said, "I've been giving a lot of thought to the Senate idea," and, at the same time, Greg said, "Have you heard that Bill Clinton might be running for president?" Greg laughed. "Good Lord, we have so much to discuss."

"How much money do you think I'd need to raise?"

"Three million for the general and half that for the primary." Greg spoke as calmly as if he were telling me the cost of a gallon of milk. I'm sure I made a face, because he added, "You definitely need the support of one or two massively rich donors. You're tight with Bitsy Sedgeman Corker, aren't you?"

"I'm not sure I'd say tight, but we're friends. And I know Pete Duvel. He's very involved with Northwestern as an alum." Pete Duvel was a plaintiff's lawyer who'd won several major class action suits and, in addition to donating to the law school, regularly hosted fundraisers for Democratic candidates in Chicago.

"You have the League of Women Voters in your back pocket," Greg said. "And you know Ivo Burgmund. Do you know anyone with the Rainbow Coalition?" Ivo Burgmund was the state party chair for the Democrats, and the Rainbow Coalition was Jesse Jackson's organization.

I said, "I know Kevin and Martine at the Coalition."

"And then we'd need a labor union leader. Maybe Hal Scott. Oh, and what flavor of Christian are you, again?"

"Methodist, but should I convert to Catholicism? Just kidding. If Thomas's hearings will probably wrap up in late September and the filing deadline is March second, when would I announce?"

"Taking into consideration how the hearings play out, I'd think early to mid-November."

"I don't want Dixon to vote to confirm Thomas," I said. "But you're scarily persuasive."

Greg laughed—he had feathery blond hair and large, very white front teeth and was the first person I knew who used teeth whitener—and said, "Are we pretending that you need to be persuaded? Sure, I'll go along." Our mai tais arrived then, and Greg held his up. "To Senator Rodham."

I laughed and clinked my glass against his. I said, "To long shots." Then I said, "Yes, I've heard that Bill Clinton is running. He called me last week to ask if I'd sing his praises to reporters."

"That's fun, right?"

I thought of contradicting him but didn't. After the '88 Democratic Convention, where Greg had heard Bill's speech from inside the Omni Coliseum, I'd told Greg that he was my law school boyfriend but I'd never explained why Bill and I had broken up. I said, "Do you think Bill could beat Bush?"

Greg sighed dramatically. "Not unless Americans

realize that the Gulf War is nothing but an oil grab."

On Sunday afternoon, before driving to my parents' house for dinner, I called my Wellesley friend Phyllis. After finishing medical school and a residency in oncology, Phyllis had joined a practice in New York. In the early eighties, she'd been married and divorced within three years, without having children, and she and I often confided on matters of being single. Shortly after breaking up with Pranath, when I'd asked Phyllis a little sheepishly if she owned a vibrator, she'd said, "Did I never tell you to buy one? My God, that's friendship malpractice."

On this August day, we'd been on the phone for fifteen minutes, catching up, when I said, "I have a question for you. Have you ever slept with a married man?"

"Of course." She sounded amused. "Have you not?"

"Are you kidding or are you serious?"

"I've turned down more invitations than I've accepted, but come on. I'm sure you've also been propositioned a million times."

"Not really. You know that I've never given off a"—I tried to think of a way to phrase it that didn't implicate her—"a sexy energy," I said. "Has it been relationships or one-night stands for you?"

"Some of both."

"Am I incredibly naïve? Am I operating by one set of rules while everyone else operates by another?"

"Well, you've certainly read the Bible more thoroughly than I have. But it's not as if people are all one thing or the other, sexually or maritally."

I thought of the conversation Barbara Overholt and I had had years before in Walker Park. I said, "Have you felt guilty?"

"I don't consider anyone else's wife to be my responsibility."

"I guess Bill's behavior way back when made me assume I'd never have an affair."

"Fair enough, but you must have friends who've had them."

Rumors had circulated about two political science professors I knew, a man and woman who'd recently divorced. "Maybe," I said.

"No, definitely. Trust me. It's not everyone, but it's a lot of people. What married man are you thinking of sleeping with?"

I laughed. "I didn't say I was."

"Right," Phyllis said. "You didn't need to."

By the Friday before Labor Day weekend, Bill still hadn't publicly announced that he was running for president, and I remained undecided about how I'd respond if a reporter called me. What, I wondered, did I owe him? Beyond that, what was my obligation as a voter and citizen? Could my words really affect the election in some small way? Certainly I was no fan of George Bush's warmongering or flip-flopping on abortion.

I spent much of Saturday and Sunday finishing my syllabi for the upcoming semester. The Rymarcsuks' cookout at which I'd meet Steve's colleague started at four on Monday. I called Maureen to ask what I could bring, which turned into a half-hour conversation about various topics, and at some point I said, "Did you ever find out from Steve whether he thinks this Chuck person and I have anything in common?"

Without changing her tone, Maureen said, "Steve, what made you want to set up Hillary and Chuck?" Realizing they must have been in the same room, perhaps for the entire conversation, I felt the tiny betrayal by the married friend who often criticizes her husband but also enacts standard domestic closeness with him. Maureen said, "Steve says Chuck isn't as smart as you, but he's great at crossword puzzles."

Driving to their house for the party, I looked down and realized I had, once again, failed to shave my legs. I was wearing a straw hat, a pink linen short-sleeved shirt, turquoise linen culottes, and sandals, and it was the bristly stretch between the end of my culottes and my ankles that was the problem.

At the Rymarcsuks', I found Maureen in the kitchen, pulling plastic wrap off a platter of deviled eggs. I set down the six-pack of beer I'd brought, and we hugged. She felt the sleeve of my shirt with her thumb and forefinger. "So pretty."

"But look." I extended one leg.

"What?"

"My hairy legs."

"If that's your idea of hairy legs, then I'm a baboon."

I lowered my voice. "What if my stubble keeps Chuck from falling in love with me?" Although I felt some feminist ambivalence about this, I'd already decided that if I found Chuck cute, I wouldn't swim. On the whole, I thought I looked pretty good. I jogged three days a week—along the lake on weekends in the summer, on a treadmill in a gym in the basement of my building otherwise—and if I felt my weight creeping up I'd go on the fourteen-day version of the Scarsdale diet. But I still did not yearn to expose my pale and lumpy thighs to a man on our first meeting.

"Do you want to go upstairs and shave really quick in my bathroom?" Maureen asked.

"Is Chuck worth the effort?"

Maureen's expression turned pensive.

"Great," I said. "In that case, I won't bother."

About twenty people sat or stood on the patio, with a handful of children swimming in the pool. I greeted the Rymarcsuks' next-door neighbors, then Maureen's mother, then Maureen set a hand on my back, and said, "Hillary, this is Chuck. He works with Steve." Steve and the man in question stood by the grill, both holding cans of Budweiser. Chuck was neither particularly attractive nor unattractive—he had salt-and-pepper hair and dark eyebrows, and he was a few inches taller than I was.

"Good to meet you," he said stiffly, and I smiled and said, "Likewise."

"What do you do at LaSalle?" I asked, and the short answer was that he was an executive vice president in the retail banking division. The longer answer, delivered over the next eighteen minutes, was that he had some complaints about his commute and also about the low quality of the pens provided in the office—the pens were retractable but so cheaply made that the barrel and tip often detached—and he'd expressed his concerns to the office manager, who appeared completely indifferent, which he assumed was attributable partly to her having had her fourth child recently and, not that he was sexist, but it was hard for him to see how a woman could have four children and still manage an office with any degree of competence. It took me several seconds to understand he wasn't joking about the pens. I had a strong suspicion he wasn't going to ask me anything, but, just to be sure, I paused and let a silence arise. He said, "Nice pool, huh?"

"You know what?" I said. "I'm going to go for a swim. Now, actually. Hey, Meredith." Maureen's daughter was playing on the side closest to us, her head bobbing, her hair slicked back like that of a mermaid. I said, "Is there room in there for me?"

In an American seven-year-old's fearless attempt at a British accent, she said, "My butler has prepared a teapot for us."

"Oh, good," I said. "Because I'm very thirsty."

"I am the queen of England and you are Darth Vader."

"Excellent," I said. "Just give me a minute to put on my suit." I found it where I'd hung it in the mudroom the previous weekend, and I changed in the bathroom next to the kitchen. But I didn't bother with the cover-up. I left my clothes, shoes, and straw hat in a tidy pile on a kitchen chair and walked out the back door, my pale forty-three-year-old thighs jiggling with abandon, my stubbly calves exposed to the world, or at least to a couple dozen cookout guests in Skokie, Illinois. There were steps leading into the pool at the shallow end, and I descended them, until I was waist-deep in the water, then held out both arms and dove forward. The immersion, the contrast of the warm air with the cool water, felt glorious.

Abruptly, while I was still submerged, Bill Clinton crossed my mind, and I thought, **I'm not talking to reporters on your behalf. How can I**

when you could be publicly accused of rape at any time? And when it could be true? From time to time over the years, I had thought about the woman in Chouteau's parking lot, and I had never resolved what I believed. This was the first time that, even in my own head, I'd used the word **rape.**

I taught a family law seminar on Thursday afternoons, and it was at the conclusion of the first class that a student asked if he could speak with me. He looked to be in his midtwenties and wore khaki pants and a light-blue polo shirt. I knew because I'd memorized all their names that his was Rob Newcomb.

"I noticed that your syllabus is really focused on women's problems," he said.

It wasn't the first time I'd received this feedback from a student, and I said, "Gender plays an important role in family law."

"But there's a difference between, like, feminist consciousness-raising and constructive legal discussion," he said.

"Yes," I said. "There is."

"I noticed that there are four separate readings on abortion," he said.

"Reproductive privacy is a complex issue."

"I'm not paying twelve thousand dollars a year to listen to straight-up male-bashing."

"Let's agree to disagree," I said. "I have a meeting momentarily, but I look forward to a semester of spirited debate."

"Not everything in law is related to the subjugation of women," he said. "And don't roll your eyes at me."

I was so surprised that I laughed.

"I'm serious," he said. "You just rolled your eyes."

"I need to get to my meeting," I said. "I'll see you next week."

But as I left McCormick Hall and crossed the path between McCormick and Levy Mayer Hall, I felt unsettled. I'd encountered truculent male students before, but the fact that this had occurred so early in the semester was a bad sign. I hoped he wouldn't poison the atmosphere of the class.

As I got off the elevator on the fourth floor, I almost collided with James. "Pardon me, Hillary," he said, and I said, "No, that was my fault." Then I blurted out, "One of my students just told me not to roll my eyes at him."

James looked horrified. "What do you mean?"

"He came up after class to tell me my syllabus is too feminist."

"What an arrogant little jerk. I'll bet he'd never tell a male professor not to roll his eyes."

"Clearly." Slowly, I added, "I'm not completely sure I **didn't** roll my eyes. I don't think I did, but he was testing my patience."

"Who cares? He's the student and you're the

professor, and you were doing him the courtesy of listening to him. The only thing he should have said was thank you."

It was notably unusual for one of my male colleagues to recognize the gender dynamics that often made their way into the classroom, let alone to be outraged by them. And because James was so polite, I might have expected him to be even likelier than most to tell me to calm down or take the high road.

"Are you going to the faculty meeting now?" I asked.

"I am."

"If you wait thirty seconds for me to drop off my briefcase, I'll walk with you."

That Saturday evening, my mother and I planned to see a production of **Così fan tutte**, but at 8:00 A.M. she called and said, "Honey, I hate to do this, but Dad is under the weather, and I need to stay home. I hope the tickets weren't expensive."

I said, "Do you want to see how he feels as the day progresses?"

"I just don't think it'll work," she said. "He's coughing quite a bit."

"Then how about if I come out there, pick you up, we go to Taco Casa for lunch, and I'll have you home in an hour?"

By 12:15, we were sitting at a table across from

each other eating enchiladas. "This is delicious," my mother said. "They do such a good job here."

"Mom, would it sound crazy to you if I ran for Senate?"

"Well, you've always been a leader."

"Not State Senate. U.S. Senate."

"That's what I thought you meant."

"My friend Greg heard that Alan Dixon might vote to confirm Clarence Thomas, so it would only be if that happens. But it doesn't seem like—I don't know—hubris on my part? To run for a national office when I haven't previously been elected to anything?"

She was calm and sincere, not sarcastic, as she said, "Men do that."

I laughed. "Yes, but they're men. Mom, I'm sorry if— I hope—" Saying this was spontaneous, which was why I was stumbling over my words. "I'm sorry I didn't give you grandchildren," I said. "I hope Hughie or Tony will, because you'd be a wonderful grandmother." At the time of this conversation, Hughie was forty-one and Tony was thirty-seven.

"If you wanted children, it's a shame you didn't get to have them." My mother's gaze was direct. "But your life is bigger than mine ever was, being a law professor and your Election Day work and your friends all over the country. If you go to Washington, you can be a voice for all the people who don't have one." She took a bite of food and added, "I don't wish that anything about you was different."

Less than sixty seconds after I arrived in my office following my family law seminar, James appeared in the doorway and said, "How was the little jerk?"

"You mean the student who told me not to roll my eyes?"

"Did he weigh in today on your tone of voice? Or maybe your hairstyle?"

"Thankfully, no. It did occur to me that he was smirking, but there was nothing overt. Did you teach today?"

"I taught Contracts and it was uneventful. I'll let you get back to work, but I'm glad that punk is showing more respect."

We smiled warmly at each other, and as James returned to his office, I wondered if we'd just pulled off a deft and mutual form of sublimation or if the awkwardness between us, the tamped-down flicker of attraction, had only ever been in my head.

I called Greg at his office—it was on the forty-fourth floor of a building on Dearborn Street—and said, "Hypothetically, if I ran, where would I announce?"

"No offense, but I don't see you doing some grand celebration at Navy Pier because at this point, you'd struggle to generate bodies. I envision a media rollout, starting with an interview with WBEZ or the **Trib**."

"Would you be willing to be my communications director?"

"I'd sabotage you if you didn't offer it to me. You know who'd be a great campaign director is Stephanie Crouppen." Stephanie had worked on the successful campaigns of a few Illinoisans in Congress. Greg said, "We can brainstorm other names, but Stephanie is my top pick."

"I'd also need a finance director, a political director, a field director, deputies for all that, a TV consultant—who am I forgetting?"

"Those are the biggies, but you need to budget for a pollster. And a body man. Body woman?"

"I'm going with body woman," I said. "Hypothetically, of course."

"Keep me posted," Greg said. "Hypothetically."

Clarence Thomas's confirmation hearings started on Tuesday, September 10, and I watched them when I could in James's office. Just after Thomas's opening statement, in which he described his upbringing in rural, impoverished Pin Point, Georgia, and conveyed his respect for Thurgood Marshall, I had to go teach Conflict of Laws. After class, I returned to my own office for long enough to set my briefcase inside the door then entered James's office and said, "What'd I miss?"

As always, James rose when he saw me. "They're on recess now, but Thomas has been very evasive. He wouldn't even weigh in on natural law." James gestured toward the left-hand chair facing the TV. "This is now yours. You have a standing invitation to watch whether I'm here or not."

"I need to meet with a student, then I'll pop back in. Let me know if it gets good." I winced. "So to speak."

When I went back to his office an hour later, he stood again, and before I could even ask, he said, "More of the same. Pontificating senators, evasive nominee."

"Have they asked him any more about **Roe**?"

James shook his head. "The Democrats are subdued, especially Kennedy. The idea that Ted Kennedy is a champion of women is just—" James grimaced. "It's a travesty. He really ought to retire."

"You won't get any argument from me," I said.

Onscreen, there was a call to order, and as the senators reemerged into the chamber, I sat. In his answers, Clarence Thomas did indeed seem wooden and rehearsed—improbably, he said that he'd never debated **Roe** during law school because he was already married and had a child—and the Democratic senators tiptoed around him.

I thought of telling James about Thomas carrying

pornographic magazines in his overalls, but I feared that mentioning it would re-create awkwardness. Instead, I said, "My friend Gwen told me Thomas was known at Yale for talking wild. Do you know what that means?"

James shook his head.

"Neither did I, but I guess it means talking about sex." As soon as I heard myself, I wondered how what I'd just said was any **less** awkward.

"I don't mean to sound prejudiced," James said, "but Thomas just doesn't seem that intelligent."

"Or maybe he was overcoached."

At the next break, I said, "How are you liking Northwestern?" James laughed, and I said, "Is that an odd question?" I'd been on the search committee that had hired him; he'd come from Wake Forest's law school in North Carolina, and, in addition to teaching, he was running Northwestern's Center for Law and Finance.

"It's going well," he said. "It's certainly more competitive here."

"The students or the faculty?"

"I suppose both. But my main concern in moving was Susie and David, and they've adjusted faster than I have. We bought a house in Naperville, and they've both made friends in our neighborhood. I'm afraid I'm one of those stereotypical men who isn't great at socializing. I was in a squash league in Winston-Salem, and that's what I miss the most, which might sound silly."

"Why would that sound silly?" I asked.

But onscreen, Senator Biden was pounding his gavel against the table. "To be continued," James said.

The hearings—what we didn't realize at the time were the first round of hearings—were often boring, with long, convoluted questions from the senators. They went on for more than a week, and it crossed my mind to show them to my students one day, as an example of democracy in action, but the hearings weren't directly related to either family law or conflict of laws.

In Family Law, during a discussion of abortion-funding cases vis-à-vis fundamental rights, Rob Newcomb said, "Fine if some welfare queen wants to get thirteen abortions, but it's not the state's responsibility to pay for them."

As so often happened in the classroom, I didn't need to rebut a student because another student did it for me. A young woman named Cathy Fernandez said, "Welfare queens are a racist Republican myth perpetuated by Reagan to erode public support for social services."

On September 27, the Judiciary Committee voted seven to seven—a deadlock—on whether to endorse Clarence Thomas's nomination to the rest of the Senate, then voted thirteen to one to send Thomas's nomination to the full Senate with no recommendation. This was an odd and surprising development on whose meaning James and I speculated.

And then I learned as any stranger might have that Bill Clinton was officially running for president—by listening to **All Things Considered** on the afternoon of October 3, 1991. By this time, in addition to Paul Tsongas, six other Democrats had entered the race, including Tom Harkin and Bob Kerrey. That evening, I made a point of watching **NBC Nightly News,** which was hosted by Tom Brokaw.

In the clip, Bill stood outside the Old State House Museum in Little Rock, a row of flags behind him, facing supporters who waved signs that read CLINTON FOR PRESIDENT and CLINTON '92. As he spoke about the forgotten middle class, social responsibility, and Republican race-baiting, his family stood a few feet to his left: Sarah Grace, to whom he'd been married for fifteen years; their fifteen-year-old son, Ricky; and their twelve-year-old daughter, Alexis. Sarah Grace had pale skin and strawberry blond hair that appeared to be permed, and she wore a floral dress with short, puffy sleeves and a lace collar, as did Alexis. Ricky wore a short-sleeved white button-down shirt and a tie. Bill looked handsome—a little injuriously so—in a dark suit, light-blue shirt, and blue-striped tie.

While I watched, I was eating dinner in my kitchen: peanut butter on toast, a sliced apple, and a glass of white wine. It was undeniably surreal to sit alone in downtown Chicago and see Bill in Little Rock, setting in motion his lifelong dream and a plan in which I'd once believed I'd play an integral part. Had it been nothing more than a youthful illusion that our meeting was fated, that we'd found in each other something unique? I tried to imagine myself outside the Old State House instead of Sarah Grace. I owned no dresses like the one she was wearing, preferring suits, but was there a version of me that existed in a parallel universe who would by this point have absorbed the customs of Arkansas, including its fashions? If I'd married Bill, would I now be Hillary Clinton? Hillary Rodham-Clinton? Would I be the mother of a fifteen-year-old boy and a twelve-year-old girl?

Had the announcement been available online, I'm sure I'd have watched it in its entirety, and perhaps have rewatched it, but I was spared such impulses toward thoroughness or masochism by the media and technology of the time. Within a minute, Tom Brokaw had moved on to describing a disagreement between the White House and the Department of Energy.

Presumably, Bill had timed his announcement to the Senate vote on Clarence Thomas's confirmation, which was scheduled for October 8; Bill had been inviting Americans to imagine how the Supreme Court might change under him in contrast to how it might continue to change under President Bush. But surely Bill wouldn't have announced his candidacy when he did if he'd known what would happen next. Just three days later, on Sunday, the country learned that a thirty-five-year-old black law professor was prepared to testify that Clarence Thomas had sexually harassed her when he'd been her boss at, of all places, the EEOC.

I first heard Anita Hill's name while listening to **Weekend Edition** on NPR; apparently, she too had gone to Yale Law, graduating in 1980.

As soon as the segment ended, I called Gwen and asked, "Do you know her?"

"The odd thing is that I heard someone might accuse him of impropriety, but it wasn't her," Gwen said. "I hope that means she won't be the only one to testify. But I don't know her. We left New Haven around the time she got there."

"This has to derail Thomas's confirmation," I said.

"I'm cautiously optimistic," Gwen said. "With the emphasis on **cautious,** not **optimistic.** If Thomas withdraws his nomination, does that mean you'll wait to see who else Bush nominates before you decide on a Senate run?"

I had been wondering the same. "I think yes," I said. "And how Dixon votes."

"How do you feel about Bill's announcement?"

"I know he'll never get your vote," I said. "I'm trying to decide if he'll get mine."

"You know what I thought when I heard he'd entered the race?" Gwen said. "I thought, There but for the grace of God goes Hillary."

On Monday morning, I was unlocking my office door when James appeared and said, "My God, the talking-wild rumors."

"I know!" I had been planning to go see him as soon as I'd set down my briefcase.

"You predicted this! Can you imagine that her legal team has, what, four days to prepare?"

We looked at each other, and the giddiness between us—it was partly the giddiness of two Democrats hoping a Republican nominee's confirmation would implode. But I did not think it was only that.

For as long as I live, I'll never forget watching Anita Hill deliver her opening statement: her aquamarine suit, her composure and seriousness, her essential isolation as she faced the row of fourteen white male senators and the many, many cameras. After she'd held up her right hand and sworn to tell the truth, she sat again and began reading her statement: "Mr. Chairman, Senator Thurmond, members of the committee: My name is Anita F. Hill and I am a professor of law at the University of Oklahoma. I was born on a farm in Okmulgee County, Oklahoma, in 1956. I am the youngest of thirteen children. . . ."

After a summary of her education, church affiliation, and professional experience, she described meeting Clarence Thomas and going to work for him at the Department of Education and then the EEOC. Three months after they began working together, she said, he asked her out, an invitation she declined. "What happened next and telling the world about it are the two most difficult experiences of my life. It is only after a great deal of agonizing consideration and a number of sleepless nights that I am able to talk of these unpleasant matters to anyone but my close friends."

In addition to continuing to ask her on dates, she said, he brought up sex frequently: pornographic films showing women with large breasts and men with big penises, bestiality, group sex, rape. He boasted of his sexual prowess and his fondness for performing oral sex. In the office, he once held up a soda can and asked, "Who has put pubic hair on my Coke?"

It was jaw-dropping—weirder and more vulgar and more specific than I would ever have imagined, and its weird, vulgar specificity had the texture of truth.

I was, of course, watching in James's office, and I

could feel him shifting, though in astonishment or discomfort, I couldn't tell. Intermittently, either he or I said, "What?" or "Oh my God," or we simply gasped. But mostly, we just listened.

Eventually, Hill said, she had been hospitalized with acute stomach pains, which she believed were caused by job-induced stress. A year later, she left the EEOC to become a law professor in Oklahoma. Before her departure, Thomas told her that if she ever told anyone of his behavior, it would ruin his career. She said, "This was not an apology, nor was it an explanation."

After acknowledging her occasional contact with him in the years since, her voice was both impassioned and contained as she said, "I have no personal vendetta against Clarence Thomas. I seek only to provide the committee with information which it may regard as relevant. It would have been more comfortable to remain silent. I took no initiative to inform anyone. But when asked by a representative of this committee to report my experience, I felt that I had to tell the truth. I could not keep silent."

She stopped speaking and tidied the stack of papers on the table in front of her. After a few seconds, it became apparent that she was finished.

Unlike during the earlier hearings for Thomas, James and I were joined that day by several colleagues; a larger television had also been set up in a classroom that wasn't being used. It was a Friday, which meant that few classes were occurring. Hill's testimony went on and on, with questions from the senators that ranged from skeptical to flat-out disrespectful. The door of James's office was open, and a colleague named Eli Disterhoft stuck his head in and said, "Can you believe what they're putting her through?" He kept watching with us for the next hour.

Around noon, an older colleague, a man named Edmund Lynham, also paused as he was walking by and said, "I don't believe a word of it. She voluntarily stayed in touch with him for years."

"She needed him as a professional reference," Eli said.

During a break, James and I went to the student union to get sandwiches, and he said, "She seems to me like she's telling the truth."

"What incentive would she have not to?" I said. "She's opened herself up to vicious criticism from the Right and from some people in the black community."

"But how could Thomas be that careless?" James said. "How could he imagine he'd get away with it?"

I thought of Bill, the tension between his private behavior and public ambition. "I wish I knew."

By the time Anita Hill's testimony ended, it was almost 7:00 P.M.—almost 8:00 on the East Coast—and James and I were the only ones left on the fourth floor. It seemed an idiotic concession on the part of the Democratic senators, but Thomas was being allowed to respond immediately. With vehement outrage, he denied everything; he called Hill's claims "a high-tech lynching."

At 9:30, the hearing finally ended, though it would resume the next morning. James said, "I assumed that to reconvene, it had to be something big, but God almighty."

We both were sitting in our usual uncomfortable chairs, and I felt as simultaneously wired and drained as if I myself had spent the day testifying. Onscreen, pundits were discussing the proceedings. I said, "A friend of mine who's very active in the Democratic party here told me he's heard Alan Dixon is planning to vote to confirm Thomas. I'm considering running against Dixon if he does."

"For Senate?" James looked aghast.

I said, "I've done election monitoring in Illinois for years, and before that I worked on several campaigns. It's not as far-fetched as it sounds."

"You'd run in the '92 election?"

"There's a rumor the Republicans are really courting Dixon, but I can't imagine he'd let himself be convinced after today."

Truly, as I spoke, it looked like James had tasted something terrible. At last, he said, "You can't run for Senate because you'd win and I'd never see you again."

Our collegiality—had it just broken open, laying

bare the true emotions that ran under it? I tried to smile at him, though I suspected my smile was more panicked than sultry.

"I like you so much, Hillary," he said.

I was looking straight ahead, at the TV screen, as I said, "I like you so much, too." The strenuous innocence between us—I had not imagined it after all, at least not the strenuous part.

After a silence, he said, "If I didn't have a family, I would definitely—" He paused. "I would love to ask you out on a date. Would **you** want that?"

"Yes," I said. "But given that you do have a family—" I was violating one of my own rules, which was not to have a significant conversation without knowing what I wanted the outcome to be.

"Given that I do," he repeated, but, for a minute, he didn't say anything else. Then he said, "You're so bright and interesting and attractive. After we have a conversation, I always think about how lucky I am to know you."

At earlier points in my life, when men had said slight variations of **You're so bright and interesting and attractive,** they'd meant it as an explanation for why they **didn't** want to date me; how odd it was that the passage of time could invert a sentiment.

"The last few months," I said, "talking to you for five minutes here or there, it's made my days feel so much more fun. But I guess I've tried to avoid thinking too deeply about why."

"I got married when I was twenty-two," James said. "That seems ludicrous now, like it shouldn't be allowed. Susie is a devoted mother. She's a good person. But I wish— I've heard that some couples grow together, but that seems much rarer than growing in different directions."

Thinking of Maureen and Steve, I said, "I agree, although I'll refrain from pretending to have any expertise."

"If I could do it again, I'd pick someone like you. Someone I could have conversations with."

There was a sadness I felt in this moment, an amalgamated sadness. I felt sad that I didn't have a true partner, with whom to share a bed and discuss daily indignities and inside jokes. I felt sad that most marriages didn't, beyond the first few years, seem very happy. I felt sad that, in the background of my life, the man I'd once been wildly excited about had become a person it would have been simpler never to have met. And I felt sad that, in the foreground of my life, the man I most wanted to kiss was another woman's husband.

It was for all these reasons that I reached out and took James's hand. I didn't intend for the gesture to be flirtatious or provocative; I meant for it to be rueful. But I suppose that, even as it seemed we were agreeing that nothing romantic would happen, I wanted some small intimacy as consolation.

It was immediately apparent that James saw what I'd done as overture rather than lamentation. He rubbed the back of my hand with his thumb, then clasped his other hand on top of mine. Were we, after all, about to kiss?

But we simply sat there holding hands for several minutes, for long enough that the physical contact went from shocking and exciting to confusing to the tiniest bit boring. Also, didn't he have a long commute to Naperville? Finally, I squeezed his hand and said, "I know we both need to go home. Let's not try to resolve this right now." I extricated my hand and stood. "I'll get my things and we can walk out together."

We made small talk as we took the elevator downstairs and left Mayer Levy Hall. After ten on a Friday night in October, the law school campus was quiet and dark. I knew he was headed to the parking garage, and I gestured and said, "I'm going along Lake Shore Drive."

"You're not walking at this hour, are you? Please let me give you a ride."

"It's safe," I said. "It really is."

We stood there for a few seconds, and again, I wondered if we'd kiss, though we were right outside the building where we both worked. I stepped forward and hugged him, and it wasn't a brief hug. But I felt a relief when I was by myself again, the vast glittering darkness of Lake Michigan to my left. The day had been filled with multiple kinds of tension, and I was exhausted.

• • •

"Wait a second," Maureen said when I called her from my apartment. "Your co-worker hit on you during Anita Hill's testimony? I wasn't an English major, but isn't that the definition of irony?"

"I sort of hit on him, too," I said. "And technically, Anita Hill was finished. Are you appalled?"

"Well, I don't think it implies anything good about his marriage."

I adored Maureen. But I was struck, not for the first time, by how casually and authoritatively dismissive of marriage married women were, except when they weren't.

I went for a run on Saturday morning, and when I returned, I had two phone messages.

From Greg: "You know that rage you felt boiling inside you as you listened to Anita Hill? A lot of other women felt it, too."

And from my brother Tony: "Who has put pubic hair on my Coke?"

The reopened hearing had lasted through the weekend, concluding in the wee hours of Monday morning. Walking to school Monday, I thought that all the turmoil would provide a cover for or distraction from what had happened between James and me on Friday evening. But a few minutes after I arrived at my office, James appeared in the doorway. "Do you have a minute?" he asked.

"Of course," I said.

He stepped inside, closed the door, and said, "I thought about you all weekend." As usual, he wore a suit and tie; his tie on this day was maroon with navy stripes.

I was sitting at my desk, and I smiled. "I thought about you, too."

"You look very pretty today," he said.

"I was just thinking how handsome you look."

"Would it be all right if I hug you now?"

I laughed, then I held the back of my hand in front of my mouth. "I'm not laughing **at** you," I said. "It's just—you're very sweet."

As he approached me, I stood, and when he wrapped his arms around me, I could feel him inhaling the smell of my hair. There was a blurriness of sensations I lost myself inside—how his physicality was both unfamiliar and comforting. That we would kiss this time seemed inevitable, even if it was eight-twenty on a Monday morning and we were in my office. It seemed inevitable until he squeezed me once more before stepping back. "I need to go meet with the provost," he said. "I can't wait to see you later."

• • •

On October 15, Clarence Thomas was confirmed fifty-two to forty-eight. It was the narrowest margin in the history of Supreme Court nominations, and, in a roll-call vote, Alan Dixon was one of eleven Democrats who voted yea. This happened a little after 5:00 P.M. central time, when normally I'd still have been at the office, but James was teaching, and I'd wanted to watch with someone, so Greg and I had both left work early and met at his apartment.

In Greg's living room, when the vote was official, I felt two distinct feelings: deep dismay that Clarence Thomas would ascend to the Supreme Court and deep curiosity about whether this fact would change my own destiny. I turned to Greg. "Can you give me forty-eight hours to decide?" Conveniently, we were having dinner at Szechuan Wok two nights hence.

"As long as you know there's only one right answer."

"Do those fifty-two senators not believe Anita Hill or do they not care?"

Greg shook his head unhappily. "Republicans are ruthless fuckers, and it's the only thing I admire about them."

The next morning, James appeared in my doorway and said, "Please tell me you're not running for Senate."

"Sometimes that's what bright women who are interesting to talk to do." I'd been joking, but he looked displeased, and I added, "I'm still thinking it over."

He closed my office door, walked to where I sat at my desk, extended his hand, and pulled me toward him when I took it. Then he hugged me tightly, and this was the moment I understood that he would never do anything that I hadn't done first. That I had taken his hand and that I had hugged him meant he would take my hand and hug me. But he would not go further. Was this impasse due to marital guilt? A fear I'd think he was being forward? Did he want or not want me to initiate more? Did he believe these were rules we had agreed upon?

On the one hand, the comparative chasteness felt absurd. We were in our forties. I hadn't had sex in three years, and he was an attractive man. And if he feared hurting or angering his wife, I couldn't imagine she wouldn't be hurt or angered by what we were already doing.

On the other hand, there was in this restraint an enticing plausible deniability. If, say, a newspaper reporter were to find evidence of everything we'd ever said or done with each other, would it count as an affair? I didn't think it would.

• • •

At Szechuan Wok, the minute Greg sat down, I blurted out, "I'm in."

"I have good and bad news. Carol Moseley Braun is running."

"Wow. Oh. Gosh. I mean—well, that would certainly be poetic justice." Carol was the Cook County recorder of deeds, a former assistant majority leader in the Illinois House, and she was black, meaning if elected she'd be the first black woman senator. I said, "I can't run now. Can I?"

"It does change the landscape."

"Do you think she can win?"

"She'll be an underdog, and in a different way than you would. But she has the magic. Everyone who meets her loves her, as I assume you've seen."

"I've heard her speak a few times at the IDA dinner." This was an annual event hosted by the Illinois Democrats Association.

"Then you know what I mean," Greg said.

"Let's not dance around this. You think she'll connect better with voters than I would?"

"Your serious-professor vibe is a strength running against men, but I fear it'd come off as pretentious or elitist contrasted with her."

"It's a shame when so few women run for national office. I shudder to think of the catfight headlines."

"Ha," Greg said. "Those would be the fun part."

I sighed. "If she has an electoral record and I don't, and if her election would represent this milestone—for me to try to stop her would give off a bad smell."

"I wish I disagreed," Greg said, and he didn't seem quite as regretful on my behalf as I might have imagined. "Hey, did you read Clinton's interview in the new **Time**? He's a funny dude."

"I missed it," I said. **If I'm not running for Senate,** I thought, **I'm definitely sleeping with James.**

But over the next few weeks, I didn't sleep with James. Was it because I was respecting his marriage? Though I knew the claim might seem risible, to some degree, yes. Was it because, while the Methodist church I attended on Sundays was progressive, it certainly wasn't **that** progressive? Yes. Was it because I worried that if we had sex I might fall in love with him or he might fall in love with me but the falling might happen unequally, and so instead I chose to enjoy this sweet purgatory? Also yes.

It often occurred to me that if either of us had a sofa in our office, sex would have been inevitable. And at times, the discomfort of the chairs notwithstanding, it was difficult to refrain from climbing onto his lap, or just from inviting him to my apartment. If he'd kissed me passionately, or reached inside my bra, I'd have been delighted and responded in kind. And on some days his restraint was, frankly, a turnoff. But on other days it was enough—it was wonderful—to hold hands with this gentle, intelligent, kind man. As the weather turned cold, that yearning I'd had since girlhood was muted by the tenderness and reassurance, perhaps especially when we weren't together, of carrying James in my heart and knowing he was carrying me in his. This was true during both mundane tasks, such as taking a trash bag down the hall to the chute in my apartment building, and during moments when I'd once have felt a heightened loneliness, such as before bed or when I could smell fall leaves burning.

Once when I left to go teach Conflict of Laws, James stood, too, and as we embraced—we had never kissed and didn't on this day—he began to cry.

"James," I said softly and, my body still pressed against him, I rubbed his back with my palm. "Sweetheart."

He reached for a tissue. As he wiped his eyes, he said, "I'm sorry that I'm being ridiculous."

"You're not ridiculous."

"I wish so much that things could be different."

"I do, too," I said.

On another day, when we were sitting side by side in his office in the late afternoon, he said, "For the whole first year here, I was intimidated by you." I laughed, and he added, "You're so cool and confident in faculty meetings. The way you stood up to the dean about changing the first-year requirements—do you remember that?"

Having been reminded, I did remember.

"And I'd heard you talking to Sheila about a trip to Paris with your Wellesley friends," he was saying. "I imagined you having this exciting single person's life, jet-setting to European cities."

"If by jet-setting you mean flying coach to Europe every three or four years, then maybe."

"I was so happy when you wanted to watch Thurgood Marshall's press conference in my office."

Jokingly, I said, "Did you have a crush on me?"

"Very much so. I never planned to act on it, but how could I not?" There was something so guileless in James's affection, so boyishly sincere, and this guilelessness in a polite law professor—I found it touching.

I said, "Well, this is all very flattering, but it's not how anyone besides you sees me. I'm actually an honorary man."

He looked bewildered. "What does that mean?"

"It's my trade-off for getting to join the boys' club. Things have changed since I started as a professor, and I'm sure they'll continue to." His expression was still so dismayed that I added, "I'm not trying to get you to tell me I'm pretty or anything like that. I'm just describing certain realities."

"Pretty?" he repeated. "You're beautiful."

I smiled. "I hope you're still intimidated by me."

He squeezed my hand. "Completely."

And once, on a Friday afternoon, he said, "I know this isn't fair, but if you told me you were going on a date this weekend, I'd be devastated."

I said, "I'm not going on a date this weekend."

In fact, I was having dinner at Maureen's that night. Steve and the boys had gotten tickets to a Bulls game, and Maureen and I ate pizza with Meredith. When she went to watch **The Little Mermaid** in the den, we stayed in the kitchen.

Maureen said, "Are you in love with him?"

Automatically, I said, "No." It occurred to me that James would be hurt by this reflexive disavowal, and I added, "There's no room, given the circumstances."

"I'm not asking if being in love with him is a good idea."

"If he were single, I'd want to date him. But there's no point wondering if I would marry him or anything along those lines."

"How's the sex?"

"No, no," I said. "We haven't done more than hold hands."

"You can't be serious."

"We haven't even kissed."

"What? Have you, you know—" She waved a hand in the air. "Heavy petting or whatever?"

"We hug each other for a long time, but nothing beyond that."

She looked like she was having trouble keeping a straight face. "Does he get an erection?"

"Sometimes, but then he pulls away." Again, I wondered whether sharing this information was a betrayal of James. "I promise it's shockingly innocent. It's like we're in grade school."

"Is that really what you think?" Maureen's expression had become skeptical.

"I'm telling you the absolute truth. Barely anything has happened."

"Hillary, this version is worse than if you were sleeping together. I'm on your team, but from the perspective of a wife—this deep, meeting-of-the-minds friendship where he's also smitten with you is more threatening."

"Do you think I should cut it off?"

"Can you? It seems like the situation has taken on a life of its own."

"I could try."

"I assume either you'll meet someone else, which will make it awkward that your offices are next to each other, or else you'll eventually have sex. I just don't see two adults who've confessed their attraction sitting there and holding hands indefinitely."

"He's different from a lot of other men. He's—" I searched for the right word. "Honorable. Not in a self-righteous way. He's just a really good, decent person. He's also really cute."

She laughed, but sympathetically rather than mockingly. She said, "Good thing you're not in love with him."

A week and a half before Thanksgiving, Carol Moseley Braun announced her candidacy from a private terminal at Midway Airport. The location struck me as strange—apparently, the logic was that she'd proceed to fly around the state introducing herself to voters—but she seemed poised and warm. She said, "I am running for the Democratic nomination to the United States Senate because I—along with everyone else—saw my senator stand on the floor of the Senate and say that it didn't matter to him what I thought. I watched him side with the people who have ruled us so badly, as he has again, and again, and again."

It would have been a lie to say I didn't feel envy and regret, certainly more than I'd ever felt watching Bill on the campaign trail. My own ambivalence about running—it was both deflating and inspiring to watch her show by example how it was self-imposed. I wondered if in the future I'd run for something, or if the stars would never quite align. The reality was that I still didn't really want to do my time in Springfield. As it happened, just a day before Carol had entered the race, another Democrat had preceded her, a wealthy personal-injury lawyer named Albert Hofeld who'd never held elected office.

After deciding against running, I'd called to tell Gwen, and the night of Carol's announcement, Gwen called from Washington. She said, "I respect the choice you made. I want you to know that."

The next morning, I mailed a check for a hundred dollars to Carol's campaign headquarters.

On Thanksgiving, I took pumpkin pie and pecan pie to my parents' house, and as I passed off the bakery boxes to my mother, my father said, "Thank God you didn't make them or we'd need to call poison control."

We were joined by my brothers and sister-in-law, and around noon the Bears played the Detroit Lions; the Bears lost, which didn't improve my father's mood. We ate early, and after the meal, while my father and I were playing Scrabble, he idly said, "I wish Carol Moseley Braun was my daughter."

"I do, too," I said.

I'd told my mother weeks ago, by phone, that I wasn't running for Senate because Carol was, and calmly, my mother had said, "That makes sense, honey." Thus I was almost sure that she'd never mentioned the subject to my father; he'd just found another prominent woman with whom to compare me unfavorably.

I was home by eight o'clock, and when my phone rang, I was shocked that it was James. He said, "My mother-in-law dispatched me to the supermarket to buy whipping cream. I'm at a pay phone, and I have ninety seconds, and I want to use them to say I can't stop thinking about you."

"I fully approve of your choice," I said, and he laughed.

"I miss you," he said.

"I miss you, too." We had last seen each other on Tuesday afternoon, a day and a half before. For a few seconds, neither of us spoke. It sounded like cars were driving by him. "It's really nice to hear your voice," I said. "I'm glad you called."

Student evaluations for the semester were anonymous, but I easily recognized Rob Newcomb's. **This course is a waste of time from start to finish,** he had written. **Placing the blame for all of society's ills on men does not achieve anything. Students would be better served if Professor Rodham sharpened her analytical skills and understanding of legal frameworks instead of trying to force-feed us her feminist agenda.**

• • •

After Meredith's grade school got out for winter break, she and Maureen came into the city, and, as we did every year, we went out for lunch and visited the Marshall Field's Christmas windows. Although it was bitterly cold, State Street was crowded, and Meredith excitedly pointed out that one of the elves in the window wore roller skates.

As we moved on to the next window, Maureen said to me, "My friend Sophia Dyson and her sister Evalyn are having a luncheon fundraiser thing for Carol Moseley Braun in early January, and they want me to be a cohost. Would you be okay with that?"

Maureen knew, of course, about my short-lived notion of running for Senate.

"Of course," I said. "You don't need my permission."

"Will you come?"

"Tell me when it is, and I'll look at my calendar." As a rule, I didn't like socializing during the day with nonworking women. Even though my schedule was flexible, their relationship to time was different from—less urgent than—mine. But I was surprised and intrigued that Maureen was involved in an event for Carol. That Carol was making inroads among white women in the affluent northern suburbs seemed promising for her.

"By the way." Maureen crooked her finger, indicating that I should lean forward, and when I did, I realized it was because she didn't want Meredith to overhear. "I read an article about what you're doing," Maureen whispered. "It's called an emotional affair."

Bill wasn't expected to win the straw poll at the Florida Democratic Convention the week before Christmas—Harkin or Kerrey was—but when he did, I heard from reporters the next day. Whether they'd found me on their own or Bill had decided I wanted to help promote him and referred them to me, I didn't know. The first to leave a message was a reporter from the **L.A. Times**, and I didn't return any of his three calls. The second reporter was from the **Arkansas Gazette**, and I didn't return her calls. The third was from **The Washington Post**, and—this was in the days before caller ID—I happened to pick up. "If you have just a few minutes, I'd love to ask some quick questions about Bill Clinton and your time in law school," she said.

"I'm not interested in being interviewed," I said.

"It will only take a few minutes."

"It's not a matter of time. I don't want to be quoted."

"Do you believe Bill Clinton wouldn't be a good president?"

"I have to go," I said.

"We also could talk on background if that would be more comfortable. That means I wouldn't include your name."

"Please don't call me again," I said.

I decided after all to go to the luncheon that Maureen was cohosting for Carol Moseley Braun, for not two but three reasons: Even though it was during the week, I was still on winter break; Maureen was involved; and I wanted to help Carol beat Alan Dixon. The suggested minimum contribution was fifty dollars.

The event was called for noon, and when I arrived a few minutes after, many cars were already parked along the gravel street where Maureen's friend Sophia lived. Sophia's house turned out to be a sprawling white colonial, and the entry hall, living room, and dining room were abuzz with women of various ages in quilted or boiled-wool jackets and pearls. I filled out a name tag, affixed it to my blouse, and went to get a glass of wine from the bartender in the living room. I then found Sophia, whom I'd met before—through Maureen, not through political circles—and thanked her for hosting. I chatted with a few other attendees, three of whom apparently didn't hold jobs and one of whom was a high school principal, and when they went to get food from the buffet in the dining room, I located Maureen.

"This is a great turnout," I said. "There must be close to a hundred people."

But Maureen's expression was grim. "Carol was supposed to arrive forty-five minutes ago, and no one has heard from her or her team since yesterday. We were planning to start the program now."

"She's probably caught in traffic or coming from another meeting," I said.

"If you were me, when would you start worrying?"

I looked at my watch, which read 12:32. "In another twenty minutes," I said. Carol's lateness struck me as odd—especially in a setting like this one, every minute that wasn't spent schmoozing was a missed opportunity to fund her campaign—but Bill had certainly run late during his first congressional run.

At 12:45, when guests were starting to leave, Carol's campaign director called Sophia from a gas station pay phone to say they expected to arrive by one o'clock. Maureen summoned me to a hushed conference in the kitchen with Sophia and her sister, Evalyn—around us, catering staff in their black aprons assembled trays of brownies and cookies—and I said, "Do you want me to filibuster until she gets here? I'm happy to."

"You really don't mind?" Evalyn said.

There wasn't a microphone, but I was accustomed to projecting my voice, from teaching. Sophia and I stood in the entry hall, which was between the living room and the dining room, and I introduced myself by saying that I was a law professor at Northwestern, a longtime member of the League of Women Voters, and an Election Day monitor. I looked alternately at either side of the entry hall as I said, "If my name sounds familiar, it's probably because I was very involved in fighting against voter suppression and intimidation during Harold Washington's first mayoral campaign." Spontaneous applause broke out, and I was surprised by how good it felt. I continued, "Today I want to talk about why electing Carol Moseley Braun, who will be here in a minute, is not only a historic opportunity but also will send the message to all Illinois officeholders that they need to take the concerns of women seriously." It was as I was declaring that economic issues and healthcare issues were women's issues because all issues were women's issues that the door behind me opened, and, along with a burst of cold air, Carol and her three-person retinue appeared.

"And here she is!" I exclaimed. "Our guest of honor!"

"Oh my goodness, I am **sorry**," Carol said loudly. "The highway out of the city was beastly. But I'm just thrilled to be here with such a beautiful bunch of women." Everyone applauded again with great enthusiasm, and Carol applauded, too, saying when the cheering quieted down, "No, I'm clapping for **you**." She hugged both Sophia and me then immediately launched into her stump speech: why she'd decided to run, how she was tired of the gridlock in Washington when the officials there were supposed to work for the American people and not the other way around. She spoke about growing up on the South Side, about the importance of education in her life and for all children, about her eventual graduation from the University of Chicago Law School and her beloved brother's fatal drug overdose in 1983 and her teenage son. The audience was rapt as she described how, as a state representative in Springfield, she'd been known as the conscience of the House. "Speaking truth to power is always important," she said. "Right now, it's more important than ever."

I'd recognized within seconds that she had the same charisma Bill did. Right away, the crowd had forgiven her tardiness and they nodded and smiled and frowned and cheered at exactly the moments they were intended to nod and smile and frown and cheer. And it was extra impressive how effortlessly she connected with them given the differences of race and upbringing. I saw a few women pulling out checkbooks even before Carol finished speaking.

And yet, standing a couple feet from her, I had a thought I couldn't suppress: **I'd** never have shown up more than an hour late to my own fundraiser. Yes, Bill had done this sort of thing, and maybe he still did. But didn't Carol know—shouldn't she—how careful women had to be?

On the weekend before the semester started, my brother Tony and I went to a movie—we saw **Bugsy**, starring Warren Beatty—and afterward, over cheeseburgers, Tony said, "Did you hear Dad got in a fender bender in the parking lot of Menards?"

"I thought he wasn't driving anymore."

"Is that what he told you?" Tony scoffed. "At night maybe, but he still drives during the day."

"Was anyone hurt?"

"Not that I know of."

"I don't think he could pass the driving test if he had to take it," I said. "Do you?"

"There's no way in hell." Tony bit into his cheeseburger and said with his mouth full, "When we're all at Hughie's, want me to steal his license out of his wallet?" Our brother and sister-in-law hosted an annual Super Bowl party, which would occur the following weekend.

"Like that would do anything," I said, and Tony laughed, then so did I. Not because it was funny—learning that our father was still driving was distressing—but because it was true. And also because it was nice to be out with my brother, eating cheeseburgers.

Bitsy Sedgeman Corker called me at the office. "I just had lunch with Ivo Burgmund, and he told me you're considering running in the Senate primary. What can I do to convince you?"

The Democratic state party chair had told one of the leading Democratic donors in the state that I might run for Senate? "I was considering it, before Carol decided to run," I said. "I'm not at this point."

"I like Carol," Bitsy said. "But her campaign is an absolute disaster. They're incredibly disorganized, and the campaign manager is a very weird South African man she's rumored to be involved with."

"I went to a fundraiser for her in Skokie," I said. "She was an hour late, but once she got there, she was terrific."

"She's late to everything. Listen. I'm not racist. Carol's a sweet person, and if I thought she could win, I'd support her. I don't think she can win."

"It's interesting to hear you say that."

"And I want a woman in that seat. Whether it's Alan Dixon or Joe Biden or George Bush, I'm so tired of these idiot men getting to make up the rules for the rest of us. They're not smarter. They're not nicer. They don't have better judgment. They're just men."

•

As soon as Bitsy and I hung up, I called Greg. "Have you heard that Carol's campaign is having problems?"

"Yes, and I was about to tell you."

I said, "If the primary is four months from now, it's too late to jump into the race. Isn't it?"

"Could you take a leave from teaching this semester?"

"Not at this point."

"How much time do you actually spend in the classroom?"

"Eight hours a week."

"Man, I want to be a law professor."

"What a coincidence," I said. "I want to be a political strategist."

•

If Carol Moseley Braun's campaign was unstable, she wasn't alone. The day after I heard from Bitsy, a tabloid published an article about a Little Rock cabaret singer who claimed she'd had an affair with Bill for twelve years. She also claimed to have recordings of their recent phone conversations, including ones in which he urged her to deny their involvement. In a statement to the media, Bill's campaign press secretary said Bill and Sarah Grace did indeed know the woman but that her allegations were false and she'd been paid by the tabloid.

Listening to this news on NPR, I didn't feel glee, or even vindication. I felt sad, and I felt uneasy. Was this because, for the first time in my life, I understood not only how organically an affair could happen but also how special and sweet—how not sordid—it could seem to the two people involved?

And yet: twelve years? I wanted to imagine I'd never have put up with such a thing. Then again, I had, in the end, agreed to marry Bill, and I'd done so knowing of his predilections. He was the one who had spared me.

"I have something to tell you that might sound strange," I said to James. We were in our chairs in his office, holding hands. "You know Bill Clinton?"

"Not personally."

"Funny you should put it that way," I said. "When I was in law school and for a few years afterward, he was my boyfriend."

"The governor of Arkansas who's running for president and is involved in a sex scandal—that was your boyfriend?"

"Well, he wasn't the governor then, and he certainly wasn't running for president. But the first law school where I taught was the University of Arkansas."

James seemed nonplussed. "And to think that you denied leading a glamorous life."

"I can assure you that Fayetteville, Arkansas, in the midseventies was far from glamorous."

"Do you think the call girl's accusations are true?"

"She's a cabaret singer, not a call girl, but yes. The reason I didn't marry him is that he was chronically unfaithful."

"You would have married him otherwise?" There was a tinge of jealousy in James's voice.

I didn't want to upset him, but I also didn't want to lie. I said, "It was a very long time ago."

"Also hypothetically," I said to Greg over the phone, "if I do decide to jump into the Senate race, how damning is it if I have a co-worker, another law professor who's married and has a child, and he and I hold hands and hug in our offices? But we don't have sex, and we've never kissed."

After a beat, Greg said, "How many people know?"

"Besides us, I think only my friend Maureen."

"Ask him if he's told anyone, and make sure Maureen can keep her mouth shut."

"She can."

"Confirm it. How long has it been going on?"

"Three and a half months."

"You just, what, feel each other up?"

"Not even that. We really only hug and hold hands, and only in our offices with the doors closed."

"I've heard of a lot," Greg said, "but I didn't know kinks could be G rated. Stop immediately. The public can barely wrap its head around a female senator, and they're sure as shit not going to put up with a female senator who's boning someone else's husband."

"I'm not remotely close to boning him."

"The nuances of this will fall on deaf ears. Stop."

"By the way," I said, "the reason Bill Clinton and I broke up back in 1975 is that he kept cheating on me."

"How ironic. Are you looking forward to **60 Minutes**?" The furor around the cabaret singer's charges wasn't dissipating, and Bill and Sarah Grace were going to address the controversy on an episode of **60 Minutes** airing after the Super Bowl.

"I'm not sure I'll watch," I said. "My whole family will be at my brother's, and there's no way I'm watching Bill's interview with my parents there."

"Then come to my place, and we'll order Szechuan Wok's finest."

"I don't know if I **want** to watch."

"Hillary, I'm not even going to waste time pretending this is a real discussion. I hate football, so come over in the last inning or whatever they're called."

When I told my parents I wouldn't be at Hughie's,

my father said with evident pleasure, "It looks like your communist boyfriend really got his tit caught in a wringer this time, huh?"

Sarah Grace and Bill sat on a pale love seat in a hotel suite in New Hampshire, and the interviewer faced them from an armchair; over the interviewer's shoulder, a fire crackled in a fireplace. Sarah Grace wore the same style of dress she'd worn for Bill's announcement, this one light pink and puffy sleeved, with a Peter Pan collar. She looked extraordinarily nervous.

As the interviewer began asking Bill questions about the cabaret singer—"How do you know her? How would you describe your relationship?"—Sarah Grace was unblinking and unsmiling.

"Her outfit is way too **Little House on the Prairie,**" Greg said. "She should be wearing a suit."

"And they're sitting too far apart," I said. There were probably three inches of space between them. "They need to present a united front."

The singer had been a friendly acquaintance, Bill was saying, but her allegations of a twelve-year affair were false. He said Sarah Grace knew her, too, and that when the media started hounding the singer, Sarah Grace had been worried for her, thinking how frightened she must be by the lies and exposure. Sarah Grace's gaze shifted grimly between the interviewer and Bill.

"He needs to let her speak for herself," Greg said. "She should be saying all this, not him."

Just then, the interviewer asked Sarah Grace if what Bill said was true.

Sarah Grace nodded. She said, "I felt sorry for the woman."

I winced. "Unfortunate choice of words."

In a soft voice, her eyes downcast, she added, "I think Bill's been a wonderful governor for the state of Arkansas."

"Jesus Christ," I said. "Did they not give her media training?" She was so—there was no other word for it—weak. Bill needed an equal who'd act like even if he'd had affairs, so what? Because they both were sophisticated and tough and the only person he was answerable to was her and if she'd dealt with it, it was no one else's business; hell, maybe she'd had affairs, too. The American public would not, of course, like such a woman, but that didn't matter. He was the one running for office, and the reality was that a wife like that would probably win him sympathy votes.

The interviewer asked Bill what he'd meant when he'd previously said his marriage had had difficulties—did it mean communication problems? Adultery? Separation?

Bill said, "I think the American people, at least people that have been married for a long time, know what it means and know the whole range of things it can mean."

"That's a good answer," Greg said.

"But she's got to jump in," I said. "It can't just be him."

For the next few minutes, it was only him.

When the interviewer asked if he was prepared to say he'd never had an affair, Bill said, "I'm not prepared tonight to say that any married couple should ever discuss that with anyone but themselves."

He said, "I have acknowledged wrongdoing. I have acknowledged causing pain in my marriage. I have said things to you tonight and to the American people from the beginning that no American politician ever has."

He said, "I think most Americans who are watching this tonight, they'll know what we're saying. They'll get it, and they'll feel that we have been candid."

The interviewer said to Sarah Grace, "When your husband sits next to you, and his answers are not a denial that he's had an extramarital affair—what's that like?"

"I love Bill very much," Sarah Grace said in a quavering voice, and then she began to cry.

"Oh my God," I said, and Greg said, "What a train wreck."

"And I love Sarah Grace," Bill said, setting an arm around her shoulders. "And together we couldn't be more excited to get back to the real problems of this country, which is helping millions of Americans fulfill their dreams and find stability and prosperity." Did Bill think he looked protective, reassuring—husbandly?—in this moment?

"Call a priest," Greg said. "Someone needs to read the last rites to Bill Clinton's candidacy."

"Greg," I said, and he turned to look at me. "I want to run for Senate."

I didn't announce until February 18, three weeks later, but by the next day, a frenzy of activity had commenced that didn't stop until the primary: I was reaching out to major donors and influential members of the party, assembling a staff, requesting a leave from committees and other responsibilities from the dean of the law school and the university provost.

As Greg had recommended, I announced I was running by sitting down with a reporter from the **Tribune**. This interview would occur at the **Tribune**'s office on Michigan Avenue and, on the way, as Greg sat in the front seat of a taxi and his deputy, Jill, and I sat in the back, Greg turned around to face us. "Good God, Hillary," he said. "When did you last shave your legs?"

I was wearing a black wool skirt suit and pantyhose—never a lucky combination for me, apparently—and when I glanced down, it was true that the blond hair on my calves swirled visibly inside the nylon.

"Pull over," Greg said to the driver. "Jill, run into that Walgreens and get shaving cream and a razor."

When Jill reentered the car, she passed a plastic bag to me, and Greg said, "No. Jill, you do it for her."

"I shave Hillary's legs?" Jill sounded uncertain. "Now?"

"I'll do it," I said.

"Take off your tights, Hillary," Greg said. "And no, you won't. I want you focused while we run through your answers."

My life had changed overnight, and this was who I had become—a person whose legs were shaved by someone else, in a taxi. If I had lost, my entry into the Senate race would, I suppose, have seemed at best quixotic and at worst humiliating. But because I won—because I beat Dixon, Albert Hofeld, and Carol Moseley Braun in the primary and then Richard Williamson in the general—my decision to run for Senate took on a retroactive sheen of inevitability. It did so in a public way, seeming to others, especially journalists, like the fulfillment of a destiny set in motion at my Wellesley graduation. But it did so in a private way, too, in how I explained my life to myself: This, it turned out, was the reason I had never married or had children; this was the reason James and I hadn't really acted on our attraction; this was the reason I had worked hard as a professor and a volunteer and made important connections, so that at the age of forty-four I had a résumé that allowed me to run for U.S. Senate.

I tried to tell as many friends and acquaintances as possible ahead of time—friends because I was excited, and acquaintances so they'd feel flattered and invested and therefore inclined to donate.

Gwen was, of course, one of the first people I called. I said, "There's been a happy change of plan. I'm running for Senate."

Gwen said, "What about Carol Moseley Braun?"

"Her campaign has very serious problems, and she might well drop out before the primary. If I thought it was realistic that she could be elected, I wouldn't challenge her."

"My friend at the Rainbow Coalition told me she's a media darling and is raising lots of money."

"Yes and no," I said. "Apparently, her campaign manager is bad news, and Carol is flaky in terms of her schedule. I witnessed it myself at an event. I just don't think she can go the distance."

"Why don't you wait and see? And if she doesn't, run next time."

"The momentum following the Anita Hill stuff—if Carol isn't going to capitalize on it, someone else should."

I was unprepared for the steeliness in Gwen's tone when she said, "You haven't convinced me, Hillary. The idea that her campaign is troubled—that sounds like a justification for you doing what you want to do."

"Just to be clear," I said, "this isn't about race."

"Well, sure." There was an edge to Gwen's voice I hadn't heard even when she'd tried to convince me not to move to Arkansas. "This isn't about race for you."

I knew in advance the conversation wouldn't go well with James. Sitting side by side, holding hands—I'd decided this would be the last time, and the truth was that Greg's disdain had seeped into the act itself, rendering it slightly foolish—I said, "This is all a bit last-minute, but I've decided to run for Senate after all."

James looked just as dismayed as he had during our earlier conversations on the subject. "But why?"

Was he expecting me to answer literally? I said, "Because our government makes lots of important decisions, and I'd like to be involved in them."

"But politics is such a sleazy business, and you're such a lovely person."

Did I bristle because of the hint of snobbishness or paternalism or was it easier to say goodbye if I found some flaws in him?

I said, "It's far from a sure thing I'll beat Dixon, but, either way, this could be an opportunity for both of us."

James looked bewildered. "How?"

"You can recommit to your marriage, and I

can—" I paused. "Step back and get some perspective. I've had so much fun with you. I don't regret a minute of it. But maybe it's time to get on with things."

When he spoke, his voice was controlled but thick with emotion. He said, "What I feel with you is the most profound connection I've ever felt with another person. Maybe that's been one-sided, but this was always much more than fun for me."

"Of course it's not one-sided. James, I adore you. I just—with Susie—and David—"

"If I leave Susie, will you not run for Senate? If you asked me to leave her, I would."

I swallowed before saying, "I wouldn't ask you to do that."

"People get divorced."

"No one has ever gotten divorced because I asked them to."

We still were holding hands, and this was when he pulled his hand away and stood.

"James, I'm sorry," I said. "The fact that I'm running for Senate doesn't mean I don't value our friendship."

He was shaking his head, looking angry and also on the brink of tears. He said, "That's an awful thing to say to a person who's in love with you."

Once I had won the primary, the general election, given the political makeup of Illinois, was a foregone conclusion. Election night 1992 was nevertheless exciting because a record-breaking four other female senators won, including Barbara Mikulski being reelected from Maryland. Counting Nancy Kassebaum from Kansas, a total of six senators would now be women, and Kay Bailey Hutchison won a special election in Texas the next year. By then, the media had dubbed 1992 the Year of the Woman, a title I found both silly and heartening. Election night 1992 was also, of course, sobering because of George Bush's reelection.

Twenty minutes after the polls closed at seven, my race was called. My victory party was at the Hyatt Regency on East Wacker, and I wore a red skirt suit—red was not yet a color that belonged to Republicans—and spoke at eight-twenty, surrounded by my parents, brothers, and sister-in-law; Maureen and her family; a few Wellesley friends; and many volunteers, including Northwestern law students and undergraduates.

"I believe wholeheartedly that Illinois's brightest days are ahead of us," I said into the microphone. "And I'm confident that together, with hard work and optimism, we will reach them."

There were, of course, many things I didn't know then about the future. When journalists or voters ask me now about my first run for office, I think less of my campaign, which frankly has blurred with subsequent campaigns, and more of two images from the fall of 1991. The first is of Anita Hill delivering her opening statement—her aquamarine suit, her composure and isolation. In the sense that Clarence Thomas was confirmed, she didn't prevail. But she did, I feel certain, change the course of history.

The second image is the framed photo next to James's TV, his family's rugby shirts and their smiles and the autumn leaves behind them. When James committed suicide in December 1993, eleven months after I'd been sworn in as a senator, I don't believe that it was because I'd broken his heart; I don't believe a person takes his life unless he has serious underlying mental health issues. And in terms of external problems, the one that probably loomed much larger than me was that earlier in the fall, he'd been accused of misusing funds in his role as director of the Center for Law and Finance. On a college-visiting trip with his son, David, James had apparently paid for a rental car, meals, and hotel rooms with a university credit card. I can't imagine this was anything other than an honest mistake—he was more scrupulous and ethical than most people—and I also assume it embarrassed him deeply. It made the news and cost him his job with the Center, though he would have remained a professor.

I will always feel a terrible sadness that James hanged himself, from a beam in his family's basement. (I suspected it was intentional that he did it on a morning when a housecleaner was there so that it was she rather than Susie or David who found him.) I learned of James's death after returning to my Senate office from voting on a transportation bill; my colleague Eli from the law school had left a message.

My father also had died in 1993, back in April. Though I certainly mourned my father's passing, it was hard to know what I could have done differently with him. I was both grateful for the lessons he'd imparted and sorry they'd been shared with so much antagonism.

In contrast, even now, twenty-five years later, I harbor regrets about James. I wish that I had kept in touch with him after I left Northwestern, that I'd suggested meeting for lunch on a weekend when I was back in Chicago or just called his office to say hello. At the time, initiating contact would have felt like opening a sealed envelope. But now that I am in my seventies, I've learned that very little from the past is truly sealed.

Bill had dropped out of the presidential race four days after the **60 Minutes** interview. Four months later, at 6:30 A.M. on the morning after my Senate primary, he called me. I'd gotten three hours of sleep the night before and was still in bed.

"Congratulations," he said. "Madam Senator has a nice ring to it."

"Thank you," I said, "although I plan to keep working hard right through to the general. I'm sorry about your campaign. How have you been?" I actually did feel forgiving, as if I didn't need to punish him, because finally karma had.

"It's because you wouldn't go on the record about what a super guy I am," he said. "That's why it all blew up." He chuckled before adding, "In all seriousness, I'm thinking it's time for me to get out of the political racket. I'm not saying this to discourage you, but it's meaner than it used to be. It's more spiteful and a lot less fun."

"What would you do instead?"

"That's the question. Turns out you can pour your heart and soul into a state for decades, only to become persona non grata. You know what? Fuck 'em." Ah, here it was—his sincere self-pity and resentment, as if the cabaret singer's accusations had been a natural disaster over which he exerted no control.

"How's your family doing?"

"Sarah Grace's relieved I dropped out. She never wanted to live in the White House, and same for Ricky. But Alexis took it harder. I think you and Alexis would get a kick out of each other. She's a spitfire."

My call-waiting had beeped repeatedly as he'd

spoken, and I said, "Bill, forgive me, but I need to take this other call."

"Oh, Hillary," he said. "You were never the one who needed forgiveness."

There was at least one person who would have disagreed with Bill's assessment. Carol Moseley Braun had called me the previous night at ten past eight to concede, after I'd received calls from both Alan Dixon and Albert Hofeld. My primary-night victory party also took place at the Hyatt Regency, and when Carol called, I was in a suite with Maureen, who was helping with my makeup.

"Congratulations, Hillary," Carol said.

"Thank you," I said. "You ran a strong campaign, and I'd love to work together going forward, because it's clear our goals are aligned. I know you understand that I had to do what I felt was best for the state of Illinois."

Carol laughed and I thought at first that it was a sincere laugh. Then she said, "I realize you have to say that when the cameras are around. But for goodness' sake, Hillary, let's not pretend that either of us really believes it."

PART III

The Front-Runner

AMERICAN PRESIDENTS AND
VICE PRESIDENTS ELECTED 1988–2012

1988: George H. W. Bush and Dan Quayle

1992: George H. W. Bush and Dan Quayle

1996: Jerry Brown and Bob Kerrey

2000: John McCain and Sam Brownback

2004: John McCain and Sam Brownback

2008: Barack Obama and Joe Biden

2012: Barack Obama and Joe Biden

CHAPTER 5

2015

Iowa
April 26, 2015
5:23 P.M.

AT THE RALLY IN CEDAR Rapids, she was standing in the second row, holding up a sign that read EVEN CANCER WON'T KEEP ME FROM VOTING FOR YOU!!! Although the crowd wasn't exactly going wild, she cheered after every positive remark or policy promise that I made. She was forty or so, with long dark hair, wearing a gray hooded sweatshirt that said OLD NAVY across the front, and she was accompanied by two dark-haired girls I assumed were her daughters; one was a teenager who looked like she'd rather be elsewhere and the other was nine or ten and intermittently joined in her mother's cheers. The event was in a union hall, and this was the second day of a four-day visit to Iowa. I had announced two weeks earlier that I was, for the third time, running for president.

I'd been starting my stump speech by mentioning a local event or issue—in this case, a nineteen-year-old from nearby Shueyville was one of three finalists in a singing-competition television show that my traveling press secretary, Clyde, loved—then I always thanked local elected officials and organizers. I then spoke about the economy, jobs, education, and national security. In Cedar Rapids, the longer I went on, the more I could feel the energy in the hall flagging, apart from the woman in the second row. Indeed, after several instances in which she was the **only** one cheering, other people clearly began to wait with amusement for her exuberant yelp or "**Yesss,** Hillary!" This dynamic improved the energy in the air, though not by enough.

It wasn't necessarily that the audience was bored—these were the people who'd chosen to attend a Sunday afternoon political rally nineteen months before Election Day—and likelier a result of the fact that the hall could have held eight hundred people, and four hundred had shown up. As with a party, the most obvious determinant of how exciting a political event feels is the proportion of bodies to space.

About 75 percent of attendees were female,

which was standard for me: a smattering of little girls in tutus and glittery shirts (the previous day, in Waterloo, a six-year-old had been wearing a blue pantsuit, making me wish the one I was wearing was also blue instead of green); teenagers, who were generally the least emotive demographic, but you never knew; poised twenty- and thirtysomethings; my jaded but nevertheless hopeful peers, with whom of course I felt a particular affinity; and women twenty or thirty years my senior, the officially old ones who often were the most unabashedly thrilled I was running. Because this was Iowa, the vast majority of the audience was white.

I finished by encouraging everyone to register to vote if they weren't registered, to register others if they were, to caucus for me when the time came, and to remember that every donation helped, no matter the size. Even before the applause ended, the speakers swelled with an upbeat pop song by a young female artist.

As my traveling chief of staff, Theresa, my body woman, Kenya, and my security agent, Darryl, led me down the stage steps toward the rope line, I gave the event a B, maybe a B-plus considering the charms of the cheering woman. The rope line was, as usual, not rope but waist-high steel barriers around and between which members of the traveling press corps, including cameramen and sound guys, were inserting themselves among the Iowans. (Increasingly, reporters were women, but camera and sound people still were almost always men.) Just before I leaned over the barrier to shake the hand of an ancient-looking woman in a wheelchair, Theresa murmured into my ear, "Mary Witberg. She's a hundred and two."

"Thank you so much for coming," I said loudly as I extended my arm. "I'm thrilled you're here."

In a warbly voice I had to strain to hear, Mary Witberg said, "I was six years old when Congress gave women the right to vote. I've been waiting for you ever since."

I could feel Darryl, who was behind me, grab the waist of my pants because I was bending so far forward. I ignored this indignity—certainly not the only one of the day—and I said to Mary Witberg, "Well, you've been very patient. I can always remember when the Nineteenth Amendment passed because it's the same day my mother was born."

Seriously, quaveringly, Mary Witberg said, "I would like for you to be elected."

"I would, too," I said. "Very much. Thanks again for coming."

Next was another woman who looked to be a comparably youthful eighty-something. My mother, who had died in 2011 and whom I thought of every day, would have been between the ages of these two women—she'd have been ninety-five. The octogenarian asked, "How long will you be in Cedar Rapids?"

"I head down to Iowa City right after this," I said. "I'm on a four-day, twenty-county tour of the state, which is such a wonderful opportunity to see all different places."

The octogenarian said, "Why, twenty counties in four days hardly gives you time to piddle around anywhere."

I laughed. "I know, but I promise I'll come back. Thank you for helping us get to Election Day together."

A fifty-something woman wanted to know what my plan was for addressing the opioid epidemic, and a forty-something woman wanted to know what my position was on the Keystone XL pipeline, and a twelve-year-old girl told me she was raising money for Ethiopian orphans with AIDS. The next person was the woman who'd been holding the cancer sign, who blurted out, "Hillary, I love you!" Her daughters stood behind her, and the older one looked mortified.

Because it always felt disingenuous to reply "I love you, too," I instead smiled extra warmly and said, "Thank you very much for your support. I'm honored that you came today." Though I'd never had much luck convincing the media of it, I usually liked other human beings and they usually liked me. I liked their specificity, their often unfashionable clothes, their accents and enthusiasms and the things they cared about enough to seek me out and tell me about, and I liked their belief that I could help them in a measurable way. I wanted—I had always wanted this—for their belief to be accurate.

The woman exclaimed, "You're so much prettier than you look in pictures! Your eyes are so blue."

This observation about my appearance occurred daily, sometimes hourly, and I accepted it in the spirit in which I believed it was intended. "Thank you," I said. "I noticed your sign. How are you feeling?"

"Oh my God, Hillary, if a Republican is elected, I'm screwed because all they want to do is take away Obamacare."

"You have health insurance?" I said, and she nodded.

"But I used up all my sick days when I had surgery, and I haven't even started chemo yet. Hillary, I had to have a double mastectomy." So it was breast cancer; I hadn't felt like it was appropriate to ask.

"I'm sorry you're going through this," I said.

"I'm a single mom, but I'm a strong person like you. My sister helps us some, but she lives in Dubuque."

"Do you live in Cedar Rapids?" I asked. When she nodded, I said, "Have you connected with local support services? The American Cancer Society can often provide referrals." I gestured to the right. "This is one of my team members, Kenya. I want you to give your name and contact information to her."

"Hillary, you have to win!" the woman said. "I mean, these are my two daughters, so for being a role model, too."

"I'm trying my hardest." I smiled. "Thank you for all your enthusiasm today." Before I moved on to the next person, I turned and murmured to Theresa, "Bring her backstage."

1993

I had thought that I'd like being a senator; in fact, I loved it. The first speech I ever gave on the Senate floor was about fair housing, and the first bill I ever co-sponsored was the Improving America's Schools Act of 1993, and I loved being able to tangibly and directly take on the problems I had spent my adult life thinking about. I loved learning about topics that were less familiar, about foreign relations and energy and appropriations, and choosing where to focus my attention. I loved analyzing policy, talking to my staff and colleagues and experts in the field—it turned out experts were not only willing but in most cases seemed pleased to be sought out by a senator—and I loved reading briefing books in preparation for committee meetings and hearings, and I loved attending committee meetings and hearings. Most of my colleagues were bright and interesting, and some were funny and charming—even the

Republicans. There was a notoriously racist and sexist seventy-eight-year-old senator from South Carolina who once said to me, in the senators-only elevator, "I heard you were a women's rights firebrand, but nobody told me how cute you are," and then he winked, and, though I feared I was single-handedly undermining feminism, I henceforth saw him as an endearing grandfather. I loved the camaraderie of the weekly caucus lunches, where Democratic senators gathered to listen to our leadership and eat from a buffet of chicken and salad and red Jell-O, and I also loved the bipartisan female senators' dinners Barbara Mikulski initiated early in '93. These dinners usually happened in a modest room in the Capitol, and we discussed policy there, too, but sometimes we discussed things like the male-only pool where our Senate colleagues swam nude (there was no female-only pool) or how many of us had, while presiding over the Senate chambers, received the same anonymous note, delivered by a page, telling us to cover our cleavage.

I usually, unless they were confrontational or unpleasantly kooky, loved meeting the Illinoisans who'd stop by my office in the Hart Senate Office Building, the families and Girl Scout troops and retirees. I enjoyed returning to Chicago on weekends or when Senate was out of session and alternating between inhabiting my former life—seeing my parents or Maureen and her daughter,

Meredith, eating at my favorite restaurants—and traveling around the state for town halls and to walk in parades and shake hands at supermarkets. I loved finding myself in places I'd never have otherwise visited, mingling with people I otherwise wouldn't have met. Although I hadn't wanted to live in Springfield, let alone in the truly tiny towns downstate, it was fun to pass through them.

My sense of purpose as a senator made me recognize retroactively that there had been a certain slackness in my life before, or perhaps it was that previously I had been imposing structure on my days and now an external structure was imposed on them. I felt busy in a good way. I also, though this would have been difficult to express without sounding obnoxious, felt important. It wasn't that I was swarmed with fans—the reality is that most Americans don't know the names or faces of their own senators—and certainly I had detractors, too. But I felt what I'd felt in fifth grade when I'd been co-captain of my school's safety patrol, what I'd felt speaking at my Wellesley graduation: that my distinct abilities were recognized and appreciated.

I did not love fundraising, which, due to the laws against campaign activity in a federal building, usually took the form of walking with an aide to a featureless room inside an office the DSCC rented for this purpose a few blocks from the Senate buildings, sitting at a desk with a call sheet, and, for several hours, begging strangers, acquaintances, and friends for money. I didn't love it early on, and the time it required only increased in the years to come. But again, I was Midwestern enough to not only accept the downside to any situation but even to experience it with relief; life wasn't supposed to be perfect.

Iowa
April 26, 2015
5:44 P.M.

Backstage anywhere tends to be decidedly unglamorous. I've spent a significant portion of my political life in the bowels of convention halls, in underground parking lots and freight elevators and climbing the steps of loading docks, in the locker rooms of stadiums or just waiting to be called onstage from windowless cinder-block hallways—many, many windowless cinder-block hallways. Even when proper greenrooms exist, they tend to be utilitarian rather than fancy; also often windowless, with stained furniture and old carpet and sometimes an adjacent bathroom, though on more than one occasion, the bathroom hasn't included a door. Fresh fruit is a luxury, and flowers are downright decadent.

The union-hall greenroom in Cedar Rapids was no exception, featuring a massive mirror, a few stackable metal banquet chairs, and a "buffet" of bottled water and individual packets of Wheat Thins crackers. Over the course of twelve minutes, I rubbed elbows with—and again expressed my gratitude to, and posed for photos with—a local multimillionaire (she was the seventy-year-old widow of a seed entrepreneur) and her daughter-in-law; two city council members; and several of my campaign's Iowa field directors and deputy directors.

This time I officially met the woman with the cancer sign from the rope line. Holding out an arm, Theresa said, "And, Senator, you remember Misty LaPointe. She's a bank teller here in Cedar Rapids, and these are her daughters, Lauren and Olivia."

Without a steel barrier between us, Misty jumped into my arms. She seemed both happy and about to cry, neither of which was unusual on the campaign trail. Multiple times a day, I was encircled in the arms of strangers, my hair was petted, my hands and arms grabbed. Sometimes I had to change my shirt or jacket because a woman's lipstick or foundation had rubbed off on the fabric, usually at my shoulder.

I said, "If you're comfortable telling me a little more about your situation, when were you diagnosed?"

"It's BRCA1." Her tone had become abruptly serious. "I didn't even know what that was, but I found a lump on Christmas Day. It was so bad, Hillary. I was so worried."

"I take it you're having adjuvant chemo?"

She nodded. "I'm doing Friday afternoons so I'll have the weekend to recover without taking off more work."

"Do your doctors know how long the chemo will last?"

"They said at least six months. Hillary, oh my God, I'm sorry, but can we take a picture with you?"

"Of course," I said.

Misty passed her phone to Theresa, and we all quickly maneuvered into place. I was between Misty and Lauren, the teenager, my arms around both their backs. Olivia, who stood in front of us, glanced over her shoulder at me and said, "Are you going to win?"

"That's the plan," I said, and all the adults in earshot laughed. I smiled as Theresa clicked the phone several times, though what Misty had told me was alarming. I had never stopped being struck by how unevenly good and bad fortune were distributed, even when you accounted for class, or maybe accounting for class was impossible. As we stepped apart, I said to Misty, "My team member Kenya is going to refer you to an aide in my Senate office, and she'll help you find some resources, stuff like if you need someone to drive you to doctor's appointments. But I want to keep in touch. Please let Kenya know how your first day of chemo goes, and she'll pass the message on to me. I really mean it. I'm rooting for you."

"Senator, it's time for us to leave," Theresa said. "Misty, thank you so much for coming."

"And for bringing your wonderful daughters," I added. Already, I was being ushered away, into a cinder-block hall that would lead to a stairwell that would lead to a rear parking lot, but in my last seconds in the greenroom, I called out "Stronger together!" and held up one fist. In reply, everyone assembled cheered.

In the stairwell, I said to Kenya, "Call Frieda at the American Cancer Society and see what support services they have in Cedar Rapids."

1994

Early on, the press and I enjoyed a cordial if not cozy relationship. As part of the Year of the Woman, I'd received an initial spike in attention before and after taking office that had mostly dissipated within a few months. Insofar as I had a national identity, it seemed I was perceived of as a hard worker, a pragmatic centrist, and a Midwestern bore. When I was the primary sponsor of a bill requiring greater accountability for government contracts and task orders, the **Sun-Times** ran a cartoon of me as a school principal exhorting my constituents to eat their vegetables; that same week, **The New York Times** referred to me as a "flat-voweled Democratic stalwart." And in January 1994, a **Tribune** profile taking stock of my first year in office was headlined "Proudly Dull, Defiantly Dowdy: Hillary Rodham Is Just Fine with Being Uncool." In equal parts, I was amused and insulted; before reading the headline, I had never considered myself especially proud, dull, defiant, dowdy, or uncool.

A particular **Tribune** reporter, a woman in her early twenties named Erin Calhoun, somehow got it in her head that I had inordinately expensive taste in restaurants, haircuts, clothing, vacation destinations, and cultural outings. The implication was that, while my preferences might be in keeping with those of a person who'd attended Wellesley and Yale, they were at odds with those of my voters, especially downstate. But the most irritating part of Erin Calhoun's preoccupation with my finances was that, though I was twenty years her senior, her tone implied that she was flagging the extravagance of a peer: "If it's Labor Day Weekend, some of us are roasting hot dogs at Lincoln Park, and others of us—yep, looking at you, Hillary Rodham—are off dining on steak tartare and caviar at Trio. . . ." I learned from an aide that, like me, Erin Calhoun had attended a public high school in an upper-middle-class suburb, in her case Buffalo Grove, before attending Loyola University in Rogers Park. I met her once at the Illinois State Fair, and she was unremarkable, with medium-brown hair, a doughy build, and an air of smugness; I presume she was present at other public events I participated in but we just didn't speak. I hope she didn't know, because I'm more than a little ashamed to admit it, that a few years existed when, to those closest to me, I'd routinely complain about Erin Calhoun for ten or fifteen minutes at a time. Later, the frustration seemed amateur on my part, even quaint, given the relative mildness of her criticism and the fact that such criticism was limited enough that I knew its main practitioner by name, age, and high school.

The strangest rumor about me in the nineties, one initially promulgated by the alt weekly the **Chicago Reader,** was that I was a virgin. Another rumor was that I was a lesbian, but the virgin one proved to have more sticking power. Though I never was asked outright about it in an interview, my communications director was asked so many times that she developed a stock answer: "That's not a question worth dignifying." Oddly, the **Reader** first floated the virgin theory in an article that rebutted its own premise by mentioning the names of a few men I was alleged to have dated. Though two of the names were accurate, to my relief, my Northwestern colleague James's was not among them. And really, from the time I took office until eleven years later, I didn't know how good I had it mediawise. I didn't understand how ugly things would get.

Iowa
April 26, 2015
8:17 P.M.

My event in Iowa City was in the student union at the university, a question-and-answer session with perhaps a hundred more people in attendance than in Cedar Rapids. It was satisfyingly substantive: Audience members asked about my policies and funding around mental health, whether I'd expand the number of families eligible for Pell grants, and how I'd address climate change. Two thirds of the way in, a man in his twenties said into the standing microphone in the aisle, "You claim to support campaign finance reform, yet you yourself are awash in dark money. You're a hypocrite," and the audience split into simultaneous applause and booing. But I suspected the booing came more from his un-Midwestern tone, name-calling, and lack of an actual question than from the issue he was raising, which was legitimate.

"I understand the disconnect that you're seeing," I said. "And I promise that I'm deeply and sincerely committed to getting special-interest money out of our political system. Unfortunately, the system is currently set up in such a way that for me not to accept PAC contributions in this election cycle would be to simply give control to conservatives using secretive back channels to do things like roll back environmental regulations and strip Americans of social services. I'm a pragmatist, and I've always been committed to working for change from within the system. But make no mistake. I believe unlimited fundraising jeopardizes our democracy, and, as your president, I will aggressively fight it."

It was by this point after 8:00 P.M., and I thought the exchange would be the emotional inflection point of the event. And I suppose that, publicly, it was. But fifteen minutes later, on the rope line, I got the bombshell. A white-haired man in a Hawkeyes windbreaker had just declared, "I don't like greedy bankers on Wall Street getting bailed out of their messes while the rest of us struggle to get by."

Before I could respond, a network reporter standing behind him, a man named Tiff whom I wasn't crazy about—he reminded me of an overgrown prep school boy with palpably high regard for his own talents—called over the hubbub, "Senator Rodham, any comment on the rumors that Bill Clinton will announce tomorrow that he's entering the presidential race?"

What the hell are you talking about? I thought. I had heard these rumors over the years but not in recent weeks or days. I ignored both the question and the mic angled a foot above my forehead. I said to the white-haired man, "I don't like it, either. And if you go to my website, you can read all about my economic plans to help the middle class."

The network reporter repeated, "Senator, any comment on the rumors that Bill Clinton will announce he's running?" The reporter's voice had taken on a tone of beleaguered amusement, as if, rather than his interrupting a conversation, he were the one being treated with disdain.

I glanced over my left shoulder and made eye contact with Theresa. Neither of us said anything, and—we had been working together for eighteen years—I was almost certain that what she conveyed in this mutual silence was **I haven't heard it, either**.

The network reporter called, "Has Governor Clinton notified you of his decision?"

"Banks should be held accountable just like people," the white-haired man said. "They shouldn't get special treatment."

"You're right," I said. "I'm going to address that, and I'll also create a lot of new jobs, increase the minimum wage, and stop multimillionaires from paying lower taxes than everyone else."

The network reporter called, "Will the fact that you and Bill Clinton dated influence the race?"

1997

Starting when she was about ten, Maureen's daughter, Meredith, would come stay with me for a night or two a few times a year—usually if Maureen and Steve were traveling (Meredith's brothers were by then in college), but in some cases just because Meredith and I had fun together. That she was a kind of surrogate daughter seemed so obvious as to not need articulating between Maureen and me, but it was the daughter part—the child part—that was as precious to me as the surrogate part. Meredith was a respite from all the adults I interacted with, with their agendas and neuroses and cynicism. Meredith did have an agenda, of course, but it was to speak in an English accent, win when we played Connect Four, and convince me to give her ice cream multiple times a day.

One evening in August 1997, when Senate was out of session, Meredith and I were in the den of my Chicago apartment, eating mint chocolate chip ice cream (hers was topped with gummy bears and mine wasn't) and watching an interview with a very famous pop singer. The singer was about to turn forty and was divorced, with one child. Near the end of the interview, the host of the newsmagazine said, "As you approach this milestone birthday, you're an international icon. You have unprecedented album sales, countless awards, and hundreds of millions of dollars in the bank. But tell me: Are you lonely?"

The singer's expression was coolly amused—if she thought the question was idiotic, I agreed—and she said, "Well, top-of-game alone. Sure."

"Top-of-game alone," the host repeated. "What do you mean by that?"

The singer said, "At times, I feel lonely because there's only one of me. But the plus side is"—she was wearing bright red lipstick and a sleeveless, low-cut black blouse, and she leaned forward and smiled—"there's only one of me. I was born with special abilities, special creativity, and if it was 1850, I'd be out of luck. But it's 1997, and the sky's the limit. I've been selling out stadiums for twenty years. I **can** do it, and I **am** doing it."

As I watched, the hairs on my arms stood up. I hesitate to say that I realized in this moment that I'd eventually run for president, because at some level it was as if I already knew, as if I'd always known. Perhaps it's more accurate to say this was when I admitted what I knew to myself.

Meredith was thirteen then. She gestured toward the screen and, with her mouth full of ice cream and gummy bears, she said, "Hillary, she's like you."

Iowa
April 26, 2015
9:40 P.M.

My traveling team, those of us making our way around the state in an armored van, numbered at eleven, including me; Theresa, who in addition to being my traveling chief of staff also held the title of campaign vice chair; my traveling press secretary, Clyde; my campaign trip director, Diwata; my body woman, Kenya; my hairstylist, Veronica; my makeup artist, Suzy; a young video director named Ellie; a not-so-young photographer named Morty; and Darryl and Phil, the two Secret Service agents who doubled as drivers. Of this group, the ones I summoned to meet in my suite in the Marriott in Davenport were Theresa, Clyde, and Diwata.

I'd already changed into my pajamas, though I kept on a bra—there were certain realities of gravity and time to which I felt it was simply cruel to subject my twenty- and thirtysomething staffers—and also donned a fleece jacket.

In the suite's living room, I was in one armchair, Clyde was in another, Theresa sat on the love seat, and Diwata sat in the desk chair that she'd turned around to face the rest of us. "I think we just say we always knew Bill Clinton's candidacy was a possibility," I said.

"I'll start doing background with the networks and the wires," Clyde said.

"Sorry, but 'We always knew it was a possibility' will satisfy the travelers for about a minute," Diwata said. "The travelers" was how we referred to the traveling press corps.

"He's out of touch with everyday Americans. That's number one," Theresa said. "And out of practice politically."

"A lot of people consider 'out of practice politically' a recommendation," I said, and, at the same time, Clyde said, "He'll for sure present himself as an outsider, and we can't give credence to it."

"Won't he mostly present himself as Daddy Warbucks?" Diwata said.

Diwata was twenty-eight, Clyde was thirty-two, and Theresa was thirty-nine. This meant that they knew him more as a tech billionaire than as a politician; when his presidential campaign had imploded, they'd been between the ages of five and sixteen. I wondered if they'd ever watched the **60 Minutes** interview. Certainly Theresa knew about my past with Bill—she even knew, as almost no one else did, about my visit to his penthouse in San Francisco in 2005—and I assumed Clyde and Diwata knew I'd dated him. I'd devoted a paragraph to it in my 2002 memoir-plus-campaign-treatise, **Midwestern Values.** I didn't include this information to boast but rather to lay to rest that stupid virgin rumor. However, from time to time at appearances or in interviews, I was asked about having dated Bill, and the implication seemed to be that it was a bit of trivia amusing exactly in proportion to its unlikeliness. **Why** it was unlikely that I'd dated Bill related, presumably, to a perceived imbalance in our appearances, or to the fact that Bill now showed up in gossip columns consorting with mildly famous and highly attractive women in their thirties or forties—TV anchors, wellness gurus, B-list actresses. Once, during an onstage conversation at a women's conference in San Diego in 2006, my bubbly interlocutor had exclaimed,

"All I can say is you must have been a fox in law school!"

In Davenport, I looked from Diwata to Clyde. "Have either of you met Bill?"

They shook their heads.

"Have you heard him speak?" I asked.

"I've seen him interviewed," Clyde said.

"At his worst," I said, "he's long-winded and pedantic, and at his best, he's dazzling. He can hold the attention of a room, but he also can connect one-on-one in a very emotional, intuitive way."

"I know what you mean," said Diwata. "But, like, post-Obama? He's just, you know—" She trailed off, and I raised my eyebrows. "Pale, male, and stale?" she said. Diwata herself was biracial, the daughter of a black father and a Filipina American mother.

I laughed—at sixty-seven, I was just a year younger than Bill, and equally white—and I said, "Again, some consider that a recommendation."

Theresa deepened her voice and said, "I just find something about him very presidential. Hard to say what."

I deepened my voice, too—this was a routine all of us engaged in—and said, "I'd like to share a beer with him."

Clyde, who normally spoke in a borderline falsetto, said gruffly, "Maybe him and me could go huntin'."

I looked at Diwata and said, "Point taken, though."

In his usual voice, Clyde said, "Here's where I think Clinton's campaign is a nonstarter. It's not just that he cheated when he was married, right? He's been accused of full-on sexual harassment." Clyde pulled out his phone, typed rapidly, and said, "Yeah, I thought so. In '93, he settled a case brought by an Arkansas state employee for $850,000."

"Plus, like, orgy parties?" Diwata said.

I could feel Theresa glance at me delicately, and I made eye contact with her. "Have our researchers focused on Bill at all?" I asked.

"I'll check," she said, "but I don't think much, so far."

By design, I didn't even know the firm's name to whom my campaign outsourced opposition research, or the acquisition of damning information about both my potential Democratic and Republican opponents. When my staff members relayed choice findings to reporters, it was through third parties, and when I learned choice findings, it was through my chief of research, a woman named Gigi Anderson, who lived in Washington.

"Regarding the elephant in the room," I said, "I trust you all know that I dated Bill in law school and afterward. We almost got married." I hadn't mentioned the marriage part in **Midwestern Values**, but none of them looked surprised.

In a neutral tone, Clyde said, "Are you in contact with him now?"

"Not often. Occasionally by email." I glanced among them. "I really don't want to spend the primary answering questions about my law school love life. Assuming he does announce tomorrow"—by this point, the rumor was all over the Internet—"let's come up with two or three anodyne sentences and repeat them ad nauseam."

"You want them tonight or first thing in the morning?" Clyde asked.

"The morning's fine," I said. I noticed that Theresa was rolling her lips inward and outward, which she did under stress. She was remarkably unflappable, but this gesture was her tell.

"Just out of curiosity," Diwata said, "**did** we always know this was a possibility?"

"Everything is always a possibility," I said. "From the minute he left politics, he's floated the idea of getting back in. I guess at some point I decided he was crying wolf."

"What about this?" Clyde said. "You address the dating stuff during an interview on an entertainment talk show. Daytime, nighttime, whatever, but it's chatty and conversational."

Theresa nodded. "That could work."

"It's just really weird," Diwata said.

We all looked at her. "What's really weird?" I asked.

Though Diwata was playful by nature, her expression was somber. She said, "It's weird you almost married Bill Clinton, because he seems so unworthy of you."

1997

On the evening that Meredith and I watched the interview with the pop singer, after Meredith fell asleep in my guest room, I sat in my nest and made notes on a legal pad. I understood that I would need to convince the American people gradually, that it was virtually impossible I'd run for president once and get elected. At that point, Jerry Brown had been in the White House for a year and a half. Based on his lack of popularity—from the start, conservatives had succeeded in depicting him as antibusiness and eccentric—I saw two paths forward. Both involved running for the first time in 2004; that would be my practice. If Jerry managed to win a second term, a Republican would likely win in '04, so I could run again in '08 against that Republican incumbent—again as a kind of practice. And then in 2012, I could run with the realistic hope of becoming elected. At that point, I would be sixty-four years old, and, assuming my own senatorial reelections, I'd have held office for twenty years. If either Jerry had just one term or a Republican president got elected for just one term, then my goal in '08 would be to join the Democratic ticket as the party's vice presidential nominee and run for president in '16. This scenario seemed preferable in terms of acclimating voters to the idea of a woman president. In that version, I'd be sixty-nine years old on Election Day 2016.

That Monday, I called Deb Strom, the executive director of the Victoria Project, which was a political action committee named for Victoria Woodhull that worked to elect pro-choice Democratic women in national races. After an introduction facilitated by my bundler, Bitsy Sedgeman Corker, they had endorsed me in '92 and helped significantly with my fundraising, and in the six years since, I'd campaigned for other female candidates endorsed by the Victoria Project and I'd also become friends with Deb.

When I reached her by phone, I said, "I want something, and I think you want it, too, and I'm wondering if you'd like to work with me to try to make it happen. I want to become president."

"Oh, Hillary," Deb said. "Be still my heart." Then she added, "We've already discussed this internally, but we decided to wait until your reelection next year to approach you about it."

In a series of confidential meetings over the next several months, six of us met in the Victoria Project's Dupont Circle office: me; Deb; her deputy; my chief of staff; Greg Rheinfrank, who still worked as a consultant in Chicago and whom

I remained close to; and Bitsy Sedgeman Corker. To me, though not to anyone else, Greg referred to us as the Itsy Bitsy Titsy Committee. In most ways, the strategy we laid out aligned with the one I'd developed in my nest, though the collaborative plan contained more specific benchmarks: which Senate committees I ought to join or bills I should sponsor to demonstrate my presidential bona fides; how much money I'd need to raise by what dates. We determined that I'd write a book prior to 2004, that I'd court particular journalists and form alliances with certain members of Congress.

One March evening, Greg and I left a meeting and walked north on Connecticut Avenue, planning to get a drink at a bar near my apartment in the Kalorama neighborhood. He said, "Don't you wish you had a crystal ball so you could see if we pull it off and make you the FWP?"

"What's the FWP?" I said. Then I said, "Oh."

Iowa
April 26, 2015
11:04 P.M.

And then, while I was lying in bed at the Marriott in Davenport, responding to emails on my iPad, my cellphone rang and the name **Bill** showed up on the caller ID. I knew many Bills, there was even a twenty-seven-year-old Bill on my speechwriting team, a man with whom I interacted frequently, but only one Bill was in my contacts without a surname. Though I didn't speak often to this Bill, he retained pride of place.

When I answered, his voice was warm. "Hillary, it's Bill Clinton," he said. "How are you doing?"

"I'm fine," I said. "How are you?"

"I'm well." It was the delivery of those two words—distant, almost impersonal, but pleasantly so—that made me know, before he said the rest. He was upbeat but not in a mood to engage; this was perfunctory, I was an obligation, and he was checking me off a list. He was calling to say that the rumors he was running against me were true.

"Listen," he said. "You know I have nothing but the highest respect for you."

I've learned over many decades that people are likeliest to declare their respect when their behavior suggests the opposite.

"You're a brilliant woman," he continued, "and you're a formidable candidate. But I trust you'll agree that robust competition in the primary is all to the good. The engagement Democrats showed in '08 was thrilling"—he was referring, of course, to Barack Obama's victory over me to secure the party's nomination—"and that's why I'm throwing my hat in the ring."

I said nothing, and, laughing a little, he said, "You haven't hung up on me, have you?"

I wasn't laughing at all as I asked, "How final is your decision?"

"Really?" he said. "Not even congratulations?"

"When are you announcing?"

"Tomorrow," he said. "Noon PST."

Fury rose up in me—fury at the lateness of this ostensible courtesy call, at his blithe tone, at the enormous personal fortune that allowed him to make such a decision without needing to show his hand ahead of time by forming an exploratory committee for fundraising. And, if I was being honest, fury at myself for not trying harder or earlier to preempt this eventuality.

For all these reasons, I made an effort to sound pleasant. I said, "I know it's been a while, but you remember how grueling the campaign trail is, don't you? Long hours, bad sleep, unhealthy food? And there are people called journalists, whose job it is to record everything you say and to wait for one throwaway comment that comes out a little wrong and lead the news with it. Then at the next event, they're shocked that you're not happy to see them."

Bill's tone was as congenial as mine. "If I didn't know better," he said, "I'd think you were trying to intimidate me."

"I doubt that's possible. These are just friendly reminders. The journalist creatures also like to dwell on the past. They have very long memories."

"You might find it hard to believe," he said, "but I miss campaigning. I remember everything you're saying, but there's the fun, too. The camaraderie, the handshaking, the stories from all those real people. I'm sure we can agree that that side of things always came more naturally to me."

I ignored the slight. "It seems like you're in a good place in your life," I said. "I'm surprised you'd want to trade that away."

"Is it nice to enjoy the fruits of my labors? You bet it is. But there's more to life than corporate boardrooms and protein smoothies. And you and I are no youngsters. It's now or never."

"Obviously, you've always been drawn to service," I said. "I don't think you've ever really left it behind." Of course I thought he'd left it behind, but I knew from Silicon Valley fundraisers that there was little a tech billionaire found more pleasing than the pretense that his innovations made life more equitable and meaningful. I added, "And that's why I'd love to offer you a position in my administration. An ambassadorship, a cabinet role—you'd be a natural as secretary of education or HUD."

"Oh, Hillary." He chuckled. "How very magnanimous of you."

"I'm serious," I said. "Skip the drudgery, enjoy the perks. I'm in Davenport, Iowa, at this very moment. For dinner, I ate a cold burrito."

"You really do think I've become a princess, don't you?"

"I'm not sure I have a handle on who you've

become," I said. "Because this nonsense about robust competition—do I need to remind you that that's the perfect way to get Jeb Bush elected? Or Mitt Romney?" Though neither of them had yet announced, these were the expected Republican front-runners. "If you actually care about your legacy, help put the first woman president in office. Do it for Alexis and for 155 million other girls and women in this country. Don't stand in my way."

"Says the woman who started her political career by cock-blocking Carol Moseley Braun." His tone was still unruffled. "You know what?" he said. "You and I are going to have a lot of fun, and so are the American people. I always loved our discussions, and now the whole country will get to watch them in real time."

You asshole, I thought. **You fucking asshole.** Aloud, I said, "In that case, best of luck to you."

1998

Eight months after I was sworn in as a senator, in January 1993, a letter from Barbara Overholt had arrived at my apartment in Chicago. **It isn't public yet,** she'd written, **but Bill and Sarah Grace have separated and will be divorced within the year.** I received this letter during a weekend I was in Chicago, and it agitated me because what I wanted to think was **Who cares?** And what I thought instead was, **Wait, Bill's single?** But I did nothing other than write back, **Thank you for the update. I wish that I were attending the Women's Law Conference with you this year and we could catch up over a drink at a very cheesy hotel bar next to some plastic ferns.** I'd been touched that Barbara and Ned had each donated a thousand dollars—the maximum then—to my Senate campaign.

A few months after exchanging letters with Barbara, while reading **The Wall Street Journal,** I learned that Bill had moved to Silicon Valley to be the CEO and eighth employee of an early web services provider—a hire made, obviously, not for his coding expertise but for his ability to work a room and inspire confidence in others. The web services provider had a silly-sounding name that seemed a bit less silly on the day of its IPO, in 1996, when shares opened at twenty-four dollars and closed at forty-two dollars. From that point on, as far as I could tell, Bill was harvesting money. As so many implausible outcomes do, his status as a tech tycoon also took on the retroactive sheen of inevitability.

It was in 1997 that I learned, in a one-sentence aside in an article about Bill's guidance of the company that ran in the business section of **The New York Times,** that he was engaged to a woman named Evangeline Cole. Despite the best efforts of Bill's own company, the Internet in 1997 was not the comprehensive and speedily accessed labyrinth it's since become. Thus, sheepishly but with faith in her discretion vis-à-vis other staff members, I asked my personal aide, Joanna, who had a plucky college student intern named Theresa, to determine exactly who Evangeline Cole was. The answer: the thirty-eight-year-old daughter of a legendary Los Angeles music producer and executive, which was to say an heiress still probably young enough to have children. She'd graduated from Harvard, had never been married, and had never really held a job, though she'd participated in job-adjacent activities, such as underwriting a documentary about elephant poaching in Chad.

A year later, I was on a plane from Denver to Jackson Hole to appear on a panel at a progressive think tank's summer conference. A few hundred presenters—people active not just in politics but in academia, public health, technology, and the arts—would be joined by an audience of very rich donors. I was accompanied by Theresa, who had graduated from Temple University and whom I'd promoted from intern to personal aide, and by my fundraising consultant Delaney Smith. During this scenic and bumpy plane flight, I looked at a briefing book Delaney had prepared that featured the photos and truncated biographies of the conference donors whom Delaney planned to nudge me toward in the hope that they might wish to support the work of a defiantly dowdy and flat-voweled Democratic centrist. When I turned a page to see separate side-by-side yearbook-style photos of Bill and Evangeline Clinton, I gasped.

Though '98 was an election year for me, it wasn't an accident that I hadn't sought out Bill to ask for money, not recently and not ever. As our plane began its descent, I explained to Delaney that I knew Bill, but some requests were simply too fraught to make.

It turned out Bill and I were on separate panels at the same time the next morning, as I realized after checking in to the resort and reading the conference program. His panel was on the digital divide, and mine was on early public education. I was relieved that the simultaneity precluded my attendance, or even making a decision about my attendance, at his. But I blurted out to Theresa, in a blushing way that made me feel a bit like I was in seventh grade, that it was very weird Bill was there.

"He was sort of the love of my life," I said. I was attempting to decrease the awkwardness, and probably managing the opposite, when I said, "Do you have a boyfriend?" Theresa was twenty-two then, and I was fifty-one.

"Yes," she said. "Bryan. But he still lives in Philly."

"Is he in grad school?"

"He's on his brother's construction crew. We went to high school together, and he started at community college but he decided to work instead." Though the way she said this was not with embarrassment, she clearly understood she was conveying slightly surprising information.

I said, "Have the two of you dated since high school?"

She laughed. "My mom wouldn't let me date." I already knew Theresa was the oldest of six sisters. "Bryan and I were friends, but we didn't get involved till I was in college."

Theresa was so good at her job—so organized and calm and easy to be around—that I hadn't realized until this moment, a year into knowing her, how pretty she was. She had delicate features and dark hair that she wore in a bun.

I said, "When he's next in Washington, I look forward to meeting him."

That night in Jackson Hole, the dinner beneath a sprawling white tent in the yard of a massive chalet-style house was one of those events with a higher proportion of famous than non-famous guests. The Grand Tetons rose behind us, a jazz quartet played on a patio near a stream, servers passed bacon-wrapped dates and tuna tartare, and an unsurpassed quality of progressive schmoozing occurred.

After making our way through the sumptuous buffet, Delaney, Theresa, and I took seats at one of the round tables for eight, joining the former ambassador to Ireland and his wife, and the CEO of a responsibly-made-athletic-clothing company and his wife; as per Delaney's instructions, I sat next to the CEO. We'd been speaking for just a few minutes when a friendly, husky, Southern voice, said, "Got room here for two more?"

"Oh my goodness, Bill," I said. "Look at you." I really was happy to see him, far less ambivalently than I'd have expected. When he'd dropped out of the presidential race in '92, it seemed he'd paid a price for his various transgressions; because of the choices he'd made, he would not get to lead the life he'd most wanted. But when he'd turned around and immediately made millions in the private sector, the price had seemed rather low.

I stood as he set down a heaping plate. Warmly, he said, "Madam Senator," and I said, "Oh, please," and he kissed my cheek. Then he cocked his head to take in the entirety of the tent and murmured so that only I could hear, "Now this is what I call an A-plus elitist clusterfuck."

Delaney moved so Bill could sit next to me, and I was describing to him the panel I'd be on when a tall, slim—and I mean slim even by the standards of wealthy mountain towns—woman with long brown hair appeared behind Bill. She wore an electric-blue cocktail dress. Before greeting anyone at the table, she gestured toward Bill's plate, which included, among piles of green salad and orzo, two slabs of prime rib and some exceptionally gooey scalloped potatoes. In a tight voice, she said, "Bill, it's a Thursday. You want to be eating fish."

Bill chuckled, gestured at me, and said, "Evangeline, this is Senator Hillary Rodham."

She regarded me coolly and simply said, "Hi." Some people are nervous or intimidated to meet a senator; Evangeline was not one of them. If I hadn't already known she'd grown up privileged, this would have been proof. When Theresa stood and gave her seat to Evangeline, Evangeline didn't acknowledge her.

But with Bill's arrival, the conversation at the table took on an effortless quality; he asked us questions, collectively and individually; he pontificated, but entertainingly; he made knowledgeable references to the Irish economy and to the Licancabur volcano, in Bolivia, which the CEO had recently climbed, and to the Workforce Investment Act, which I was co-sponsoring. Through all of this, Evangeline sat in silence and picked at her food. Before dessert, the hostess whose enormous yard we sat in, who'd made her fortune in a frozen yogurt chain during the eighties and nineties, gave a toast congratulating all of us and herself on our magnificence. As soon as she finished, before the dissipation of the applause, Evangeline set her hand on Bill's forearm and mouthed, **Let's go**. It still took another fifteen minutes for them to depart because of Bill's long goodbyes to us and those at nearby tables; to his credit, he even found Theresa at the next table, apologized for causing her to move, and inquired where she'd grown up and how long she'd worked with me.

As soon as he and Evangeline were out of sight, I said to Theresa, "Wow."

"Well, it is Thursday," Theresa said. "Which apparently is a fish day."

"That must be what he wants," I said. "Because he's always had plenty of women to choose from."

How strange that Bill had ended up married to a woman who clearly hated him! Granted, he was probably cheating on her and she probably knew it. But the intensity of her antipathy suggested that she'd never experienced an affection for him abundant enough to mitigate his flaws.

Delaney, Theresa, and I stayed at the party for another hour. I chatted with a world-famous violinist and a geneticist who was also a professor at Princeton, and it was Delaney's job to delicately interrupt, gesture a few feet to my left, and murmur, "That's the shipping heir Karl Zinsser, and he's obsessed with solar panels."

Then we boarded one of several shuttles departing from outside the front door of the chalet. It was a two-mile ride back to the resort, during which our driver pulled over twice because black bears were frolicking in the road. A playwright who had won the Pulitzer the previous spring was drunk enough that he attempted to exit the shuttle and introduce himself to the bears, but the driver talked him out of it, and I felt a peculiar lightness, a merriment even, at the many interesting places my life had taken me.

Iowa
April 27, 2015
6:45 A.M.

I had texted Diwata and asked her to stop by my suite, before my team met in the lobby but after my hair stylist, Veronica, finished blow-drying my hair; yelling over the hair dryer's roar was not my favorite way to conduct a conversation.

When Diwata appeared, I was sitting in the desk chair in the living room, reading news on my iPad while Veronica rubbed texture cream through my hair and Suzy, my makeup artist, sat on the love seat looking at her phone. Diwata greeted all of us and said, "Boss, are you feeling ethanol-ish?"

"Well, always," I said. "But especially today." On my schedule for the next fourteen hours was a morning visit to an ethanol plant, an afternoon roundtable with community college students, and a stop-in at a yarn shop to discuss my proposed standard tax deduction for small businesses. How much, I wondered, would Bill's entry into the race hijack the news cycle? I said to Diwata, "At our meeting last night, you made a reference to orgy parties, and I couldn't tell if it was a joke. What did you mean?"

Diwata looked as if she'd detected a bad odor, but she spoke matter-of-factly. "Supposedly, Bill Clinton attends Silicon Valley sex parties with other very rich men, and there are drugs and group sex."

"Good God," I said. "Does everyone except me know about this?"

"There was an article a few months ago that was, ah—vivid? It only mentioned Clinton in passing, but I'll send it to you."

"Do you mean the men have sex with each other? Or are women there?"

Diwata smirked. "There are definitely women there. Like young hotties is my impression."

In the mirror above the desk, I made eye contact with Veronica and said, "Have **you** heard of this?"

"Not till now." Veronica was in her forties, the lesbian mom of a teenage boy, and she lived in Chicago and sometimes did my hair there, too. Suzy, who would do my makeup when Veronica finished, was in her fifties, worked on film and TV sets around the world, and was a woman whose credibility was enhanced by the fact that her own skin glowed. Whenever our campaign plane touched down, before I emerged onto the tarmac, she'd spray mineral water on my face and also, for fun, on the faces of whoever else happened to be nearby. The extra time female politicians were expected to spend on our appearance, known as the pink tax, amounted to an hour a day for me, but I'd learned the hard way that it was necessary. In the past, whenever I didn't have my hair and makeup professionally done, the media would speculate about whether I was ill or exhausted.

"Suzy," I said, and when she looked up from her phone, I said, "have you heard the sex party rumor?"

She winced and said, "It actually does sound familiar."

I had the impulse to shake my head, but I didn't want to mess up Veronica's handiwork. I said, "You know when true equality will be achieved? When a woman with these kinds of skeletons in her closet has the nerve to run for office."

2004

On August 9, 2003, at a rec center on Chicago's South Side, surrounded by children of many ages and skin colors, I announced that I was running for president. I was not the first woman in recent years to do so—Pat Schroeder had run briefly in '87 and Elizabeth Dole in 2000—and, if anything, I tried to treat my gender as peripheral rather than momentous. "People in this country are ready for change," I said into the microphone on the podium. "For universal healthcare and better schools and lower taxes for the middle class. I'm a proud Midwesterner, and I'm bringing my can-do Midwestern spirit to running for president because I want to make life better for all Americans."

A few hundred supporters had turned out and were waving HILLARY FOR PRESIDENT signs. Already, my campaign had paid a consultant fifteen thousand dollars to tell us that my surname was too harsh-sounding, especially in tandem with my harsh professional record (in this instance, apparently "harsh" meant "in a male-dominated field") but also that being called by my first name undermined my seriousness. Given that we were damned if we did and damned if we didn't, we went with first name. Among the supporters was my mother, who, after I spoke, handed me a box of six energy bars and said, "Honey, just put these in your purse because I know you won't always have time to eat when you're on the go."

I soon discovered that running for president was more humbling than coasting along as a respected if not nationally known senator. At early events in Iowa and New Hampshire, at diners and bars and bowling alleys, I routinely spoke to groups of fewer than twenty people. The goal was to stay in the race until Super Tuesday; not coincidentally, dropping out by early March would still allow me to make the filing deadline for my third Senate run.

Jerry Brown had indeed turned out to be a one-term president, beaten by John McCain in 2000.

Though my secret brain trust revisited my 2004 run after 9/11—surely some people would speciously argue that it was unpatriotic or just foolhardy to challenge a veteran following the tragic attacks, and some did—I proceeded. And my long-term plan coalesced. It was increasingly plausible that a Democrat would win in '08, solidifying my goal to ascend to the presidency via the side door of the vice presidency.

From the minute I declared in '03 that I was running, critiques of my voice, clothes, and demeanor were daily occurrences. Newspaper editors often chose photos where my mouth was open, as if I were yelling. I was asked about the brand of the pantsuits that had become my uniform, about whether never having married or had children made me unable to understand the concerns of regular Americans, and about whether the country was ready for a female president. But still, this was all a kind of ambient sexism; though I thought I'd been initiated, I hadn't.

In a field of eight Democratic candidates, I came in sixth in Iowa, by which point, with Super Tuesday six weeks away, I was rapidly running out of money. The campaign was alternately demoralizing and inspiring—demoralizing because the small turnouts made me realize how much work I needed to do to ever have a shot at winning, inspiring because when I actually spoke to people I always remembered why the work was worth it. Plus, by the time of the Iowa caucuses, I'd stood on a stage five times for debates with my male opponents. Hadn't the seed been planted, even if the plant would take another eight years to flower?

But knowing 2004 was the foundation for the future didn't make watching the New Hampshire primary returns at my Manchester headquarters, which was a storefront in a strip mall, any less dispiriting than Iowa had been. On such nights, interacting with my own staff felt almost socially awkward. We as humans tend to look away from the explicit failures of others, and my staff and volunteers' discomfort over the course of the evening was palpable. As the night wore on, our exchanges grew increasingly terse and factual—I'd received just 5.4 percent of the state delegates, then 5.1 percent of the state delegates, then 5.2 percent of the state delegates—and, along with Theresa and Greg Rheinfrank, I retreated from the headquarters' open space to a private office in the back before reemerging to speak to about thirty supporters around nine o'clock. I said I planned to keep fighting.

The next morning, in the parking lot of Manchester's Hilton Garden Inn, a CBS News correspondent named Pierre Bouce, who was standing next to a van with a film crew, said, "Senator, can we steal a minute of your time?" It was an overcast fifteen degrees, and my team and I were on the way to the airport and then on to a rally in Phoenix. I think Pierre had approached me spontaneously; I wasn't much of a get at this juncture.

When the camera was rolling, Pierre said, "Last night was rough for your campaign. How are you feeling now?"

I said, "As I told supporters, I'm really focused on Super Tuesday. I've met so many voters who are looking for solutions and who trust me as an experienced, reasonable voice to lead all Americans."

"Realistically, your chances at this point—" Pierre paused and motioned for me to respond.

I've always found nonquestion questions lazy, as if the speaker can't be bothered to specify the last few words and expects the subject to do the work of transforming vague verbal gesturing into cogency. Or maybe it's that this nonquestion was, if accurate, insulting, but for once I didn't take the bait. I just gazed at Pierre.

"A lot of people look at you and wonder why you're running," he said.

I raised my eyebrows. "Do a lot of people wonder that?"

Seeming unperturbed, he said, "I think they do."

"You see—" I paused. "I prefer questions like 'What's your vision?' Or, 'What will your leadership bring to the presidency?' This more fundamental question, this request for self-justification—Pierre, why do you think it is you ask that of me but not of my opponents? Why **wouldn't** I run for president?

I've been a senator for two terms. I love this country, and I'm committed to making it even stronger and more equitable for everyone." I could have stopped there; as the record reflects, I did not stop there. I added, "Sure, I could have gotten married and had kids. I suppose I could have stayed home, baked cookies, and had teas. But what I decided to do was fulfill my profession. The work that I have done as a professional, a public advocate, has been aimed to assure that women can make choices, whether it's a full-time career, full-time motherhood, or some combination."

Many, many news clips and articles sprang from those thirty-one words, those three sentences that started with **Sure** and ended with **profession;** the sentences flanking them on either side were rarely included. Running for president actually hadn't made me a household name, but my comments in New Hampshire did. Through the jokes of late-night television hosts and the talk show roundtables and the think pieces in newspapers, I was introduced to America, and it was as a supercilious, antifamily bitch. A female columnist for **The Wall Street Journal** declared that due to my various off-putting qualities, my campaign would only make elections harder for women candidates in the future. A mother of three in South Carolina told **Time** magazine, "I was planning to vote for Hillary Rodham, but now that I know she thinks

I have nothing better to do than throw tea parties, I've changed my mind."

Even as I experienced self-doubt, the furor made me determined not to drop out for the very reason that I didn't want to seem as if I'd been driven from the race by fear or weakness. By the skin of my teeth, which is to say, thanks to a PAC called Hillary for America that was funded almost single-handedly by Bitsy Sedgeman Corker, I made it to Super Tuesday. One day later, I announced at a press conference in Chicago that I was ending my bid and throwing my support behind Dick Gephardt.

Sometimes I look back and think that I was bound to blurt out an ill-considered remark at some point and if it had happened later, it probably wouldn't have caused less damage. Or perhaps it would have—perhaps the public would have been more familiar with me and the remark would have represented a smaller fraction of the sum of what they knew of my identity. Sometimes I wish I'd left my room at the Hilton Garden Inn in Manchester just a few minutes later that morning, that I'd been constipated or spilled coffee on my pants. Sometimes I think I've made so few mistakes that the public can remember all of them, in contrast to certain male politicians whose multitude of gaffes and transgressions gets jumbled in the collective imagination, either negated by one another or forgotten in the onslaught. The less you screw up, the more clearly the public keeps track of each error.

It was Greg's idea to send cookies to the political desks at the big three networks and certain cable channels. I also not only appeared on-air on a late-night television show holding a platter of cookies, but I even, after a ten-minute argument with Greg, did so wearing an apron. That is, he won the argument.

In the moment, that morning in New Hampshire, I could feel a shift in the air: the contained glee of the reporter, the contained dismay of Theresa and Greg, standing outside the shot. I knew right away that I'd screwed up, though I didn't know how extreme the consequences would be, and presumably neither did Pierre or my staff.

As if any of it was in my control by then, I added, "And now I'd like to get back to talking to voters in Missouri and South Carolina and Arizona about the things they really care about, like how we can balance the budget for all Americans."

Pierre nodded with a faux earnestness that did not conceal his excitement about the unexpected and juicy morsel I'd just bestowed. He said, "Thank you, Senator Rodham, for your time."

Iowa
April 27, 2015
10:44 A.M.

We shot the clips outside the ethanol plant in Mount Joy, Iowa. The job of my video director, Ellie, who was twenty-six, was to capture or just stage anything funny, heartwarming, or inspirational on the campaign trail and share it in the hope that it would go viral.

By 10:30, I had donned a green hard hat, toured the plant, met with senior employees and hourly wage workers alike, affirmed my commitment to the federal renewable fuel standard, and posed for two hundred selfies. In the parking lot, before my team climbed back in the van, Ellie filmed me on her iPhone, with the plant's tall white tanks and columns visible in the background. I still wore the hard hat.

In the first video, I said, "Hello, Iowa. I'm here at Mount Joy Renewables, and it's great to see up close just how corn can help all of us reduce greenhouse gas emissions!" In the second, I said, "Does this hat make me look corny?" In the third, which I ad-libbed, I said, "Does this hat make me look on fleek?" The previous day, in the van, Diwata had used the phrase **keeping it 100,** the meaning of which I had absolutely no idea, which had led to a discussion of other millennial terms. At the ethanol plant, when I said "on fleek," everyone on my team, even the security agents, burst into laughter; that was the only video that didn't require more than one take.

2005

The next time I saw Bill was at a glitzy party in Manhattan celebrating the fiftieth anniversary of a culture-and-fashion magazine. This was in September 2005, a little less than a year into my third Senate term and eighteen months after my first presidential bid. Once again, the room was thick with prominent people of all stripes, most of whom made politicians seem frumpy—Hollywood actresses, Olympic athletes, Grammy-winning musicians—and then, just a few feet from me, chuckling with the mayor of Los Angeles, there was Bill. He was completely white-haired and the slimmest I'd ever seen him, including as far back as our law school days. I wondered if he could be sick, but there was also a cheer about him that made me almost sure he wasn't. He'd recently left the web services provider and become a partner at a venture capital firm in Menlo Park.

This time, I was the one who approached him. When his eyes landed on me, he beamed. "Hillary!" he exclaimed and threw his arms around me with such enthusiasm that I feared spilling champagne on his jacket. I could swear that with that hug, he transferred a bit of his giddiness into me.

The mayor of Los Angeles was soon swept up in another conversation, and it was just Bill and me. He said, "So, one of us might end up in the

White House after all." Because of how loud and crowded the party was, we had to speak into each other's ears; his breath was warm and champagney, as, presumably, was mine.

I said, "How come you didn't tell me that running for president is kind of hard?"

He laughed. "But kind of exhilarating, too, right? Everyone should do it at least once. Sometimes I'm tempted to try again, then I think about the dickhead Republicans and gotcha journalists, and I think, Fuck 'em all. I assume you're in for '08, though. '04 was just your dry run, yeah?"

"You know," I said, "a long time ago, a wise man once told me that the way you can tell if someone is truly thinking of running for president is that she'll never admit it until she announces."

"Ha!" he said. "Touché!" He looked truly delighted. "Hey, who's your Silicon Valley bundler? Have him call my assistant, and we'll set something up. I'd love to help."

Even after our pleasant interaction in Jackson Hole seven years earlier, I hadn't asked Bill for money. But for him to **offer**, and at this golden juncture in his own career—I was genuinely appreciative. I said, "It's Danny Welch, and I can't tell you how grateful I am. What's your assistant's name?" We both pulled out our BlackBerries, and he said, "And when you're next in the Bay Area, will you let me buy you dinner?"

"Would it be calling your bluff if I told you I'll

be in the Bay Area in two weeks? I'm speaking at the law school at Stanford."

"Fabulous. I'll have Raj make a reservation for us somewhere. Who are you here with tonight?"

"My deputy chief of staff, Theresa Ramirez. You actually met her in Jackson Hole."

"Sure, sure." He nodded. "From Philly, right? Oldest of six sisters?" Truly, he was remarkable; I could do this because I prepared, but he could just do it.

"Is Evangeline here?" I asked.

"You haven't heard? We're divorced." The expression on his face could have been discomfort, mild amusement, both, or neither.

I said, "Oh, I'm sorry."

With unmistakable mischief, he said, "You know what else I remember from that night in Jackson? That was some damn good prime rib they served, which I say with the nostalgia of a vegan."

"You can't be serious."

He held up his right hand. "As God is my witness."

I said, "Is it insensitive to say I'm more surprised that you're vegan than that you're divorced?" But he didn't have a chance to respond because a large man, a man almost as tall as Bill, had just appeared and inserted himself between us. The man's back was to me, and the first thing I noticed was his golden hair. The second thing I noticed, after I'd taken a step back, was that he was Donald Trump. I had never met him. "Bill Clinton, it's good to see you," he said in a loud voice, and the two men shook hands vigorously and at length.

Warmly, Bill said, "Donald, how are you?"

"When are we playing golf? You come to my club, we'll play. It's a beautiful club, it's newly reopened, everyone who plays there says it's the nicest course they've ever seen."

Bill and Donald were still shaking hands. Then Bill set his arm around my shoulder and said, "Donald, this is Senator Hillary Rodham, who I know you know ran for president."

Donald turned and squinted at me, his expression undisguisedly evaluative. He did not attempt to shake my hand. Instead, skeptically, he said, "President of what?"

"The United States," I said, and because his expression was unchanged, I added, "I'm a U.S. senator representing Illinois."

"And she does a terrific job," Bill added. "A true leader in the Democratic party."

"Every day, people beg me to run for president," Donald said. "I think about it seriously, very seriously. I'd be the greatest president this country has ever seen. But do I want to? I don't think I do."

I wondered if he was kidding, offering up some parody of male egomania, but it didn't seem he was. I said, "Well, no one should run for president if they don't want to," and I could feel a current of amusement between Bill and me.

"If I did run, I'd win," Donald said. "No one could do a better job."

Theresa had caught my eye and held up her right hand, signaling that she wanted to introduce me to someone; at the same time, a photographer had just taken a candid shot of Bill, Donald, and me and was asking for a posed shot in which I stood between the two men, as if we all were great friends. I was so much shorter than both of them that I felt a bit like a child. As the flash of the camera went off again, a gorgeous woman in her twenties who wore a black strapless gown slit up to her thigh—she was an actress I recognized but didn't know the name of—walked behind the photographer. On one side of me, I felt Bill perk up, and on the other side of me, Donald said, "That's very nice, isn't it?" Then he answered himself. "Yes, it is. It's very nice."

Bill said to me, "I've gotta go say hello to Henry Kissinger—Hillary, see you in a couple weeks?"

"I'm counting on it," I said, and he leaned in and down to kiss my cheek.

Donald did not bid me farewell, but as Theresa approached, I heard him say to Bill, "Come to my beautiful golf course. You won't believe how beautiful it is."

It occurred to me only later, when the assembled guests were watching a beloved rock star perform his greatest hits while we ate panna cotta with berry sauce, that I'd been told in the span of five minutes by two different men that running for president wasn't worth their time.

Iowa
April 27, 2015
11:40 A.M.

Ellie had posted the "on fleek" video from outside the ethanol plant on social, as my team referred to it, while we rode in the van to Muscatine; by the time we arrived at the community college less than an hour later, the video had been viewed more than four hundred thousand times on seven platforms, but instead of seeming excited, Clyde, Diwata, and Ellie were visibly nervous. "You think it's doing more harm or good?" Clyde asked Theresa.

"Shouldn't it be clear?" I said. "What do the comments say?" Anyone with any public identity and a modicum of savvy knows, of course, that you don't read the comments except when you do.

Ellie was scrolling rapidly on her phone. She said, "The take on it is like—"

But she paused, and it was Diwata who finished the thought. "They're calling you out on trying too hard, like hipster grandma. They don't get that you're making fun of yourself."

"Hmm," I said. "Is that because I don't have a sense of humor?"

Diwata passed me her phone, open to the Snapchat app, where the comments included **just no** and **cringing/crying with laughter** and **Is ANYTHING less on fleek than hills rods in iowa?** Followed by three emojis of a face squeezing its eyes shut and sticking out its tongue.

Ellie was looking from Theresa to Clyde as she said, "Should we—"

Firmly, Theresa said, "Let's not overthink it. And anyway, the toothpaste is out of the tube."

2006

One afternoon when Theresa and I were riding the Senate monorail to the Capitol in order to attend the markup of a bill, I noticed that her face looked flushed and swollen. When I asked if things were all right, she said in a tight voice that she and Bryan, her longtime boyfriend, had decided over the weekend to break up. I said, "Should I ask why or would you rather not get into it?"

"He wants to get married."

"And you don't?"

"I want to be a workaholic."

She obviously wasn't joking, but I laughed. "Really?"

She was blinking back tears as she said, "I've never wanted children. I'm sure of it. Being the oldest sister, by the time I was in first grade, I was changing diapers and getting other people's sandwiches ready and tying their shoes. Everyone always thinks not wanting kids is a temporary phase, which is so condescending. I don't dislike them, but I don't want my own."

"And Bryan does?"

"He's okay not having kids, but he just proposed." Theresa was twenty-nine.

"I'm trying to understand," I said. "If he's fine not having children, what's the reason not to marry him?"

She looked at me sideways. "You didn't."

"Oh," I said. "Well, no. But not because I objected philosophically to the institution."

"It's bad for women. With housework, emotional labor, all of it."

"Statistically, yes, but not necessarily individually. Doesn't Bryan actually do all the cooking and cleaning?" He had moved from Philadelphia to Washington years before, and he and Theresa shared an apartment on Capitol Hill. He still worked in construction, which meant he worked shorter hours than she did. Also, as I'd observed several times, including when I'd eaten dinner at their place, he was warm and funny and clearly adored her.

Theresa said, "But what if that changes?"

"Can you convey that you don't want it to?" We had reached the Capitol Building, and we stood. "There was only one person I ever wanted to marry, and there were warning signs that it would be a bad idea. A lot of warning signs. I'm not trying to convince you to do it, but I don't think you need to avoid marriage for the sake of avoiding it." As we exited the monorail, I playfully whispered, "Sure, I could have gotten married, had kids, and stayed home baking cookies, but I decided to fulfill my profession." It worked—Theresa laughed.

Four months later, on New Year's Eve, I was the officiant for Theresa and Bryan's wedding ceremony. It occurred in their apartment and was attended by just forty people, most of them family members.

Iowa
April 27, 2015
1:48 P.M.

Good hitting from Kris Bryant last night, my brother Hughie had written in a text that arrived as our van parked behind a yarn shop in Des Moines. My brother Tony immediately replied, **Joe Maddon is working his hippie magic!**

For several years, my brothers and I had maintained a group text chain that consisted of 90 percent the Cubs and 10 percent everything else. From preseason, in March, until the World Series, in late October, we discussed baseball; from November to February, we had little contact outside of planning whether we were getting together on Thanksgiving or Christmas.

I almost never watched games in their entirety but tried to catch the ninth inning whenever I could. Often, after I finished a speech or fundraising dinner on a night when the Cubs were playing, I'd check my phone and find thirty or forty messages from my brothers, many of them along the lines of **Awwww SHIT!**

I typed, **This season does seem promising, but I'm trying not to get my hopes up.** Then, because I'd learned from giving speeches that ending with the negative half of a mixed sentiment made the whole thing seem pessimistic, I deleted what I'd written and typed instead, **I'm trying not to get my hopes up, but this season does seem promising.**

2008

Between the day that I dropped out of the 2004 presidential race and the day I entered the 2008 one—I announced in January 2007—I privately courted as many rich Democrats as were willing to talk to me, and I publicly conducted a charm offensive. By the time of my official announcement, in a feat of hard work and meticulous coordination between my team and the Victoria Project, I had raised $10 million and planned to raise $70 million more. Meanwhile, though I was careful not to let these extracurricular activities get in the way of my Senate work, or keep me from Washington during votes, I accepted just about every speaking invitation I got in Iowa, New Hampshire, or any swing state. An aide created social media accounts for me. I worked with a ghostwriter to complete a second book, **Midwestern Optimism**—this one was heavier on policy than memoir—and went on a fourteen-city book tour that included stops in Cleveland, Columbus, **and** Cincinnati. On one late-night talk show, I submitted to an on-camera haircut from a beloved gay stylist; on another, I danced the tango with the host (an instructor named Raoul provided a one-hour lesson in my Senate office before the host and I more briefly rehearsed on set in New York, and, though news of the lesson never got leaked, I felt regretful about it—I paid for it myself, but I still feel I should have met Raoul in my apartment rather than my office). I also continued not only to eat crow on the cookie-baking front but to pretend that I found the opportunities to do so hilarious.

Despite my multifronted efforts, I was both surprised and overjoyed by my polling numbers in the early days of 2007. I had unusually high favorable **and** unfavorable ratings—this was the time when media references to me as "divisive" and "polarizing" became de rigueur, perhaps mandatory—but my candidacy was taken seriously in a way it hadn't been in '04. I still didn't realistically expect to be elected in 2008, but I thought I had a very strong shot at being the Democratic VP, especially if the nominee was either Chris Dodd or Joe Biden.

All of which is to say that I was never under any illusions about the shifting nature of campaigns. It wasn't that I failed to anticipate wild cards generally. It was that I failed to anticipate the rise of Barack Obama specifically.

Perhaps I underestimated Barack because of his very proximity and familiarity. He'd become a U.S. senator from Illinois in '05, taking Dick Durbin's seat after John McCain appointed Dick as his one Democratic cabinet member. Barack and I regularly found ourselves on the same plane from Washington back to O'Hare on Friday afternoons or evenings—we both flew coach in those days—and I appreciated both his sense of humor and, notable among male senators, his listening skills. I also was aware of a kind of withheld or quietly coiled ambition in him; if I'd been aware of the magnitude of it, I might have enjoyed his company less.

When Barack declared he was running for president in April 2007, I found the news irritating and—because of his relative lack of national experience, race, quirky upbringing, and strange name—not particularly threatening. Certainly I recognized his oratorical skills and general charisma, and I never ruled out the possibility that he'd be president eventually, but I thought 2008 for him would be the bruising rite of passage 2004 had been for me. Plus, he was fourteen years younger than me. On the night of the Iowa caucuses, when I came in first and he came in second, it occurred to me that Barack's campaign was not a test run after all. Five days later, when he came in first in New Hampshire and I came in second, I was doubly disoriented—I was again startled by how well I was doing, and I was even more startled by how well **he** was doing.

I suspect that the simultaneity of our historic campaigns hurt both of us and benefitted both of us—that we boosted each other because our dual presences made it seem plausible the country was changing rather than making either of us, as an individual, seem like an outlier or novelty. We also, no doubt, took votes from each other. And for voters averse to seeing the country change, together we elicited an antipathy more intense than either of us might have alone. Perhaps I believe the greater portion of the antipathy landed on me only because I am me.

But from Iowa on, the floodgates of truly vicious coverage opened; I entered a period of bifurcation from which I have never emerged, an either/or landscape in which I was celebrated or lambasted. My comments about baking cookies were invoked constantly, usually preceding or following musings about my likability or lack thereof. Dozens of investigative reporters at different newspapers devoted months of their lives to determining whether the $29,000 I'd made by investing with my 1980s futures trader boyfriend, Larry, was ill gotten. Larry had ended up serving five years in federal prison, starting in 1998, for trading fraud, so the interest he generated wasn't incomprehensible. But I was mystified by the fact that the conclusion to the question was always no, yet this finding never dissuaded the next reporter from reinvestigating.

It was also 2008 that saw the explosion of a cottage industry in clothing and tchotchkes whose existence hinged on my awfulness: T-shirts showing my face with the words RHYMES WITH WITCH or HILLIARY; nutcrackers made to resemble me, with plastic legs serving as the spring joints. And in February 2008, I received my first—but not my last—credible death threat. It came from a twenty-two-year-old pizza deliverer in Florence, South Carolina, who owned a firearm and who frequently posted in an online forum about his anger at so-called radical Islam and government-controlling Jews. This forum was where, a few hours prior to a prayer breakfast I was to attend in Louisville, he announced his plan to show up at the breakfast and kill me and any members of my staff who were present. Because his whereabouts were unknown when the breakfast started, I did end up skipping it, though I participated in other planned events that day while wearing a bullet-resistant vest—law enforcement never referred to it as bulletproof—which meant I needed to change into my loosest clothing: a long A-shaped jacket and floral-patterned scarf that wound around my neck and draped over my back. That also was the day I was assigned a round-the-clock security detail funded by American taxpayers. By nightfall, the man had been taken into custody. By the next morning, a spate of articles and TV segments mistaking my bullet-resistant vest for weight gain examined why eating balanced meals on the road was so challenging for presidential candidates. The three hosts of a morning news show conducted a pseudosympathetic discussion of what one of them termed "Hillary's changing physique" and had even invited a nutritionist on the air to recommend healthy snacks. It turned out—who knew?—that hummus and carrots offered both protein and fiber and that a handful of almonds was lower in sugar than a granola bar. Given that security threats tended to inspire copycats, no one on my team refuted the weight-gain story.

And then there was the public fascination with my friendship with James, first described in the **Tribune**. The rumors that we'd had an affair were persistent, and I read a few articles, including in respected publications, in which unnamed former Northwestern colleagues swore we had—that in the fall of 1991, both James's and my office doors had constantly been closed while we had sex. Too bad we hadn't, I sometimes thought, though it also was a relief to be able to honestly deny it on the rare occasions I was asked directly. The situation was further complicated by the facts that James's widow, Susie, as evidenced by her on-the-record comments, clearly believed that we had been involved and clearly was a Republican.

But what truly astonished me were the suggestions that I had killed James, either with my own hands or through an intermediary. How could anyone in their right mind believe such a thing? But people did; they genuinely did. And these delusions had the strange effect of transforming James into a symbol, a stand-in in some people's eyes for my utter corruption and amorality and in my own eyes for the paranoia and ignorance of certain voters. In either case, he was stripped of his personhood, the distinctive qualities and habits that had made him him—his formal clothing and courtly manners, his intelligence and sweetness and wry sense of humor. First I had lost him when I'd run for Senate; then I had lost him when he'd died; and I lost him the final time when he was converted into political fodder.

To think I'd once been bothered by a twenty-four-year-old reporter who chided me for buying expensive opera tickets!

Iowa
April 27, 2015
1:53 P.M.

The owners of the yarn shop in Des Moines were two men in their sixties who'd been a couple for forty years. One of them, Henry, was tall and slim, with a gray mustache, and the other, Norman, was short and heavy, with a black mustache. While we were still shaking hands, Norman gripped my left shoulder, peered into my eyes, and said in an impassioned tone, "Hillary Rodham, you are a beautiful goddess, and you must use your divine powers to vanquish the blight of Mitt Romney or whomever else the Republicans inflict upon us."

I laughed loudly—this encounter was being documented by a dozen print and television reporters and photographers—and I said, "It's such a pleasure to meet you. Tell me about your shop." The store was tiny, probably ten by twenty feet, and the members of the media occupied at least half of it, with the travelers standing and kneeling very close to one another. My team hovered by a large shelf where brightly colored skeins of yarn were stored.

Norman, who was considerably more voluble than Henry, said how important my healthcare tax credit would be, and it was after he told me about their wool made from recycled water bottles that I purchased a small knit bear. I hadn't carried a wallet for years; my body woman, Kenya, not only kept money for me but meticulously documented how it was used.

Back in the van, I sat, as I always did, in the

second row, and Theresa sat beside me, as she always did. Clyde, who was in the row behind me next to Ellie, said, "Senator, I just want to update you on something," and his tone made me wonder if there had been a school shooting. Instead, he told me that the "on fleek" video had been viewed more than a million times, inspired a multitude of mocking memes, and was generating nonstop calls to my media team at headquarters, in Chicago, which they were ignoring.

While he spoke, I was turned around to face him, and I glanced at Ellie and said, "Be careful what you wish for, huh? If you'd put out the video where I talked about reducing greenhouse gas emissions, how many views do you think that would have gotten?"

"I'm very sorry that I guessed wrong on this," Ellie said.

"No, I'm asking literally."

"A few thousand?" she said, then she burst into tears. Darryl was pulling out of the parking lot behind the yarn shop, and abruptly, the van was completely silent.

"Oh, Ellie!" I said. "Oh, please. I've withstood so much worse."

She was sniffing intensely, and I was reminded just how young she was. I tended to use Maureen's daughter, Meredith, as a frame of comparison for my team members, and Meredith was now thirty-one—five years older than Ellie.

"Truly," I said. "This is background static. When there are nutcrackers made in your image, trust me, you're not fazed by online commenters saying you're uncool."

From the third row, Diwata said, "Boss, at least Norman in the yarn shop seems to have a major crush on you."

Amid the laughter of the others, Ellie very quietly and very stiffly said, "But really. I'm **so** sorry." I could see the internal debate she was having play out on her face, her embarrassment at crying in front of all of us competing with her wish to convey remorse.

"You know what?" I said, and, unfortunately, I knew I was telling her something true. "No one will even remember how on fleek I am once Bill announces."

2008

I dropped out of the presidential race in early June 2008, and, as the world knows, Barack was elected on November 4. Though I had, in the end, campaigned vigorously on his behalf, I allowed myself the reprieve of attending neither his victory speech in Grant Park, which was a mile from my apartment, nor the celebration held afterward at a hotel. On the morning of Election Day, I'd been photographed duly casting my ballot at Ogden

Elementary School, accompanied by Theresa. Two members of my security detail, Darryl and Chris, then drove us to Chicago Executive Airport, where Bitsy Sedgeman Corker's private jet waited. Bitsy was already out in Taos, and the four of us flew to New Mexico and drove on to her adobe house situated on her twenty-thousand-acre ranch. Starting in the midafternoon mountain time, Bitsy, Theresa, and I watched the returns in the den, joined by Bitsy's daughter, Sally, who was Theresa's age. At intervals, Bitsy's housekeeper, Fernanda, who was watching something in the kitchen that wasn't in English and also wasn't the election, brought out trays of carne asada and salad, then cookies and fruit; she continuously replenished our wineglasses.

As an MSNBC anchor discussed the surprisingly high number of Southern states in play for Barack, Sally said, "And all these years I believed Americans were more racist than sexist."

"Did you really?" I said. "Given when the Fifteenth Amendment passed and when the Nineteenth did?"

Some of my supporters were resentful or disappointed that Barack hadn't selected me as his running mate, but I'd known he wouldn't, known that when he secured the party nomination, my hopes of becoming president or vice president had both been thwarted at once. How could one Illinois senator possibly select another, and, frankly, how could one historic nominee select another? Many voters still needed the soothing presence of a white man on the ticket. I wouldn't have asked him to be my VP.

Anyway, as much as it was about sexism, the story of 2008 was about the ascendancy of data analytics, which Obama's team had proven distressingly more adept at than mine. They'd also, thank goodness, been more adept at data analytics than the team of Vice President Sam Brownback, who was the Republican nominee.

A little after seven mountain time, New York, Michigan, Minnesota, Wisconsin, and Rhode Island were all called for Barack. "This has to be tough for Hillary Rodham, wherever she is," one of the talking heads on MSNBC said. "That tonight will quite plausibly be historic but not in the way she hoped."

"Hmm," Bitsy said to the TV pundit. "You think you and your colleagues had anything to do with that?"

Another pundit—the first had been a man, and this was a woman—said, "Well, Hillary, don't be too discouraged. There's always 2016, right?"

A strange feature of fame is the way that on television or in print, individuals sometimes address you directly but rhetorically-directly, clearly without imagining that you'll ever see or read their message.

Onscreen, the other pundits groaned, and one said, "Let's just get through tonight, okay, Sheena?"

A few minutes after nine mountain time, the networks called it: Barack Obama had been elected president. Bitsy, Sally, Theresa, and I all looked at one another, and Sally burst into tears, and the rest of us got choked up, too. It **was** an extraordinary moment. I could feel how they were looking to me to acknowledge the night's profundity and magnitude; they were looking to me both because I was the political stateswoman and because they loved me and didn't want to offend me as Barack's former opponent. I smiled and said, "This is a remarkable milestone. I'm happy for the country." After a few seconds, I added, "And for Barack."

I became aware that Darryl, one of the two Secret Service agents who'd traveled with us to New Mexico, was standing in the threshold between the hall and the den, watching the TV, and when I glanced at him, we made eye contact. Darryl was black, and his counterpart on the trip, Chris, was white. I stood, walked to Darryl, and hugged him. "Congratulations," I said, and he nodded once in a manner that made it clear he, too, was struggling to contain his emotions. But he said nothing; agents don't tend to be loquacious.

For his concession speech, Sam Brownback stood onstage at a Topeka hotel with his running mate, Jim Gilmore, the Virginia governor. Brownback and I had been in the Senate together, and he was one of those men who was polite enough to interact with directly while being so conservative on matters of taxes, healthcare, and reproductive and LGBTQ rights that his disdain for anyone unlike himself was a form of cruelty; as such men often are, he was also deeply religious. Years before, a legislative assistant of mine had referred to these type of men, who were always at least fifty, always white, and only ever of middling intelligence, as PE-teacher politicians. The name was, of course, an insult to PE teachers.

Following Brownback's speech, which was gracious enough considering the circumstances, MSNBC switched back to the in-studio panel, whose participants talked more about the historic nature of the night. Several of the pundits were themselves visibly moved. Then we saw the stage at Grant Park where Barack would appear imminently. American flags lined the rear and sides of the stage, and bullet-resistant glass panes flanked the podium. The Obama family entered from the back, between flags, and there was thunderous cheering; well over two hundred thousand people were estimated to be in the park, which was to say a crowd fifteen times larger than my largest ever. The Obamas' clothes were coordinated in shades of red and black: Barack's dark suit and red-striped tie, Michelle's black dress with bold red splashes above and below the waist, Malia's red dress and Sasha's black one. Barack held the hand of Sasha, the younger of the two girls, and Michelle held the hand of Malia, and they waved as the crowd began to chant, "Yes, we can!"

How bittersweet this was to watch! Though all of us in politics must routinely perform the role of ourselves, there was a closeness and sweetness about their family that couldn't be faked. What, I wondered as Sasha clasped her father's hand, was it like to get both, to have a family **and** be elected president? All his predecessors had, too, except James Buchanan and, 140 years later, Jerry Brown, though Jerry's girlfriend had acted as first lady. Even Grover Cleveland, who'd been elected as a single man, had during his first term married the twenty-one-year-old daughter of a friend and eventually had five children.

And yet I couldn't fathom standing on a stage like that next to these young humans with their personalities and appetites, their favorite TV shows and snacks, the goggles they needed for swim lessons. Even with nannies, wouldn't I always have wondered if my ambition was detrimental to them, if the exposure was fair, if the times I was away were excessive and damaging? Did men wonder this? Not, it seemed, in such a way that it immobilized them or precluded their advancement. And even if I could have made peace with my decisions, the media wouldn't have been able to—they'd have wondered for me, incessantly.

Onstage, Michelle Obama beamed and waved. I'd known Michelle even before Barack entered public office—back in the nineties, she'd worked in the mayor's office and later at a nonprofit for young people—and, like everyone else, I thought she was terrific. But for her, now what? I'd read that prior to taking a leave from her hospital-executive job, she'd earned almost double the $157,000 salary her husband and I made as senators, and, as first lady, she would be paid nothing. I knew I shouldn't project, but did she really want to oversee White House Christmas decorating, to be Barack's accoutrement? Maybe the opportunity to eviscerate ugly stereotypes just by existing made the personal sacrifice worth it, or maybe influencing policy through back channels didn't seem to her like a second-rate option. But seeing her onstage was strangely like watching a younger version of myself—a taller, far more glamorous, African American version—and I wasn't envious. Or I was envious, watching as she and Barack exchanged kisses on the cheek before she escorted their daughters backstage and he began his speech. But not envious of her. I was envious of him.

As the camera panned the massive cheering crowd, I caught sight of three people I recognized, all of them near the stage, all of them prominent Barack supporters: Oprah Winfrey, Richard Greenberger, and Gwen Greenberger.

Bitsy held out her wineglass toward mine. As our glasses clinked, she said, "To 2016."

Iowa
April 27, 2015
2:41 P.M.

Of course we watched Bill's announcement—we watched it on Clyde's iPad in the van—and of course it went on for much too long. My own announcement had taken the form of a crisp and, if I did say so myself, beautifully shot six-minute video that started with me at Maureen's kitchen table and concluded with a cheery pop song over a montage of Americans who were old and young and straight and gay and every shade of skin color. Bill gave a twenty-five-minute speech on the steps of City Hall in San Francisco in which he promised to bring the innovative spirit of Silicon Valley to climate change, education, and job creation, then told a few meandering and self-indulgent anecdotes about his various start-up successes and close friendships with leaders of other countries. The assembled press lobbed softballs at him about taking a pay cut as president.

Standing behind a podium, Bill wore a cerulean blue short-sleeved button-down shirt and no tie; he looked, I thought, particularly Californian, which I hoped would work against him, though it was rare for any man's appearance to be critiqued with real vigor.

Theresa said, "I wish there was one word for **smug San Francisco billionaire.**"

"Vegan?" suggested Suzy.

Clyde said, "I swear to God the first time he uses the phrase **plant-based diet,** we're celebrating by going to KFC."

I said, "And tweeting a picture of me gnawing fried chicken, I hope?"

"No, no," Diwata said. "Plant-**forward.**"

"If he says 'plant-forward,'" said Clyde, "we're opening a bottle of Veuve Clicquot and **not** tweeting it."

But as I watched him onscreen, I honestly had no idea what motivated Bill Clinton. Was he driven by sincere patriotism and idealism? Was he bored? Was the presidency an unchecked item on his bucket list? Was his failure to be elected in 1992 his greatest regret? If my candidacy represented a bid for gender equality seventeen years in the making, his represented—what? A nostalgia tour? Surely he didn't understand the implications of how media, social and otherwise, had changed—perhaps he understood them as a VC but not as a presidential candidate. How easily people could now record whatever you said and did, how directly an anonymous individual could now contact a journalist, how quickly rumors now spread, and how impulsively they were reported even by credible outlets. Or did none of this matter with Bill? Were there rules that applied to me but, because of his charisma and his wealth and his gender, not to him?

And yet I was surprised when I heard myself say aloud, "The reason he shouldn't be president isn't that he's vegan. It's that he's a sexual predator."

CHAPTER 6

2015

THE STUDIO AUDIENCE CHEERED WARMLY as I walked onto the Burbank, California, set of **Beverly Today** and toward an armchair facing that of Beverly Collins, the show's host and a woman I'd known for almost twenty years. Before I sat, the audience continued to cheer and clap, and I waved in various directions, smiling broadly. Even when I took my seat, they still clapped, and when finally they were quiet enough for Beverly to speak, she said to me, "It's almost like they're excited that you're here."

Again, they cheered wildly, and, though we had to wait for them to calm down, I can't lie—it was nice to be in friendly territory.

Turning back toward me, Beverly said, "You were last on the show in 2014. What have you been up to since then?"

Yet again, the crowd cheered.

After a minute, I said, "Beverly, I don't know if you know this, but I'm running for president."

There was more boisterous cheering. Beverly said, "What's that like?"

"It's a lot of fun," I said. "Have you ever considered it?"

"Now that you mention it, maybe I will," Beverly said. "It seems tiring, though. Is it?"

"It's tiring sometimes," I said. "But it's also energizing. I meet so many wonderful people every single day, so many Americans who are working hard and who are optimistic about a better future."

"I'm trying to remember," Beverly said. "Are you the only one running for president?"

The audience chuckled, and I said, "Well, that's not how it works in the United States. In fact, I have three Democratic opponents, and there could be as many as ten or twelve candidates in the Republican primary."

Her playful ignorance was, of course, planned, but it was working better than I'd expected; I could feel how much the audience was enjoying it.

I'd first appeared on **Beverly Collins Cooks!**, her Chicago-based cooking show, in 1998, when I was up for Senate reelection, and we'd become fast friends both on and off the air. On that particular day, I'd joined Beverly in preparing deep-dish pizza. Standing behind a Formica counter, facing an audience, both of us wearing matching yellow aprons, I shook the oregano bottle over the pan of simmering onions and, with what appeared to be sincere alarm, she exclaimed, "Good Lord, are you not familiar with measuring spoons?" A few minutes later, as I grated mozzarella, I drew blood when I also grated my knuckle. At this, Beverly giggled and said, "The secret ingredient." With a Band-Aid over my knuckle, I helped her punch the dough to eliminate air bubbles, and she said, "Tell the truth—are you picturing Newt Gingrich?" After the filming concluded, when we were backstage, a producer in a headset said to her, "The Newt stuff, Beverly—ideally not, okay?" To which Beverly said, "But he's a depraved gargoyle!"

In the years after my first appearance, Beverly's show had expanded from the Chicago market to dozens of other cities, switched formats from a half-hour cooking show to a general hour-long talk show and from live to recorded, been renamed **Beverly Today,** and moved to California. But I still cooked with her whenever I returned, including making blueberry-strawberry muffins one Fourth of July. That time, I dropped the glass measuring cup in the whirring stand mixer, causing shattered glass to fly into the air. No one was hurt, and neither Beverly nor I could speak coherently for thirty seconds because we were laughing so hard.

At last, while tears ran down her cheeks, Beverly said, "Obviously, that never would have happened with cookies because of how much you love baking them."

In 2008, Beverly came out as a lesbian in an article in **People** magazine, and in 2010, when she married a pediatrician named Sheila, I was a guest at the wedding, in Vermont. Beverly's was the first gay wedding I'd attended.

In this moment, on her set in Burbank, Beverly was saying, "Now on the Democratic side, who's running other than you?"

"There are four of us," I said. "There's me. There's Jim Webb, who used to be a senator from Virginia. There's Martin O'Malley, who was the governor of Maryland. And there's Bill Clinton, who was governor of Arkansas." A pollster named Henry Kinoshita had run focus groups to determine how I should refer to Bill. **Sparingly** was the obvious answer, but in cases where I needed to, I was to eschew **billionaire, entrepreneur,** and even **businessman**.

"Now, this is interesting," Beverly said. "I've heard a rumor that you and Bill Clinton once dated. Is that true?"

How many times in the last few days had Clyde, Theresa, and I rehearsed this moment? "Occasionally, rumors you hear on the campaign trail are true." I paused good-humoredly, or at least this was supposed to be the effect. "Very, very occasionally. Yes, I did date Bill Clinton, but here's the crazy part. It was more than thirty years ago." In fact, he had set his head on my shoulder in the museum courtyard forty-four years before; it had been forty years since I'd driven away from Fayetteville. But my team had decided on thirty years so as not to emphasize my age.

"It was when we were in law school," I said, and an enormous photo of me not at Yale but standing behind the podium at my Wellesley graduation appeared on a studio screen, next to an equally enormous photo of Bill that I recognized from his Rhodes scholar days. My team had turned down Beverly's producers' requests for a law school photo of Bill and me together.

As if Bill and I were adorable puppies, the audience made a collective cooing "awww" sound.

"Look at those two young kids," Beverly said. "Is it odd now to be running against him?"

"You know," I said, "it really isn't a big deal. I just feel so focused on what I can do to improve the lives of everyday Americans through jobs and education and healthcare that I don't give a lot of thought to things from three decades ago. It's like if I said to you, 'Do you think about the person you went to high school prom with?'" This, too, was semiscripted, and when a photo of Beverly from her prom appeared on the screen—her male date wore a maroon tuxedo—the audience roared with delight. Beverly and I made eye contact, both of us smiling, and I felt very grateful. I often was struck by the generosity and competence with which other professionally successful women my age extended a helping hand.

And Beverly did not, as a follow-up question, say, Okay, but what if you're running for president against your prom date?

Instead, she said, "I often think about my prom date, Evan Gustafson. I bet he misses me." The audience laughed and clapped, and Beverly said, "Hillary, I know you'll be crushed to hear this, but we don't have a cooking segment on the show today."

"Beverly, I'm so disappointed," I said.

"Oh, you are?" She smirked. "Because I lied. We do have a cooking segment. Hey, Ryan—" And then a curtain was pulled back on the kitchen, revealing a counter set up for us to make apple pie. Once again, the audience cheered ecstatically.

Whenever I entered my apartment after being away, my own home always seemed shockingly clean and quiet and familiar. The décor of the rooms struck me as exceptionally attractive, as if I'd had no hand in selecting it: the sunny yellow walls of the living room and the long, skirted sofa covered in a pattern of oversized red and pink roses that matched the curtains; the large maple dining room table, which was where my staff and I held meetings; my bedroom, with its tufted headboard and throw pillows. In 1999, I'd bought the smaller apartment next door to mine and knocked down the wall between them, so I now had three guest rooms, and they were often used by staffers crashing after meetings that had lasted into the wee hours.

No matter what time of day or night I returned home, my housekeeper, Ebba, was awake to greet me and, no matter how many times I'd conveyed that it was unnecessary, to offer a snack. On this particular Saturday in early May, after the plane from Los Angeles landed at 2:40 A.M., my body woman, Kenya, and I rode through a warm rain in an armored SUV driven by my security agent Phil, and I entered my apartment at 3:30. Kenya had texted Ebba to let her know we were near, and Ebba opened the door for us and led us to the kitchen. (Past the lovely dining room and living room—what good taste the woman who lived here had!) On the kitchen counter was a dish of mixed nuts, a quartered orange, and two glasses of water. I glugged down the water, but it was only to humor Ebba that I also took an orange quarter. Ebba had been working for me for twenty years and was close to my age, and, as always—even though it was the middle of the night—she wore black slacks and a black collared shirt. She said, "When Maureen comes tomorrow at nine-thirty, do you want breakfast first or just coffee?"

"I'll set my alarm for nine and have a vegetable

omelet," I said. "Kenya, you're welcome to spend the night here."

Kenya shook her head. "I'm good, but need anything before I take off?"

"Any word from Misty LaPointe in Iowa? She was going to check in after her first chemo session."

"I haven't heard from her. Want me to reach out?"

"Just text me her contact information." I yawned, and said, "Clearly, what all of us need now is sleep."

By 3:45, I'd removed my makeup and contacts and brushed my teeth while gazing, as I usually did, at Barbara Overholt's **Venus of Willendorf** replica. She'd sent me the statue, which I kept on the bathroom countertop, after I was elected to the Senate, along with a note that read **Hurray for tough broads!** Barbara was in her nineties and suffering from dementia; I no longer heard directly from her, though I occasionally exchanged emails with her daughter.

When I entered my bedroom, I saw that Ebba had already turned down my sheet and cover and made my white-noise machine purr. The next thing I knew, the chimes ringtone of my phone was awakening me. Ebba, who hadn't necessarily slept any more than I had, prepared an omelet with spinach and mushrooms. I read briefings from my staff as I ate, but—wondrously—I did not need to have my hair or makeup done, nor did I need to marshal energy for a speech or to shake hands or smile for photos with hundreds of people I'd never met. It was a Saturday, and I'd be attending a fundraising reception that evening at a country club in Lake Forest, but I was free until 4:00 P.M., which felt decadent to an almost unsettling degree; during my initial hours of downtime, it was always jarring to not be a few feet away from Theresa, Clyde, Diwata, and Kenya. With whom was I supposed to share incisive or preposterous tweets I saw or thoughts I'd just had about infrastructure funding? Admittedly, by the time Maureen arrived, I'd exchanged texts with all of them, as well as with Greg and my campaign manager, Denise Jacobs.

Maureen said as we hugged, "I can't even say how good you were on **Beverly**. You were perfect."

I grinned. "And the amazing part is that you're totally impartial. Wait, show me the pictures from Nate's birthday."

Maureen was a grandmother of six—though Meredith didn't have children yet, both her brothers had three—and Maureen saw her children and grandchildren several times a week. They all lived in the area, and on Fridays she took care of the youngest, a two-year-old girl named Harper.

Maureen pulled out her phone, tapped the photo app, and scrolled through images. Nate had just turned five and held a pirate-themed party, though truthfully, the pictures I most wanted to see weren't of kids but of Maureen herself, in a tricorn hat, eye patch, and billowing blouse. The images exceeded my expectations.

"This is **amazing,**" I said. "Did you really make the hat?"

"I just followed instructions on a website. But you know I bought the hook, right? It's plastic."

"Oh my God," I said. "I hadn't even noticed." I enlarged the image: The part that covered her hand was black, and the hook itself was curving silver.

"By the way," Maureen said, "have you talked to Meredith lately?"

"Not for a few weeks. Is everything okay?"

"No, things are fine. I was just wondering. You know, if you want, I can make you a pirate hat. You can wear it for a big speech or something."

I laughed. "Strangely, no one has ever offered that before."

Maureen and I were having a Pilates lesson with an instructor named Nora who came to my apartment whenever I was back in Chicago. Ebba always pushed the glass table out of the center of the living room, and we did it there, in our bare feet. There had been a few years after my first election to the Senate when Maureen and I had needed to navigate the shifting terms of our friendship. I saw the shifts as purely logistical; yes, I was busier, but our closeness was, if anything, **more** important to me now that I was in the public eye. To a degree I understood only after an emotional conversation we had by Maureen's pool in the summer of 1993, she felt hurt by my decreased availability and also threatened by my friendship with Bitsy Sedgeman Corker. At the end of that conversation, during which we both cried, Maureen said, "I wanted to be your rich friend, but now that there's Bitsy, I guess I have to settle for being your oldest friend."

"Maureen, you're my **best** friend," I said.

In the twenty-plus years since, Maureen and I had rarely been out of contact, whether by phone, email, or text, for more than a day or two. On this Saturday in early May, after Nora had led us through the exercises and the cooldown, Maureen and I continued to lie on our backs on the cream-colored living room rug, and Maureen said, "Nora, you've relaxed me so much I think I'll stay here all day."

"That's a great idea," Nora said. "I'll just see myself out." After she'd collected her resistance bags and balls, I could hear her talking in the hall to Ebba, and I whispered to Maureen, "When we were doing the hundred, I peed a little bit."

"Oh, please," Maureen said. "I've been peeing in my underwear a little bit since I first gave birth in 1975."

"Do you do Kegels?"

"I mean to. You know how articles say, 'Do Kegels anywhere! No one will know'? When Steve and I flew to Oahu, I could swear the woman in front of me in the security line was doing them, or else she was just clenching her bottom."

I laughed. "Maybe the advice should be 'Do Kegels anywhere except when eagle-eyed Maureen is standing behind you.'"

"Speaking of which, I caught a little of Bill's rally on CNN yesterday, and whoever is responsible for his nips and tucks deserves a medal. God knows I don't like him, but he's had impeccable work done."

"Bill's rally was televised?" I said. I knew he'd held a rally in Oakland, and I knew two thousand people had attended it—a higher figure than anticipated—but the fact of it being broadcast had escaped me.

Maureen said, "I only watched a few minutes, so I don't know if they aired the whole thing."

I wanted to hold on to the good feeling accrued during Pilates and time with Maureen, but the tense alertness of campaigning had reasserted itself already, even as I lay on my living room floor. Maureen was leaving in a few minutes, and I willed myself to wait until she had—I succeeded, but barely—before texting Theresa, Clyde, and Greg **How the hell did BC get his Oakland rally aired on CNN?**

Using the phone number Kenya had given me, I texted Misty LaPointe on Saturday afternoon; texting seemed better than calling because I didn't want to catch her at a bad moment. **Misty, this is Hillary Rodham,** I wrote. **I have been thinking of**

you since we met and am wondering how your first chemo session went.

A reply came immediately: **GTFO who is this really and what do u want**

After googling **GTFO**, I wrote: **It's really me** and added a smiley-face emoji, which was the only emoji I ever used.

From Misty: **Ok then tell something olny Hillary would know**

From me: **Well, a lot of information about me is widely available so how about that when we met, your daughters were with you and you told me I'm much prettier in person?**

This time, about three minutes passed before Misty's response: **Miss Hillary I am so sorry I hope u will accept my sincere apologies from the bottom of my heart I just couldn't believe it u**

From me: **Please don't worry at all. How did your chemo go?**

From her: **It was ok**

From me: **I understand that Leslie in my Washington office told you that the American Cancer Society provides referrals to a financial counselor w/ knowledge about planning for health-related expenses.**

From her: **Yah maybe**

From me: **And that a nonprofit in Cedar Rapids offers free dinner delivery service 3 times/week for people with illnesses.**

From her: **Yah but my girls like my cooking ☺**

Was she telling me to back off?

From her: **I saw you on Beverly, LOL**

From her: **Is she as funny in real life**

From me: **Yes, Beverly is very funny.**

From me: **I'm afraid your girls would not be at all impressed by my cooking.**

From me: **If you think of it, please text me in a few weeks and let me know how you are.**

From her: **Ha ha if I think of it yah I have a feeling I remember**

From her: **For real I can't believe u texted me it's amazing Miss Hillary** and then there were several emojis—a face with heart eyes, a birthday hat, an American flag, a flexing biceps.

From me: **Please just call me Hillary.**

My campaign headquarters was on the eleventh floor of Prudential Plaza, a large open space with my logo painted on the wall visitors saw when they stepped off the elevator. A few senior staff members worked in offices with windows, and many junior staff members sat at cubicle desks or on beanbags, laptops open in front of them. There was usually a dog or three on the premises and both mass-produced and handmade signs from rallies adorning the walls, along with other paraphernalia featuring my name or face—pins, masks affixed to Popsicle sticks—and sometimes there was music playing from one of the departments.

In other words, the headquarters was a vibrant, buzzing place, and I was almost never there, unless I went specifically to boost morale. Otherwise, I kept a small, nondescript private office in the same high-rise on Dearborn Street where Greg Rheinfrank had for years rented his office. This was also not where we held the oppo meeting. Instead, a small group of us gathered Sunday morning at my apartment, in the dining room: Theresa; Greg, who was acting as my chief strategist and media adviser; my campaign manager, Denise; Aaron Villarini, who was my communications director; and Gigi, who was my director of research. The meeting had been called to discuss Bill.

"I'll go least incendiary to most," Gigi said. "There's the obvious. He's been married twice. He's on good terms with both ex-wives and his two kids, who are from the first marriage. He's now dating a woman named Kristin Bowen, a forty-year-old software engineer. This is where things start to get interesting. At least until recently, they've had an open relationship, and they've also been quote-unquote experimental, including participating in threesomes with other women."

There was a brief silence, the silence of not just my colleagues but my employees digesting this bit of information about a man they knew to be both my political opponent and my ex-boyfriend. Calmly I said, "I'm impressed he has the energy."

Gigi continued in a level tone. "The rumors

about the so-called orgies or sex parties in Silicon Valley are also true. Sometimes the parties last a few hours, sometimes a few days, but essentially, it's high-profile, superwealthy men, both married and unmarried, then there are couples, then there are young women. The parties happen in fancy, very private locations, everyone takes ecstasy, sometimes along with other drugs, and a lot of sex occurs. It often culminates in something called a cuddle puddle."

Several of us yelped simultaneously, and Denise said, "I need a barf bag."

"But the problem," Greg said, "is that he's living the dream of a lot of American men." He glanced around the dining room table. "Isn't he? Not that I'm an expert in the ways of heterosexuals."

"Gigi, please continue," I said.

"There's a strict code of confidentiality," Gigi said, "but it isn't because people are ashamed. If anything, as Greg is alluding to, they're proud. The men perceive themselves as disrupting sexuality and monogamous marriage just like they've disrupted the taxi and hotel industries."

Around the table, there was scoffing and laughter, and Aaron said, "I just want to make sure I understand. These people are tripping, they're having group sex, then they all see each other again a few days later in a boardroom?"

"Apparently so," Gigi said. "And experimentation takes other forms, like bondage."

"Are the young women prostitutes?" I asked.

"Not in most cases. They might be there to make professional connections, but they're not usually paid outright."

"Call me a prude," Aaron said, "but I don't think disrupting monogamy will play in Iowa and New Hampshire. Plus, this is consistent with what made things unravel for Clinton in '92."

Greg said, "But haven't mores shifted a lot since then?"

"Can we back up for a second?" I asked. "Ecstasy is MDMA, correct?" When Gigi nodded, I said, "What's the penalty for MDMA possession in the state of California?"

"Possession is a misdemeanor that comes with a fine of up to a thousand dollars and a year in jail," Gigi said. "It rarely happens, though."

"Is ecstasy now like what pot used to be?" I asked.

"Obviously, it depends who you're talking to," Denise said. "But once Obama admitted to cocaine use, things did kind of change."

I said, "But Barack's use was long before he was running."

Gigi said, "Believe me, we're doing all we can to find a witness to say they saw Clinton doing ecstasy, or having group sex. We have a couple leads, one being a young woman and one being a caterer working one of the parties. But no one has committed yet. Let me pivot a little. In 1993, Clinton settled a case for sexual harassment brought against him by a former Arkansas state employee named Sharalee Mitchell. The alleged encounter took place in 1990, when Mitchell was twenty-five, and it involved members of his security detail taking her to his hotel room, where she says they chatted for a few minutes before he exposed his genitals to her. His supposed quote was, 'Kiss it.' "

Again, a few people in the room groaned or winced. I was grateful that Gigi continued speaking matter-of-factly. "This is different from the cabaret singer who came forward in '92 to say she and Clinton had had a twelve-year affair. To this day, Mitchell is the only woman to seek damages. Ultimately, Clinton settled for $850,000. Both of these women have granted interviews in the past, in some cases paid interviews."

Would Bill really have said "Kiss it," just like that, as a command unaccompanied by flattery or self-deprecation? I could more easily imagine his saying, with some blend of feigned and sincere sheepishness, "Will you kiss it?" He was a confident man, yes, but didn't you have to be a brute to simply issue such a decree? And yet they'd known each other for a few minutes, and then he'd unfastened his pants and shown her his presumably erect penis. Had he not understood or not cared that she didn't want to see it? I thought how I **had** kissed Bill Clinton's penis, and far more than once, and usually without his asking. Was the lesson to draw that he'd probably treated me with more respect than he had the state employee? That she was more discerning or less lucky than I had been?

Denise was saying, "Granting that men running for office get far more leeway than women, isn't the combination of this stuff going to bring him down? Known adultery plus settling in a sexual harassment case plus sex parties plus drugs? Unless he's Teflon."

Greg said, "You know two thousand people just showed up at his rally in Oakland, right?"

To Gigi, I said, "You're sure he doesn't have any children besides Alexis and Ricky? I don't mean with his second wife but with anyone."

"There are persistent rumors, including that he fathered a black child in Arkansas years ago, but there's no proof."

"At one point, I heard he might be a sperm donor for a lesbian couple or just a single woman," I said. "He may have been the woman's sperm donor or her boyfriend."

"You say tomato, I say tomahto," Greg said in a singsong.

"I'll look into that," Gigi said. "The final lead we're pursuing is the rumor that in the seventies, he raped a woman in Fayetteville, Arkansas. Her name is Vivian Tobin, she's now seventy-six, and at the time, she was a volunteer for his congressional campaign."

I gasped, as did Denise, but I think she was gasping about the rape part; I was gasping because after all this time, I knew the woman's name.

"She never pressed charges," Gigi said, "and I have the impression she has no desire to talk to the media, but she told a few friends right after it happened. And frankly, someone who's sexually assaulted one person has usually sexually assaulted others, so if this woman won't cooperate, it's possible we'll find others."

It was shocking to hear Gigi's words, their dispassionate tone, their optimism even. **It's possible we'll find others.** The woman's claim—Vivian Tobin's claim—had been the secret of my adulthood, the thing I'd told no one except Lyle Metcalf, Bill's campaign manager at the time. Forty years earlier, I had wanted desperately for her to be lying, or at least exaggerating; did I now want her to have been telling the truth? It was all so sordid, so sad. And I actually believed that Bill believed what he'd said the night he'd urged me to leave Arkansas—that he'd never forced himself on anyone. But that didn't mean he hadn't.

Theresa lingered as the others left the oppo meeting. When my apartment was empty except for Ebba in the kitchen, Theresa said, "How are you doing?"

I shrugged. "I wouldn't rank that as my favorite meeting ever."

"Yeah, understandably."

"The rape rumor," I said. "It wasn't the first time I've heard it. She never told me her name, but the woman Gigi mentioned, Vivian Tobin, came up to me in a parking lot, when I was by myself, right before Election Day in Bill's first congressional run. She said she'd been one of his campaign volunteers and that he'd quote-unquote forced himself on her. It must be the same woman, right? Jesus Christ." I shook my head.

"That was when you still lived in Fayetteville?"

"A few months after I'd moved there." I laughed bleakly. "Remember when I told you there were warning signs about the one person I thought I'd marry? And I didn't even know in the seventies how rare false sexual assault accusations are." In fact, rather belatedly, some of my education had come in the last few years when two of my fellow female senators had introduced a bill to address the problem of sexual assault in the military. I added, "But I admit that I still wonder if some of this can be chalked up to it being a different time. Or did Bill do it but he only did something like this once?"

"I wish I knew the answers to any of that."

"Do you think I should tell Gigi I spoke to the woman forty years ago? And I told Bill's campaign manager about her. Should I give Gigi **his** name?"

Theresa was rolling her lips in and out. Finally, she said, "The only reason that I can see for involving yourself is if the woman makes a statement that mentions you and you're vulnerable to people saying you sat on the story all this time, until it served your purposes, and didn't care about the woman.

I wouldn't say anything for now, though, even to Gigi. It's all so explosive, but if the woman doesn't want to talk to reporters, maybe it's moot."

"I don't think it's fair to say I sat on the story all this time and didn't care about the woman," I said. After a few seconds, I added, "And I'm sorry to say I don't think it's completely unfair either."

The Harriet Tubman Leadership Academy was a charter school in North Philadelphia serving students between seventh and twelfth grades, almost all of them girls of color with an aptitude for science, technology, engineering, and math. It was in the school gym that, on a Tuesday morning, I was officially announcing my education platform, which included universal computer science classes, modernized school buildings, and reduced reliance on standardized tests.

The PE teacher's office served as the greenroom. For social media, Ellie took pictures of me beside a framed poster of a basketball going through a hoop and the words WINNERS NEVER GIVE UP. First I posed smiling and with a thumbs-up, then again without a thumbs-up, raising my eyebrows to imply, I inferred, some knowing irony—perhaps, I thought but did not say to Ellie, the knowing irony of a sixty-seven-year-old burned by having used the phrase **on fleek**.

The school principal, a woman about ten years younger than I, led me into the gym proper, where the air was charged with the energy of four hundred girls in white polo shirts tucked into navy-blue slacks. The students were crowded onto rows and rows of bleachers, still talking to one another, a mass of adolescent exuberance and laughter, with teachers interspersed among them. The press corps stood to the side of the bleachers, and I passed them, just behind the principal and buffered by two security agents and Theresa, en route to a dais.

I stood beside the dais as the principal stepped to the podium, held her arms up, and snapped three times with both hands. Surprisingly quickly, the gym quieted, the students mimicking the snapping. The principal spoke slowly and clearly as she welcomed everyone and described the history and mission of the school. She introduced the student who would introduce me, a senior named Aisha Ilwaad, who was the president of the student body. A girl in a long-sleeved white polo shirt and a hijab walked from the front row of the bleachers up to the dais accompanied by avid applause from the other teenagers.

The girl was a few inches taller than the principal, and when she—Aisha—stood at the podium, she raised the microphone a little. In a very loud, very enthusiastic voice, she said, "Here at the Harriet Tubman Leadership Academy, we are all about learning to be strong women." She turned her head to the side and looked directly at me. "Hillary Rodham, thank you for being a strong woman." At this, the students erupted.

The cheering hadn't completely dissipated when Aisha began speaking again. "My classmates plan to be doctors and lawyers, engineers and coders. As for myself, I plan to be mayor of Philadelphia." The cheering started up again, and I happily participated. "To any boy or man who says that a girl can't code or a girl can't lead, this is what I say: 'Watch me.' " By this point, we were all—all except of course the press—hooting and applauding ecstatically.

"I am seventeen years old," Aisha said. "I was born on October second, 1998, which I know, Ms. Hillary Rodham, you also have an October birthday. I will turn eighteen one month before the 2016 election, and do you want to know who I'll cast my first vote for?" The cheering ramped up even more, and Aisha nodded at the crowd, grinning and unflappable; in addition to being a better speaker than her principal, she was a better speaker than I was. She said, "Hillary Rodham, I am going to vote for you."

Four hundred girls rose to their feet and cheered their hearts out, and it was an extraordinary sight to behold, these rows and rows of students in their matching polo shirts and slacks. They were thin and heavy and short and tall, dark-skinned and light-skinned, with hair in scarves and ponytails and cornrows, and they were so excited and so full of promise. They were, I thought, not much younger than I'd been when I'd delivered the commencement address at Wellesley.

On the campaign trail, I didn't always feel it, but I felt it on this day—how close we were to the barrier that was often referred to as a glass ceiling but that I instinctively pictured as a large grassy field that, through some combination of fate and ambition, I was the likeliest person to get across first. And I thought I could do it, but I wasn't sure; there was no guarantee, nothing I alone could force. At moments like this, both the closeness and the urgency were palpable. There were so many of us who wanted this, and we wanted it so badly. I'd been asked countless times **why** I was running for president, and I'd answered countless times, seemingly never to anyone's satisfaction. I think the problem was that journalists and voters were asking an individual question that had a collective answer. I did want to help people, and I wanted to help as many people as possible. I did like the work of holding elected office, and I liked doing things I was good at, and I liked being recognized for doing things I was good at. But as much as I wanted to be president, I wanted a woman to be president—I wanted this because women and girls were half the population and we deserved, as a basic human right and a means of ensuring justice, to be equally represented in our government. Yet it was hard to explain because no man had ever run for president for this reason; even Barack, who'd surely run in part for the racial version of it, had never to my knowledge articulated it as such. Some presidents cared about improving the world, and all of them had egos; but none of them had run because they hoped to gain entry to the highest office of power on behalf of an entire gender. Yes, I was me, Hillary, but I also was a vessel and a proxy.

I walked up the three steps to the dais and embraced Aisha, and after I was at the podium and she was back in the bleachers, the audience cheered for a bit longer, which gave me time to collect myself. Briefly, I pressed one fingertip below my right eye and then below my left. This image would be widely reproduced, maybe because when I finally spoke, there was still the smallest catch in my voice; my sincerity would be widely debated.

"Thank you, Harriet Tubman Leadership Academy, and thank you, Aisha," I said. "I think you'll make a superb mayor, but if you ever decide to run for national office, I'd also love to vote for you."

It happened for the first time at Bill's rally in Youngstown, Ohio, which occurred two days later. All three of Bill's previous rallies—in Oakland, then in Des Moines, then in Manchester—had aired live on multiple cable networks, thereby allowing the pundits to marvel at the increasing sizes: four thousand people in Des Moines, five thousand in Manchester, and seven thousand in Youngstown. Even more alarmingly, a new poll showed 31 percent of Iowa Democrats voting for Bill and 38 percent for me, in contrast to 43 percent voting for me just two weeks earlier, before he'd entered the race.

I didn't watch the Youngstown rally live—I was back in Iowa visiting a dairy farm—but I watched part of it later in the day, as my team drove from Sioux City to Council Bluffs. Bill's event was in a gym on the campus of Youngstown State University, and he stood onstage at a podium with a crest affixed to the front. Behind him, on risers, were people waving signs: BILL! in red against a blue background. The crowd was young—many of them looked like college students, in baseball caps and hoodies—and mostly white and male. They were fired up, grinning and nodding and clapping and hooting. Bill seemed to convey with his very presence that neither he nor his audience could possibly have anywhere better to be, and his confidence made it true. I couldn't pretend not to understand, because hadn't he once conveyed the same to me, and hadn't I believed it?

He spoke in his Bill-ish way, expansive and smart but folksy, with ostensibly spontaneous off-script interjections that were as well worded and insightful as the rest of his speech. The gist was that places like Youngstown could be every bit as innovative, dynamic, and prosperous as Silicon Valley; that if you were a miner, a factory worker, or a student, you already had the intellectual tools to become a coder, and hell, maybe an entrepreneur, too. Sure, you might need some training, but your work ethic and your intelligence were just waiting to be utilized. This was a message to which the residents of Youngstown were, apparently, highly receptive.

After wild cheering, he said, "Now, I'm not the only Democrat running. And I respect my opponents. But one in particular, she's been in Washington for decades. And I think it's time for some innovation, some disruption of politics as usual. If we stick to the same-old, same-old of lobbyists and special interests, we'll get the same old results."

There was intense booing.

He said, "I'm a self-made man, and I'm a free agent. I'm not beholden to anyone. I'm not in this race for **me**. I'm in it for **you**."

I was watching on an iPad in the second row of the van, sitting next to Theresa. The implication that, in contrast to Bill, I was some sort of raving egomaniac made me snort.

From the row behind me, Diwata said, "Just wait."

"All the good things that have happened in my career," Bill said, "I want those things to happen to you, too. I want you to get your rightful share of the American dream. You're going to hear a lot of talk from my opponents about the economy, a lot of fancy terms and complicated policies. But what does it all mean for **you,** the hardworking people who form the backbone of our country?"

It was at this point that someone in the audience shouted, "Hillary sucks!" It wasn't audible in the video, but, according to the tweets and subsequent dispatches of reporters who'd been present, the person who yelled was a middle-aged man.

Bill shook his head. He said, "Now, now," but even in those initial seconds (was this visible to people who knew him less well than I did?), he was smirking a little. He added, "You know why there's no need for personal insults? Because we can beat her on the issues. You may wonder what she's talking about when she mentions things like short-term capital gains or tax inversion. These complicated terms she throws around—"

The person who shouted out "Shut her up!" was not the same person who had shouted "Hillary sucks!" The second person was a younger man, and his outburst also was not audible on TV. Bill ignored the "Shut her up" and kept speaking. He said, "I pledge not only that I'll talk to you plainly, but I'll substitute action for talk and innovation for the status quo." But more people were shouting, "Shut her up!" Others were booing again. Watching the footage, I wouldn't necessarily have understood what they were saying if I hadn't been told. All at once, the individual shouts coalesced into a chant, and for a solid ten seconds, a gym in Youngstown, Ohio, was chanting—about **me**—"Shut her up!" The expression on Bill's face was nonplussed. When the cameras scanned the crowd, the chanters seemed upbeat, as if rooting for their team at a sports event. Who were these people? Were they Democrats? Republicans? Independents? Libertarians?

"All right, now," Bill said. "All right, now." He had to say it four more times before they quieted down. Theresa touched her fingertip to the screen, pausing the video.

"Wow," I said.

Sarcastically, Clyde said, "It's almost like the subtext is becoming text," and I replied, "Yeah, almost."

Presumably, I was not the only one frustrated by the media attention abruptly lavished on Bill. Though I'd been the first Democrat to announce my presidential bid, I'd actually been the third candidate—both Ted Cruz and Rand Paul had announced in the weeks before I did, and in the month after, they were followed by four other Republicans, including Marco Rubio and Carly Fiorina. "She's drafting on your wind resistance," Clyde said. I'd met Carly, who had extensive corporate experience and had never held elected office, a few times over the years and I didn't care for her or her political platform—she was a virulently antichoice war hawk. Several media outlets, usually women's magazines, floated the idea of Carly and me filling out the same questionnaire so our answers could run side by side, a request to which my communications director, Aaron, would say, "In Carly's dreams."

As for Ted, Rand, and Marco Rubio—all my colleagues in the Senate—Marco had a youthful energy, but something seemed a bit off, which is to say unelectable, about Ted and Rand. I found Ted smart and unappealing, and Rand egotistical and just plain weird. The opponents who posed the biggest threat were Marco, Mitt Romney, and Jeb Bush, the latter two of whom still hadn't declared by mid-May. Mitt and Jeb both were men I could, in a parallel universe, imagine as the husbands of my friends. No matter how insidious their politics, they knew how to conduct themselves in public settings. But none of these men had the magnetism that Bill had. None of them were anywhere close.

It had been a few weeks since my text exchange with Misty LaPointe, and I reached out again: **Misty, it's Hillary Rodham. How are things going?**

From her: **I'm ok just had my 3rd chemo my hairs falling out:(**

From her: **But guess what I convinced one of nurses to vote for u!!!**

From me: **Oh my goodness, that's above and beyond what I could ask of anyone. Thank you!**

From me: **Are you still able to work full-time?**

From her: **I went on disability after surgery when sick leave used up but disability 40% pay cut so . . . not doing that for now**

From me: **When I'm back in Iowa, would you be interested in introducing me before I speak at an event? No pressure if you don't want to, but you have such a compelling story and great energy.**

From her: **OMG yes . . . I would so nervous . . . but yes!!**

From her: **Not sure how great energy is rn.**

She added an emoji whose meaning I didn't know, a sort of cringing face. I regretted my word choice.

From me: **That makes sense. I hope things continue to go as well as possible for you and please keep me posted. Someone from my team will reach out about the introduction.**

The second episode of the chanting happened while Bill was speaking in Nashua, New Hampshire; again, it started slowly and gathered force. Cameras panned the auditorium of the community college, where some members of the audience stood, pumped their arms, pointed their index fingers, and waved their BILL! signs. "Shut her up! Shut her up!"

It wasn't that everyone seemed deranged or rabid; some people were looking at their phones, some stood with their mouths closed. Maybe half were chanting? And the ones that did seem deranged or rabid—if they'd been chanting something else, something where the **her** did not refer to me, would I simply have thought they seemed impassioned? What if they'd been chanting "No more coal!" or perhaps "Not the church! Not the state! Women must control our fate!" But, of course, they hadn't been.

There was also the matter of the expression on Bill's face—what **was** his expression? It was slightly self-conscious but also pleased. It was (could this be?) flirtatious. He was smiling the way a successful man might smile if an attractive woman told him he was the handsomest man in the world. He wasn't sure it was true. He knew it probably wasn't. But still, it was awfully nice to hear.

He said, "We don't need to—you know what let's do? Let's beat her in the primary nine months from now. That'll be here a lot sooner than you think."

But much later, in the night, something occurred to me, though I waited until the morning to rewatch the rally footage and confirm it. When the chanting had begun, he had paused. He could have kept speaking, but he had paused to let it build.

• • •

I texted him that night, after eleven, from my hotel room in Denver. I did it impulsively, without consulting anyone on my staff. **Can we have a quick and confidential conversation?**

A few seconds later, he texted back, **When?**

I texted, **Now.**

My phone rang, and I said, "You need to make the chanting stop."

He laughed. "I'm well, thank you. How are you?"

"It's ugly," I said. "And think of the message it sends to girls and young women interested in running for office."

"That's who you're worried about? Girls and young women?" I said nothing, and he added, "Candidly, I don't like it any better than you do. But I think the best thing is to ignore it instead of making a fuss and fanning the flames."

"The woman who came up to me in Chouteau's parking lot in 1974—" I paused. "I assume you know that people know her name."

"Are you threatening me, Hillary?" He sounded halfway between amused and disgusted.

"I'm just amazed that you act like a person with nothing to hide," I said. "That you're so cavalier about everything."

"I **am** a person with nothing to hide. Listen—" If we'd been in the same room, presumably this was when he'd have stuck his pointer finger at me. "You claim someone told you something damning about me forty years ago. Yet you continued to date me for months, you accepted my goddamn marriage proposal, and based on what happened in 2005, there's pretty strong evidence you never stopped carrying a torch for me. For you to admit I'm a good guy when it's fun but claim that I'm an affront to feminism when it serves your purposes—come on, Hillary. Have some self-respect."

Presumably, I had known that calling him was misguided; I hadn't consulted anyone on my staff because they'd have told me not to do it.

I said, "An affront to feminism is an interesting way to describe sexual assault."

Aaron, my director of communications, had convinced me it was time to host an OTR—off-the-record—with the traveling press corps. Though Aaron usually worked out of the Chicago office, he'd flown down to Miami that Thursday morning. I was delivering a lunchtime speech to attendees of a national conference for people with developmental disabilities and their caregivers, visiting a brewery in the afternoon, and attending a $1,000-a-head evening reception on Belle Isle.

At 9:00 P.M., following the reception, Aaron, Theresa, Clyde, two agents, and I left my suite on the tenth floor of our Miami hotel to join a dozen of the travelers on a patio outside the lobby restaurant. We were hopeful that the warm breezes of Biscayne Bay—in contrast to, say, an Applebee's in Iowa—would soothe the travelers' crankiness and perhaps even flatter their elitist pretensions. In their articles and on the air, political journalists loved including local color (meat on a stick at the state fair, polka bands, caucuses held in a gun shop or grain elevator) in inverse proportions to how much they'd disdain such spectacles in their actual lives, off the job. A reporter had once told me that if she was getting dinner on her own on the road, she would choose a restaurant by googling the zip code and **kale salad.**

It really wasn't that I loathed the press, as was often reported by members of the press; it was that I profoundly distrusted them. They were, for the most part, funny, observant, and intelligent—many had degrees from fancy universities—and I knew they were hardworking because, for much of the time, they literally kept the same schedule I did, attending the same rallies, driving between the same small towns in Iowa or New Hampshire, flying in and out on the same early-morning and late-night flights (though not literally on the same plane—at this point in the campaign, my team still flew on a relatively small Gulfstream, and it wouldn't be until the general election that, God willing, the travelers would be invited onto my campaign's 737).

But most political journalists were so childish, so distracted by shiny objects in the forms of gaffes or scoops or arbitrary details they imbued with meaning that simply wasn't there. The journalists' desire not to be bored was palpable, but campaigning, like life, was often boring. Thus, in their hunger for novelty, they read shifting alliances and enmities into minor personnel changes, described mindsets they guessed at based on posture or body language, competed with each other for meaningless scraps that they could present as breaking news. They constructed elaborate narratives based on scant evidence. They also were self-righteous and self-congratulatory; they assumed that, in other fields, they could make salaries many times what they currently earned, but they believed that journalism was a noble calling. And yet, on a day-to-day basis, they were people who fought over electrical outlets, who were simultaneously obsessed with their—and my—campaign weight gains **and** with the availability of meals and snacks. They shamelessly critiqued my appearance while, in some cases (this was true of both men and women) visibly going days at a time without washing their hair or changing their clothes. Like children, the journalists wanted to say and write whatever they wanted about me and then for me to be glad to see them, for me to **like** them. Unlike children, the journalists drank a lot and sometimes had romances with each other.

My entourage stepped off the elevator, crossed the lobby, and was led by the restaurant's maître d' to the back patio, beyond which was the glittering black water of the bay, bisected by the lights of two bridges. Four small round tables had been pushed together into a square, and all except two of the chairs around them were occupied. With forced cheer, I said, "Hi, guys. Is there room for me?" Clyde was the one who took the other open seat, while Aaron and Theresa stood at the edge of the patio, as did the security agents.

Immediately, the journalists were talking to me over one another. After a few seconds, the others deferred to a woman named Elise from **The Washington Post**, who said, "Senator, have you had the chance to enjoy any spa treatments at the hotel?"

"I haven't," I said. "Have any of you?"

"No, but Caitlin and I took a Zumba class at the gym down the street," said Helena. She worked for an online magazine for which she'd once written a fourteen-paragraph article about a coughing fit I had during a rally. "Have you ever done Zumba?"

"I haven't had the chance to try it." I smiled. "I've been a bit busy."

"The chanting at Governor Clinton's events," said a **New York Times** reporter named David. "What do you think is up with that?"

I raised my eyebrows noncommittally and said, "What do **you** think is up with it?"

Only half-sheepishly, David said, "I asked you first?"

I said, "Obviously, it was peculiar to hear. But you know what I found inspiring is meeting people today with developmental disabilities at the ADN conference. I thought the question about self-advocacy from that ten-year-old boy was wonderful."

"Just to piggyback on what David was asking," said Helena, "are you surprised by how much momentum Bill Clinton's campaign has gained so quickly?"

"You know, it's standard for there to be a bounce when a candidate declares," I said. "And especially with Bill, there's a nostalgia. We'll see how long that lasts." A mojito appeared in front of me, presumably ordered by Theresa, and I nodded in thanks to the waitress before taking a sip. It was so delicious—and the setting was so lovely—that I wished I were drinking it with actual friends, or at least with just my own staff.

"Will it be strange to be onstage with Bill Clinton at debates? Emotionally strange?" This came from Tiff, the preppy correspondent for ABC.

"I'm focused on larger issues," I said. "So much is at stake in this election in terms of the economy, education, climate change, that"—I made air quotes—" 'emotionally strange' doesn't really figure into it for me." I scanned their faces. "I also loved visiting the Harriet Tubman Leadership Academy, and I look forward to the pieces you'll be doing on my education platform. I'd be delighted to answer any follow-up questions."

A few of them chuckled, then a man named Roberto from a weekly newsmagazine said, "The coincidence of your having dated Governor Clinton—do you see it as evidence of elite law schools as political feeders? Does it reveal that the Democratic party needs fresh blood?" It was hard not to wonder if they'd coordinated this line of questioning before my arrival.

I said, "Roberto, I don't know if you had a chance to watch **Beverly Today**, but I really have said all I have to say on this topic."

"Seriously, guys," Clyde said, "isn't there **anything** else you want to talk about?"

"Your host today at the Belle Isle reception," Helena said, "is it troubling to you that in the late eighties, he was convicted of three counts of tax evasion?"

"Helena, I think you can do better," Clyde said.

My communications director, Aaron, was standing about twelve feet away, but I couldn't make eye contact with him because he was looking down and typing on his phone. I wondered if he still thought this OTR was wise, or whether it had already done more damage than good.

"I need to respectfully disagree with you that the financial history of a major donor is irrelevant," Helena said. "But okay—looking at Republican candidates, is there anyone you especially hope will or won't jump into the race?"

"I'm prepared to take on whomever the Republicans offer up," I said. "I'm feeling really energized by the everyday Americans I've been talking to on the campaign trail. Aisha in Philadelphia knocked my socks off, and so did today's small-business owners Leticia and Igor Arias with their brewery." I noticed Helena and Caitlin exchange a glance that I could have sworn contained the cattiness of the worst kind of seventh-grade girls. Had I pronounced the Cuban names displeasingly to them? Had they just remembered my "on fleek" disaster?

"If you don't mind," a woman named Anna from the **Tribune** said, "I want to circle back to the chanting at Bill Clinton's rallies. If that happens again—" But Theresa had already stepped forward and said, "Hey guys, we have a surprise tonight. David, we understand that tomorrow is a big day for you." At that moment, the waitress from earlier walked onto the patio carrying a sheet cake topped with lit candles and we all began singing "Happy Birthday."

When the waitress set the cake in front of David, he breathed in just before blowing out the candles, and Caitlin, who was across the table from him on my right said, "Wait a sec—" She pulled off her wedding ring, leaned forward, and dropped it around one of the still-lit candles. Theresa had taught me the phrase **wheels up, rings off;**

apparently, it could apply to journalists, security agents, or campaign staffers, though Theresa had assured me that it didn't apply to her.

David blew out the candles, and Tiff said, "Where does that come from, the ring thing?" and Helena said, "It's to make your wishes come true," and Elise said, "I thought just blowing out the candles made your wishes come true."

"Elise," I said, "surely you know it's hard work that makes wishes come true." Gratifyingly, everyone laughed.

As David cut the cake, Anna said, "Senator, where were **you** on your fortieth birthday?"

"Oh, gosh," I said. "I hardly remember back that far." This **was** something I wouldn't have said on the record, having been cautioned not to draw attention to my age. I said, "Well, I was a professor then. And let's see, for the actual night, I had dinner with my family, and I'd spent the weekend before with some college friends in rural Virginia." I looked around the table. "Who else here is forty?"

Three of them raised their hands; of those three, it turned out all were still under forty-five, and one had been reporting from Tahir Square in 2011 on her fortieth birthday.

David's cake was chocolate with chocolate frosting, and I ate two bites. If I consumed the whole piece and drank the mojito, I'd give myself a headache. But as I set down my fork, I thought that some of the earlier acrimony had lifted. Aaron had been right after all. "David," I said, "thank you for being born."

But that question about the chanting that Anna had been prevented from asking in Miami—it may have been the only relevant question of the OTR. Because the chanting did happen again, a third time and a fourth, and then it was understood to be a standard feature of Bill's events. Quickly, it went from a shocking aberration to a new norm.

When asked about it, I'd shrug and say, "Running for president isn't for the faint of heart." I watched the chanting the third time—it was in Waterloo, Iowa, and included the same mix of mobbish bloodlust and mundanity as before—and didn't watch it again. But I confess that even as I found the phenomenon disturbing, a part of me felt vindicated. Generally speaking, complaints about sexism were perceived as sour grapes. Proof was elusive, situations subject to interpretation. Yet was this not the starkest proof?

Bill was asked about it, too. During a sit-down interview with CNN, he said, "You know, I'd rather be gentlemanly. I'm more than comfortable fighting Hillary on the merits of our candidacies."

For the interview, Bill had worn a slate-gray shirt with an iridescent sheen, and it was unbuttoned one more button than might have been considered standard, though I don't think I'd have noticed if not for what happened afterward, or really during, which was that social media, especially Twitter, became obsessed with how attractive Bill looked in the shirt: Memes and hashtags were spawned, and tweeters of every age and gender declared their crushes. Within the hour, online articles featured headlines such as "18 Times Bill Clinton Made Me Thirsty" and "I Want Bill Clinton As My Sugar Zaddy." Naturally, I needed to have Diwata define **zaddy** and, in this context, **thirsty**. But the most jaw-dropping part was when a female columnist whose work I'd enjoyed in the past tweeted **Sexually harass ME, Bill!** Only slightly less egregious was a tweet from an actress on a reality show (I had not enjoyed her work in the past) who wrote **Cuddle puddle curious and my DMs are open.**

"So it's not that they don't know about his history with women," I said to Clyde. We were on the plane again, flying to Cincinnati for an evening fundraiser and a Planned Parenthood breakfast the next morning. "It's that they don't care."

The voicemail was from Meredith, Maureen's daughter. In an unconvincing but enthusiastic English accent that I knew well, she said, "Hello, Darth Vader. It is the queen of England, and I am calling with some **veddy, veddy** exciting news. Call me when you have a chance."

From my hotel room in Cincinnati, I called her immediately, and when she answered, I said, "It's Darth Vader. What's going on?"

"I'm pregnant," she said, and I said, "Oh my goodness, this is so exciting! How far along are you?"

"Ten weeks, so we're not telling most people, but I've already gained seven pounds. Which I think might be because of, like, Dove bars and not the pregnancy. My due date is January second."

"How are you feeling?"

"Super tired. I've been going to bed by eight o'clock every night, but I haven't puked or anything."

"How's Ben?" This was Meredith's husband. He worked for an investment advising firm, and she was a real estate agent, and they lived two blocks from the house in Skokie where she'd grown up.

"He's nervous and very excited. Did you know that a euphemism for 'pregnant' used to be 'stung by a serpent'? Which is actually so much grosser than just saying 'pregnant,' when you really think about it."

I laughed. "I've heard 'with child' and 'in the family way,' but I've never heard 'stung by a serpent.' It's funny because in a yarn shop in Iowa a few weeks ago, I bought a little knit bear, and I didn't know who it was for. I just thought it was cute. But now I know."

“Oh, I love that,” Meredith said. “You had a premonition. You know what’s crazy? It’s crazy that an embryo can form, turn into a baby, gestate, and be born, and there’ll **still** be ten months left before the election.”

“Tell me about it,” I said.

In the morning, in Cincinnati, I had the TV on as I got dressed, and it happened that Donald Trump was a guest on the morning news show. I hadn’t spoken to him since our meeting at the magazine gala in 2005, though in 2011, we’d both been at the White House Correspondents’ Dinner, where he’d been mocked from the stage by both President Obama and the host comedian for his birther claims.

The news-show hosts were a man and woman, sometimes joined by other panelists and guests; I myself had appeared as a guest a handful of times. On this morning, at 6:15 A.M. eastern time, they chatted with Donald about whether he was going to continue his reality show, then about a Twitter feud he was embroiled in with a sitcom actress, and then the man said, in a preemptively amused tone, “Do we have a possible Trump presidency to look forward to? I know you’ve considered it for years, and I’m wondering if you’d like to take this moment, among friends, to announce anything to the American people.”

Donald smiled a sneering smile. "You'd like that, wouldn't you?" he said. "Good for your ratings, right?"

"I can't lie," the man said. "If you run for president, it'll be one hell of a ride for all of us."

"Everyone's asking," Donald said. "All the press, all my guys on Wall Street, they say, 'We need you, we want you, can you run?' And I'm thinking about it. But I've got a lot of big stuff coming up, a lot of deals, China wants us to build thirty, forty hotels. There's my TV show. So I don't know."

"If you did run," the female host said, "you'd be an Independent? Or a Republican? Would you consider running as a Democrat along with Hillary Rodham and Bill Clinton?"

Donald held his hands in front of him, fingers toward the camera, palms facing each other. "They're all bad," he said. "The Democrats, they're weak, they're soft. I shouldn't say it, but I'm gonna say it. They're stupid. This country is in trouble, and we need real leadership, not stupidity."

The man asked, "Do you know either of them, Clinton or Hillary Rodham?"

"He's a real ladies' man." Donald raised his eyebrows and pursed his lips insinuatingly. "I know him, he's always wanted to join my clubs, but you know what? Sometimes you have to wait in line. Sorry, Bill! Her—Hillary—I've never met her. She lives out there, wherever it is, out there in the middle of the country. She's not a New York kind of person."

It was actually less surprising to me that Donald did not, apparently, recall meeting me than that he seemed critical of Bill. At the magazine gala, Donald had been the one pleading with Bill to come play golf.

"It's true," the female host said. "Bill Clinton's a smart guy, he's made a ton of money, and I know a lot of people think he's a silver fox, but you mention his name to any woman my age and what does our mind go to?"

"I assume you're referring to the **60 Minutes** interview," the male host said.

"The **60 Minutes** interview!" the woman repeated. "It was a legit train wreck. And back in the day, maybe you could bury that kind of thing, but now anyone who missed it the first time around can call it up in three seconds on YouTube."

Cheerfully, Donald said, "Bill Clinton, he's made some bad choices, but the women stuff—is that such a crime? If that's a crime, I tell you what, a hell of a lot of us are criminals."

All three of them laughed, including the woman. And then, as I sat on the edge of the bed and pulled on the nylon footies I wore with heels, I thought, What if Donald really did run for president? It was impossible to take him seriously as a candidate, with his bloviating and his preposterous hair, but what if he made a vanity run and he and Bill duked it out for the media attention and male ardor while I stood above the fray? Was it possible they could mitigate each other? Could some unholy alchemy of testosterone occur, a destabilizing blaze that incinerated Bill but left my own campaign intact? Because, really, weren't they two sides of the same coin, wasn't Donald simply a far less palatable version of Bill? Rich and narcissistic and verbose, charismatic, and transfixing? Bill was far smarter, but was he really less sleazy?

To speculate about the consequences of Donald running was a parlor game. To take steps to make it happen—to try, via layers of surrogates, to persuade him to enter the race—was a gambit I couldn't see risking. Just to consider it made my pulse quicken. I heard a knock at the door and my security agent Darryl's voice saying, "Ma'am, Veronica and Suzy are here for hair and makeup."

"Send them in," I called.

The text was from Nick Chess: **What the fuck is Bill thinking?**

I had reconnected with Nick at our twenty-fifth law school reunion in 1997—not attended by Bill because he was in the class behind us—by which point I was well into my first Senate term and Nick had left politics, moved from Arkansas back to his hometown of Short Hills, New Jersey, and reinvented himself as an author of legal thrillers.

In late 1992, a few months after Bill had ended his presidential campaign, Nick had written a soul-searching and disillusioned essay for **The New York Times Magazine** about working for Bill, and Nick had told me at the reunion that they hadn't spoken since.

It was inordinately satisfying to receive Nick's text because of how upside down the campaign coverage seemed—because, frankly, I kept reading news articles and watching TV clips and wondering **What the fuck is Bill thinking?**

I called Nick, and when he answered, he said, "With the caveat that when I worked for Bill I turned a blind eye to a lot of things as a survival strategy, I'd love to help you however I can."

"Does the name Vivian Tobin ring a bell for you?"

"Yes."

"Do you think it's true?"

Nick hesitated. "Probably?"

"Do you think it was an isolated event or a pattern?"

"I really, really want to think it was an isolated event."

I sighed and said, "Even given everything, so do I."

"It's odd," Nick said, "because do you remember when you and I overheard Bill talking about watermelons in the law school lounge? Before I knew him, I thought he was a horse's ass. Then I got to know him and decided he was truly exceptional. Then I went to work for him and decided, no, I was right the first time—he's a horse's ass. Now, seeing his smug face onscreen while he jeopardizes Democratic unity for some kind of hand job from the media, all I can think is that this is an invitation for a Republican spoiler."

"Would you mind having all of that engraved on a marble tablet and sending it to me?" I said. "Just to look at for my own enjoyment."

"I'll make one for each of us," Nick said.

Back in Chicago, Greg came to my apartment. "I know this might sound like it's out of left field," I said, "but what if we try to convince Donald Trump to enter the race so he'll take attention away from Bill?"

"Wow," Greg said. "That is **not** what I thought you were about to say."

"Obviously not in a way that's traceable to our people. Setting aside the feasibility, what would happen if one day everyone wakes up and Donald has announced?"

"I've heard his threats to run, of course, but I've never bought it. I want to check something." Greg typed on his phone then said, "Yeah, this is what I thought—historically, he's given more money to

Dems than Republicans, but since 2011, he's given more to Republicans. Just $8,500 to Dems and $630,000 to Republicans."

"I assume he's an empty vessel politically. My goal here is to fight fire with fire. Fight a rich blowhard with a rich blowhard."

"Interesting factoid," Greg said. "My understanding is Trump wasn't actually rich until he became a reality TV star. His real estate deals are smoke and mirrors."

"Does this idea seem like a nonstarter to you?"

"I like how conniving it is, I'll give you that. But I worry it involves too many factors beyond our control. And if it gets back to Obama, you can kiss his support goodbye."

"Here's a question for you—is there some kind of feud between Bill and Donald? I saw Donald on TV the other day, and he seemed very anti-Bill."

"How gratifying." But then Greg sighed. "This makes me nervous."

"At least it's an interesting thought experiment, huh?"

"Much like the question of whether you'd run for Senate in '92," Greg said. "Remember how that turned out?"

"It turned out gloriously," I said.

In the morning, I woke up to a text from Theresa: **Just a heads-up Gwen Greenberger wrote op-ed**

for today's Wash Post endorsing Kamala Harris. To my surprise, tears filled my eyes. Kamala Harris, whom I'd met just once, was the attorney general of California, had announced her Senate bid in January, and was of black and Indian descent.

In early 1992, a week after I'd told Gwen Greenberger that I was running for Senate but before I'd publicly announced, I'd received a long letter from her. **I implore you to reconsider your decision to oppose Carol Moseley Braun in the primary,** Gwen had written. **This is an opportunity for you to help lift not only another woman but a Black woman. To compete against her is a betrayal of your principles and undermines your commitment to both racial advancement and feminism.**

Receiving this letter devastated me—there was no one whose opinion I respected more than Gwen's—but it didn't change my mind, for the reason I'd already conveyed to Gwen: Although I liked Carol, I just didn't think she had a shot at beating Alan Dixon in the primary. I wrote back saying as much, and then I didn't have contact with Gwen until almost a year later. My campaign literature and eventual ads prominently mentioned my time with the National Children's Initiative, but I neither asked for nor received any financial or verbal support from Gwen. When Deb at the Victoria Project suggested that we ask Gwen to cohost a fundraiser for me in Washington, I explained that I didn't feel I could. At various junctures during the campaign—when I won the primary, when I won the election—I'd thought I'd hear from Gwen; I'd hoped that the way events unfolded would vindicate my argument.

But I was the one who initiated contact again; in December '92, I sent a Christmas card to the Greenbergers along with another letter just for her. **I'm so sorry that we never saw eye to eye on my Senate run,** I wrote. **The idea of moving to Washington (three weeks from now!) and not getting to see you on a regular basis breaks my heart. After I arrive, can I please take you out for lunch and express in person how important you are to me? I sincerely believe that our friendship transcends any political or personal disagreements.**

Gwen's response was two typed sentences: **Hillary, I see nothing more for us to discuss. I hope that your time in the Senate will serve to remind you of the ideals you embraced as a young woman.**

But I knew I'd run into both Gwen and Richard eventually, and about six weeks after I was sworn in, Gwen and I attended the same reception for a teachers' federation. When I approached her, I deliberately didn't hug her, but it seemed preposterous to pretend we didn't know each other well. "You can't avoid me forever," I said in a friendly tone, and she looked at me with an expression of contempt that I had seen before on her face but never for me. "I certainly can," she said. From then on, on the two or three occasions a year we were in the same place, I gave her a wide berth, and the same was true with Richard, though he'd at least acknowledge me with a nod. A few years later, I had the surreal experience of asking Gwen questions when she testified before the Senate Committee on Health, Education, Labor, and Pensions, of which I was a member. Gwen was acting as an expert witness prior to the reauthorization of the National School Lunch Program. I sat at the horseshoe-shaped dais and addressed her as "Dr. Greenberger"—more than one university had given her an honorary doctorate—and she sat behind the witness table and addressed me as "Senator Rodham." I recalled driving with her to Fayetteville twenty years earlier, feeling pulled between her and Bill; it would have been unfathomable if I'd been told that two decades later, my relationships with both of them would be somewhere between distant and nonexistent.

As another ten years passed, the sting of my estrangement from Gwen decreased without ever disappearing; on a long drive during my first presidential campaign, I once told Theresa the story of my friendship with Gwen, thinking that doing so would be cathartic, but instead I felt a renewed sadness. A few days later, Theresa gave me a memoir she'd read by a black woman who had grown up attending private schools where almost all the other students were white, and who had eventually become the first black law partner at a firm in

Manhattan. Though Theresa didn't flag it, there was a passage where the woman described her difficulty having deep friendships with white women, how betrayed she'd feel by their casual comments that dismissed the complexity of race for her. I read the passage several times.

Over the next decade, I continued to reassess the falling-out between Gwen and me. I was spurred partly by how Barack Obama's election, superficial predictions aside, did **not** usher in a post-racial utopia, and I saw up close how he was treated with less respect than his predecessors; I was genuinely shocked when a Republican congressman from South Carolina shouted "You lie!" during a 2009 healthcare speech Barack gave during a joint session. I also was spurred by the rising attention to police shootings of unarmed black men and boys, and the way that more and more of such shootings were captured on cellphone cameras. After the 2013 fatal shooting of a sixteen-year-old black boy in the Fuller Park neighborhood of Chicago, I participated in a community dialogue hosted by Trinity United Church of Christ. A week later, I wrote to Gwen once more.

> I regret that back in 1992, when I called to tell you I was entering the Senate primary, I didn't convey the news with greater sensitivity. At the time, I considered myself almost immune to racism, in part due to

> my work with <u>you</u>, and I thought that my dismissal of Carol's candidacy was wholly unrelated to race. As the years have passed, I have come to see that almost nothing is wholly unrelated to race.

I received no response, and I understood that I wouldn't try again.

It was too painful for me to read Gwen's new piece in the **Post**. I started it, but I couldn't get past the first few sentences. But the fact that it was 2015 and Kamala Harris would, if elected, be the first black female senator—I saw at last how this vindicated Gwen's perception of my original Senate race more than my election vindicated mine.

This time, Theresa and my campaign manager, Denise, along with Greg, were part of the discussion about trying to draw Donald Trump into the race. The meeting happened at my dining room table.

"I see the logic," Denise said. "Don't think for a minute I don't. But isn't he a literal criminal? Like a contractor-stiffing slumlord?"

"What if people take him seriously?" Theresa said. "And he gains actual supporters?"

"That's the point," I said. "He steals from Bill's base. Either way, whether he runs as a Democrat or a Republican."

A poll released the day before showed 34 percent of Iowa Democrats for Bill and 35 percent for me, with similar figures in New Hampshire. That is, the numbers were trending in the wrong direction.

Greg cleared his throat. "Incidentally," he said, "I found out why Trump doesn't like Clinton. In 2011, Clinton was on **Good Morning America,** and he answered a question about Trump's birther accusations by saying Trump is morally bankrupt. Then Bill goes, 'And financially bankrupt, too, I hear.' Trump lost his shit on Twitter."

"See?" I said. "Let them duke it out, and we stand back and watch."

Denise said, "I just wonder how Jeb Bush will shake things up." Bush was expected to announce Wednesday, and was rumored to have already raised close to eighty million dollars.

"Here's the thing," Greg said. "Who does it? Who recruits Trump?"

We were all quiet, and then I said, "Maybe I do."

Greg said, "And this is consistent with your leave-no-fingerprints strategy how?"

"What if Donald and I cross paths ostensibly by coincidence? On the tarmac at an airport, or I have a donor luncheon at one of his clubs on a day we know he'll be there. I'm very careful with the language I use but very flattering to his ego."

"And then he turns around and tells the **New York Post**?" Denise said.

"Would anyone believe him?" I asked.

"But it'd be true," Theresa said. "And presumably there'd be witnesses."

"Then I say he misunderstood me. Why on earth would I try to get Donald Trump to run?"

"Let's imagine for a minute that you succeed," Greg said. "You convince him to run yet no one has a clue you did. Clinton and Trump are yelling at each other, and it becomes a three-ring circus that drowns out all other voices, including yours."

Was I in fact being hubristic? Had I lost my perspective, either abruptly or, after my previous campaigns, cumulatively?

I said, "I don't think Trump could last more than one debate, so he's out by mid-August at the latest. By then he'd have done damage."

Greg said, "We can run polls. Mix in Trump's name with other outsiders like Mark Cuban."

"You know what this reminds me of?" Theresa said. "Shooting the moon in hearts. Either winning becomes inevitable or you end up with twelve out of thirteen hearts and the queen of spades."

I glanced among them. "If all of you are convinced it's a bad idea, I'll drop it. But we need to throw out the rule book. I don't want a replay of '08." There was an energy, a momentum, I had watched Barack Obama take from me, and it had felt disorienting, unpleasant, and unfamiliar. Now I was watching Bill Clinton do the same, and it again felt disorienting and unpleasant. But it did not feel unfamiliar.

Greg sighed deeply. He said, "Men are such assholes."

Both Clyde and Theresa told me that my appearance on **Hey From My Mom's Basement,** aka **Hey FMMB,** had been scheduled weeks earlier and not in reaction to the chanting. It was just a coincidence, but a serendipitous one, that the satellite radio show's core audience was decidedly bro-ish, as was the host himself, a thirty-one-year-old comedian named Danny Danielson. The show enjoyed an average of 1.2 million listeners per episode, the vast majority of them white men between the ages of eighteen and thirty-four. In preparation for my interview, I listened to two earlier episodes, one in which Danielson interviewed a Hollywood actor and one in which he interviewed a fellow comedian, also male.

Its name notwithstanding, **Hey FMMB** was not recorded in a basement, Danny Danielson's mother's or otherwise; it was recorded in an office on the second floor of a building in downtown Los Angeles. The show would air live as well as being recorded on video for YouTube.

A producer introduced Danny Danielson and my team, and as we shook hands, Danny greeted me by saying, "Hey." He wore a faded black T-shirt, jeans, and flip-flops, and the scent of pot wafted off him. In the studio, Danny and I sat facing each other across a table, mics in front of us, and the production engineer was visible through a window. Theresa, the only member of my staff in the studio, sat behind me in a chair against the padded wall. Danny and I donned headphones, and I dutifully recited what I'd eaten for breakfast—a vegetable omelet with hot sauce—so the engineer could adjust my levels.

"Heyyyyyy, Basement Nation," Danny said when the recording had started, and I wondered how stoned he was. "You might know her as the Cookie Monster. Today we've got Hillary Rodham on the show, but before we get to that, lemme tell you about some other cool stuff." He was selling tickets to a live show in Austin, apparently, and then he touted a meal-kit service. Then, for the first time since we'd sat, he made eye contact with me.

"A lady president." He paused. "It's an oxymoron, right? Like jumbo shrimp? Or amicable divorce?"

In an upbeat voice, I said, "The qualities necessary for leading our country are experience, preparedness, and an ability to listen. Neither gender has a monopoly on attributes like that. And I trust you know that women are or have been heads of state in lots of other countries, including Germany, England, India, and Liberia."

"Have you ever borrowed a tampon from Nancy Pelosi?"

I honestly wasn't sure if the members of my media team would have advised me to smile or if Danny was being more extreme than they'd expected. "You know, Danny," I said, "Representative Pelosi knows how to work across party lines to get things done for the American people, and that's something I've also spent a lot of time doing."

"Huh," he said. "Do you braid each other's hair?"

Had Danny been this rude to the Hollywood actor or the other comedian? I didn't think so. Coldly, I said, "That's something we haven't done."

"I dunno, maybe you should?" He widened his eyes, flared his nostrils, and smiled with closed downturned lips, and the expression seemed like an acknowledgment of the degree to which his performance had nothing to do with me and instead was for the benefit of his audience. In some ways, this had always been the case with entertainers and politicians alike, but in the current election cycle, with the dominance of social media, it felt truer than ever.

"When you look at Bill Clinton," Danny said, "are you like, **Dude, that guy boned me**? And if so, how does that distinguish you from most other American women?"

Coming on the show had been a mistake; he was simply too obnoxious. I thought of removing my headphones and walking out of the studio. In thousands of interviews, I'd never done this. And I didn't in this moment, though I did look over one shoulder at Theresa, whose lips were rolled in so far they weren't visible. Then I said, "I realize that you're a comedian, and I guess that's your idea of humor. But are you sure you don't have any questions about my policies on healthcare or small businesses? I suspect that you're an independent contractor, and perhaps your show is an LLC."

"Nice try." Danny smirked. "You and Bill Clinton met in law school. Did women have orgasms in the seventies?"

I looked him in the eye and said, "I find that incredibly inappropriate."

"That's a no?"

"I was elected to the U.S. Senate in 1992," I said. "At the time I took office, I was one of six female senators. I've spent my entire career trying to improve the lives of women, children, and really all Americans. I've always cared passionately about making our country better for everyone. That's what I'll keep doing as president. I'll establish job training programs, I'll make college affordable, I'll end tax cuts for the rich. I'll fight for cleaner air and water and safety from terrorism." I was glaring at him, and I didn't care. "And you know what? You're not parodying sexism. You're just sexist. I know we live in ironic times, but if you think elections don't matter and there's no difference between me and anyone else who might become president, the person you're kidding is yourself."

There was, of course, a tiny part of me that

thought I'd persuade him. But I should have known better. "Damnnn," he said. "Snap. Are the men you work with scared of you? 'Cause I kind of am."

The reason I gave myself permission to yank off my headphones and walk out is that if I stayed any longer, I truly thought I might tell him to go fuck himself. But I wasn't yelling as I stood. "This might not be a waste of your time," I said. "But it's certainly a waste of mine."

I was shaking as I turned—Theresa had also stood—and pushed open the door of the studio. In the hall, Clyde, Diwata, Ellie, Kenya, and my agents were all waiting, and I said, "Get me out of here."

"Wait, seriously?" I heard Danny say.

"I'll deal with him," Clyde said. He entered the studio (this meant he'd make a cameo in the YouTube recording), and the rest of us, joined by the producer, walked toward the bank of elevators.

"Senator Rodham, what if we take a break and go back for another"—the producer began; he also looked to be in his thirties—and Diwata turned to speak with him, pausing so that he had to pause, too, while I continued walking. When the elevator doors closed on Theresa, Ellie, me, and the agents, Theresa and I looked at each other and I said, "I certainly hope I didn't just create another New Hampshire primary moment. But I just couldn't—sitting across from him—"

Theresa reached out and squeezed my hand. "Danny Danielson sucks," she said.

I said, "Find a way for me to meet with Donald Trump."

Among the online headlines in the hours after we left the studio: "Hillary's Meltdown"; "Hillary's Tantrum"; "Hillary's Tirade"; "Hillary's Worst Week Ever?"; "Shrillary Yells at Comedian." And from **The New York Times:** "For Some, Hillary Can Do No Right." Often, it was the pseudo-impartiality of the **Times** that rankled me the most, its veneer of elegance and restraint as it led readers to disapprove (for some!). I loved reading **Times** articles that weren't about me, which only made its negative portrayal sting more.

But also: Particularly on Twitter and Facebook, women were celebrating my response to Danny. Within twenty-four hours, two videos sampling my longest remarks had gone viral. In one, a bald black man in Atlanta sang a gospel version of my words while wearing a pink three-piece suit, and in the other, a lithe young white woman from Dallas, outfitted in a blond wig and a pantsuit, writhed, gyrated on a beige carpet, and lip-synched my words over a techno beat.

So some people thought it had been a catastrophic self-immolation and others a moment of transcendent greatness. Mostly, the admirers had admired me already—women old enough to have eaten shit in their own careers, which was to say women of any possible age—though apparently I'd won some new female (but not male) millennial admirers. **Really feeling this new IDGAF Hillary,** a Twitter user named @PictureofWhorianGray had written, and the surprising part was not just that I recognized this assortment of letters as a sentence but that I actually understood what it meant. Though, at the risk of parsing its sentiment too finely, @PictureofWhorianGray was wrong. If I didn't give a fuck, I wouldn't have been running for president.

When Maureen came over for Pilates, she handed me a large yellow paper bag with pale-blue tissue paper sticking out the top.

"What is it?" I asked, and she grinned.

"You have to open it."

I nudged apart the tissue paper and saw dark, soft material that I thought might be a shirt. When I pulled it out, I was holding a tricorn pirate hat, complete with a skull and crossbones affixed to the brim. I laughed very hard, and Maureen said, "Aye, matey! Put it on." When I did, she said, "Beautiful. Now say, 'Arrgh!' "

"Arrgh!" I said. "But what if you need it?"

"I made you your own. It took about fifteen minutes."

"You're so impressive."

This time, she laughed. "I know," she said. "But thank you."

We were in my living room, waiting for our instructor, Nora, to arrive momentarily. As Maureen sat to unlace her shoes, she said, "That little turd on the podcast—you handled him so well." Though **Hey FMMB** wasn't actually a podcast, I knew she meant Danny Danielson.

"Did you watch the whole thing?" I asked.

"Every second of it, and I cheered when you walked out." After she'd removed her shoes, Maureen said, "I was thinking about when you had dinner at Bill's place in San Francisco. What year was that?"

I made a face and said, "2005." Maureen was the only person, including Theresa, who knew everything that had happened that night.

"Is that why he's running? Because he's mad at you?"

"Oh." I paused. "I don't think so. If anything—well, obviously, it's not why I'm running, but it does make me more motivated to try to beat him."

"You don't think he's trying to get revenge?"

It was surreal that Bill was my Democratic opponent, almost inconceivable. But if I thought about it, it was surreal that I was running for president.

For the third time! I said, "I honestly don't think I loom large enough in Bill's life for him to want revenge against me."

The plan was that I would run into Donald Trump in the greenroom of the morning show I'd been watching when the idea to enlist him had occurred to me. The show filmed in New York, in a Midtown studio.

"I know you perceive him as not completely normal," Greg said as we rode the elevator up to the studio, accompanied by only Theresa and my agents. "But think of how not normal you imagine him to be, then multiply it by ten. He's a walking ego."

"I've met him," I said. "I'll be fine."

"He's obsessed with his TV ratings, so if there's any trouble, revert to that." Musingly, Greg added, "I wonder if this is the part in the movie where the scientist spills the teensiest bit of radioactive slime on the floor of the lab."

As the elevator doors opened, I said, "Thank you for the resounding vote of confidence."

I had rehearsed in my head the first words I'd say to Donald, which was something I'd trained myself to do for professional interactions with men, as a way of not slipping by default into a dynamic in which they controlled the situation. I planned to firmly shake his hand and say, "Donald, what a pleasant coincidence. Congratulations on everything you've been up to, especially this season of **The Apprentice**." In preparation for the moment, I'd watched an episode and found it both bombastic and silly.

But I realized quickly that my concerns about the dynamic had been misplaced. He burst into the greenroom with two assistants in tow, and it was immediately clear, in a way that had been obscured by the size of the crowd at the magazine gala ten years earlier, that he himself was a force field. This happens with some famous people, that their entrance into a room is like a sailboat tilting sideways—the mood of the room is now their mood, the very conversation is an exercise in deference. This could, in fact, happen with me, but it had started happening only after '08, when I'd won the Iowa caucuses, and certainly I still had both the willingness and the ability to revert to being the beta dog.

He was as tall as I remembered, nearly as tall as Bill, and his skin was a strange peach shade. This wasn't shocking given that he'd just been on the air, but he was definitely wearing more makeup than I was. His teeth were large, and his hair was, in its style, odd but (I have mentioned this to a few friends since, and no one has believed me) in its texture and shade, it was rather lovely, a rich and Rapunzelish blond; I didn't doubt that it was as expensively colored as my own. Just as some people emanate serenity, he emanated a smug, acrid jitteriness. As he approached me, he said loudly, "Hillary Rodham. I hear you're planning to be the first woman president."

I'd stood when he entered the room, and he took my hand, gripped it tightly, and shook it vigorously.

I said, "I certainly hope so."

"A lot of people want me to run for president," he said. "I'd definitely win, I'd be the greatest president ever."

How boyish he was! He reminded me of a boy in my elementary school class named Roger Hobson, who in third grade, on a field trip to the Museum of Science and Industry, had told me that if he really concentrated, he could knock down one of the massive columns at the museum's entrance with just his pinkie.

Donald still was gripping my hand tightly, still shaking it, looming above me, as he said, "I'm too busy, though. I've got a TV show that's breaking records with high ratings. I've got hotels and golf courses being built all over the world. Did you hear about my new hotel in Vancouver?"

"Congratulations on all of it," I said. "Especially on this season of **The Apprentice**."

A palpable softening occurred within or around him; whether consciously or not, he'd been waiting to see if I was a friend or adversary. At last he dropped my hand.

"Season fourteen was amazing, wasn't it?" he said. "Such high ratings. NBC was thrilled, they think it's the best show ever. People love it. It's huge."

"I know," I said, again with enthusiasm. "It really is. But do **you** ever really think of running for president? Maybe you should." I didn't dare make eye contact with Theresa or Greg for fear of bursting into laughter.

Donald looked suspicious. His eyes narrowed, and his mouth tightened. "You don't want to win?"

"Oh, I absolutely want to win," I said. "But voters deserve a choice. And you bring something to the table that none of the other Republican candidates do—the way you really say what you think, your passion and candor." He was still glaring as I added, "I wouldn't be running if I didn't believe I'm the right person for the job. But let's say I'm not elected. I don't spend a lot of time dwelling on it, but if I'm not, I don't want the person who **is** elected to be one of those—" I almost couldn't bring myself to say it, but I did. I said, "One of those losers. I look at some of the Republicans, and I don't know if they're strong enough. Do they really have the courage, the smarts?"

"You and Bill Clinton," Donald said. "You used to date, didn't you?"

I laughed. "Years ago."

A PA opened the door of the greenroom and said, "Senator Rodham, you're on in two." Theresa stood.

Donald said, "You still have a thing for Clinton?"

I ignored the question and said, "Frankly, I don't see him as a legitimate threat in this race. He's got that early spike now, but I suspect it'll fizzle in a couple weeks. He's not someone the American people really connect with in that visceral way. Now, **you**—" My propensity for bullshit was appalling and impressive, even to me. And then I did something that I still don't know if I'm proud or ashamed of: I brought my right hand to my forehead and, as if I were a private and he were a sergeant, I saluted him. I said, "I know, as a business leader and a celebrity, you have so many demands on your time. But promise me you'll give it some thought."

I don't usually find it difficult to focus on the person in front of me on or off the air, but during the television interview that followed, I did; adrenaline was coursing through me. When we left the studio, in the elevator, I said, "Did I lose my moral compass?"

Theresa said, "You want to win."

"That was beyond weird," Greg said. "But I don't think anyone who's lost their moral compass wonders if they've lost their moral compass."

The town hall in Bettendorf, Iowa, was at a synagogue, and when I entered the greenroom, Misty LaPointe exclaimed, "Hillary!" and hurled herself into my arms before drawing back, grabbing a lock of her dark hair and saying, "Can you tell this is a wig?"

"You look lovely," I said. "Thank you for being part of today's event."

"I'm so nervous I might pass out. I practiced a million times, but I still might pass out."

"You'll be fabulous," I said. "Just be yourself." In the six weeks since our first meeting, Misty had lost a significant amount of weight. She had previously been plump, and she was now thin. Her wig was long, straight, and almost black, with heavy bangs. She wore a blue-and-white-striped dress, and in her left hand, she held the rolled-up papers that I assumed were the introduction. Though I hadn't read it, I knew it had been vetted—and probably edited—by two members of my speechwriting team. Diwata had just told me that about three hundred people were in the audience; my media team's efforts to get any network to air the event in its entirety had been unsuccessful, and it was plausible that no one outside the synagogue would ever see Misty's introduction, but I didn't mention this to her because it seemed that it might be more deflating than reassuring. Instead, I said, "Are your daughters here today?"

"They're in the front row with my sister. Lauren was supposed to work, but I said, 'Tell your boss when your mom is introducing freaking Hillary Rodham, you need the day off.' "

I smiled. "How are you feeling?"

An expression of trepidation passed over her face, a trepidation that seemed separate from her public-speaking anxiety. But she said, "I feel good right now."

Theresa, Clyde, and Diwata walked with us from the greenroom to the wings of the stage in the synagogue's sanctuary, where a podium waited in the bimah. After the upbeat introductory video about my campaign, which was a variation on my original campaign announcement, my Midwest regional director introduced Misty, and as the director spoke, I reached out, clasped Misty's right hand, and squeezed it; I could feel that she was shaking. Then, as I had done so many times, she walked alone onto a stage.

The applause wasn't exactly fervent—no one knew yet who she was—but she still hesitated for a few seconds before speaking into the microphone. "Hello, ladies and gentlemen," she said. "Thank you for coming today. My name is Misty LaPointe. I was born and raised in Cedar Rapids, Iowa, and I work as a bank teller. I never thought I would find myself in the position I am in right now. I am forty-three years old, and I am fighting for my life." Again, she paused unnecessarily before continuing. "I'm the proud single mom of Lauren, who is sixteen, and Olivia, who will turn twelve on Thursday. They are both here today." She paused again and gave a shaky smile, and this time the audience clapped. Misty continued, "Olivia does gymnastics, and Lauren works at Cinnabon, and they both get straight A's. We are a small but close family. My goal is for my daughters to graduate from college, and I used to think paying for that would be my biggest challenge. But on Christmas day 2014, everything changed. That's when I first felt a lump in my right breast.

"Two weeks later, after a biopsy, a doctor told me I needed to have a double mastectomy as soon as possible. This happened in February, and I began chemotherapy infusions at the end of April. Because I had to take five weeks off of work after my surgery and my employer gives eighty hours of sick leave for the whole year, I had already used up my sick leave before I ever returned to work, and I had to go on disability. Even though I will continue chemo for up to seven more months, I can't afford to take more leave. I schedule my chemo infusions for Friday afternoons so that I will have the weekend to recover. My doctor recommends that I should take eight milligrams of the medicine Ondansetron three times a day for three days after chemo, but my health insurance will only pay for seven four-milligram pills per month. That means I am getting half the antinausea medicine I need." By this point, the synagogue had become very quiet. "Unlike the Republicans, who want to repeal the Affordable Care Act, Hillary Rodham wants to strengthen it. Under her plan, I will receive a tax refund to pay for out-of-pocket medical expenses.

I will pay less for my prescription medicine, less for copays, and less for deductibles. I will know there is someone in the White House who cares about people like me." Again, there was applause, and when it settled, Misty said, "I do not want handouts. I do not expect a free ride. But getting sick isn't something anyone can control. Over 1.5 million Americans a year are diagnosed with cancer. We need leaders who will fight for all of us, and that is why I am supporting Hillary Rodham for president of the United States of America."

There was a standing ovation, and just before I walked onstage to embrace Misty and give my stump speech, Clyde leaned toward me. "Wow," he whispered. "That was intense."

Once, I'd have believed it was impossible for a ten-person fundraiser to generate $2.5 million, and I'd have been correct in that it would, until 2010, have been illegal. But after the Supreme Court's Citizens United decision, campaign fundraising had basically become a free-for-all, and if I disapproved—I'd also have thought that extracting $2.5 million from ten people was obscene, legal or not—I was, as I'd told the question asker at the Iowa City event, a pragmatist.

This particular dinner was in Truro, on Cape Cod, and Theresa; Kenya; the agents; my national finance director, Emma Aguilera; and I flew into the tiny Provincetown airport, gliding over the Atlantic in the early-summer afternoon. Sometimes on rope lines, I shook hands with voters for whom I was the most famous, perhaps the only famous, person they'd ever meet. At fundraisers that were $250,000 a head, the guests were accustomed to fame. The host of this dinner, held at an oceanfront vacation house worth $10 million, was a thirty-eight-year-old hedge fund manager named Harris Fulkerson. I'd met him before, in New York, and for this visit, he'd invited me to spend the night in a private wing of his home, but, citing a scheduling conflict, I'd declined. I knew Bill relished such opportunities, establishing the bonds that arose when you shared scrambled eggs in your pajamas, but the thought of sharing scrambled eggs in my pajamas with an extremely rich person that I was only pretending to be friends with exhausted me.

The house was vast but minimalist, a shingled rectangle with a driveway of crushed white clamshells. As my team and I climbed out of the SUV that had transported us from the airport, Harris was waiting to greet us, and holding a cocktail that, he announced after kissing my cheek, was a Hillarytini. He was tall and wore a green-and-white seersucker blazer over a white T-shirt. He led us on a path around the side of the house and up a half flight of steps onto a deck that displayed a breathtaking view of the ocean. The nine other guests were all waiting. Harris said, "I present Hillary Rodham, the first woman president," and they applauded.

I held my Hillarytini aloft and said, "Harris, from your mouth to God's ears." Even given the small guest list, I then segued, as it was understood that I would, into an abbreviated and slightly juicier-than-usual stump speech; the slightly juicy part, where I was far franker about my opponents than I'd be in public, was why no press was allowed. And in fact the setting, with the distant crashing waves and lovely light, was too elitistly beautiful for Ellie to document for social media, which was why she wasn't in attendance, either.

After I spoke, there was a Q and A session with all the guests, during which a man around my age named Albert Boyd asked about the Trans-Pacific Partnership. At dinner, I was seated between Harris and Albert, and Albert said, "I have to tell you that my wife, Marjorie, was a great fan of yours." Being told by a man that his wife was a fan was something I heard as frequently as I heard that I was prettier in person, though I heard the former almost exclusively from white men and the latter almost exclusively from women, gay men, and people of color. But then Albert added, "And it was through her that I became such an admirer. Marjorie passed away in 2011, after ten years with lung cancer."

"I'm sorry," I said.

"Thank you. She was wonderful and quite politically active. In the hospital, she liked to have me read out loud to her, and one of the books we read was your autobiography. I know there's an audio version of you reading it, and I'm sure your version is far more proficient than mine, but I really enjoyed it."

"That's lovely," I said. "I'm honored."

"Political memoirs get a bad rap for being propaganda, but I find them very interesting. How a person constructs their life, who they're influenced by, and that sort of thing."

"I agree," I said. "Although there's a chance I'm a tiny bit biased."

He laughed. "Impossible!"

"Do you have ties to the Cape?" I asked.

He was still smiling as he said, "I'm glad that I do tonight." Was he **flirting**? And was it a coincidence that this was the first time it registered with me that he was handsome? He was mostly bald, with a closely cropped ring of silver hair, and had lively hazel eyes. He added, "Marjorie and Harris's mother were roommates at Vassar, and he's my godson. I visit Harris every so often, but I live outside New York. If this doesn't sound too appallingly WASPy, my own family has gone to Maine in the summers for several generations, to Biddeford. Have you been there?"

"I haven't," I said. "Though I've had the pleasure of meeting many appalling WASPs."

"I'm curious—does running for president feel like a variation on running for Senate or is it its own animal?"

"Some of both. The scope is broader, obviously, the whole infrastructure of the campaign. But, and I'm not just saying this, it's fascinating. I mean, apart from getting to participate in the great democratic experiment, we saw a whale as we flew in today."

"Oh, I love when that happens," he said. "Did your pilot swoop down?" He really was strangely easy to talk to, or I was strangely comfortable. It was somewhat unusual, at this point in my life, for a person I'd just met to talk to me normally, with give-and-take—my prominence made it hard for most people to fathom asking me a question that didn't relate to them or something they wanted, hard to fathom that I had a self separate from their impression of me, our fleeting interaction. "Now, would it be appropriate or inappropriate," he was saying, "if I made a criticism of Bill Clinton?"

"Since we're far from any media, I think it's permissible." Was I **attracted** to him? If so, was it due to the fact that I was on my second Hillarytini, or was it hormonal? Which hormones was I even still in possession of?

Albert said, "He could shut down the chanting."

"He absolutely could."

"I know politics have always been cutthroat, and nostalgia for a more decorous time is a bit delusional, but the chanting really seems barbaric."

And then Harris said, "Uncle Albert, you've got to share her with the rest of us. After the entrée, everyone is going to change seats except the senator."

Albert looked into my eyes and said, "How regrettable yet understandable," and the next thing I knew I was between the COO of a tech firm in Cambridge and his wife. But I kept glancing at Albert, who was sitting three guests to the left of me. I wondered, as I almost never did anymore, if I had kissed a man on the lips for the last time. How could I have, but how could I not have? Setting aside the impossible logistics, who would want to date a woman whose likeness was replicated in nutcrackers?

My team and I were the first guests to leave, but I shook hands and posed for photos with everyone before we did. When I got to Albert, he said, "I didn't have the chance to mention earlier that we know someone in common. Your Wellesley friend Nancy was also a friend of my wife's."

"Small world," I said. "Do you know that Nancy's son just got engaged?"

"I'll be at their party in October. Will you?"

"Unfortunately, I can't make the engagement party because it's just before the first debate. But I plan to be at the wedding." This would be in April.

Albert smiled. He said, "I'll very much look forward to seeing you there."

• • •

I did my best to practice good sleep hygiene, and not to check devices in the middle of the night, but around 2:00 A.M., in a hotel room in Boston, I made an exception. In an email to Nancy, I wrote, **I just met Albert Boyd at a fundraiser. Not to sound like we're back in the dorm at Wellesley, and please don't tell anyone I'm asking but . . . does he have a girlfriend? Or whatever the word is when we're in our sixties?**

No girlfriend that I know of, Nancy had written back by 7:00 A.M. **But I will discreetly do some sleuthing. For the record, I loved Wellesley Hillary and I love 2015 Hillary even more.**

Greg called me that afternoon. "Trump's not gonna run. He's afraid that if he does, everyone will think it's because a girl told him to."

"Does he not get that the way it works is that others enlist you? Or at least you pretend they did? Hillary for America, anyone?"

"I don't think we can overestimate the magnitude of the dude's insecurity, and it seems like there's something about **you** in particular that he's intimidated by."

"My X chromosomes?"

"My hunch is your credibility," Greg said. "If you tell people his presidential run was your idea, they'll believe you."

"First of all, it was **his** idea! He's been talking about it for, what, thirty years? And my God, I'd lose easily half my base if they knew I'd encouraged him."

"Yeah, but if you could spend your days sitting on a gold-plated shitter, fucking hookers, and getting paid millions to appear on TV for a few minutes, would **you** run for president? Did you know **The Apprentice** films in Trump Tower? If that was my setup, I wouldn't run. Here's where things get weird. You ready?"

"Probably not."

"He wants to be your surrogate. It's not clear he knows the word **surrogate**, but he wants to appear at your events and talk you up to the press."

"You can't be serious."

"He has the attention span of a flea, so he might forget about it, but you have to admit it's intriguing."

"I'm absolutely not allowing Donald Trump to appear at my events."

"Let's say you're never on the same stage. I thought you wanted to fight testosterone with testosterone."

"No," I said. "There's just no way. Besides, what's in it for Donald? Clearly, he's never done anything out of the goodness of his heart."

"You know how he owns the Miss Universe pageants? It sounds like he has visions of cross-branding dancing in his head, but we—"

"Have you lost your mind?"

"I'm not saying it would happen. I'm saying we'd string him along."

"Maybe after I'm elected I can judge the swimsuit competition **during** the State of the Union," I said. "Just spitballing here."

"Tell me you see the irony of the two of us having switched positions."

"I wanted him as Bill's foil! Not as my sidekick. For Christ's sake, Greg, no."

"Would you do it if you knew it would work? He supports your candidacy, a little of the rancid smell of Donald Trump rubs off on you, but you beat Clinton in the primaries and go on to win the general?"

"How would I explain to Barack that I'm accepting Donald's support?"

"Those of us from Chicago know Barack isn't as pure as we all pretend. Besides which, none of it is personal, and he'd rather elect you than Jeb Bush. The latest polls—"

I interrupted. "I realize Bill and I are neck and neck, but this is insane."

"No," Greg said. "We just got new numbers a few minutes ago. Bill is two points ahead of you in Iowa."

By the light of day, I focused on the concrete: what was actually happening as opposed to what might happen, what I could do to affect outcomes. I sometimes envisioned the events that unfolded in a day or a week or a season as a wave washing over me. The water wasn't nothing. But it also was only water. Even if it knocked me down, I could stand again. I was always still myself, and resilient.

Sometimes in the night, however, in an unfamiliar hotel room, I'd wake with a start and wonder if running for president was a bad idea. I didn't doubt my ability to do the job. After all, I understood the way government worked. I was able to listen to other people, was respectful of cultures and countries not my own. I could endure stress. I was, especially for a sixty-seven-year-old, healthy and energetic.

But the bullshit and ugliness, the battles with journalists and Republicans, the idiocy of social media—that, I questioned. I knew from reading Wellesley's alumni magazine that many of my classmates, including the ones who'd led interesting lives and been professionally successful, were now retiring, moving from bigger houses to condominiums, relaxing in gardens or with grandchildren or by taking trips to, say, China to visit the Chengdu Panda Research Base. Whereas if I traveled to China, it would be on a forty-eight-hour state visit in which I met with President Xi to discuss trade and North Korea and human rights. I would, while massively sleep deprived, attend late-night ceremonial dinners and early-morning meetings and pose for thousands of photos shaking the president's hand. If I visited the Forbidden City, it would only be for as long as it took to get footage showing that I had visited the Forbidden City.

Might someone else, someone more extroverted, be better suited to such tasks? Might Bill Clinton? Policy-wise, Bill and I were more similar than different, so didn't it come down to temperament, to which of us was more presidential? Or was it which of us was more electable? Or was it which of us was more likable?

Was it possible that, if elected, he'd be less divisive than I was, likelier to bring back into the Democratic fold the rural and working-class white men who had been defecting to the Republican Party? On the other hand: Was appeasing rural and working-class white men more important than inspiring women and girls? I'd once heard that little girls would read books and watch TV shows that featured either girls or boys as the main character but that little boys preferred male main characters, and that this phenomenon influenced the creative decisions of authors and TV producers. How were such patterns anything but self-reinforcing? How likable did a woman need to be in order to earn the right to run and not be accused of undermining her party?

And really, wasn't this endless ruminating over my own likability in itself a thing only a woman would do? Did Bill—or Ted Cruz or Rand Paul—ever ponder their likability, or did they simply go after what they wanted? Did Bill ever stop to think about which of us was more qualified, did he question his own motives for entry into the race? The idea was laughable. And for God's sake, his history with women would be a national security issue.

But more than one thing could be true at the same time. It could be true that I knew in my heart I was more qualified to be president than Bill, and it also could be true that, for reasons that had nothing to do with this election, a part of me despised him.

Back in 2005, after Bill and I had run into each other at the magazine soirée, he had indeed followed up on dinner plans for when I'd be in the Bay Area two weeks later. His assistant had made a reservation for us at a restaurant, then Bill had emailed just me: **You know what, fuck that stuffy French food, I'll make you dinner at my place. Healthier and more intimate.**

I was in my office in Washington and had just greeted a fourth grade class from Danville, Illinois, when I received the email. There was a jolt I experienced on reading that one word—not **fuck**—that was both distant from my present life and deeply familiar. Was it possible that this was to be a date? That we both were putting out feelers, reassessing each other?

In the thirteen years I'd been in the Senate, I'd experienced little in the way of dating or sex. Though

I suppose it's not a widely applicable tip, becoming a female senator is actually a decent method to take the pressure off romantically. Although I met men constantly, few were appropriate. I did have my admirers: I'd regularly receive letters from constituents, felons, or, in the case of parolees, both. **Dear Hillary, you are such a beautiful, special, and attractive woman, I know we'd really get along if I can take you out for dinner.** Unless they posed a security threat or were deemed outlandishly hilarious by my staff, I didn't see the majority of such letters. Sometimes I felt a flare-up of attraction to, say, another senator's sixty-something chief of staff who'd made insightful points in a meeting without grandstanding, then I'd notice the wedding band on his left hand. Or an unexpectedly handsome photographer would be sent by a magazine to take my picture at my desk, we'd banter, then it would occur to me that he was twenty-five years younger than I was.

For New Year's Eve in 1996, I'd traveled to Bitsy Sedgeman Corker's vacation home in Hobe Sound, Florida—not to be confused with Bitsy's other vacation home in Taos, nor with her **other** other vacation home in northern Wisconsin—where, among the dozen guests celebrating New Year's Eve, was her divorced cousin Charles, who lived in Minneapolis. Charles was a tall, slender man with thinning blond hair and a penchant for pink Oxford cloth shirts. I can't deny that the idea of dating a Sedgeman was both odd and intriguing—would I never need to fundraise again?—and we ended up kissing at midnight, and, after a few weeks of emailing, sleeping together when he visited me in Washington. This was my first postmenopause sex, and I was delighted to discover I still had the knack, as long as there was lubricant nearby. Over the next few years, Charles and I saw each other every three or four months for a night or two, which was infrequent enough for it not to matter that I quickly realized I found him boring. We tried to talk on the phone, but in one of our early conversations, I fell asleep while he was describing the exquisite design of classic Bugatti cars and woke up again without any indication that he'd noticed. Though, if I were being honest, Charles's monologues about vintage cars were less objectionable than his seemingly apolitical outlook. Once when I referred to Slobodan Milošević, Charles appeared not to know who he was. When I delicately expressed to Bitsy that I suspected things between her cousin and me wouldn't last, Bitsy said, "Oh, Charles is dull as dishwater. None of us could believe it went on this long."

By the time Bill and I were arranging our dinner, another four years had passed during which I hadn't had sex. What if, as with circling a globe, Bill and I had gone so far in opposite directions that we could meet again in mutually congenial circumstances? Was this a preposterous notion or was it reasonable? The night before Theresa and I were to fly from Washington to San Francisco, the wisdom of procuring not only lubricant but also condoms occurred to me; getting chlamydia from Bill Clinton was not part of my plans. Another single female senator whose state included a famously liberal city had once told me that, as casually—even festively—as possible, she collected condoms at gay pride parades. Given that my dinner with Bill was imminent, this wasn't an option. I could have run into a drugstore myself, and there was a 98 percent chance I wouldn't be recognized. But that other 2 percent, especially after my cookie comments debacle—it would be humiliating if it became a gossip item in a newspaper.

Already, in our years together, Theresa had purchased Pepto-Bismol on my behalf and had instructed me that I needed to clear a nostril before I went onstage. In our hotel in San Francisco, after we returned to the city from my afternoon speech at Stanford followed by a fundraising reception at a private home in Menlo Park, she handed me a Walgreens bag containing two different brands of condoms and a five-ounce container of K-Y jelly with as little fanfare as she would handing me Purell. My dinner with Bill was the next evening, and as I turned out the light to go to sleep, I thought about arriving in Berkeley with him in May 1971, thirty-four years prior: his orange station wagon and our rental apartment in the stucco building on the hill; how much I had loved living with him and exploring the Bay Area; how devastated I'd been the day I'd found him kissing my boss's daughter. We'd been so young then, and there had been so much neither of us knew. I wondered if unbidden memories from that summer had played out in his mind when he'd moved to California. If so, surely in the last decade the details of his present life had replaced them, or diminished their potency.

The next day, I ate breakfast at my hotel with two entrepreneurs who wanted to discuss common carrier regulations, and then I spent the rest of the morning in the hotel room calling prospective donors. At lunch, when Theresa got takeout salads for both of us, I told her to hold the raw onion on mine, and also requested that she purchase a bottle of white wine. At four, I walked on the hotel treadmill then showered, brushed my teeth with extra vigor, and used mouthwash. The idea of kissing someone, kissing **Bill,** felt almost as momentous as the idea of having sex. Would my mouth really touch Bill's, or was it all in my head? Before showering, I'd laid my best lingerie, a blue lacy matching bra and underwear set, and my nicest pantsuit and shell blouse on the made bed, on top of the white duvet. I applied makeup while still in my robe. As I dressed, I intermittently caught sight of my reflection in the mirror: There was more flesh than I wished for around my upper arms and between my bra straps and my armpits. Though I refused to use the word **cellulite** because it was a pseudoscientific term created by the cosmetics industry, I wished for a little more smoothness in my thighs. Would I, in the next few hours, end up naked in a bed with Bill? As I pulled on my pants, I noted that I still had a nice waist and my hair had never been more artfully cut or golden in color. Also, though my neck, particularly just under my chin, had a crepey quality no dermatologist could fix, thanks to the Botox injections that I and just about every woman in the public eye underwent every four months, the skin on my face was smoother than I had any right to expect. And several years before, I had undergone thorough, painful laser hair removal, so at least I was prepared on that front. I didn't mistake myself for beautiful, but, all things considered, I thought I looked attractive.

At six-thirty, Theresa sent me a message on my BlackBerry: **Your car is outside.**

I replied, **Leaving room now.**

Have fun, she wrote back.

Sitting in the backseat of the town car, I could, to my surprise, feel the feeling, that charge familiar from other important moments in my life: the anticipation and focus, the elimination of all other obligations and ephemera, the reduction to just this moment, looking out the window at the sunny September evening, riding away from Union

Square and toward whatever it was that was about to happen. On the sidewalk at the corner of Grant and Pine, a dark-haired woman in exercise clothes pushed a stroller containing a child I couldn't see except from the knees down, in the form of a small pair of jeans and two little calves sticking out, the feet clad in brown leather slippers. The woman spoke animatedly to the child, and I thought of the minutiae and specificity of all our lives, how tightly fixed we are within the present moment even as the moment passes.

Bill's apartment was a penthouse in Nob Hill. When I stepped off the dedicated elevator, which itself was large enough to include a bench and fancy enough to include a chandelier, I was in a vast open space that led on the left to a kitchen and on the right to a living room. Straight in front of me were floor-to-ceiling windows overlooking the financial district, including the Transamerica Building, and beyond it, the San Francisco Bay, the Bay Bridge, and Oakland.

"You made it!" Bill approached from the kitchen wearing a royal-blue apron over a dress shirt and jeans. He really was incredibly handsome: tall and slim and white-haired, with that familiar smile. I set my purse next to a red porcelain lamp on an ornate wooden table and, as I held the bottle of wine Theresa had selected, he leaned in to hug me and kissed the top of my head. Upbeat classical music played in the background, no doubt on a state-of-the-art sound system, and the sweet smell of something baking filled the air.

As I passed him the wine, I said, "Quite a view you've got."

He grinned. "Not bad for a boy from Hope, Arkansas, huh?"

I grinned back at him. "Does that country boy shtick still work for you?"

"Better than ever. But not with everyone, apparently. You look great, by the way."

"You look great, too. California must agree with you."

He opened a bottle of his own wine, a red, saying, "It's one of my favorites, very velvety but structured." When we made eye contact, he added, "Does saying that make me sound sophisticated or like an asshole?"

"Why choose?" I said, and he laughed. "I'm teasing," I said. "You don't sound like an asshole, and I'd love a glass of something velvety and structured."

After he'd poured, we clinked our glasses together. "To the past **and** the present," he said, and I said, "Hear, hear."

I sat on a barstool at the granite island while he stood facing me with the bay behind him, dicing an onion on a cutting board. Barstools are dreadful onstage, even worse than director's chairs and even if you favor pantsuits—you need to hoist yourself backward onto them and keep your legs crossed, and after twenty minutes, my legs often start shaking. But in Bill's kitchen, I could lean my forearms against the counter, and I was comfortable and content. Various appetizers were laid out: a small bowl of olives, a bowl of pretzels, two pastel dips that I guessed to be some variation on hummus. The sun setting over the water became almost unbearably beautiful.

After Bill poured olive oil into a saucepan, he set the saucepan on a burner on the granite island; a minute later, using the knife, he swept the diced onion into the pan and it sizzled a little. The next vegetables he cut were eggplant, zucchini, and red pepper.

"When did you learn to cook?" I asked.

"After my second divorce, I decided not to be one of those bachelors with nothing but a six-pack and a jar of mustard in the fridge. Turns out cooking is kind of fun."

"I'll bet I haven't touched a stove in a decade."

"Would you like for tonight to be the night?"

Yes, I thought, **but not with the stove**. "You look like you've got things under control. What are you making, anyway?"

"You ever had a ratatouille tart?"

I shook my head.

"You're about to."

"It sounds fantastic."

"Full disclosure, the crust that's in the oven as we speak was made earlier today by my housekeeper,

Elena. I still want you to be impressed by my slicing and dicing, though."

"I'm **very** impressed," I said.

"I assume this is rare, but if it's just you at home, what do you have for dinner?"

"If I'm feeling really lazy, cottage cheese. If I'm feeling only moderately lazy, toast and peanut butter, with a side of baby carrots. If I'm not mistaken, that covers most of the food groups."

"And it's vegan to boot."

"That hadn't occurred to me."

"Do you still sit in your nest at night?"

Something inside me clenched. So often, people let you down; so often, situations turn out disappointingly. But occasionally someone recognizes, acknowledges, your private and truest self.

"The short answer is yes," I said.

"What's the long answer?"

"Well, there are briefing books involved. And electronic devices. It's less pure than it once was."

He chuckled. "Aren't we all?"

The smell of the baking crust competed pleasantly with the savory scent of the simmering vegetables. I was hungry but too keyed up to eat the olives and pretzels in front of me; also, of course, I didn't want to be full if we had sex. I took another sip of wine and said, "If there was ever a time when you were pure, Bill, I think it was long before we met." He looked a little hurt, and I added, "But I've come to think purity is overrated. Do you know what I was just reminded of? Do you remember when you told me about going home with Kirby Hadey for Thanksgiving your first year at Yale? You were very impressed that his parents' penthouse had its own elevator, and look at you now."

"It's funny," he said, "because I don't think I ever ride up here without recalling that." He looked at me intently. "What you and I had," he said, "I never found that with anyone else. I mourned it for so many years."

"I did, too."

"And it seems like it should be weird as hell to be standing across from you right now, but it feels totally natural."

"I agree," I said. The intensity of his expression made it difficult to maintain eye contact, and with feigned casualness, I said, "Tell me about a day in the life of Bill Clinton circa 2005."

"I bet it's a heck of a lot less interesting than a day in the life of Hillary Rodham."

"I'll be the judge of that. Start with when you wake up."

"I've got a yoga instructor who comes here three mornings a week at seven. Mostly Vinyasa, a little Kundalini. Is this too much detail?"

I shook my head. "Although I won't pretend to know which style of yoga is which."

"Vinyasa is more athletic, Kundalini is more spiritual. But Kundalini still gives you a workout. You've never tried yoga? It really is fantastic."

"I've taken a few classes over the years, but I always feel bored and uncomfortable. Do you remember my friend Maureen? She's gotten me into Pilates, which seems close enough."

"You know that finding yoga boring and uncomfortable means you should be doing more of it, right? You should be sitting with your boredom and discomfort."

I laughed. "Should I politely pretend that I'll follow your advice?"

"That's all right." He was laughing, too.

"Back to your schedule, then—"

"It takes an hour or so to get to Menlo Park in the morning, so I arrive in the office at nine-thirty or ten. I've got a driver." His smile was sheepish. "I confess I feel self-conscious around you with regard to some of this. But a lot of our dreams came true, didn't they? That's part of why it's nice to see you, because it reminds me how lucky we both got."

"Or is it that—" I paused before saying, "I like the sentiment you're expressing. But am I parsing it too much if I argue that it's more complicated than that? It's like the dreams we didn't even know to dream came true. I'm not disagreeing about the lucky part."

"That's what I meant, that we've both risen to the highest level of our fields. Or you're damn near it.

My God, I know it didn't happen in '04, but if you do become president, Hillary, it'll be the greatest fucking thing. You'll be so good at it, and just think of making history like that. I can't pretend I won't be envious."

"Honestly, I try not to think too much in those terms. It makes me feel as if everything that comes out of my mouth should be written in calligraphy, with a quill pen, which is immobilizing. I'm not, you know, George Washington."

"Not even Georgia Washington?" Bill grinned.

"Is that George's sister?"

"Or him when he lets his wig down?"

We both were smiling, and I said, "Almost all my advisers recommend downplaying anything about gender or firsts."

"But symbolism is what inspires people," Bill said. "Sure, you've got the folks who won't vote for a woman unless hell freezes over. And you've got the folks who need to be cajoled. But you've also got folks for whom you're a dream come true."

"Unfortunately, polls indicate that the thrilled group is only seventeen or eighteen percent of the population. What you're saying is accurate, but the middle group is closer to thirty percent. And cajolery was always something you were better at than I am."

Fondly, he said, "I was good at it, wasn't I?" He was opening a can of crushed tomatoes, and he dumped it into the saucepan over the vegetables.

"Do you know the number one predictor of whether a woman approves of the idea of a female president?" I said.

"A college degree?"

"That's a factor, but it's not the biggest. It's whether she's married, and there's an inverse correlation. Married women vote with their husbands." I watched as Bill shook some oregano into his palm and dropped it into the mixture. "Back to your schedule," I said. "It's nine-thirty or ten and you get to the office. Then what?"

"Then meetings. Meetings and meetings and more meetings."

"These are with people pitching start-up ideas they want you to fund?"

"Or we've already funded them and they're updating us on their progress, or they're trying to go from their seed round to series A."

"Are the meetings interesting?"

"Some of the entrepreneurs are brilliant. And it's exciting getting sneak peeks at the technology everyone will be using eighteen or thirty-six months from now. Other times, you know ten seconds into a pitch that nothing will come of it, and you still need to sit there for twenty minutes."

"It's a very male world, isn't it? Numbers-wise?"

"It is, and we've got to do better. There's really a pipeline problem, where only about a quarter of computer science majors are women. Then there's the leaky pipe problem, which is retention."

"Because women quit when they have kids?"

"Or because they aren't the right fit with a company's culture. The ping-pong tables and whatnot. Hey, I hear that Tara and Pete Fourgeaud held a fundraiser for you at their house last night."

"News travels fast."

"The Fourgeauds are terrific. I was invited, but I had a conflict, and I thought, hell, I get you all to myself for dinner tonight."

There was a happiness I felt in this moment, a pure, warm, unambivalent animal happiness; I just really, really enjoyed being in Bill Clinton's company.

And then, sitting there on his barstool, listening to his classical music, I thought, What if I didn't run for president again? What if I didn't even run for Senate again after this term? Let some other woman make history while having her clothes and voice and intellect and voting record picked apart. Let **me** have great sex and stimulating conversations; let me travel to foreign countries not to meet with dignitaries and eat chicken in ballrooms but to swim in fancy pools at expensive hotels and read novels while lying on enormous mattresses. Let me be a well-paid lawyer or consultant or lobbyist, let me be Bill Clinton's girlfriend again, let me finally be Bill Clinton's wife.

Aloud, I said, "That's true. You do get me all to yourself tonight."

This is when he said, "I have a story that I think

you'll appreciate." He reached for the wine bottle and refilled my glass. "You may have heard that I've started a foundation. We're still getting our sea legs, but we're focusing on all the big issues. Climate change, poverty, biomedical research. Eighteen months ago, I hired a woman named Kira Duncan to run the foundation. She has a stellar record, went to Stanford for undergrad and business school. After B-school, she worked for a gay rights advocacy group so I assume she's a lesbian even though she's gorgeous. Long red hair, milky white skin, very slender."

Really? I thought. **Long red hair, milky white skin, very slender? Now?** Wryly, I said, "I've heard that it's possible for a woman to be gorgeous and gay at the same time."

He laughed. "Just wait. Now, I'm not usually in the foundation office, but Kira and I talk five, six times a week. She's very on the ball, always prepared, a tireless worker. In a lot of ways, she reminds me of you. And she's pretty buttoned-up about her personal life, but bits and pieces emerge. She does indeed have a female partner, a gal named Louise. We—Kira and I—go to Haiti together to meet with Dan Jacobs, who runs Global Health Mission. Do you know Dan?"

"Yes," I said. "GHM does wonderful work."

"Dan's fabulous. I'll tell you what, if I were picking a surgeon general, he'd be on my shortlist."

"We might be getting ahead of ourselves just slightly," I said. "But good to know."

"When Kira and I are in Haiti, she tells me she and Louise want to have a baby. They're going back and forth about who should carry it and who the donor will be. If that's not the quintessential modern problem, huh?"

"Well, there've always been divisions of childcare." Although I was speaking in what I hoped was a normal tone, my wariness was increasing; I wanted to go back just a minute or two to when he'd said, **I get you all to myself.**

"Now, I've met Louise by this point," he continued, "and she's smart, but a tough customer. Very butch. A few weeks pass, and Kira and Louise invite me over for brunch and say they have something to ask me. They've decided Kira will carry the baby, and they want me to be the sperm donor."

"What'd you tell them?" Was Bill the biological father of a Bay Area baby? Was a Bill baby, at this very moment, in utero? I tried to do the math—hadn't he said he'd hired Kira eighteen months ago?

"I can't deny I was flattered. It also, though I didn't put it like this to them, seemed like opening a can of worms. The idea is I'd be like a godparent, with absolutely no expectation of financial support, let alone changing diapers. Now, I'd be a fool not to realize laws can change, and could I get stuck with college tuition or what have you twenty years down the line? Of course. Then again, we're talking about them becoming parents, about the miracle of life."

"Remind me how old your kids are now?" I said.

"Alexis is twenty-six and Ricky is twenty-nine. That was a consideration, too, absolutely—how would this look to them? Ricky is very relaxed, very accepting, but Alexis can be judgmental. I say to Kira and Louise, 'Let me take a week to think about it.' "

Why did I so dislike the turn our conversation had taken? Was it jealousy? The reminder of my age? Or the reminder of Bill's narcissism? As if his sperm—his fifty-nine-year-old sperm—was uniquely worthy.

"The day after brunch, Kira calls me up sobbing," he continued. "She's crying so hard I can scarcely understand what she's saying, but I make out that Louise has accused her of wanting me to be the donor as a way of creating intimacy with me. Kira says, 'I felt so angry when Louise said this. I went for a run, just feeling furious, and that's when I realized she's right. I'm in love with you.' Kira offers to resign effective immediately, which I don't allow."

"Wow," I said. "Where do things stand now?" At least the mystery of why I disliked hearing all this had been solved.

"We're taking things slow. Just enjoying being together, not rushing to any decisions."

"Wait a second. You're in a relationship with Kira?"

"She's not big on labels. And here she is, this sexually fluid individual. She hasn't dated a man since she was a teenager. But the energy between us, the connection, it's truly incredible. Kira's extraordinary in the way she sees the world, her creativity and compassion. Hopefully, she'll pop in later tonight and I can introduce the two of you."

"She'll pop in **tonight**?" I said.

He looked at his watch. "She has a dinner meeting, so probably not before nine."

"And she is or isn't pregnant?"

"For now, we've hit Pause on that. We've got a trip together to Namibia in November, and we'll discuss it after we get back."

One of the most important lessons I've learned in life is this: Do not preemptively take no for an answer. Do not decide your request has been rejected before it officially has. As with so many other lessons that involve assertion, this one applies far more to women than men. Thus I took a sip of wine and said, "Surely, you and Kira aren't monogamous."

He squinted.

"Your tart smells delicious," I said. "But just to give ourselves time, let's go to bed now and eat afterward."

He blinked, then smiled a little, questioningly.

"For old times' sake," I said. "For fun, with no

strings attached. I told you I'd decided purity is overrated."

"I'm certainly flattered," he said. "And surprised."

"Are you?"

"Hillary, you know you've always, always held a special place in my heart. Having you in my home now, it's a true joy. I've thought about you so many times over the years."

I wondered if I ought to stand and walk around the granite island.

Then he said, "For anything physical to happen between us, that's just not where I am."

So now my request **had** been officially rejected. There were other things I thought, in this moment and later, but the main one was what a giant fucking waste of time and energy it had been to worry over the acquisition of condoms and lubricant. This was the man for whom, not five minutes earlier, I'd pondered chucking my presidential aspirations, my entire career? Setting aside what was wrong with him, what was wrong with **me**?

Yet even, or maybe especially, in disequilibrium, I experienced an impulse toward fact-gathering. I heard myself ask, "What is it about that story of you and Kira that made you think I'd particularly appreciate it?"

His tone was wary but cheerful—he couldn't discern if we were moving away from or deeper into a fraught topic—as he said, "The feminist angle, for one thing. Sisters are doing it for themselves.

And her directness, her lack of gamesmanship. Do I mean gameswomanship?" He smiled. "I remember how frustrated you felt by the narrow expectations for women when we were in law school."

"And what did you want from tonight? Why am I here?"

He bit his lower lip, and I could see that my opinion mattered to him, that he sincerely wanted my approval or at least feared my opprobrium. But hadn't this been Bill's genius as a politician, that he was this way with everyone? And it was always sincere. He said, "When two old friends have the chance to catch up, that's something I value more and more as the years pass. And I thought we were having a nice time." **Old friends**—it was hard to know which word was more insulting. Then he added, "I also wanted to float the idea of you joining my foundation's board. As we've discussed, there can be a shortage of female leadership, the female perspective, in these parts. But God knows I didn't mean to be confusing."

I said, "Just out of curiosity, how old is the oldest woman you've slept with?"

"I don't see what that has to do with anything."

"Forty-five?" I said. "Forty?"

"Evangeline was forty-four when we separated last year." He bowed his head. "If I gave you the impression this dinner was romantic, I'm sorry."

"In the last few days, did it cross your mind we'd have sex tonight?" Given the inherently loaded nature of the question, I asked as neutrally as possible.

"I just— I wasn't thinking in those terms. What with being in a brand-new relationship."

The oven timer beeped then, and we didn't speak as he slid on an oven mitt, opened the glass door, and removed the crust. He set the crust on a stove burner. We still didn't speak as he began spooning the ratatouille into the crust, and finally, when he was finished, he said, "That doesn't look half-bad, does it?"

But I didn't want to eat his food. I didn't want to join his board. I didn't want to be in his penthouse, and I didn't want to be in his presence. It wouldn't, I thought, be difficult to remain on good terms with him; salvaging this moment would require little effort. Perhaps in the future he'd even feel a guilt he wouldn't want to name and be more generous in donating to my campaign or more helpful in soliciting others. But backpedaling, restoring the goodwill between us, would be difficult for **me**. Putting up with Bill Clinton's bullshit—hadn't I earned the right never to do it again? Sometimes speaking your mind is expensive, which doesn't mean it's not worth it.

"There's nothing you did wrong tonight that's provable in a court of law," I said. "Which is your specialty. But I do think you led me on.

It's funny because all those years ago, when you proposed, I remember thinking, On the one hand, he'll never be faithful, but on the other hand, he'll never not be attracted to me. He just loves women and sex. But now I think I was wrong. If we'd gotten married, you eventually would have traded me in for a new model."

His face flushed as he said, "What our marriage would have looked like is immaterial, and you're the one who made it immaterial. I was prepared to do my best as your husband. Was my best, is my best, perfect? No. Was it enough for you? Also no. Therefore the subject of whom I've chosen to be involved with since is none of your business."

"Except," I said, "for your decision to invite me over for an intimate dinner." I swept my arm through the air, taking in the tart, the music, the view. "Is it that you wanted to leave your options open, but now that I'm here, I look too wrinkly to you? Is my skin not milky white enough?"

He bit his lip—he actually had two bitten-lip modes, one pensive and one angry, and this was the angry version—and said, "You've never understood that you can't litigate the human heart."

"Spare me." I slid forward on the barstool. "I know we didn't get through a typical day for you, but I hope that on a regular basis, seeing a therapist is part of your schedule because without question, you're a narcissist. And I mean that in the clinical sense."

"What diagnosis would you give to a woman who tries unsuccessfully to seduce a narcissist?" If he wasn't shouting by this point, he was close.

"Fuck you," I said.

"I believe I made it clear I'd rather not."

"You know," I said, "if you're trying to humiliate me, I **am** ashamed of myself. But not for thinking you'd find me attractive. I'm ashamed because you've given me so much evidence for so many years about what a piece of shit you are, and once again, I ignored it." I stood. "Goodbye, Bill." I didn't wait for him to respond before I turned and strode toward the elevator.

"You think that's how it works?" he yelled. "I welcome you into my home, and when things don't go exactly how you imagined, you get to impugn my character?"

I glanced over my shoulder. "I don't impugn your character," I said. "You do that all by yourself."

If we'd been on the ground floor, my dramatic exit could have been more efficient. As it was, after reaching the elevator, grabbing my purse off the table, and pressing the call button, I didn't need to wait longer than a few seconds, but any delay, as I stood there with my back to him and those enormous windows, imbued the situation with a certain absurdity. Behind me, I heard him say, "You've always gotten off on making me feel bad about myself. Holding me to your impossible standards then scolding me when I don't meet them.

You know what you are? You're a self-righteous cunt."

I looked over my shoulder and said, "And you're a spoiled, selfish child."

This is when he threw the serving spoon. Was he throwing it **at** me? I'd never known him to be violent, though I'd also never seen him this enraged. He hit the red porcelain lamp on the table, knocking it to the floor and shattering it. I was shocked, and when I looked at him, it seemed he was, too.

The elevator doors opened, and I stepped inside then turned around. I held the doors open as I spoke. "Did you say your housekeeper's name is Elena? You're so good at getting other people to clean up your messes."

The male host of the morning show whose greenroom I'd been in a week prior said to Donald Trump, "Are you officially endorsing Hillary Rodham?"

"What you have to understand about me," Trump said, "is that I've always been a feminist. Whether it's my beautiful daughter, Ivanka; the girls in my pageants; or the ladies who work for me at my hotels, no one supports women more than I do. As a mentor, as a boss—no one. I can't even count the number of girls and women who say to me, 'Mr. Trump, nobody in my life has ever given me opportunities like you.' They say this, and there's literally tears running down their face."

"Wow," I said. "We are down the fucking rabbit hole."

Diwata said, "The way he pronounces **feminist** makes me feel like I need to take a shower."

We were back on the plane, flying to Greenville, South Carolina, and watching on an iPad.

"But you are or aren't endorsing Hillary?" the female host said.

"No, no." Donald smirked. "If she wants that, she has to work for it, you know what I mean? But we've been very close for some time. I'm one of her most trusted advisers." I waited for them to remind him that in an earlier appearance on their show, he'd claimed never to have met me. Instead, the screen cut to the photo taken at the magazine gala in 2005 of me standing between Bill and Donald, all three of us with our arms around one another, wearing fancy clothes and beaming.

"Oh, dear God," I said.

" 'Very close,' what does that mean?" the male host said. "Does that mean private dinners? Golfing together at Mar-a-Lago?"

"All of it," Donald said.

"When the two of you are together, what do you discuss?" the woman asked with faux earnestness. "Healthcare? Foreign policy?"

"Exactly." Donald nodded emphatically. "She says to me, 'What should I do about business, what should I do about the economy?' And I say, 'Don't worry about it. You do what I say, I can get you into the White House.' "

It was impossible to hear what anyone onscreen said next because Diwata, Theresa, Clyde, Kenya, and I all simultaneously groaned.

"Did I have a psychotic break?" Clyde asked.

"Ask him the most rudimentary question about the economy!" I said. "Ask him to define the budget reconciliation process."

"You know what, though?" Theresa said. "If he can't speak for more than one sentence about anything but himself, he can't really put words in your mouth."

Onscreen, the male host was asking, "Donald, have you left the door open even a crack to running yourself?"

"Listen," Donald said, and his pleasure in having the question posed to him was palpable. "I'd be so good at it. I'd be better than Hillary if I'm being honest. But I have other things to do, so many things, such good business." He leaned forward conspiratorially, as if this whole exchange were not being broadcast on television. "Bill Clinton, he's such a dog. He's a dog and you know how I know? Because I'm like that, too. Men like us, we love women, and that's great. But you can't have threesomes with models when you're president."

I said, "I could swear I heard him defend Bill's womanizing a few weeks ago."

Diwata said, "Oh, he's totally inconsistent. Whatever comes out of his mouth is whatever comes out of his mouth."

"No pervs allowed in the Oval Office," Donald said. "I didn't make the rules."

"Needless to say," Clyde said, "we'll come up with a strategy of intense verbal jujitsu to signal to your supporters that you're using him."

"Who's the blues musician who supposedly sold his soul to the devil?" I said.

Diwata laughed. "Robert Johnson, but have you ever listened to his stuff? It was totally worth it."

CHAPTER 7
2015

OVER THE SUMMER, MY TEAM had held several strategy sessions for the first Democratic debate, but we didn't hold a mock debate until Thursday, October 8—five days before Bill Clinton, Martin O'Malley, Jim Webb, and I would appear together on a stage at the Wynn Las Vegas resort. So that I could be as focused as possible, my schedule had been cleared until the debate, and, as in 2008, we'd rented a two-hundred-seat amphitheater, in addition to a few conference rooms, in a suburban Chicago hotel. At 8:30 A.M., the person running debate prep—my policy aide, Clarissa Jovicich—gave me and three dozen staffers an overview of the logistics and format. By a few minutes after nine, I and the men playing my opponents were backstage preparing to walk out one by one: An aide named Clay was acting as Martin O'Malley, who was currently polling among Iowa voters at 4 percent; an aide named Bob was acting as Jim Webb, who was currently polling among Iowa voters at 1 percent; and Nick Chess, my long-ago Yale classmate, was playing Bill, who was currently polling among Iowa voters at 40 percent. I was playing myself, and I was currently polling among Iowa voters at 43 percent; that is, I had regained my slight lead over Bill in Iowa and also New Hampshire. For the real debate, four CNN correspondents would moderate. To Greg's delight, he was playing Anderson Cooper.

I actually liked debates; they tended to feel like tests I'd studied hard for. And because there was so much free-floating criticism of me, because the Americans who had a low opinion of me had **such** a low opinion, postdebate polls usually showed that I'd won over some viewers simply by not behaving like a schoolmarm or dragon lady.

Clarissa wanted us to go through one timed debate without stopping, no matter how many gaffes occurred: from the entrance onto the stage to the intracandidate handshakes to assuming our positions behind the lecterns to making opening statements to the barrage of questions.

In the interest of verisimilitude, Clay, Bob, and Nick had been kept out of my sight up to the point when we all met backstage, when they were in character. But it was hard not to laugh when I saw

Nick, who in real life had a thin, hippie-ish ponytail but on this morning wore a white wig meant to resemble Bill's hair, and also a red tie with the image of a Razorback, tusks and all. I appreciated the effort, and in fact I was wearing a silk pantsuit. I walked onto the stage third, and the staffers applauded wildly—the sound of about forty people cheering in a two-hundred-person auditorium is a specific one—and I waved and beamed and pointed at imaginary audience members. As in a real debate, there was a box-like clock at the front of the stage, facing away from the audience, that would count down the seconds for our answers in digital red numbers.

In my opening statement, drafted by two speechwriters after several rounds of discussion, I talked about jobs, education, and clean energy, though, above all, I was trying to seem warm and positive. Nick-as-Bill focused on the unprecedented problems and opportunities before us, and celebrated how the tech revolution was just beginning; Nick also emulated Bill's confident, long-winded speaking style, his tendency to use his hands and intermittently hold up his pointer finger. Bob–as–Jim Webb described his military experience, and Clay–as–Martin O'Malley spoke of how his time as a mayor and governor made him qualified for the presidency.

Then Greg–as–Anderson Cooper, along with three other faux moderators, asked us about the economy and gun control, about immigration and financial reform and reproductive freedom and zero-carbon power and ISIS. When I responded to a question on healthcare, I mentioned Misty LaPointe, who would be one of my three special guests in the audience, all of them people I'd met campaigning; the others were a veteran-turned-teacher from Lebanon, New Hampshire, and a construction worker from Chicago.

CNN would be partnering with Facebook to host the debate, and some questions would come from ordinary voters. During the last few minutes of the mock debate, the ordinary voters were played by various staffers raising their hands. An attorney named Maryanne said, "Governor O'Malley, you have a strange accent that I can't place. Are you part elf?" My communications director, Aaron, said, "Senator Rodham, Donald Trump is now both your very close friend and your spiritual adviser. Can you tell me from first-hand experience if his famous toilet is gold plated or actual solid gold?" And a campaign consultant named Rebecca said, "Governor Clinton, we know you're fond of orgies. Do you use Viagra?"

But the silliness aside, answering the real questions was invigorating. On planes and in my bed at night, in my nest, I had pored over green binders containing briefings on policy of every topic. In some cases, I'd asked questions and been provided with additional information; it was possible that

Bill could come off better in the debate than I did, but it was not possible that he could have prepared more thoroughly.

At last, Greg–as–Anderson Cooper said, "Thank you, candidates and voters alike, for joining us," and everyone clapped and cheered.

"Fantastic job, Senator," Clarissa said, and Greg-as-himself said, "That was very impressive." I knew the compliments were a prelude to extensive criticism.

Still in a Bill accent, Nick Chess said, "Hillary, was the sound of my voice as mellifluous to you as it was to me?" and everyone chuckled. I was still onstage as, one by one, my staffers were checking their phones then looking at one another. Prior to the mock debate, I had given my phone to Kenya, and I said, "Did something happen?"

I made eye contact with Theresa, who was in the amphitheater's front row and who looked at Clarissa then back at me. It was Denise, my campaign manager, who spoke. She said, "A piece was posted a few minutes ago on American Truth alleging that you sexually harassed a member of your staff in the early nineties."

"Jesus, Mary, and Joseph," I said. "Is the man claiming this was someone who really worked for me?" American Truth was a fringy, ultraconservative website.

"It's actually a woman named Jill Perkins." The expression on Denise's face was uneasy. "She's saying that during your first Senate campaign, you forced her to shave your legs."

I heard Greg say, "Wait, do you mean Jill Rossi?" Though I didn't recall either the first or last name of the young woman who in 1992, in a taxi on the way to my interview with the **Chicago Tribune**, had shaved my legs, the surge of indignant anger I'd experienced just seconds before changed into a sickened dismay. There was a part of me that wanted to laugh because the situation was so preposterous. But the grain of truth in this distortion, and the colorful nature of the story and the irony and the timing—all of these factors meant it was likelier to stick. Truly, there was no bottom to the coarseness, ruthlessness, and disloyalty in politics.

"Jill Rossi, you little bitch," Greg was saying. "You trashy, whorish conservative pawn."

"Easy, Greg," I said.

"Do you remember her?" Denise was looking between us.

Greg said, "She was my assistant for about ten minutes, until I fired her for gross incompetence."

We needed to evaluate how the mock debate had gone, while it was still fresh in all our minds, because the real debate was arguably the single most important event of the campaign. And we also needed to do triage on this breaking scandal. We needed to do both right away.

I breathed as my Pilates instructor, Nora, had taught me—in through the nose, out through the mouth. "Let's all take a ten-minute break," I said.

"Listen," Bill told one of the television reporters traveling with his campaign after an eight-thousand-person rally in Madison, Wisconsin, that had, of course, aired in its entirety on multiple networks. "Did Hillary exercise bad judgment? Clearly. Is she a bad person? Absolutely not. Times have changed, and there are ways people acted twenty years ago, or, hell, even ten years ago that just don't fly anymore. And yes, I'm including myself in this assessment. Brave individuals coming forward and speaking out help our society move forward together, and that's all to the good. By the same token, do you throw out anyone who's ever made a mistake? I don't think you do." He paused and smiled. "Let he who is without sin cast the first stone, you know?"

Debate prep had finished, after eight hours, at close to 4:00 P.M., and I was in my armored SUV on the way to my apartment with Kenya, Theresa, and Denise. We'd be joined by a handful of other high-level staffers for a strategizing session. When we finished watching the clip of Bill, Denise said in a fake-Southern, fake-husky voice, "Just call me False Equivalence Clinton."

Obviously, the scandal had been engineered by

Bill's campaign, and obviously they had created it to get ahead of accusations of sexual harassment or sexual assault about him; in fact, there were rumors that a big interview was about to run in **Vanity Fair** with a young woman who'd had a sexual encounter with Bill at a Silicon Valley sex party. I felt fury, and also a peculiar respect for his team's nefarious cleverness.

Already, the media had a name for it. They were calling it Razorgate.

Seven of us were assembled around my dining room table, and Gigi, who was in Washington, was joining in on speakerphone from Theresa's iPhone in the table's center. The consensus was that I needed to categorically deny sexually harassing any person in any form ever. I had described to everyone present what had actually happened in the taxi twenty-three years prior, and from that point on, none of us at the table used the word **lie**. Of course we didn't.

The questions under discussion were where, when, and how this categorical denial should be issued: Aaron, my communications director, could release a statement calling the claims meritless. I could speak in an ostensibly off-the-cuff moment to a reporter, as Bill had done after his Madison rally, though I had no public events scheduled before the debate. In the next day or two, I could hold a press conference at which I'd address the claim as one among an array of topics. But press conferences often didn't go well for me—I had difficulty concealing my irritation with the journalists' ridiculous questions. We also could simply ignore the story and hope it went away, especially given its dubious origins. In general, directly addressing accusations, even in the form of denial, almost always conferred legitimacy on them and extended their lives. Finally, we could pretend to ignore the story while having surrogates deny it.

It was almost 8:00 P.M., and my dining room table was strewn with pizza crusts on paper plates and cans of Coke and Diet Coke. Around the table, my staffers looked as tired as I felt. Directing my voice toward Theresa's iPhone, I said, "Gigi, can you give us what you have on Jill Rossi Perkins?"

"We'll keep digging, but so far, the basic outlines are, she's forty-eight, married to a dentist, three teenage kids. After Greg fired her, she worked for the PR firm Blaise Cartwell for seven years, until her first child was born, then she stayed home. From 2005 to 2009, she wrote a column for a Chicago-based parenting magazine. The columns are about stuff like driving her kids to sports practice and how hyper they got after eating Halloween candy."

"That sounds riveting," I said.

"Although she voted consistently, it doesn't appear that she was actively involved in any campaigns. But, Senator, she made a $250 donation to your Republican challenger in '98."

"This is so unsatisfying," Greg said. "Can't you find anything about her selling edibles out of her station wagon?"

"Sorry to interrupt," Denise said, "but I just got a text from someone at ABC, and the bad news is that Jill Perkins and her lawyer will be on **Good Morning America** tomorrow."

I sighed. "What's the good news?"

Denise looked confused. "What do you mean?"

"If that's the bad news, what's the good news?"

"I'm so sorry," Denise said, "but at this point, I wouldn't say there is any."

Quickly, Theresa said, "The good news is that you're the front-runner to be the Democratic nominee for president."

On the night in September 2005 when I left Bill's penthouse after our disastrous nondinner together, the doorman of his building called a taxi for me, and I sat in it feeling embarrassment, anger, and, above all, astonishment. I was stunned that my feeling on the way to see Bill had been wrong. My own prescience, reliable since my youth, had failed me. I had thought that something good and special had been about to happen, and I'd been wrong. I considered calling Maureen, worried I'd break down when I heard her voice, and instead emailed her from my BlackBerry. **It turns out there's one woman on Earth who Bill Clinton doesn't want to have sex with,** I typed. **The woman is me.**

Another five years had passed when I once again found myself at a large and rarefied event with him, in this case a cybersecurity conference in San Diego. Bill and I stood thirty feet apart and didn't speak. Though the sight of him made me shaky, it did not make me hopeful. I suspected he didn't notice my presence. Ten months later, at a tech summit at the White House, we made eye contact and again didn't speak. The next day, an email from him appeared in my inbox: **Thought you'd enjoy this if you haven't seen it.** The attachment was a white paper on artificial intelligence and populism.

We then, to my surprise, entered a new epoch of distant but collegial contact, exchanging emails every two or three months that included an attachment or link to the findings of an academic study or an article from **The New Yorker** or **The New York Times.** The topics could be anything from tax regulation to substandard federal prison conditions to the future of NATO. Always, the emails contained a slight variation of the words **Thought you'd find this interesting.** The recipient would read the article within a day or two—sometimes I'd already read what he sent and had even considered sending it to him—and reply with a similarly brief bit of editorializing: **Astute analysis of limitations**

of zero tolerance policies or **Fails to acknowledge China's role in supplying arms.**

This contact, with its external focus and regularity that wasn't frequency, achieved something that had for me proven elusive: It demystified Bill. When I saw him in Davos in 2013, we casually chatted for ten minutes, and the stakes felt blessedly, unprecedentedly low. In 2014, I was using the elliptical machine in the female senators' gym when I realized I'd forgotten to acknowledge an email he'd sent more than a week before. Wasn't this lapse proof that I was—finally—over him? And perhaps my prescience that night in San Francisco hadn't been wrong; perhaps that **had** been a night of significance because it was when my true liberation from Bill began.

Our mostly digital contact of the last few years was also the reason that I'd thought if he decided to run for president, I'd know well in advance. I hadn't only been exchanging articles; I'd also been keeping tabs on him.

Jill Perkins had wavy dark-brown hair, wore a cream-colored blouse, and seemed anxious in a way that came off as sincere as she said, "Watching Hillary Rodham pretend to be a champion of women, I just couldn't stay silent. No matter who you are, that doesn't give you the right to abuse other people."

She and her lawyer, a man with a neatly trimmed brown beard, sat together on a short couch, and the anchor interviewing them sat on a chair to their left, emoting concern; though it was 7:20 A.M. on the East Coast, she wore what appeared to be a turquoise cocktail dress. The anchor said, "You're alleging that more than twenty years ago, when you were an aide on Hillary Rodham's first Senate campaign, she subjected you to severe and pervasive sexual harassment. One of your most provocative accusations is that Senator Rodham once required you to shave her legs. Can you take us through how this happened?"

Jill Perkins glanced at the lawyer, who nodded once. In a shaky voice, Jill Perkins said, "We were in a taxi. Hillary Rodham was wearing a skirt and nylons, and she realized she hadn't shaved her legs and her leg hair was visible. She told me to kneel on the floor of the taxi and shave her legs for her. I immediately was very uncomfortable, but I didn't think I had a choice. I felt humiliated and violated."

The lawyer said, "Jill was twenty-five years old at the time."

Denise, Theresa, and Kenya all had stayed over at my apartment after the meeting, and before we returned to debate prep, we were watching this on the television in my den. In their presence, my embarrassment at the picture of me being painted in front of TV viewers nationwide intensified. Were these female staffers whom I liked and respected appalled by me? Did they identify with Jill Perkins? I also felt anger at Jill Perkins's disingenuousness, her misrepresentation of the spirit of the moment, as well as her misrepresentation of the facts, her omission of Greg's presence and role in instigating the moment. Ironically, this misrepresentation would be helpful in issuing a denial—my campaign hadn't yet done so—and I already, reflexively, was composing the wording in my head. ("The story that Ms. Perkins told is simply false. . . .") And yet I also felt remorse. If my boss had asked me to shave her legs when I was twenty-five, I didn't know if I'd have done it—I thought with a pang of Gwen Greenberger, though I always thought of Gwen with a pang—but either way, I'd have found the request distasteful and extraordinarily awkward. It was possible that the reason Jill Perkins seemed sincere was that she was.

"But, Jill, I want to ask you," the anchor said, "what makes this sexual harassment rather than workplace harassment?"

It was the lawyer, not Jill, who responded. He said, "Senator Rodham showed a pattern of sexually suggestive behavior and remarks. The physical aspect of what she did, the inappropriate touching and unwanted contact—this was a person in a position of power creating a hostile work environment for a subordinate." The chyron beneath the man read ROB NEWCOMB, ATTORNEY

FOR RODHAM ACCUSER. The name sounded familiar, but I couldn't place it; perhaps I had met so many people that every name sounded familiar.

The anchor said, "When you say 'pattern,' can you give other examples?"

Again, Jill Perkins glanced at the lawyer before speaking. "I felt unsafe," she said. "I realized very quickly that working for Hillary Rodham, I'd always have to keep my guard up. I didn't know what she'd do next, if she'd try to kiss me or—" She paused. "Anything else."

"Oh, wow," I said, "Subtle."

In the chair beside me, somberly, Theresa said, "How can that woman live with herself?"

The anchor said, "You worked for Rodham's campaign for just two weeks. Is this why you left?"

"It just felt unsafe. I just—the way Hillary Rodham is—I wasn't used to a woman like her."

"Hoo boy," Denise said. "Don't hold back, Jill."

My phone had been buzzing repeatedly, and when I looked at it, the most recent text was from Greg: **Welcome to Team Homo!** I found this faintly amusing, and I also wondered if Greg would apologize to me for his role in the current mess. I shouldn't have gone along with his suggestion that Jill shave my legs, but he shouldn't have suggested it.

The anchor said, "Jill, thank you for sharing your story, and Rob, thank you. We'll all continue to follow Razorgate with great interest. It's been an unusual presidential campaign in so many ways, and it doesn't look like that's about to change anytime soon."

"Oh my God," I said. "Her lawyer—Rob Newcomb—he's my former student. He was at Northwestern in the early nineties, and he hated me even then."

But it wasn't just that I was a lesbian; apparently, for years, I'd been involved in a clandestine love affair with Beverly Collins, my TV host friend. Within an hour of the **Good Morning America** interview, stills of my appearances on Beverly's shows over the years—images in which we shared a laugh or looked fondly at each other—were plastered all over the Internet. The mainstream media was handling the implication of my gayness with marginally greater restraint than the right-wing websites, substituting insinuations for declarations:

There's a lot we've never known about Hillary's private life.

Rodham, who has been single for her entire adult life . . .

Her intimate longtime friend Beverly Collins . . .

At the hotel where debate prep was occurring, as we all stood around drinking coffee before Clarissa called us to order, I said to Greg, "Do people know Beverly is married?"

"A minor detail," Greg said. "Because it's a weirdly linear story when you think about it. You and Bill date for a few years, but you break up because you're gay. That's why he goes on to marry and reproduce, and you never really date again."

"Ouch."

Greg laughed. "If the foo shits."

I said, "Anyway, isn't my lesbianism at odds with my having murdered my married boyfriend?"

Though he'd never met my Northwestern colleague James, Greg was one of very few people who knew the real version of what had happened between us. And though I thought I'd been joking, enacting my thick-skinned resilience, I was taken aback when Greg said, "Remind me—did you do that with a gun or a knife or what?"

Did he think I didn't have a heart, or did he not have one? Again, I was struck by the absence of an apology for his involvement in the incident with Jill Perkins. We looked at each other—we had known each other a long time, at good and bad junctures—and it occurred to me that I might cry. That would be highly inconvenient, with my entire debate-prep team milling around.

Either by coincidence or necessity, my own brain rescued me. "Wait," I said. "I have an idea."

The idea involved making a phone call. But before I could do this, certain vetting had to occur, and while it occurred, a linguist I'd worked with over the years was giving feedback. Nan Abelson was a professor and author who'd flown in from Seattle to observe the mock debate the previous day and offer advice on not just the words I used but which ones I emphasized, how I modulated volume, even the way I breathed. I'd originally sought out Nan after mentions in the '04 race of my voice as shrill, strident, nasal, and screechy.

On this morning, she made a forty-minute PowerPoint presentation, which boiled down to the recommendation that I tell more stories about both myself and voters. "Even in your opening statement, Senator Rodham, I'd love for you to talk about your parents or your grandparents. Really make it personal from the outset."

In an only half-joking tone, Clarissa said, "Who's your poorest ancestor?"

Nan said, "I'd also like you to explicitly invoke the historic nature of your campaign in your opener. Not at length, but just a sentence or two where you pay respect to the people for whom that's important."

The first time Nan and I had ever spoken by phone, a decade before, I'd said, "The problem is that when I don't project my voice, the feedback is that I don't seem sufficiently tough. But when I do project it, the feedback is that I'm angry."

"I have a diagnosis," Nan had said. "You're female. In all seriousness, the important thing to understand is that people believe they're making specific observations about you, but they're just unaccustomed to hearing the voice of a woman running for president. Have you ever seen someone with a facial tattoo?"

"Maybe once or twice." It had seemed strange she was asking.

"Think of it this way," she'd said. "People who attend your events are self-selecting and largely predisposed to like you. But whenever you're on TV, imagine you have a huge tattoo across your face. You're discussing healthcare, and people can hardly listen because they're so busy thinking, **Why did she get that tattoo?** That's how unfamiliar voters are with a woman running for president."

In the amphitheater, Nan was saying, "Senator, as always, don't speak too quickly, and don't be afraid to interrupt the men."

I said, "Didn't we decide yesterday that I'm not supposed to interrupt because it's aggressive and off-putting?"

"Interrupt calmly," Nan said.

Aaron, my communications director, said, "The test of a first-rate intelligence is the ability to hold two opposed ideas in mind at the same time and still retain the ability to function."

"Except backwards," said the consultant, Rebecca. "And in high heels."

• • •

Razorgate lesbo scandal is much adieu about nothing! Donald Trump tweeted at 12:33 P.M. **Sorry it's not PC but all jr employees work there way up with tasks that are No Fun.**

Theresa said, "Autocorrect can happen to anyone, but I seriously don't understand what goes on between him and his phone."

In the almost four months since Donald had appointed himself my surrogate, he'd routinely made jaw-dropping statements about both Bill and me, statements that the media then discussed ad nauseam, with barely concealed glee. On the morning talk show where he'd first declared his support for me, he had said, "Hillary's no beauty. She's no beauty. But she's smart, and that's what we need for president." He had said, "If Hillary was younger, I'd worry about her going crazy once a month. You know what I mean. Everyone knows! But she's old, she's past all that." At all hours of the day and night, he'd issue tweets that weren't just unfathomably crude but brazenly hypocritical.

At 3:12 A.M. on July 17, 2015: **Everyone knows Cheatin' Bill lied about his marriages, why would we Believe anything he says about the election?**

At 1:01 P.M. on August 10, 2015: **Sleazy Bill Clinton should drop out of the race, unless you want Blowjobs in the oval office!**

At 11:43 P.M. on September 4, 2015: **Hardball Hillary is a great leader that wants to put our economy first. Do not vote for Cheatin' Bill!**

Initially, I and my team had been inundated with questions about my relationship with Donald. As with making statements about having dated Bill, my strategy was to offer one comment and from that point on to say, with an exasperation that I didn't need to feign, "I've addressed this question in the past and I'd refer you back to what I said before." The thing I'd said about Donald—on camera, to an ABC correspondent, while leaving a town hall in Mason City, Iowa—was "I'm glad to have the support of anyone who recognizes that I'm the candidate best equipped to take on the challenges facing our country today." That evening, at an event at a Lutheran church in Charles City, Iowa, two women stood outside with homemade signs: One featured Trump's face, with the words SHAME ON YOU, HILLARY underneath it, and the other sign read THE ENEMY OF MY ENEMY IS NOT MY FRIEND.

As some in the media began referring to my improved polling numbers in Iowa and New Hampshire as the Trump effect, I'd realized that Donald wanted to flaunt our closeness in public but seemed not to wish for direct contact with me. Greg communicated on occasion with a media executive who knew Donald well, but Donald and I had never spoken on the phone and my team had never tried to influence his remarks because of how likely the effort was to backfire. At some point, I suspected he'd say something so incendiary that I would need to publicly disavow it, at which point

I might well draw his wrath—perhaps he'd even defect and become a supporter of Bill's—but I'd cross that bridge when I came to it.

In the amphitheater, Greg had pulled out his phone and was looking at Donald's latest tweet. "That should be the title of a French prostitute's posthumously published memoir," Greg said. "**Much Adieu About Nothing.**"

In the last several hours, Theresa had, from someone on my finance team, tracked down the email address of Albert Boyd, the man from the Cape Cod fundraiser in June, and sent him a message asking if he'd be available to talk to me. In the meantime, Gigi had found that he had no criminal record, massive debts, or damning social media posts. Most reassuringly, she'd spoken to my Wellesley friend Nancy, who'd vouched for his character.

When I called from an empty conference room at the debate-prep hotel, he answered after the first ring by saying, "This is Albert."

"Hello, Albert," I said. "It's Hillary Rodham. I believe my aide Theresa mentioned you'd hear from me."

"I'm delighted." This was gracious given that he probably thought I was about to ask for a campaign donation, on top of what he'd paid to have dinner with me—obviously, anyone with $250,000 to spare had more where that came from.

I said, "I'm getting in touch for a somewhat silly reason." In the minute before pressing the green phone icon, I had rehearsed what I'd say, but even so, I hesitated for a few seconds. "You may have heard some rumors swirling around my campaign. My team and I talked about it, and we feel—this is a bit awkward—but we thought it would be good for me to go on a few dates with a man who could be a plausible romantic partner. And I thought of you." On its own, against my volition, my mind summoned from its depths the letter I'd written to Bruce Stappenbeck in 1960: **If you ask me to be your girlfriend, I will say yes**. I wondered if in contacting Albert Boyd I was doing something extraordinarily stupid—if I should have asked this favor of someone for whom I had no sincere feelings. It was both mortifying and mildly interesting to observe the extent to which, after fifty-five years, I remained romantically incompetent.

Then Albert said, "I would absolutely love to go on a few dates with you."

"Really?" I said.

"Well, who wouldn't?" he said, and I laughed.

"I can think of a few people."

"I don't mean to be impertinent, but this bears more than a passing resemblance to the plot of a movie my daughter, Carson, used to watch over and over when she was about twelve. It featured two high schoolers who pretend they're dating."

"Should I ask how things turn out for them?"

"How about if I tell you on our date?"

"It's a deal. In the interest of full disclosure, if I say Razorgate, do you know what that refers to?"

"I do, and it sounds like nonsense."

I winced, above all because it wasn't **complete** nonsense. I said, "Another component of this, to make sure you understand—I'm thrilled you're game, but to make sure—if we walk down the street together, photos of you, of us, will appear in publications all over the world. I'm not being hyperbolic. And you'll hear from your friends who aren't crazy about me, both Republicans and Democrats."

"Please know I'm much too old to be bothered by that sort of thing." Thanks to Gigi's research, I knew his date of birth—April 26, 1947, meaning he was six months older than I was to the day—but I refrained from revealing this fact.

I said, "I have one more ask. I don't know what your schedule is like, but the goal is for us to go out as soon as possible, ideally this weekend." It was Friday afternoon as I spoke. "Is there any chance you can fly to Chicago tomorrow? My team will arrange your flights and accommodations."

"I was supposed to attend a very dull-sounding cocktail party tomorrow, and this gives me an outstanding excuse to skip it."

Had he been grown in a lab just for me? Or was he secretly a Republican operative plotting my exposure and humiliation?

I said, "Theresa will follow up, but I'll give you my number, too. I believe it showed up for you as unlisted." After I'd recited the digits, I said, "I can't thank you enough. I really look forward to this, and I also really appreciate it."

"I'm honored. It sounds like a great lark."

There was an argument, certainly, that if I genuinely liked him, the last thing I should subject him to was the scrutiny he'd get for being associated with me. The counterargument was that I had devised not just an ideal way to see him but perhaps the only way.

Among my emails that evening were one from Beverly Collins and one from my Wellesley friend Nancy.

From Beverly: **Hillary, no offense but you were never my type.**

From Nancy: **Now I'm confused—is intel on Albert Boyd being gathered for him to be your boyfriend or your VP??**

The goal was to engineer a viral moment in the debate, and toward this end, in the amphitheater, my team had been trying to generate zingers for me to use against Bill. I stood behind my lectern—though we'd have one more mock debate, my ersatz opponents had been given Saturday morning off—and it was Greg who was acting as Bill while no one acted as Jim Webb or Martin O'Malley.

Someone had suggested that when Bill spoke about his sympathy for, say, laid-off coal workers, I'd chuckle and declare, "Coming from a person in the one percent, all I can say is . . . that's rich!"

I delivered the line a few ways—with amusement, with sarcasm, with reproach—and they all fell flat. "It's too contrived," I said.

We'd already rejected "Shut me up? How about shutting **down** the Keystone XL pipeline?"

From the amphitheater's front row, Dave, a debate specialist popular among Democrats, said, "Senator, I agree that none of these is perfect, but don't forget that you also have soft power. Even more than what you say, your reactions really matter, and a disapproving expression when the men are battling it out, or when Clinton says something ludicrous, could become a sensation. It'd be like, Mom's pissed and she's not taking any more of this shit." To demonstrate, Dave raised his eyebrows and pursed his lips.

Skeptically, from behind my lectern, I repeated, "Mom's pissed and she's not taking any more of this shit?"

"Pardon the gender stereotypes, obviously."

"Which gender stereotypes are you referring to? You're invoking so many at once that it's hard to tell."

No one said anything.

I deepened my voice, projecting it out into the amphitheater where perhaps twenty staffers sat, in most cases with a seat or two between them. "It's a shame that Hillary Rodham is so unlikable, isn't it? I'd love to vote for a woman for president, but I just can't see voting for **her**. She's so ambitious and power hungry. What kind of woman would rather have a career in politics than a family? Couldn't she find a husband? And the vibe she gives off—she's cold and she's not funny at all. She's uptight, like my high school principal. Except at least my high school principal was honest, and I don't trust Hillary. How did she really make that money she claims was from futures in the eighties? What's she not telling us? How does a woman who went to fancy schools and lives in Streeterville know anything about the struggles of ordinary Americans? I respect it when men are rich, but when a woman has money, it just feels wrong."

My staff was watching me with alarm; they didn't know what would happen next, though truly, neither did I. Still in the deep, fake voice, I said, "Can I tell you anything about Hillary's voting record? No. Can I tell you what subcommittees she's served on? No. Have I ever listened to one of her speeches in its entirety? Well, they're not televised, but even if they were, her voice—it's so hard on my ears. Really, when I think about

Hillary, what I think is—" I looked around the amphitheater, took a deep breath, and said, "Shut her up! Shut her up! Shut her up!"

There were stairs on either side of the stage; Theresa ascended the ones on the right and Denise ascended the ones on the left, and they reached me at the same time. They acted as if I were drunk. Denise bent the microphone away from me—I didn't fight her—and Theresa stood beside me and put her arm around my shoulder.

Speaking into the mic, Denise said, "There are sandwiches in conference room A. Let's all meet back here at one o'clock."

No fewer than seventy emails had been exchanged in twenty-four hours by eight members of my staff about what Albert and I should do for our date on Saturday night: The ballet, the symphony, and a sushi restaurant were all deemed too elitist; a bluegrass show was deemed too risky securitywise because of the layout of the venue; Mexican food was deemed too blatantly pandering just prior to my arrival in Nevada. I also rejected bowling as pandering, and even if it wasn't, I'd have refused on the grounds that I didn't wish to publicly stick my rump in the air. Also vetoed were upscale hamburger or fried chicken restaurants, which could backfire when articles pointed out that I'd eaten a $17 grass-fed cheeseburger rather than a $3.79

Quarter Pounder with cheese from the McDonald's two blocks away.

At last, a reservation was made at an American bistro in Lincoln Park at which I'd order grilled chicken thighs ($15) and a glass of the house cabernet ($8). After discussion, my staff decided it was okay to leave it up to Albert what he'd order.

Donald sent the tweet at 4:02 P.M. central time, as I was riding back from the amphitheater to my apartment to get ready to meet Albert: **Hardball Hillary is staying at Trump Las Vegas for debate and that's not all. Major announcement coming soon!**

Theresa and Kenya were in the SUV with me, and I said to Theresa, "Is he coming to the debate? Could someone at the DNC have given him tickets?"

"I'll find out." Theresa was already typing on her phone. "Don't worry, you're staying at Caesars Palace."

"Would he know a person needs tickets?" Kenya asked.

"True," I said, and my phone buzzed with an incoming call from Aaron.

"Apparently, Trump's been telling people you want his daughter Ivanka in your cabinet, so that could be the so-called announcement," Aaron said. "Greg's calling his Trump contact now."

"Wow," I said. "Is he crazy or a pathological liar?"

Aaron chuckled. "With Trump, you get a twofer."

Albert Boyd was supposed to arrive at my apartment at seven for a glass of wine; at seven-thirty, we'd be driven to the restaurant; at nine o'clock, we'd leave the restaurant. I barely remembered what one did to get in the mood for a date, but certainly analyzing Donald Trump's tweets wasn't it.

In my walk-in closet that doubled as a dressing room, Suzy and Veronica did my makeup and hair, Theresa and Kenya breezed in and out on their phones, and I asked Ebba to open two bottles of white wine for all of us. I deliberately didn't read emails or news stories on my iPad, though it was almost physically difficult to refrain.

Suzy and Veronica left, and I called Maureen. "The thing I'm confused about," Maureen said, "is, does he see this as a real date or a fake date?"

"That's an excellent question."

"Maybe a fake date is preferable. All of the fun and none of the messiness."

I heard the security agents and Ebba let Albert in, and I said, "I feel more nervous right now than I did when I spoke at the Democratic Convention in '08."

Maureen laughed. "Of course you do."

Theresa and Kenya stayed out of sight—they'd

wait at the apartment to debrief on my return—and when I walked into my living room to see Albert in khaki pants, a blue blazer, and a blue-and-white-striped shirt, I felt a surge of surprising and genuine happiness. He looked very handsome. He stood, and we clasped hands and leaned forward to kiss each other's cheeks.

"You're an awfully good sport," I said, and he said, "It's my pleasure."

I sat in a chair and he sat on the couch. Ebba had set out a dish of mixed nuts and a tray of cheese and crackers, neither of which we touched, and she brought him a glass of wine; I still had mine. I asked about Albert's flight, and he described the book he'd been reading on the plane—nonfiction that had been shortlisted for the Pulitzer Prize, by a writer whose articles I'd read, though I hadn't read the book.

"Did you end up going to John and Kate's engagement party?" I asked. This was the son and future daughter-in-law of our mutual friend, Nancy, and the party had happened the previous weekend in New York.

"I did," he said. "Do you know how they got together?"

"I don't think I do." (What a relief it was not to be pleading with an Iowan to caucus for me!)

"Apparently, they connected on a dating website and decided to meet at a bar in Brooklyn. At the appointed time and place, they showed up, introduced themselves, began chatting, and hit it off. But twenty minutes into the conversation, they realized he was supposed to have met a different woman named Kate, and she was supposed to have met a different man named John. They assumed their counterparts must be elsewhere in the bar, so they all found one another and decided to make it a double date. But the die was cast. Our John and Kate were already smitten. At the party, they gave a very funny joint toast in which they admitted that, after they discovered the mix-up, they both considered suggesting sneaking out together to a different bar."

"That's incredible," I said.

"It does make you wonder about fate, doesn't it?"

"Do you believe in fate?" Our eyes met, and I added, "Just a little lighthearted predinner banter."

He laughed. "Certainly there are coincidences that are otherwise difficult to explain."

"Although, I suspect you're referring to happy coincidences. I've also met so many people in such difficult situations that to claim their struggles were determined by God seems callous. And not very Methodist, either. Do you go to church?"

"Only on Christmas and Easter. I know you go regularly." He made a sheepish expression. "We're not on a level playing field, are we? In terms of the amount of information about you that's out there."

I smiled. "I don't know if you'll find this unsettling

or reassuring, but my research team has looked into you thoroughly."

"I hope it was worth the effort. I fear I'm a bit boring."

"You don't seem that way to me." To my own amazement, I felt the heightened feeling I'd had on Cape Cod, the astonishing hunch that there was between Albert and me a genuine connection. At this almost comically inopportune moment! I said, "Even as I resist the notion of predestination, I do sometimes wonder—this isn't the sort of thing I can discuss in public, but if I'm elected, it's certainly a consequence of choices I've made. But was my ability to make those choices a form of destiny? Starting with being born in the right place at the right time."

Albert said, "I'm trying to think how that squares with the sense most of us have that there are other lives out there we could have led, if circumstances were only slightly different. My Dartmouth roommate was from the Central Valley in California, and when we graduated, he tried to convince me to move to San Francisco with him. I was tempted, but I ended up taking the far more conventional route, living in Manhattan and working for Morgan Stanley. And that's how I met Marjorie, who was what we then called a secretary."

"Was she your secretary?"

He shook his head. "I didn't have one at Morgan. I stayed only two years before I went to Citicorp."

"In my alternate life, I would have been an astronaut," I said. "I wrote to NASA when I was in eighth grade, and they wrote back saying the space program didn't take women."

Albert smiled. "I suppose that would have been a different kind of trailblazing."

"Did your marriage feel fated? I hope that's not intrusive to ask."

"Let me think about how to answer." But he did not appear offended. "We had, on balance, a good and solid marriage. We were compatible in that daily way that makes life run smoothly. But I don't think it's disloyal to Marjorie to say that it didn't seem as if only we could have made each other happy. I know some people talk about soulmates, but I don't think she'd have claimed that for us."

"Ironically, I thought Bill Clinton and I were soulmates," I said. "Not recently, but in my twenties."

"And now?"

"Isn't there a country song about thanking God for unanswered prayers?" We both laughed, and I said, "But this gets to my point about the tension between fate and free will. Is there a parallel universe where I married Bill, and if there is, did we stay married? If you'd gone out to San Francisco in 1969, would you have moved back east after a year and met Marjorie anyway? Or would you now be, I don't know, running a winery in Sonoma County?"

"Exactly. Though it does feel like my daughter, Carson, is the one predestined aspect of my life, that **she** was meant to be mine. I suppose that's a function of the intensity of parental love. Did you ever want to have children?"

"Absolutely. There are a few young women I think of as almost surrogate daughters"—Theresa, along with Kenya, was somewhere in my apartment, probably but not definitively out of earshot—"and having biological children was certainly part of what I originally pictured for my life. But I made peace with not taking that path. I don't think other things would have been possible if I'd been a mother. For all that Americans are suspicious of a woman who doesn't marry or have kids, I suspect that they also want or even need the first woman who'll be elected president to seem different from other women."

"As penance for ambition or as proof of exceptionalism?"

"Probably both." I tried to sound casual as I said, "Have you used any of those dating websites like Kate and John did?"

"Carson has tried to get me to, but the idea of meeting a stranger at a Starbucks—I fear this sounds pathetic, but I'd rather spend the evening with my golden retriever. I don't suppose you could have given online dating a whirl whether or not you wanted to."

"Some of my staffers once showed me the apps on their phones, and I found them anthropologically fascinating, but I wasn't jealous. It seems very stressful. What's your dog's name, by the way?"

"Her name is Annabel. She's excellent company, in my defense. She's with a house sitter now."

"Do you and Annabel live in a house or an apartment?"

"The same house Marjorie and I bought in 1971. Carson has encouraged me to sell it, but I enjoy the space, the yard. Maybe I could show it to you sometime."

"I'd like that very much." It was almost time for us to leave the apartment, to go on the public portion of the date, and I gestured around the living room—it was hard to say at what—and said, "Did you mention that you were doing this to Carson? Or your godson?"

"Carson is very amused, and I'll let Harris find out. But, Hillary, at the risk of sounding boastful, this won't be my first fifteen minutes of fame. Years ago, before a blizzard, I was getting milk at the supermarket and a reporter from the **Times** interviewed me. I was quoted saying something profound, like, 'I hope the power doesn't go out.'" He leaned forward, set his wineglass on the table, and looked at me intently. "When I told you on the phone I thought going on this date sounded like a lark, I just—I want you to know that I assumed you were far too busy making history to go on a date with an ordinary man from Westchester County. Otherwise, I'd have asked you out right after we met in Truro."

How generous he was, and how lovely this was to hear. I said, "Well, in the same spirit of candor, for me, tonight isn't a transaction pretending to be emotional. If anything, it's something emotional pretending to be transactional." Was this what dating was in your late sixties, the dispensing of subterfuge? Or was it Albert-specific? I nodded my head toward the front hall and said, "Shall we?"

Between the presence of my security detail, the palpably self-conscious waitstaff, and the other patrons pseudodiscreetly using their phones to take our picture, being at the restaurant felt like being in a play. We stayed an hour and ten minutes, Albert ordered scotch and pan-seared salmon, and although I'm not sure other diners could hear us, we spoke as if they could—we spoke about food and travel and prestige television shows, none of which I'd seen. When we emerged from the restaurant onto the sidewalk, the flash of camera bulbs in the October darkness was blinding. Although we were ushered by my agents, Darryl and Phil, into the back of the waiting armored SUV, it wasn't as if I could complain about the paparazzi; this was ostensibly the point of the date, and the photographers had been tipped off by members of my media team, though it was likely the date had also been live-tweeted by other patrons.

When the doors were closed and the SUV was moving, I said, "Are you okay?"

"That was . . . something." He sounded a bit stunned.

And then, at the same moment, I reached out to set my left hand on his right forearm, and he reached out with his right hand to take my left one. As we held hands, I felt, in spite of everything, a calmness and a comfort. Albert was speaking quietly—he might have felt constrained by the presence of the two agents in the front seat—as he said, "I'm not sure at what point either of us turns into a pumpkin, but if you're interested, we could go to your apartment and watch one of those shows now. I have a Hulu account." He added, "Obviously, by telling you that, I'm trying to impress you."

I laughed. "I'm very impressed. And I so wish we could do that. But believe it or not, I have a meeting tonight." Forty-five minutes into dinner, my phone had exploded with texts, and when I'd apologetically checked it, I'd learned from my brothers that, in a playoff game against the Cardinals, the Cubs had scored five runs in the second inning and from Denise that a meeting had been scheduled for 9:30 at my apartment; obviously, the latter wasn't a good sign. I said, "But what if, as soon as possible after the debate, we see each other again?"

"That sounds perfect," Albert said.

"In the meantime, will you tell me the plot of your daughter's favorite movie?"

"Ah. It's about a nerd who pays a beautiful cheerleader to pretend to be his girlfriend. Should I tell you what happens or not spoil it?"

"You should definitely tell me."

"Under her tutelage, he becomes cool, and it goes to his head."

"Of course it does," I said.

"He starts behaving badly, so she gets even by revealing the deal they made to everyone at their school. But after the boy's comeuppance, he remembers who he is, and they fall in love." He paused. "If it isn't abundantly clear," he said, "I'm the nerd here."

"That's chivalrous," I said, "but I don't think it's true."

"Then maybe we're both beautiful cheerleaders," he said, and when I laughed, he leaned over and whispered in my ear, "If we were alone, I would try to kiss you now."

I turned my face toward his; I found his lips with mine. It was exhilarating—delicious!—to kiss this man. In the front seat, Darryl and Phil did not react at all.

Denise had scheduled the meeting because Donald Trump wanted to officially endorse me;

Donald wanted to do this at the Trump Las Vegas, before the debate, with me by his side. And, incredibly, most but not all of my senior staffers thought I should cooperate. A few minutes earlier, Theresa and Kenya had been waiting for me in the basement parking garage of my building when, still inside the SUV, I bade farewell to Albert. Darryl and I exited the car; Phil would drive Albert back to his hotel. When I entered my apartment, nine staffers were waiting around my dining room table.

"The Interweb is beside itself with excitement about your date," Aaron said. "That was genius."

"But focusing on Trump, here's how the endorsement would work," Greg said. "Instead of flying to Vegas on Tuesday morning, a few of us fly out Monday. Monday afternoon, you hold your nose and appear with Trump for ten minutes while he sings your praises. White working-class men in Michigan, Wisconsin, and Pennsylvania decide, Hey, what's good enough for Donald Trump is good enough for me! You wash the Trump cooties off your hands, and on Tuesday, you kick Bill Clinton's ass."

I said, "What could possibly go wrong?" Looking at Denise, I said, "You're on board with this?"

It was Aaron who answered. "The media loves an unlikely friendship, and if you and Trump make just one appearance together, I suspect that'll get them through the primary."

"I want Obama's endorsement," I said.

"Obama will endorse the nominee," Greg said. "When you're the nominee, he'll endorse you. We'll finesse the Trump stuff with him down the road."

I said, "This feels like some kind of hostage situation. The idea that Donald can back me into appearing with him, at his hotel no less—" I paused, and my political director, Ben, said, "I agree. It sets a dangerous precedent."

Denise cleared her throat and said, "Let's bring Henry in for a second."

I had noticed that my top pollster, Henry Kinoshita, was at the table, which was slightly surprising; he wasn't typically in the inner circle. "What the numbers boil down to is that the Trump effect is real," Henry said. "Between June and September, your stats improved so significantly in categories like 'willing to listen to opposing viewpoints,' 'can improve the economy,' and 'shows strong leadership' that we ran another poll specifically asking about Trump, since those are his main talking points about you. This was 811 registered voters, 430 Democrats and 381 Republicans, with a 2.2 percent margin of error. For 'Do Donald Trump's tweets make you see Rodham in a more favorable or unfavorable light?' 72 percent said favorable. For 'A friendship between Hillary Rodham and Donald Trump is—' then we supplied positive adjectives like **funny** and **uplifting** and negative ones like **hypocritical** and **immoral**, and the agree rate for the positive adjectives are through the roof. Like, 77 percent, 82 percent, et cetera. The numbers aren't great for black voters and only a little better for Lantinx, but for whites, they're incredible."

Once again, I thought of Gwen Greenberger; I thought of what she'd think if she saw me standing next to Donald.

"Here's the thing," Greg said. "We can spend hours pondering why American voters can be dipshits or we can take advantage of it. I'm not saying you don't have a choice. We can convey to Trump that you're thrilled he wants to endorse you, but your schedule doesn't allow you to visit his hotel in person. Needless to say, what he does—or tweets—next is anyone's guess. And if you ask me, you'd be shooting yourself in the foot. But it's your call."

"Where does it end, though?" I said. "Aaron, you say I appear with Donald once, but what happens when he announces on Twitter that I'm doing a fundraiser at Mar-a-Lago?"

"We should be so lucky," Denise said.

"Fine, then what if he decides he wants to be my VP?"

I hadn't been joking, but everyone at the table laughed, even Theresa. Greg said, "Donald Trump would **never** agree to be your vice president."

Before I went to bed, I skimmed my brothers' texts—**We can do this! Goooo Jorge Soler!!! World**

Series here we come!!!!—and I almost missed the final one, which was from Tony and wasn't baseball-related: **Hillary do you have a boyfriend?**

I wrote back: **Maybe?**

By Sunday morning, hundreds if not thousands of articles about my date were online. My favorite—one for which my communications team had, off the record, supplied details—ran on the website of a celebrity-and-human-interest publication with the largest circulation of any American magazine. "Five Facts to Know about Hillary Rodham's Boyfriend," read the headline, and the facts, each accompanied by a few sentences of explication, were:

He supports Democrats!

He loves dogs!

She can discuss economic policy with him (he co-founded an investment management firm)!

He's a widow and a dad!

They met at a fundraiser last summer!

Naturally, no one on my team had specified the amount Albert had paid to attend the fundraiser, though I assumed that, as with so many other tidbits I'd rather keep private, this one would also emerge in the fullness of time.

I was waiting until 9:00 A.M., meaning after I'd arrived at the hotel amphitheater and half an hour before he was being picked up and taken to the airport to return to New York, to text Albert; I planned to thank him again for the date, reiterate what a good time I'd had, and ask if he'd seen the coverage and, if so, how he was feeling about it. But a text from him arrived at 8:20, while I was still en route to debate prep: **Dear Hillary, please don't answer this if you're busy, which I'm sure you are, but I can't stop myself from saying I had a wonderful time. —Albert**

Dear Hillary! And actual punctuation! And a sign-off! In a text! What a charming man he was.

Dear Albert, I texted back immediately, **I had a wonderful time, too. I can't thank you enough. I hope all goes well with your travel. Let me know when you arrive east this afternoon? —H**

"I'm sorry to say I just heard Misty LaPointe can't come to the debate," Theresa told me when we broke for lunch. "She's taken a turn for the worse. Diwata is working on finding a demographically similar Las Vegas person as your guest, but I know you like Misty."

"Thank you for letting me know." I had just used the bathroom inside a greenroom off the amphitheater, and I decided to text Misty before getting food with the others. I sat on a couch through which I could feel the springs and wrote, **Misty, I'm sorry to hear you can't come to the debate, although of course I understand.**

Usually, she replied right away, but more than two hours passed before her text arrived: **In hospital since Thurs. Not doing good.**

From me: **I'm really sorry to hear that.**

From her: **Drs found it in my ovaries.** She added a crying emoji.

From me: **Gosh, that's a lot to deal with.** This development seemed to be incredibly bad news, and it occurred to me to ask when the most recent diagnosis had happened or how her daughters were, but I wasn't sure that explaining such things to me was a good use of her energy. I wrote: **I hope you feel that you're in good hands with the doctors and nurses.**

She didn't reply and I considered not telling her, but then I did; when I'd known other people who were very sick, their sickness had almost never precluded an interest in gossip. I wrote: **When you have a moment, you might get a kick out of seeing that I went on a date last night! His name is Albert Boyd.**

From her: **OMG**

Thirty seconds later: **He is cuuuuute**

And: **Nice job**

And: **Go on with you're bad self,** followed by a winking emoji.

I was standing next to the stage, and it was time to run through my opening statement once more, but before I took my place behind the lectern, I said to Theresa, "Will you send something from Las Vegas to Misty LaPointe? Or, no, call a florist and send her a cactus."

Our plane left Chicago at eleven o'clock on Monday morning and arrived, after the three-hour flight, at 12:20 local time in Las Vegas. Veronica and Suzy had done my hair and makeup as we'd flown west, and, before we deplaned, Suzy sprayed mineral water on my face, then on Theresa's, then on Kenya's, then on Greg's. On the tarmac, my team and I climbed into three black SUVs. Unfathomably, we were headed to the Trump Las Vegas, where Donald Trump had called a press conference for two o'clock.

Out the car windows, the sky was pale blue and vast, and the mountains behind the cityscape were dun colored. How exactly had I arrived at this moment? Was I being pragmatic or just deeply cynical?

Built in 2008, the Trump Las Vegas was one of the tallest buildings in the city, its glass supposedly containing actual gold. Though the hotel didn't feature a casino, its entrance couldn't have been gaudier: Over glass and gold-plated doors, Trump's name appeared in large gold letters against a gold panel. Even seen from the outside, the lobby was already visibly crowded, with a chaotic air, and news vans with satellite dishes waited in the parking lot. We bypassed the main entrance, riding around to the building's rear, and entered through a loading dock.

My ears popped as we rode the elevator to the penthouse condo where I'd meet Donald before our public appearance. And then eight of my staffers and I, counting my security detail, were in a living room with a view of the Strip, including the Eiffel Tower replica. The décor of the living room was upscale but generic: lots of beige furniture and a fuchsia-and-white orchid on a glass coffee table. We'd been ushered in by a short man wearing a white-and-gold uniform, and Greg asked him, "Is Ashley here?" Apparently, Ashley was Donald's assistant.

The uniformed man went to find her, and we took seats on the sofa and chairs, all of us pulling out our phones. We'd been offered neither drinks nor food, not even water. Sixty-four stories above the earth, the condo was quiet. Where was Donald's staff?

Minutes passed. My team joked that I should use the time to call donors, and Kenya offered me a PowerBar, and other people were debating ordering from room service. Greg had texted Ashley repeatedly and finally received a response that she'd arrive momentarily. As more minutes ticked by, dread gripped me.

At last, Ashley entered through the same entrance door of the condo we had. She looked to be in her early twenties and was as stunning as a model—tall, slim, with long lustrous auburn hair—and she thanked us for coming and asked if we needed anything. In a snippy tone, Greg said, "Some waters would be great."

"Sure." She counted our heads then disappeared down a corridor and reappeared carrying Styrofoam cups, ice free; she brought these out two by two, as unapologetically as if my team were a suburban family who'd locked ourselves out of our house and she was the next-door neighbor letting us wait in her kitchen. Diwata approached Ashley and spoke in a hushed but urgent tone, and a few seconds later, I heard Ashley say, "What's a run of show?"

Donald entered the condo at 1:55, massively tall, preternaturally blond, his face a powdered orangeish tan. He wore a navy suit, white shirt, and red tie, and he was accompanied by just one other person, a younger man.

"Hillary Rodham," Donald said in a booming voice. "You like my beautiful hotel? It's beautiful, isn't it?" He strode toward me, vigorously shook my hand, and said, "Are we gonna do this? We're gonna do this. We're gonna get you elected, and after that, the sky's the limit."

A shift in the physics of time occurred, wherein Donald's presence made the seconds and minutes spin forward. Abruptly, we were riding back down the elevator, toward the lobby. The elevator doors opened onto pandemonium: a crowd that surely exceeded the fire code, with many people holding up their phones to record the moment; the song "Rockin' in the Free World" blasting over a sound system; a row of American flags with a podium in front of them. I followed Donald toward it, my agents flanking me. When we stood side by side in front of the podium, as hundreds of media camera flashes popped, I noticed the sparkliness of the lobby—the chandeliers, the many marbled and mirrored surfaces, the gold and white and gold and white. The crowd was roaring. Instinctively, I was smiling and waving, and in my peripheral vision, I could see Donald holding out both hands in thumbs-up gestures. Then he reached for the microphone and said into it, "Wow. Whoa. That is some group of people. Thousands.

"It's great to be at Trump Las Vegas. It's great to be in a wonderful city. And it's an honor to have everybody here. This is beyond anybody's expectations. There's been no crowd like this.

"Our country is in serious trouble. We don't have victories anymore. We used to have victories, but we don't have them. When was the last time anybody saw us beating, let's say, China in a trade deal? They kill us. I beat China all the time. All the time.

"When do we beat Mexico at the border? They're laughing at us, at our stupidity. And now they are beating us economically. The U.S. has become a dumping ground for everybody else's problems. When Mexico sends its people, they're not sending their best. They're sending people that have lots of problems. They're bringing drugs. They're bringing crime. They're rapists. And some, I assume, are good people.

"Islamic terrorism is eating up large portions of the Middle East. They just built a hotel in Syria. Can you believe this? When I build a hotel, I pay interest. They don't have to pay interest, because they took the oil that, when we left Iraq, I said we should've taken. Our enemies are getting stronger and stronger, and we as a country are getting weaker. Even our nuclear arsenal doesn't work.

"Now, our country needs a truly great leader, and we need a truly great leader now. We need a leader that can bring back our jobs, can bring back our manufacturing, can bring back our military, can take care of our vets. Our vets have been abandoned. And we also need a cheerleader. We need somebody that can take the brand of the United States and make it great again. So, ladies and gentlemen—I am officially endorsing Hillary Rodham for president of the United States, and she is going to make our country great again.

"We have to rebuild our infrastructure, our bridges, our roadways, our airports. You come into LaGuardia Airport, it's like we're in a third world country. You look at the patches and the forty-year-old floor. And I come in from China and I come in from Qatar and I come in from different places, and they have the most incredible airports in the world.

"Sadly, the American dream is dead. But if Hillary gets elected president she will bring it back bigger and better and stronger than ever before, and she will make America great again.

"Thank you. Thank you very much."

I was in a state of shock. I was in a state of shock, and I also understood I needed to speak. I leaned forward, and he didn't move—he seemed barely aware of me next to him—and I bent the microphone down. "Wow," I said. "Wow, that was truly unforgettable. Donald, you and I are such different people, but I'm glad we can agree on the promise of this great country. Now, from my perspective, and there's a lot of data to support this, immigrants bolster the American economy and actually commit fewer crimes than people born in the United States. I firmly believe that diversity is a strength, and the idea that we have to pick either financial security or open borders—that's a false choice. And other countries are our allies, not our enemies. My administration will build and maintain coalitions to tackle problems that affect all of us, like climate change. One of our core American values, and I absolutely plan to uphold this as president, is that every person, no matter who they are or where they were born, deserves to be treated with dignity."

Donald elbowed me and grabbed the microphone

back. Laughing, he said, "Folks, she has to say that. When you're a politician, you have to toe the line." He smiled at the crowd. "When you're a star, you can do anything you want."

Then he grabbed my hand and lifted my arm into the air next to his.

My schedule on Tuesday had been kept clear before the debate, though Diwata, Theresa, Ellie, and I did visit the Caesars Palace laundry room, where I introduced myself to the housekeepers, thanked them, and encouraged them to register to vote immediately and to caucus in February. As it happened, of the five housekeepers, all were immigrants, and at least one did not know who I was. Ellie immediately posted the photo she took of all of us on social media.

Otherwise I stayed in my suite, practicing my opening statement and studying my green binders. The debate started at 5:30 Pacific time, and for lunch I ate salad and a chicken breast; I had what I thought of as my ritual predebate diarrhea an hour later; I did a five-minute guided meditation on my iPad; I ate a handful of mixed nuts and drank a glass of water; I brushed my teeth; and by 2:00 P.M., Veronica and Suzy were at work on my hair and makeup. By three, my team and I were in our black SUVs headed north on Sammy Davis Jr. Drive.

Sometimes on debate days in the past, I'd awakened with the feeling—the anticipation and preparation and loneliness, the sense that I was about to enact my own destiny—but the truth was that on this day I hadn't. I did have a strange feeling entering the Wynn, but it was not the feeling; what I felt was the awareness that Bill might well be under this same roof, breathing this same air. That if he wasn't already in one of the greenrooms, he would be soon.

In my greenroom, I examined the papers I'd take onstage, and I took small sips of water; Veronica touched up my hair and Suzy touched up my makeup. And then I was being led through a maze of hallways to the wings of the stage, I was seconds from laying eyes on Bill (and also Martin O'Malley and also Jim Webb, though, really, I didn't care about them), and suddenly there we all were, the candidates and our aides and a pop singer in leather pants who would be performing the national anthem. I could see the instant when Bill leaned down to kiss my cheek out of impulse or habit but caught himself. "Good to see you, Hillary," he said, as casually as if we were former co-workers. "So you and Trump, huh? Politics really does make strange bedfellows."

I said, "Oh, I hardly think that's the most surprising part of this race."

A strange effect of having interacted with Donald such a short time ago was that Bill's presence seemed comparatively refined and intellectual. Where Donald was physically beastly, Bill was handsome. But I was not attracted to him. Once we had been so close, so rapturously close, and that closeness had been poisoned. But if it was irretrievable, its irretrievability did not strike me, as it had during earlier times, as tragic. It had taken most of my life, but I finally found it harder to believe that Bill and I had ever been a couple than that we hadn't stayed together.

And then I was shaking hands with other people, Martin O'Malley, his chief of staff, the pop singer. This singer wasn't the one I'd seen interviewed all those years ago—though that other singer was older now, she'd always been perceived of as controversial in a way that made it unlikely she'd be invited to perform the national anthem before a debate—but I fleetingly thought, **Top-of-game alone**. Would the goal I had set for myself watching TV with Meredith in 1997 come to pass? Either way, hadn't I tried, wasn't I trying, as hard as I knew how?

We walked onstage just as I'd practiced, and it was impossible to see the audience because of the bright lights directed at us. The Wynn auditorium held 1,400 people, a mass of shadowy bodies. When all four of us had emerged—the applause for me was of a different magnitude than for Jim or Martin, and the applause for Bill was of a different magnitude than for me—the singer followed. An enormous screen at stage left showed a billowing American flag, and we all faced it, our hands over our hearts, as she sang.

After we'd taken our places behind the podiums, Anderson Cooper established the debate's rules—a minute to answer the questions, thirty seconds for follow-ups or rebuttals—then we made our opening statements. Jim Webb was in full PE teacher mode. Martin O'Malley was more endearing but somehow hollow or generic, like a movie version of a president. Plus, he **did** sound elfin. They both invoked their children, of which Jim had six and Martin four. Bill went third, and the difference between him and the other men was striking, his comfort and confidence and eloquence as he declared that the American dream had always been about innovation.

And then it was my turn. I introduced myself as the granddaughter of a factory worker. I spoke about children fulfilling their potential, about making America fairer for families by closing tax loopholes and creating paid leave. I concluded by saying that in electing me, fathers would be able to say to their daughters, You, too, can be president.

Often the first question in a debate was related to a current event and put to everyone, but instead Anderson asked each of us individual questions tailored to our candidacies, which had a cut-to-the-chase quality. He started with Bill, pointing out that the top 1 percent of American households owned 40 percent of the country's wealth and asking whether a billionaire could understand the plight of voters struggling to pay for groceries. Bill described his humble childhood, how he'd lived with his grandparents in Hope while his mother got her nursing degree in New Orleans so that she could support him as a single mother. Raising the minimum wage was important, he said, but he didn't want Americans to just get by; he wanted them to thrive. As he was wrapping up his response, he added, "Now, if any of you don't know this, I'd be remiss if I didn't mention that Hope, Arkansas, grows the world's sweetest watermelons. Since my boyhood, nothing's ever tasted better to me." The audience chuckled.

"Senator Rodham, just over twenty-four hours ago, you stood next to Donald Trump, receiving his endorsement," Anderson said. "In the same remarks, he denigrated immigrants, which follows on what some find to be offensive tweets he's written about President Obama and about women. Are you willing to publicly condemn these statements by Donald Trump, and if so, how can you accept his support?"

"Let me be crystal clear," I said. "To suggest that Barack Obama was born outside the United States, and thereby to question the legitimacy of his presidency, is deplorable. Xenophobia and racism in all forms are deplorable. Sexism is deplorable. That said, when anyone's views evolve and become more enlightened, it's to be celebrated. We're all products of particular circumstances, of times and places and ways of thinking, but our minds and hearts can be opened. If Donald Trump wants to embrace feminism, I welcome his evolution. I don't believe in permanently writing someone off because of things they've said or done in the past." I felt okay with my answer, but there was no time to dwell on it; Anderson was putting questions to Jim and then Martin, and I needed to remain attentive to every word.

Quickly, a rhythm was established, with the bulk of questions going to Bill or me. When Jim or Martin tried to break in, or even overtly complained about the uneven allotment of time, it mostly underscored their peripheralness. We were forty minutes in when Anderson said, "Senator Rodham, a woman named Jill Perkins recently accused you of sexually harassing her, including demanding that she shave your legs in a taxi in 1992. Did this incident happen, and was it sexual harassment?"

In prep sessions, we had settled on "Jill Perkins's accusations are categorically false. I have never sexually harassed her or anyone else, and in fact, I've sponsored multiple bills that fight workplace harassment and discrimination and protect harassment and discrimination victims. . . ."

But all at once, I felt the feeling that had been absent earlier—the Wellesley feeling, the urge to take a risk beyond which, perhaps, lay my destiny.

I said, "It's confounding to me that I'm standing onstage with a man who settled a sexual harassment lawsuit against him for $850,000, yet I'm the one who's asked about this issue. But I will try to do something radical up here. I want to try to describe a complicated situation in an honest way.

"In February 1992, on the day that I declared I was running for Senate from the state of Illinois, I was riding in a cab to do an interview at the **Chicago Tribune**. The people in the cab with me were a man named Greg Rheinfrank, who was then my communications director, and a woman named Jill Rossi, whose married name became Perkins, who was Greg's assistant. I was wearing sheer pantyhose, and Greg noticed that it had been a few days since I'd shaved my legs. Out of a concern that this would look unattractive or be embarrassing, he asked the taxi driver to stop. He sent Jill Perkins into a drugstore to buy a razor and shaving cream, and when she returned, Greg suggested that she shave my legs so that I could focus on practicing my responses for the upcoming interview. For many reasons, I wish now that I'd shaved my own legs or left them unshaven. I apologize to Jill Perkins for creating an uncomfortable situation. I understand why she felt that way. At the time, I didn't perceive what I was doing to be harassment, and certainly not sexual harassment. The reality is that an interaction can involve close physical proximity and not be inappropriate, as with a doctor or nurse, or even a barber shaving a man's beard. Or as with tonight, when a hair stylist, Veronica Velasquez, and a makeup artist, Suzy Gunther, helped me prepare. Nevertheless, I acknowledge that in that taxi, I exercised poor judgment, and I regret it. It was an isolated event, and never in my long career as a law professor or elected official has anything remotely comparable happened.

"Have I made mistakes? Yes. We all make mistakes. But I strongly believe that I haven't made that many, that I've learned from them, and that I'm consistently respectful of other people.

"Now, there's a larger issue I want to address. I want those of you here tonight in Las Vegas, as well as those of you watching at home, to think of the first time you heard my name. Unless you're from Illinois, it was probably in 2004, when a comment I made about not having stayed home to bake cookies resulted in a national backlash. It's likely that there was never a time that you were aware that I existed without also being aware that I'm supposedly controversial, untrustworthy, or unlikable. And it's very normal that if we're told many times over many years that a person is untrustworthy or unlikable, we'll believe it.

"But why are Americans so fixated on my likability? Do we ask ourselves if Jim Webb is likable, if Martin O'Malley is likable, if Bill Clinton is likable? If you want someone very funny, you can go to a comedy club. If you want someone very attractive, you can watch a Hollywood movie. If you want someone to enjoy a beer with, you can go to a bar with your friend. But if you want someone to look out for the interests of the American people, for your family, for **you**—someone who understands the economy and education and healthcare and foreign policy, who has common sense and decency, someone who **doesn't** believe that the normal rules and laws don't apply to her—then vote for me. You can vote for me because you're excited to elect a female president, but you also can just vote for me because I'll do a good job. I promise that at every opportunity, for as many Americans as I can, in as many ways as I can, I'll fight to make life better for you."

I had gone over my allotted time by more than twenty seconds, and Anderson hadn't interrupted me. When I finished speaking, there was applause, the most applause I received that night. And I cannot lie: I felt exhilarated, but I also felt uncertain. Some haze had burned off, some distillation had occurred, and I wasn't sure how the public would react.

Afterward, back in the greenroom, Greg said, "Thanks for throwing me under the bus," then he said, "You did good, Rodham."

"Thank you for encouraging me to run for

Senate," I said. "And for a few other things along the way."

Apparently, as several pundits would later point out, it was the first time the word **pantyhose** had been used onstage at a presidential debate.

The narrative of my eventual election and presidency is that the first Democratic debate was when I found my voice, demonstrating an authenticity and candor that had otherwise eluded me for decades. I consider this narrative apocryphal, but when I reflect back—more than two years have passed since the debate and more than a year since my inauguration—I do think of the days after the debate as the point when I suspected I'd win, when I felt some confidence or optimism that had previously been beyond my grasp. It was when I began to securely inhabit my own lead.

But to the extent that speaking frankly about Jill Perkins was a defining moment in the 2016 election, it's for a reason both more concrete and more convoluted than that I abruptly became authentic. Among the fifteen million viewers of that night's debate was Vivian Tobin—the woman in Chouteau's parking lot—and, as she said later, the combination of my public apology to Jill Perkins and my acknowledgment of culpability motivated Vivian to come forward and tell the story of what had happened so many years before between her and Bill Clinton. She didn't like me, Vivian Tobin told reporters, but she **hated** Bill. She decided to do what she could—at a high personal cost—to prevent his presidency. I will always be grateful to her, though I could only shake my head whenever I heard her oft-repeated on-the-record comment that the person she really wished would run was Donald Trump.

Ultimately, even with a woman credibly accusing him of rape, Bill and I fought it out until early June 2016, when I officially won the majority of delegates and became the presumptive nominee. The battle preceding the general election was as ugly as the primary. My Republican opponent was indeed Jeb Bush, and the media followed his example on behaving as if his being five years my junior put us in two different generations. There were rumors that I had Parkinson's and a traumatic brain injury and syphilis, and even Jeb himself, who was routinely congratulated in the press for his impeccably WASPy manners, regularly declared that I seemed "worn out."

There was also, in August 2016, a scandal when Bitsy Sedgeman Corker's troubled forty-year-old son, Jesse, who was a major donor of mine, was arrested for involuntary manslaughter after providing the opioids that a friend of his overdosed on. Naturally, this initiated another wave of stories about my Northwestern colleague James and my supposed role in his death.

And Donald Trump remained a thorn in my side right up until Election Day. When the race was called around 9:00 P.M. eastern time on November 8, he tweeted, **Hardball Hillary, who owes her victory to me, is President. But where is my 'Thank you' Hillary?** Now that he's been indicted for tax fraud in New York—his trial isn't for another few months—he's obsessed with my pardoning him, which I absolutely won't do.

In spite of all this, once Bill was out of the race, everything was easier and more predictable. Certainly debating Jeb was far less stressful than debating Bill; Jeb was less charismatic, less intelligent, and I'd never had sex with him. Plus, his supporters had never chanted "Shut her up!" at rallies. Sometimes when I saw Jeb and his VP pick, John Kasich, the governor of Ohio, I'd think of Diwata saying that Bill was pale, male, and stale. Though I had seriously considered picking Barack's HUD Secretary Julián Castro as my VP, I ended up going with the Virginia governor, Terry McAuliffe, which is to say—Terry is a decade younger than I am—we are just pale and stale. But I genuinely like Terry's energy and sense of humor, and he's phenomenal at fundraising.

It had seemed that Election Day would never arrive, and then it arrived. In the end, I won by 2.9 million votes.

• • •

In the White House, on a typical weeknight, I make my nest in the Living Room, which is in the residence between the Master Bedroom and the Yellow Oval Room. Apparently, many presidents and first ladies didn't share a bedroom, and the Living Room was used as sleeping quarters by, among others, Mary Todd Lincoln, Harry Truman, and John F. Kennedy. The designer I worked with—truthfully, it was primarily Maureen who came to Washington for several months to oversee his redecorations—didn't put a bed in the room but did find a very large, comfortable tweed couch, which is where I sit at night to drink tea and read briefing papers in a leather binder and news articles on my iPad. The room's other décor includes a seventeenth-century still life of a fruit bowl borrowed from the National Gallery of Art; on the mantel, a matching pair of ceramic horses given to Ulysses S. Grant by a Chinese diplomat; a mahogany table on which rests the white crocheted tablecloth sent to me by the Suarez family in 1971 and, set atop it, framed photos of family and close friends; and floor-to-ceiling toile drapes in a lovely seafoam shade. I try to get in bed by eleven, spend another fifteen minutes reading a book of devotionals to unwind, and turn the light out by eleven-twenty.

My days are so hectic and stimulating and interactive, so relentless, that if I didn't have this private evening peace, I suspect I'd become a kind of automaton, a figurehead, to the exclusion of being a person. The time alone gives me the tranquility to recollect not just my emotions but also my experiences. I know better, of course, than to try to convince the public that policy as well as poetry can arise from Wordsworth's "spontaneous overflow of powerful feelings." I know that something being true can't make people believe it.

And yet, if my Living Room nest is essential to my equilibrium, and if being president is necessarily lonely, I am less personally alone than I've been for much of my adulthood. For the last two years, my relationship with Albert has developed in a surprisingly natural way. He visits from New York almost every weekend, as well as acting as my date for state dinners and White House receptions around the holidays. Though I avoided taking him on international trips for the first year, I've relaxed my stance, and he recently accompanied me to, among other places, the G7 summit in Italy. Albert is extraordinarily accommodating of my schedule, and I honestly don't know if this is because I'm the president, because he's retired, or because this is who he'd always have been, if we'd met earlier and under other circumstances. We have discussed the question—one of the things I like best about him is that we can discuss anything—and we've both admitted we have no idea. We simply enjoy each other for now, and I think we're both amused and grateful to experience true companionship. And also, though I've never mentioned it to anyone besides Maureen, fabulous sex. It's not acrobatic, it always involves lubricant, and in Albert's arms, under the covers, I'm overwhelmed with a particular physical happiness that I thought I had left behind long ago. Why did it take more than fifty years for me to meet a person who is kind and interesting and attractive; who is faithful; and who is single? If I wonder this occasionally, I can say with confidence that I wonder about it less than the journalists who, collectively, have written millions of words of speculation about what resides within my heart.

At night, Albert goes to sleep earlier than I do. When he's in New York, before he turns in, he texts me while I'm in my nest, always a variation on the same message: **Goodnight, my darling, and sweet dreams.** (Though I found it cute, he no longer uses salutations or sign-offs in texts, though he does still use punctuation. He also on principle refuses to even try to comprehend Albert Boyd "stanning.") In the morning, I am generally awakened with a phone call from a valet at six-fifteen, and for this reason, Albert sets his alarm for six-ten. That way, when I wake, there's always, in addition to my briefings, a text from him. Usually, it's **Good morning, my darling, and I hope you slept well.**

I consider the range and depth of not just my friendships but also my many work relationships to be one of the great gifts of my life; if I hadn't met Albert, I'd still have been lucky. But there is something about another person caring when you go to sleep at night and when you wake up in the morning—caring not because of what they need from you but just because they love you—that is a novelty for me. There's a sweetness and solace in it that I don't take for granted.

My inauguration took place on January 20, 2017. I wore a gray suit with—to symbolize the melding of blue and red America—a purple collar and a purple shell beneath it. It was unseasonably warm in Washington, almost fifty degrees. I know that many women, and also some men, wept as they watched me place my left hand on a Bible that had been given to my mother when she was a teenager and repeat the oath administered by Supreme Court Justice John Roberts: "I, Hillary Diane Rodham, do solemnly swear that I will faithfully execute the office of president of the United States and will, to the best of my ability, preserve, protect, and defend the Constitution of the United States, so help me God."

I had decided ahead of time not to cry. The presidency is a strange blend of the bureaucratic and the symbolic, and Inauguration Day was the height of symbolism; it was downright cinematic, which didn't mean that it was false. To stand on the west front of the Capitol, facing both the Washington Monument and the Lincoln Memorial, to publicly enact the peaceful transfer of power that is the hallmark of a democracy—it was profoundly moving.

Though other presidents have been flanked during the swearing in by family members, I chose to stand alone. But the closest seats were occupied on one side of the aisle by my brothers, their wives, and Tony's children, and, on the other side, by Maureen and Meredith and their husbands and baby Hillary, Meredith's one-year-old daughter. Also nearby were Theresa, Greg, Denise, Clyde, Diwata, and other staffers; and my Wellesley friends Nancy and Phyllis. Albert and his daughter, Carson, sat next to Nancy. The oath itself took about thirty seconds, and my speech afterward took twenty-three minutes. It was during the musical performances before the oath that I thought of the many people who had longed for this day and not lived to see it: the suffragists, of course, Susan B. Anthony and Elizabeth Cady Stanton and Frederick Douglass; more recently, Misty LaPointe, who passed away in May 2016; and, in the middle, my mother, born in 1919 on the day that Congress gave women the right to vote. **Oh, Dorothy Rodham,** I thought. **Oh, Mom. How I wish you could be here.** I have always been particularly touched by the proverb about the purpose of life being to plant trees under whose shade you do not expect to sit.

I knew, on Inauguration Day, that challenges lay ahead, including gridlock in Congress and a divided electorate. Such challenges make me even prouder of the legislation my administration has gotten passed without Republican support: reversing the Hyde Amendment to allow poor women access to abortions through Medicaid; creating a path to citizenship for undocumented immigrants; exceeding the climate-change commitments in the Paris Agreement; and requiring background checks on all gun sales. There have also, of course, been disappointments and failures. None of it has been easy, even the successes. There have been good and terrible days.

But the grassy field I often pictured while campaigning—I've made it to the other side. This is miraculous! Or is the miracle in how quickly it came to seem ordinary? At first, when reporters on NPR or ABC said "President Rodham," those words together, the honorific and my surname, sounded strange, but within a few days, they didn't.

If I'll never know how much this was my path because of fate and how much because I willed it, the question is less important than that I made it across. Now other women know they, too, can make it, and not because I or anyone else tells them. They know because they've seen it happen.

ACKNOWLEDGMENTS

For facts, anecdotes, and analysis, I am indebted to the following books and their authors: **Living History** by Hillary Rodham Clinton; **What Happened** by Hillary Rodham Clinton; **My Life** by Bill Clinton; **Chasing Hillary: On the Trail of the First Woman President Who Wasn't** by Amy Chozick; **A Woman in Charge: The Life of Hillary Rodham Clinton** by Carl Bernstein; **Strange Justice: The Selling of Clarence Thomas** by Jane Mayer and Jill Abramson; **Behind the Smile: A Story of Carol Moseley Braun's Historic Senate Campaign** by Jeannie Morris; **Good and Mad: The Revolutionary Power of Women's Anger** by Rebecca Traister; **Brotopia: Breaking Up the Boys' Club of Silicon Valley** by Emily Chang; **Dear**

Madam President: An Open Letter to the Women Who Will Run the World by Jennifer Palmieri; **Plenty Ladylike: A Memoir** by Claire McCaskill; **Off the Sidelines: Speak Up, Be Fearless, and Change Your World** by Kirsten Gillibrand; **The Truths We Hold: An American Journey** by Kamala Harris; **The Senator Next Door: A Memoir from the Heartland** by Amy Klobuchar; and **This Fight Is Our Fight: The Battle to Save America's Middle Class** by Elizabeth Warren. I am similarly indebted to the following podcasts: **With Her,** hosted by Max Linsky and the Clinton Foundation; **Slow Burn: Season 2,** hosted by Leon Neyfakh and **Slate** magazine; and **Making Obama,** hosted by Jenn White and WBEZ Chicago.

In a few instances, this novel incorporates verbatim words spoken during real-life public events. Passages include Thurgood Marshall's 1991 retirement press conference; Bill Clinton's 1991 presidential campaign announcement; Anita Hill's testimony during Clarence Thomas's 1991 confirmation hearing; Carol Moseley Braun's 1991 Senate campaign announcement; Bill Clinton's 1992 **60 Minutes** interview; and Donald Trump's 2015 presidential campaign announcement.

As I wrote, I asked many questions of various people. I truly don't have the words to express to Rebecca Hollander-Blumoff and Susan Appleton my gratitude and respect for their intelligence and good humor. P. G. Sittenfeld and Ellen Battistelli also gamely answered countless text queries. Diana Mallon, Sarah Sittenfeld, and Paul De Marco let me interview them about their areas of expertise. Kim and Chris Smith gave permission to borrow a good story, as did Susanna Daniel. In early 2016, Tyler Cabot and David Granger offered a magazine assignment that became part of my inspiration for this book. And since the mid-1970s, Betsy and Paul Sittenfeld have provided encouragement, literary and otherwise.

My smart early readers included Emily Bazelon, Jennifer Weiner, Emily Miller, Tiernan Sittenfeld, Josephine Sittenfeld, P. G. Sittenfeld, Matt Carlson, and Julius Ramsay.

One might say that the publication of a novel takes a village. I'm so lucky to be part of a village that includes my brilliant editor Jennifer Hershey and my exceptionally talented publicist Maria Braeckel. I'm deeply grateful for the wisdom and competence of Marianne Velmans, Patsy Irwin, and Tabitha Pelly. And I am awash in excellent agents, including Jennifer Rudolph Walsh, Tracy Fisher, Claudia Ballard, and Jill Gillet. Also looking out for me at WME are Suzanne Gluck, Fiona Baird, Alicia Everett, Alyssa Eatherly, Camille Morgan, and Sabrina Taitz. Also looking out for me at Random House are Gina Centrello, Andy Ward, Avideh Bashirrad, Susan Corcoran, Theresa Zoro, Leigh Marchant, Barbara Fillon, Jessica

Bonet, Sophie Vershbow, Vincent La Scala, Janet Wygal, Benjamin Dreyer, Jordan Pace, Erin Kane, Paolo Pepe, Robbin Schiff, and Elizabeth Eno. Also looking out for me at Transworld are Larry Finlay, Jane Lawson, and Jo Thomson. See? It really does take a village.

Finally, I'm thankful to my family. You're so creative and funny, and you fill my life with joy.

ABOUT THE AUTHOR

Curtis Sittenfeld is the **New York Times** bestselling author of the novels **Prep**, **The Man of My Dreams**, **American Wife**, **Sisterland**, and **Eligible**, and the story collection **You Think It, I'll Say It**, which have been translated into thirty languages. Her short stories have appeared in **The New Yorker**, **The Washington Post Magazine**, **Esquire**, and **The Best American Short Stories**, of which she is the 2020 guest editor. Her nonfiction has appeared in **The New York Times**, **The Atlantic**, **Time**, and **Vanity Fair** and on public radio's **This American Life**.

curtissittenfeld.com
Facebook.com/curtissittenfeldbooks
Twitter: @csittenfeld

LIKE WHAT YOU'VE READ?

Try these titles by Curtis Sittenfeld,
also available in large print:

You Think It, I'll Say It
ISBN 978-0-525-59035-4

Eligible
ISBN 978-0-399-56684-4

For more information on large print titles, visit
www.penguinrandomhouse.com/large-print-format-books